THE
MAVERICK DOCTOR
AND MISS PRIM

&

ABOUT THAT NIGHT...

BY
SCARLET WILSON

MILLS & BOON

REBELS WITH A CAUSE

A fabulous new linked duet by Scarlet Wilson

Doctors on a mission to eradicate infectious diseases…
Their work is life-changing and often heartbreaking.
But for these rebel heroes and bravehearted heroines
their work with the DPA (Disease Prevention Agency)
isn't just about making a difference and saving lives—
because they are all running from something, and
facing a crisis together puts their own hearts on the line!

THE MAVERICK DOCTOR AND MISS PRIM

and

ABOUT THAT NIGHT…

THE
MAVERICK DOCTOR
AND MISS PRIM

BY
SCARLET WILSON

All ... ... the imagination
... ... bearing the
... ... by any
... ... ncidents are

... ... whole or
... ... ment with
... ... cation or any
... ... form or by any
... ... , recording,
... ... without the

First published in Great Britain 2013
by Mills & Boon, an imprint of Harlequin (UK) Limited.
Harlequin (UK) Limited, Eton House, 18-24 Paradise Road,
Richmond, Surrey TW9 1SR

© Scarlet Wilson 2013

ISBN: 978 0 263 89906 1

Harlequin (UK) policy is to use papers that are natural, renewable
and recyclable products and made from wood grown in sustainable
forests. The logging and manufacturing process conform to the
legal environmental regulations of the country of origin.

Printed and bound in Spain
by Blackprint CPI, Barcelona

Dear Reader

When I was asked by my editor if I would be interested in writing a duet I was delighted and jumped at the chance. The Center for Disease Control in the US has always fascinated me. I work in public health, and love all the work around infectious diseases and immunisation campaigns. The CDC always features heavily in any plague/outbreak/epidemic films that are made, and I was excited at the prospect of having a story along those lines and set about creating my own fictional organisation, the Disease Prevention Agency, for my *Rebels with a Cause* duet.

But all stories need to have fabulous characters, and I instantly fell in love with my hero in THE MAVERICK DOCTOR AND MISS PRIM—Matt Sawyer, wounded bad boy and very much like his namesake, Sawyer in *Lost*. He's the kind of guy you know deep-down has real good in him. It's just going to take a special woman to unearth it.

My sassy heroine Callie is a girl out of her depth. She takes the initial call at the DPA and assembles the team, but her mentor is taken unwell on a plane and she's left in charge of a situation that is clearly bigger than any she's coped with before.

Her only option is to turn to Sawyer for help. After all, he worked in the DPA previously and has the expertise she needs. So why doesn't he want to help? It makes quarantine very interesting…

Both my characters in this story are grieving. And both deal with their grief in their own way. Needless to say I let them get their happy-ever-after. It just takes a while to get there!

Please feel free to contact me via my website: www.scarlet-wilson.com. I love to hear from readers!

Scarlet

Scarlet Wilson wrote her first story aged eight and has never stopped. Her family have fond memories of *Shirley and the Magic Purse*, with its army of mice, all with names beginning with the letter 'M'. An avid reader, Scarlet started with every Enid Blyton book, moved on to the *Chalet School* series, and many years later found Mills & Boon®.

She trained and worked as a nurse and health visitor, and currently works in public health. For her, finding Mills & Boon® Medical Romances™ was a match made in heaven. She is delighted to find herself among the authors she has read for many years.

Scarlet lives on the West Coast of Scotland with her fiancé and their two sons.

Recent titles by the same author:

AN INESCAPABLE TEMPTATION
HER CHRISTMAS EVE DIAMOND
A BOND BETWEEN STRANGERS*
WEST WING TO MATERNITY WING!
THE BOY WHO MADE THEM LOVE AGAIN
IT STARTED WITH A PREGNANCY
The Most Precious Bundle of All

These books are also available in eBook format from www.millsandboon.co.uk

Dedication

This book is dedicated to my two fabulous and entrepreneurial brothers-in-law, who have put up with me for more years than I care to remember. For Sandy Dickson and Robert Glencross, thank you for everything that you've done for me and my family and for taking such good care of my sisters!

CHAPTER ONE

Chicago

"OKAY, BEAUTIFUL, WHAT you got for me?" Sawyer leaned across the reception desk as the clerk glared at him.

Miriam cracked her chewing gum. "You've been here too long—you're getting smart-mouthed."

"I've always been smart-mouthed."

"And get a haircut."

He pushed his shaggy light brown hair from his eyes then tossed his head. "The long-haired look is in. Be-sides—I'm worth it."

The clerk rolled her eyes and picked up three charts. "You can have two sick kids with chicken pox in room six or a forty-three-year-old female with D&V behind curtain two." They lifted their heads in unison as the noise of someone retching behind curtain two filled the air.

He shuddered. "Give me the kids." He grabbed the charts and walked down the corridor. His eyes skimmed the information on the charts. Ben and Jack Keating, aged six and seven, just returned from abroad with chicken pox.

He pushed open the door. Unusually, the lights were dimmed in the room. The two kids—brothers—lay on the beds with a parent at each bedside. Alison, one of the nurses, was taking a temperature. She walked over to him, her pregnancy bump just starting to emerge from her scrub trousers. "Sickest kids I've seen in a while," she murmured.

He gave her a smile, his natural instinct kicking in. "You safe to be in here?"

She sighed. "After three kids of my own it's safe to say I'm immune."

Sawyer crossed the room quickly, leaving the charts at the bottom of the beds. Alison was right. These kids didn't look good. Chicken pox could be a lot more serious than a few itchy spots.

"Hi, I'm Matt Sawyer, one of the docs. I'm going to take a look at Ben and Jack." He extended his hand towards the mother then the father, taking in their exhausted expressions before turning to the sink, washing his hands and donning some gloves.

He walked over to Ben. In the dim light it was difficult to see his face, but it looked as if it was covered in red, bumpy spots. "Hi, Ben, I'm just going to have a little look at you."

The six-year-old barely acknowledged that he'd spoken. He glanced at the cardiac and BP monitor, noting the increased heart rate and low blood pressure. At first touch he could feel the temperature through his gloves. He pressed gently at the sides of Ben's neck. Unsurprisingly his glands were swollen. There were a number of spots visible on Ben's face so he peeled back the cover to reveal only a few angry spots across his chest but a whole host across his forearms.

The first thing that struck him was that all of the spots were at the same stage of development. Not like chicken pox at all—where spots emerged and erupted at different times.

Alarm bells started ringing in his head. *Be methodical.* He heard the old mantra of his mentor echoing around him.

He moved to the bottom of the bed and lifted Ben's foot.

There. The same uniform spots on the soles of his feet. He stretched over, reaching Ben's hand and turning his palm over. Red vesicular spots.

He tasted bile in the back of his throat and glanced across the room to where Alison had switched on her telepathic abilities and had already hung some bags of saline and was running through the IV lines.

"Where were you on vacation?"

The boys' father shook his head. "We weren't on vacation. I was working. We've just come back from three months in Somalia. I work for a commercial water-piping company."

Somalia. The last known place for a natural outbreak of this disease.

"Were any of the locals you came into contact with sick?" There were a million different questions flying around his head but he didn't want to bombard the parents.

Mrs Keating nodded. "We were in the highlands. A lot of them were sick. But we didn't think it was anything too serious. We actually wondered if we'd taken a bug to them—we were the first people they'd come into contact with in years."

His reaction was instinctive. "Step outside, please, Alison."

"What?" The nurse wrinkled her brow.

He raised his voice, lifting his eyes and fixing them

on her, praying she would understand. "Wait outside for me, please, Alison."

The atmosphere was electric. She was an experienced nurse and could read the expression on his face. She dropped the IV lines and headed for the door.

"Is something wrong?" Mr. Keating started to stand.

Sawyer crossed to the other bed. Jack was lying with his back to him. He wasted no time by pulling the white sheet from across Jack's chest and tugging gently on his shoulder to pull him round.

Identical. His face was covered. Red, deep-seated round vesicles. All at the same stage of development, a few covering his chest but mainly on his forearms. He opened Jack's mouth. Inside, his oral mucosa and palate were covered. He checked the soles of his feet and the palms of his hands. More identically formed red spots.

He could feel chills sweeping his body. It couldn't be. *It couldn't be.* This disease had been eradicated in the seventies. No one had seen this disease since then.

Then a little light bulb went off in his head. Hadn't there been a suspected outbreak a few years ago that had turned out to be chicken pox? The very thing that this was presumed to be? He ran the list of other possibilities in his head. He knew them off by heart. Anyone who'd ever worked in the DPA did.

But the more he stared at the spots the more convinced he became that it was none of the alternatives.

"How long since the spots appeared?"

The mother and father exchanged glances. "A few days? They had a rash at first then the spots developed. They've got much worse in the last day. But the boys had been feeling unwell before that—headaches, backaches, vomiting. We just thought they'd picked up a bug."

Sawyer felt as if he was in a bad movie. Why him? Why did this have to happen while he was on duty?

Would someone else recognize this? Realize the potential risks? Or would they just chalk it up to a bad dose of chicken pox and discover the consequences later? He'd put all this behind him. He'd walked away and vowed never to be involved in any of this again. He was in the middle of Chicago—not in some far-off country. Things like this didn't happen here. Or they *shouldn't* happen here.

And right now that was he wanted to do again. To walk out that front door and forget he'd ever seen any of this.

He looked at the long inviting corridor outside. He wasn't a coward. But he didn't want this. He didn't want *any* of this. The kind of thing that sucked you in until it squeezed all the breath from you.

A shadow moved outside the door.

But there was the killer. A pregnant nurse standing outside that door. A nurse who had been working with him and had contact with these children. Could he walk away from her?

He glanced upwards. It was almost as if someone had put her here so he *couldn't* walk away. His conscience would never allow him to do that.

If only he didn't know she was pregnant. If only that little bump hadn't just started to emerge above her scrub trousers. That would make this a whole lot easier.

Then he could walk away.

He took a deep breath and steeled himself. He was a doctor. He had a duty of care. Not just to his colleagues but to these kids.

These very sick kids.

He looked back at the parents. "I need you to think

very carefully—this is very important. Did you fly home?"

They both nodded.

"When, *exactly*, did you first notice the rash on the boys? Before or after you were on the plane?"

The parents looked at each other, screwing up their foreheads and trying to work it out.

A detailed history could wait. He knew enough already. He wasn't part of the DPA any more. This was their job, not his. The notification part he could handle—setting the wheels in motion so the processes could take over.

Isolation. Containment. Diagnosis. Lab tests. Media furore.

In the meantime he had two sick kids to take care of and staff members to worry about. Let the DPA do their job and he could do his.

He pulled his smart phone from his pocket and took a picture of Jack's spots and then Ben's. "Wait here."

Alison jumped as he flung the door open. "What on earth's going on?" She matched his steps as he strode down the corridor to Reception. "Don't you think you can get away with speaking to me like that. I want to know what you think is wrong." He watched her as subconsciously her hands went to her stomach. This day was just about to get a whole lot worse.

"Did you touch them?"

"What?" She wrinkled her nose.

"The spots. Did you touch the children's spots?"

She must have read the fear he was trying to hide behind his eyes. "I think I did." She looked as if she might burst into tears. Then realization dawned. "I think I had gloves on." Her voice grew more determined. "No, I'm *sure* I had gloves on."

"And when you took them off, did you touch any other part of your skin?"

Her face crumpled. "I don't think so. But I can't be sure."

His hands landed on her shoulders and he steered her into the nearest free room. He knocked the water on with his elbows and pulled the hand scrub over, opening up a scrub brush for her. "Scrub as if you were going to Theatre and don't stop until I tell you."

She looked pale, as if she might keel over. But her reactions were automatic, pumping the scrub, covering her hands, wrists and forehands and moving them methodically under the running water.

He watched the clock. One minute. Two minutes. Three minutes. Four.

"Sawyer?"

He nodded. "You can stop now."

"Do you know what it is?" She was drying her hands now.

"I think I do. I'm just praying that I'm wrong. Come with me."

They reached the desk. Miriam had her back to them and was chatting loudly on the phone.

Sawyer leaned across the desk and cut the call.

She spun around. "What are you doing?"

"We're closed."

"What?" Several heads in the surrounding area turned.

"You don't have any authority—"

"I do. Get me Dr. Simpson, the chief of staff, on the phone." He turned to face the rest of the staff. "Listen up, folks. As of now, we have a public health emergency. The department needs to close—right now." He pointed at Miriam. "Let Dispatch know not to send us any more patients."

He turned to one of the security staff. "Lock the front doors."

The noise level around him rose.

He put his hand on Alison's arm, pulling her to one side. "I'm sorry, honey, but that isn't chicken pox. I think it's smallpox. And we need to contact the DPA."

Atlanta

Callie Turner stowed her bag in her locker and nodded at a few of her colleagues getting changed. She glanced in the mirror and straightened her skirt, taking a deep breath as she gave herself a nervous smile and pulled at her new haircut—an asymmetric blonde bob.

It was meant to signify a new start—a new beginning for her. It had looked fabulous in the salon yesterday, expertly teased and styled. Today it just looked as if she was halfway through a haircut. This would take a bit of getting used to.

First day at the DPA.

Well, not really. An internship and then a three-year specialist residency training program completed within the DPA. All to be part of the Disease Prevention Agency. Eleven years in total of blood, sweat and lots of tears.

All to fulfil someone else's dreams. All to pay homage to someone else's destiny.

Today was the first day of the rest of her life.

She pushed open the door to the telephone hub. "Hi, Maisey."

The short curly-haired woman looked up. "Woo-hoo! Well, look who picked the lucky bag on her first day on the job." She rolled her eyes at Callie. "Go on, then. Who did you upset?"

Callie laughed and pulled out the chair next to Maisey. "No one that I know of. This was just my first shift on the rota." She looked around. "It's kind of empty in here. Where is everyone?"

Maisey gave her a sympathetic glance. "You should have been here two hours ago. They're assembling a team next door. We've got a suspected outbreak of ebola."

Callie's eyes widened. First day on the job and she was assigned to the phones. The crazy calls. While next door the disease detectives were preparing to investigate an outbreak. She bit her lip. "Who took the call?"

Maisey smiled again. "Donovan."

Callie sighed. Typical. The person who took the call usually got to assemble and lead the team. Donovan had a knack of being in the right place at the right time.

Unlike her.

She stared at the wall ahead of her. Someone had stuck a sign up: "NORMAL PEOPLE DON'T PHONE THE DPA."

Never a truer word was said. The phone next to her started ringing. She bent forward and automatically picked it up. It would be a long day.

Four hours later she'd spoken to three health officials, crazy bat lady—who phoned every day—two over-anxious school teachers, five members of the public, and two teenagers who'd obviously been dared by their friends to ring up. Right now all she could think about was a large cappuccino and a banana and toffee muffin.

Her stomach grumbled loudly as she lifted the phone when it rang again. "DPA, Callie Turner, can I help you?"

"This is Matt Sawyer at Chicago General. I've got two kids with suspected smallpox."

She sat up instantly as her brain scrambled to make sense of the words. All thoughts of the muffin vanishing instantly. This had to be a joke. But the voice didn't sound like that of a teenager, it sounded like an adult.

"Well, aren't you going to say anything?" He sounded angry. Patience obviously wasn't his strong point.

She took a deep breath. "Smallpox has been eradicated. It's no longer a naturally occurring disease, Mr. Sawyer."

"Listen, honey, you can call me Doctor. Dr. Matt Sawyer. Ringing any bells yet?"

She frowned. Matt Sawyer? The name seemed familiar. Who was he? And why was he speaking to her like that? She put her hand over the receiver and hissed at Maisey. "Hey, who's Matt Sawyer?"

Maisey's eyes widened instantly, the disbelief on her face obvious. She skidded her wheeled chair across the room next to Callie. "You're joking, right?"

Callie shook her head and pointed to the phone.

Maisey bent forward and pulled the phone away from her ear, replacing it with her mouth. "Outbreak, dead pregnant wife, disappeared off the map."

The pieces of the puzzle started to fall into place and become vaguely familiar. Of course. She *had* heard of this guy. In fact, everyone in the DPA had heard of this guy. He was like a dark, looming legend. But it had been way before her time.

Her training and natural instincts kicked in. There was a protocol for this. She pushed her chair under the desk and pulled up a screen on her computer. "Hi, Dr. Sawyer. Let's go through this."

The algorithm had appeared in front of her, telling her exactly what questions to ask, why and when. She started to take some notes.

"You said you're at Chicago General. Whereabouts in the hospital are you?"

She could almost hear him sigh. "The ER."

"What are the symptoms?"

"Two kids, returned from Somalia a few days ago. Ages six and seven. Very sick. Febrile, uniform red spots mainly on their faces, forearms, palms and soles. A few on their trunks. Low blood pressure, tachycardic, swollen glands."

She was typing furiously. Somalia. The last known place to have a natural outbreak of smallpox. It did seem coincidental.

But there were a whole host of other diseases this could be. She started to speak. "Dr. Sawyer, have you considered chicken pox, herpes, scabies, impetigo—"

"Stop it."

"What?"

"I know you're reading from the list. I've considered all those things. It's none of them. Check your emails." He sounded exasperated with her.

"What do you mean?"

"Lady, do I have to tell you everything twice? Check your emails. I just sent you some photos. Have you ever seen spots like that?"

She clicked out of the algorithm and into her emails. Sure enough, there it was. Everyone in the DPA had a generic email address starting with their full name. He was obviously familiar enough with the system to know that. There was no message. She opened the attached photos.

Wow.

The phone was still at her ear and she moved her face closer to the screen to examine the red spots. No.

She hadn't seen anything like that before—except in a textbook.

"Show the photo to Callum Ferguson," the low voice growled in her ear.

Callum Ferguson. The only person in their team who'd actually been through the last smallpox outbreak. The only person who'd seen the spots for real. Only someone who'd worked here would know something like that. This phone call was definitely no hoax.

"Give me two minutes." She crossed the room in big strides, throwing open the door to the briefing room where the ebola team was assembling.

"Callum, I need you to take a look at something urgently."

"Kind of busy in here, Callie." The large Scotsman looked up from the floor, where he was packing things into a backpack. Callum was well past retirement age but nothing seemed to slow him down, and his age and experience made him invaluable on the outbreak team.

She lowered her voice, trying to avoid the glare coming across the room from Donovan.

"It's Matt Sawyer on the phone. He needs you to look at something."

Callum looked as though he'd just seen a ghost. His hands froze above his pack. He started to stutter, "Wh-what?"

She nodded and he stood up wordlessly and followed her out of the room.

In the few seconds she had been away from her seat, everything had changed. Her boss, Evan Hunter, was standing in front of her computer, staring at her screen, his two deputies and Maisey at his side. The phone receiver was still lying on the desk.

No one spoke. They just moved out of Callum's way

as he reached the screen. His heavy frame dropped into Callie's chair and he glided under her desk.

"Well?"

Evan Hunter wasn't renowned for wasting time. The scowl on his face was fierce and made Callie raise her eyebrows. Hadn't someone told her there had been no love lost between him and Matt Sawyer in the past?

Callum, normally red faced, looked pale. He turned to Evan Hunter and nodded. "I'm sure. I never thought I'd see this again," he whispered.

Everything around them erupted.

Evan pressed his hand on Callum's shoulder. "You're off the ebola team. This is yours—it couldn't possibly be anyone else's, seeing as Matt Sawyer is involved. You're the only one who's ever managed to assert any control over that loose cannon. I want you all over him. Pick your team." He looked at his watch. "It'll take ninety minutes to fly to Chicago. I want you packed and ready to go inside four hours."

He turned and swept out the room, his deputies scurrying after him. Callie was shaken. Had this really just happened?

Callum's voice continued in low tones on the phone. He wasn't even looking at the algorithm she'd pulled up on the screen. His eyes were still fixed on the photo.

"You're sure there's no possibility that this could be intentional—a biological terrorist attack?" He was scribbling notes as he listened. There were a few more mumbled questions before he replaced the receiver.

"Was it him? Was it definitely Sawyer?" Maisey looked fit to burst.

Callum nodded. "It was him." He stood up slowly, obviously still in thought. "I guess that means he's all right, then." He touched Callie's arm. "Get ready, Dr. Turner. This could be the experience of a lifetime."

"I'm on the team?" She could barely contain her excitement. It was only made slightly better by the look of disgust on Donovan's face over the other side of the room.

Callum smiled at her. "You know the rules, Callie. You took the call—of course you're on the team."

"I'll be ready in half an hour. Let me get the updated plans." She rushed off, her heart thumping in her chest.

First official day on the job and she was on the outbreak team investigating an apparently eradicated disease. Isabel would have loved this.

Callie shoved her bag in the overhead locker and sat down next to Callum. Everything was happening so fast. She hadn't even had time to think.

The doors of the plane were already closed and they were starting to taxi down the runway. The cabin crew was already in their seats—the safety announcement forgotten. The normal rules of aviation didn't seem to apply today.

This was the biggest team she'd ever been part of. There had to be around thirty people on this plane. Other doctors, epidemiologists, case interviewers, contact tracers, admin personnel and, most worrying, security.

Callum had the biggest pile of paperwork she'd ever seen. He was checking things off the list. "Vaccines—check. Protocols—check. N95 filtered masks—check. Symptom list—check. Algorithm—check. Three-hundred-page outbreak plan…" his thumb flicked the edges of the thick document "…check."

He leaned back in his seat. "And that's just the beginning." A few minutes later they felt the plane lift off. Ninety minutes until they reached their destination.

"What have you done about containment plans?"

He nodded at her question. "I've identified a suitable building for a Type-C containment. Arrangements are currently being made to prepare it. In the meantime we've instructed Chicago General to switch their air-conditioning off. We don't want to risk the spread of the droplets. They don't even have suitable masks right now—only the paper ones, which are practically useless."

He shook his head. "Those spots were starting to erupt. These kids are at the most infectious stage of this disease."

Callie shuddered. A potentially deadly disease in an E.R. department. Her mind boggled.

It didn't matter that she was a completely rational person. It didn't matter that she specialized in infectious diseases. There was still that tiny human part in her that wanted to panic.

That wanted to run in the other direction.

The strange thing was that there were colleagues at the DPA who would kill to be in her shoes right now. Her very tight, uncomfortable shoes. Why hadn't she changed them before they'd left? Who knew how long she would be on her feet?

She hesitated. "Who are you relaying the instructions to right now?"

His eyes fixed on the papers in front of him. He didn't look so good. "The chief of staff at Chicago General is Max Simpson. He's following our instructions to the letter. Or rather Matt Sawyer is following our instructions to the letter. He's the only one with any experience down there."

There were small beads of sweat on his brow. He reached into his top pocket and pulled out some antacids.

"You okay?"

He nodded as he opened the packet and popped three in his mouth.

Callum was the calmest, most knowledgeable doctor she'd ever worked with. She'd worked side by side with him through lots of outbreaks. She couldn't ask for a better mentor. But even he looked a little scared. Maybe it wasn't just her after all?

Or maybe it was something else entirely.

She lowered her voice. "He was your protégé, wasn't he?"

"My what?"

"Matt Sawyer. I heard he was your protégé."

Callum grimaced and shook his head. "Do me a favor. Don't let Sawyer hear you call him that. That would tip him over the edge that I presume he's currently dangling on."

"What do you mean?" During all the frantic preparations Callie hadn't had any time to find out more about Matt Sawyer. Only a few whispers and hurried conversations here and there.

This was her first real mission. She'd been out as a danger detective before—when she'd been completing her specialist residency training. But this was her first real chance to prove herself. To prove that she was a worthy member of the team. To prove to them—and herself—that she deserved to be there.

It didn't sound promising if the doctor who'd made the initial call was unstable.

She looked at the pile of papers on Callum's lap. The outbreak plans, the containment plans, the paperwork to use for contact tracing, the algorithms. A plan for everything. A piece of paper for every eventuality. Just the way she liked it. Just the way she'd learned to function best.

Rules and regulations were her backbone. The thing that kept her focused. The thing that kept everyone safe.

Callum followed her gaze. "This could get messy."

"What do you mean? With the disease? The casualties?" She hadn't even stopped to think about that yet. She still had her public health head on, the one that looked at the big picture. She hadn't even started to consider the individuals.

Callum looked kind of sad. "No." He gave a little grimace again. "With Sawyer."

"Sawyer? Aren't you happy to see him again?" She was confused. Hadn't they been friends?

"Under any other set of circumstances I would be. But not here. Not like this. This will be his worst nightmare. Sawyer walked away from all this. The last thing he wants to do is be involved in another outbreak. I can't imagine how he's feeling."

"He's a doctor. He has responsibilities. He has a job to do." She made it all sound so straightforward. Because in her head that was the way it should be.

He sighed. "Things change, Callie. Life gets in the way. Sawyer doesn't live by anybody's rules but his own. He didn't even follow protocol today. He should have notified the state department first but he didn't. He just called the DPA. He called *you*." He emphasized the word as he placed a hand on his chest.

She'd missed that. Miss Rules and Regulations had missed that. In her shock at the nature of the call it hadn't even occurred to her that Sawyer should have contacted the state department first and *they* should have contacted the DPA.

How could she have missed that?

She didn't need anyone to remind her that things could change—that life, or lack of it—could get in the way. She was living proof of that.

Seeds of doubt started to creep into her mind. She'd missed the first rule of notification. And if she'd missed that, what else would she miss? Should she even be on this team?

Rules were there for a reason. Rules were there to be followed. Rules were there for everyone's safety.

Then it really hit her. What was happening before her very eyes.

The last thing she needed to do right now was look at the wider picture. She needed to concentrate on the picture right before her.

Callum was turning gray, with the slightest blue tinge around his lips. His skin was waxy and he was still sweating. His hand remained firmly on his chest.

"Callum? Are you okay?" She unfastened her seat belt and stood up, signaling to some of the other members of the team. "That's not heartburn, is it?"

He shook his head as she started barking out orders to the rest of the team. "Get me some oxygen. Find out how soon till we get there. Can we get an earlier landing slot? Speak to the pilot—it's a medical emergency."

They literally had every piece of equipment known to man on this plane. Unfortunately, most of it was in the hold. And none of it was to treat a myocardial infarction.

She cracked open their first-aid kit, monitoring his blood pressure and giving him some aspirin. She pasted a smile on her face. "Things will be fine, Callum. We'll get you picked up at the airport and taken to the nearest cardiac unit."

His hand gripped her wrist. "I'm sorry, Callie. I shouldn't be leaving you to deal with this. Not with Sawyer. You two are like oil and water. You won't mix. Not at all." His head was shaking.

Callie's stomach was churning. The thought of facing the legendary Sawyer herself was not filling her with confidence. But right now she would do or say anything that would relieve the pressure on Callum. Anything at all.

"Everything will be fine. You'll see. Don't worry about a thing, Callum. I can handle Sawyer."

Famous last words.

CHAPTER TWO

"WHO ARE YOU and where is Callum Ferguson?" Not waiting for an answer, the man with the shaggy hair pushed past her and looked behind her. With his broad frame and pale green eyes, on another occasion she might have looked twice. But she didn't have time for this.

Great. The welcoming party. And he was obviously delighted to see her.

She struggled to set the box down on the reception desk. There was only one person this could be. And she intended to start the way she meant to continue. This was business.

"Here are the N95 masks. Make sure anyone that goes into the room with those kids wears one. And make sure it's fitted properly, otherwise it will be useless."

He hadn't moved. He was still standing directly in her path. "I asked you a question."

She almost hesitated but that would do her no good. She needed to establish who was in charge here. And it was her.

"Matt Sawyer? I'm Callie Turner and I'm leading the team." She turned towards the door as the rest of the team fanned in behind her, carrying their equipment.

It was like an invasion. And the irony of that wasn't lost on her.

She tilted her head. "I'd shake your hand but you're already an infection control hazard, so forgive me."

Did she look confident? She certainly hoped so, because her stomach was churning so much that any minute now she might just throw up all over his Converses.

She walked around behind the desk and started pulling things out of the boxes being deposited next to her. "Lewis, Cheryl, set up here and here." She pointed to some nearby desks.

"I'm only going to ask you one more time. Where is Callum Ferguson?"

He was practically growling at her now. And that hair of his was going to annoy her. Why didn't he get a decent haircut? Wouldn't long hair be an infection control hazard? Maybe she should suggest he find an elastic band and tie it back, though on second thoughts it wasn't quite long enough for that.

She drew herself up before him. This man was starting to annoy her. *Did he think she was hiding Callum Ferguson in her back pocket?* "I'm sorry to tell you, Dr. Sawyer, that Dr. Ferguson became unwell on the plane en route."

He actually twitched. As if she'd just said something to shock him. Maybe he was a human being after all.

"What happened?"

"We think he had an MI. He's been taken to the cardiac unit at St John's. I heard it's the best in town."

She waited for a second while he digested the news. Would he realize she'd checked up on the best place to send her colleague, rather than just send him off to the nearest hospital available? She hoped so. From the expression on Sawyer's face she might need to win some points with him.

Why did the thought of being quarantined with this man fill her with impending doom?

Sawyer was about to explode. And Miss Hoity-Toity with her navy-blue suit, pointy shoes and squinty hairdo was first in line to bear the brunt of the impact.

It was bad enough that he was here—but now to find out that the one person in the DPA he absolutely trusted *wasn't* going to be here?

The thought of Callum Ferguson having an MI was sickening. Sawyer had almost fallen into the trap of thinking the man was invincible. He'd spent the last forty years investigating outbreaks and coming home unscathed.

Please let him be okay.

He scowled at Callie Turner as she issued orders to those all around him. Did she realize her hand was trembling ever so slightly? Because he did. And it wasn't instilling him with confidence.

He planted his hand on his hip. "How old are you *exactly*?"

He could see her bristling. Her brain was whirring, obviously trying to think up a smart answer. She walked straight over to him and put both of her hands on her hips, mirroring his stance.

"Exactly how old do you want me to be, Sawyer?"

He couldn't wipe the smile from his face. Smart and sassy—if a little young. The girl showed promise.

"So what happened to the hair?"

He'd already caught her tugging self-consciously at one side of her hair. As if she wasn't quite used to it yet. "Were you halfway through when you took my call?"

He took a piece of gum offered by nearby Miriam and started chewing as he watched her. He could tell she was irritated by him. Perfect. Maybe if he annoyed Miss DPA enough, he could get out of here.

Except it didn't work like that and he knew it. Still, he could live in hope.

She dumped a final pile of papers on the desk from her box, which she picked up and kicked under the desk. Yip. She was definitely mad.

She grabbed the heavily clipped document on the top of the pile, strode over and thrust it directly against his chest. It hit him square in the solar plexus, causing him to catch his breath.

"My haircut cost more than you probably make in a month. Now, here—read this. And it isn't from me. It's from Callum. He said to make sure it was the first thing I gave you—along with the instructions to follow it to the letter."

He pulled the document off his chest. The DPA plan for a smallpox outbreak. All three hundred pages of it. He let it go and it skidded across the desk towards her.

"I don't need to read this."

She stepped back in front of him. "Yes. You do. You've already broken protocol once today, Dr. Sawyer. You should have contacted the state department *before* you contacted us. But, then, you know that, don't you? You don't work for the DPA anymore, Dr. Sawyer."

He cracked his chewing gum. "Well, that's at least one thing we agree on."

She glanced at her watch. "So, that means, that as of right now—five thirty-six p.m.—you work for me. You, and everyone else in here. This is my hospital now, Dr. Sawyer, my jurisdiction, and you will do exactly what I tell you." She jerked her thumb over her shoulder. "And it's all in that plan. So memorize it because there'll be a pop quiz later."

She kicked her navy-blue platforms beneath the desk and started to undo her shirt. "Where are the scrubs and protective clothing?" she shouted along the corridor.

"In here," came a reply from one of the nearby rooms.

"Let's go see these kids," she barked at Sawyer over her shoulder as she headed to the room.

Organized chaos was continuing around him. Piles upon piles of paper were being pulled from boxes, new phones were appearing and being plugged in all around him. He recognized a couple of the faces—a few of the epidemiologists and contact tracers—standing with their clipboards at the ready.

He could hear the voices of the admin staff around him. "No, put it here. Callie's very particular about paperwork. Put the algorithms up on the walls, in the treatments rooms and outside the patient rooms. Everyone has to follow them to the letter."

So, she was a rules-and-regulations girl? This was about to get interesting.

He wandered over to the room. Callie was standing in her bra and pants, opening a clean set of regulation pale pink scrubs. Last time he'd worn them they'd been green. Obviously a new addition to the DPA repertoire.

The sight made him catch his breath. It was amazing what could lurk beneath those stuffy blue suits and pointy shoes. The suit was lying in a crumpled heap on the ground, discarded as if it were worthless when it easily clocked in at over a thousand dollars. He could see the label from here. Maybe Miss Hoity-Toity did have some redeeming features after all.

Her skin was lightly tanned, with some white strap

marks on her shoulders barely covered by her bra. She was a matching-set girl. Pale lilac satin. But she didn't have her back to him so from this angle he couldn't tell if she favored briefs or a thong...

Her stomach wasn't washboard flat like some women he'd known. It was gently rounded, proving to him that she wasn't a woman who lived on salad alone. But the most intriguing thing about her was the pale white scar trailing down the outside of her leg. Where had that come from? It might be interesting to find out. His eyes lifted a little higher. And as for her breasts...

"Quit staring at me." She pulled on her scrub trousers. "You're a doctor. Apparently you've seen it all before." She tossed him a hat. "And get that mop of yours hidden."

She pulled her scrub top over her head and knelt in the corner next to her bag. She seemed completely unaffected by his gawping. Just as well really.

Sawyer reluctantly pulled on the hat and a disposable pale yellow isolation gown over his scrubs. She appeared at his side a few seconds later as he struggled to tuck his hair inside the slightly too big cap.

"Want one of these?" She waved a bobby pin under his nose with a twinkle in her eye. She was laughing at him.

"Won't you need all of them to pull back that one side of your bad haircut?"

She flung a regulation mask at him. "Ha. Ha. Now, let's go."

They walked down the corridor where the lights were still dimmed. She paused outside the door, her hand resting lightly on his arm.

"Let's clarify before we go in. How many staff have been in contact with these kids?"

He nodded. He would probably answer these questions a dozen times today. "Main contact has been myself and Alison, one of our nurses. We're estimating they were only in the waiting room around ten minutes. One of the triage nurses moved them through to a room quickly as the kids were pretty sick."

Her eyebrows rose above her mask. "I take it that you've continued to limit the contact to yourselves?"

"Ah, about that."

"What?" Her expression had changed in an instant. Her eyes had narrowed and her glare hardened.

"There's a problem."

"What kind of problem?"

"Alison's pregnant. Eighteen weeks."

She let out an expression that wasn't at all ladylike. He hadn't known she had it in her.

"Exactly. I haven't let her go back in. She's adamant. Says there's no point exposing anyone else to something she's already breathed in anyway. But I wasn't having any of it."

He could see her brain racing. There was the tiniest flicker of panic under that mask. "But the vaccine..."

He touched her shoulder. "I know. We don't know the effects it could have on a fetus." He shrugged. "I don't know if you've come up with any new research in the last six years, but I wouldn't want to be the doctor to give it to her."

She nodded. "Leave it with me. I'll take it up with the team." She turned back to the room. "We need to get some samples."

"It's already done."

"What?" She whipped around. "Why didn't you say so?"

He sighed. "What do you think I've been doing these

last few hours? I'm not that far out of the loop that I don't know how to take samples. Besides, the kids were used to me. It was better that I did it."

She nodded, albeit reluctantly. "And the parents?"

"I've taken samples from them too. They're all packaged and ready to go. Let's find out what we're dealing with."

"I want to see the kids first."

Now she was annoying him. "You think I made their spots up? Drew them on their faces and arms?"

"Of course I don't. But, like or not, I'm the doctor in charge here. I need to see the spots for myself. Get some better pictures than the ones snapped on your phone. I need to be clear that you've ruled out everything."

She was only saying what he would have said himself a few years ago. She was doing things by the book. But in his eyes, doing things by the book was wasting time. That was why he hadn't bothered with the call to the state department. Best to go right to the source.

And this family might not have that time to waste. Just like his hadn't.

It made him mad. Irrationally mad. And it didn't matter that the voices in his head were telling him that. Because he wasn't listening.

"For goodness' sake. Don't you have any confidence in my abilities? I've been doing this job since you were in kindergarten. I could run rings around you!"

She pushed her face up next to his. If it weren't for the masks, their noses would be practically touching. "You're not quite that old, Matt Sawyer. And it doesn't matter what I think about your doctoring abilities. I'm in charge here. Not you. We've already established you don't work for the DPA any more and I do. You know how things work. You know the procedures and protocols. You might not have followed them but I do. To the letter." She put her hand on the door. "Now, do your job, Dr. Sawyer. Take me in there and introduce me to the parents."

Callie leaned back against the wall in the sluice room. She'd just pulled off her disposable clothing and mask and dispensed with them in line with all the infection control protocols.

She let the temperature of the cool concrete seep through her thin scrub top. Thank goodness. With the air-conditioning turned off this place was getting warm. Too warm. Why couldn't this outbreak have happened in the middle of the winter, when Chicago was knee deep in snow, instead of when it was the height of summer? It could have made things a whole lot simpler for them. It could also have made the E.R. a whole lot quieter.

Those kids were sick. Sawyer hadn't been kidding. They were *really* sick. She'd really prefer it if they could be in a pediatric intensive care unit, but right now that was out of the question.

And even though it seemed like madness, in a few minutes' time she was going to have to inoculate them and their parents with the smallpox vaccine.

Then she was going to have to deal with the staff, herself included.

There wasn't time to waste. The laboratory samples were just away. It could be anything up to forty-eight hours before they had even a partial diagnosis and seven days before a definitive diagnosis. She didn't want to wait that long.

She knew that would cause problems with Sawyer. He would want to wait—to be sure before they inflicted a vaccine with known side-effects on people who might not be at risk. But she'd already had that conversation with her boss, Evan Hunter. He'd told her to make the decision on the best information available. And she had.

She wrinkled her nose, trying to picture the relationship between the man she'd just met and Callum Ferguson, a doctor for whom she had the utmost respect. How on earth had these two ever gotten along? It just didn't seem feasible.

She knew that Sawyer had lost his pregnant wife on a mission. That must have been devastating. But to walk away from his life and his career? Why would anyone do that? Had he been grief stricken? Had he been depressed?

And more to the point, how was he now? Was he reliable enough to trust his judgment on how best to proceed? Because right now what she really needed was partner in crime, not an outright enemy.

If only Callum were here. He knew how to handle Sawyer. She wouldn't have needed to have dealt with any of this.

Her fingers fell to her leg—to her scar. It had started to itch. Just as it always did when she was under stress. She took a deep breath.

She'd made a decision. Now it was time to face the fallout.

"Are you crazy?"

"No. I'm not crazy. I've already spoke to my boss at the DPA. Funnily enough, he didn't want you sitting in on that conference call. It seems your reputation has preceded you."

"I don't care about my reputation—"

"Obviously."

"I care about these staff."

He spun around as the crates were wheeled into the treatment room and the vaccine started to be unloaded. One of the contact tracers came up and mumbled in her ear, "We're going to start with a limited number of people affected. The kids, their parents, Dr. Sawyer, yourself and these other four members of staff who've had limited contact."

"What about Alison?"

The contact tracer hesitated, looking from one to the other. "That's not my decision," he said as he spun away.

Callie swallowed. She could do with something cool to drink, her throat was dry and scratchy. "Alison will have to make her own decision on the vaccine. There isn't enough data for us to give her reliable information."

She saw the look on his face. He looked haunted. As if he'd just seen a ghost from the past. Was this what had happened to his wife? Had she been exposed to something that couldn't be treated because of her pregnancy? This might all be too close to home for Matt Sawyer.

"Okay." He ran his fingers through his hair. It hadn't got any better now it had been released from the cap. In fact, it seemed to have grown even longer. "Do me a favor?"

She lifted her head from the clipboard she was scribbling on. "What?"

"Let me be the one to talk to Alison about it. If there hasn't been any more research in the last six years, then I'm as up to date as you are."

She took a deep breath. She didn't know this guy well enough to know how he would handle this. He was obviously worried about his colleague. But was that all? And would his past experience affect his professional judgment?

"You can't recommend it one way or the other, you understand that, don't you?"

She could tell he wanted to snap at her. To tell her where to go. But something made him bite his tongue. "I can be impartial. I'll give her all the facts and let her make her own decision. It will come better from someone she knows."

Callie nodded. He was right. The smallpox vaccine came with a whole host of issues. She was already questioning some of the decisions that she'd made.

Alison was at the end of the corridor in a room on her own, partly for her own protection and partly for the protection of others. She'd been in direct contact with the disease—without any mask to limit the spread of the infection. In theory, because she hadn't had prolonged exposure in a confined space, she should be at low risk. But she'd also been exposed to—and had touched—the erupting spots. The most infectious element of the disease. Pregnant or not, she had to be assessed as being at risk. "You know I have to do this, right?"

He was glaring at her, his head shaking almost imperceptibly—as if it was an involuntary act.

"We have the three major diagnostic criteria for smallpox. This is a high-risk category. Those parents look sick already. They're probably in the prodromal stage of the disease."

The implication in the air was there, hanging between them. If they waited, it could result in more casualties and the DPA being slaughtered by the media for wasting time. That was the last thing anyone wanted.

"Callie? We have a problem."

Both heads turned to the DPA contact tracer standing at the door. "What is it, Hugo?"

She stepped forward and took the clipboard from his hand.

"It's the parents. They can't say for sure if the rash came out during or after the plane trip home."

"You're joking, right?" Callie felt the hackles rise on the back of her neck. This was one of the most crucial pieces of information they needed. Once the rash was out, the person was infectious. This was the difference between three hundred passengers on a plane being at risk or not.

Hugo looked pale. "Mrs. Keating is sure they didn't have a rash before they got on the plane. And she's almost sure they didn't have it on the plane, because the kids slept most of the journey. They went straight home and put the kids to bed—she didn't even get them changed. It wasn't until the next day she noticed the rash, but it could have been there on the plane."

Callie cringed, as Sawyer read her mind. "Prodromal stage. Did they sleep because they were developing the disease or did they sleep because it was a long flight?" He put a hand on Hugo's shoulder. "You have to establish if she noticed either of the kids having a fever during the journey." He paused, then added, "And make sure they didn't change planes anywhere." Sawyer rolled his eyes to the ceiling, "Or our contact tracing will become a nightmare."

Hugo nodded and disappeared back through the door.

Sawyer watched her as she fiddled with the clips in her hair. She was consulting the plan again. There seemed to be one in every room he entered. A list of procedures. A multitude of flow charts.

She didn't like it when things weren't exactly to plan.

Then again, she'd never been in charge of an epidemic before.

He could be doing so much more for her. He could be talking her through all this, helping her out. Liaising more with the team back at the DPA—even if that did mean dealing with Evan Hunter.

He knew all this stuff inside out and back to front.

But he just couldn't.

It didn't matter that he was stuck in the middle of all this. There was a line he didn't want to cross. He had to take a step back. He had to focus on the sick children.

He picked up another disposable gown and mask. "The IV fluids on the kids probably need changing. I'm going to go and check on them." He paused and turned his head just as he left. "You need to go and make an announcement to all the staff. You need to bring them up to date on the information that you have." He hesitated, then added something else.

"It's not only the natives that will be getting restless. We've got patients here who've been quarantined. They won't understand what's going on. They won't know what to tell their relatives."

She gave the slightest nod, as if the thought of what she was going to say was pressing down on her shoulders. He almost withered. "There's a public address system at the front desk—use that."

His phone beeped and he headed out of the room and down the corridor, pulling the phone from his pocket.

Violet.

He should have known.

No, he should have texted her first. She must be frantic.

He flicked the switch to silent and pushed it back into his pocket. She would just have to wait. He would deal with her later.

* * *

Callie could hear the raised voices as she strode down the corridor. "Why can't I leave? I'm fine. If I stay here, I'll get sick. You can't make me stay!"

It was inevitable. People always reacted like this when there was an outbreak. It was human nature.

The hard part was that Callie didn't want to be here any more than they did. But she couldn't exactly say that, could she?

The reality check was starting to sink in. She was in a strange city, in the middle of a possible outbreak of a disease that had supposedly been eradicated. She wasn't ready for this. If she closed her eyes for just a second, she could see Isabel in the middle of all this. This had been her dream from childhood—to work at the DPA at the cutting edge of infectious disease. She wouldn't be feeling like this. She wouldn't be feeling sick to her stomach and wanting to go and hide in a corner. Isabel would be center stage, running everything with a precise touch.

But Isabel wasn't here.

And that was Callie's fault. Her beautiful older sister had died six years earlier. Callie had been behind the wheel of their old car, taking a corner too fast—straight into the path of someone on the wrong side of the road. If only she hadn't been distracted—been fighting with her sister. Over something and nothing.

That was the thing that twisted the most. It was the same argument they'd had for years. Pizza or burgers. Something ridiculous. Something meaningless. How pathetic.

She fixed her gaze on the scene ahead. Isabel would know exactly how to handle a man like Sawyer. She would have had him eating out of her hand in five minutes flat.

Okay, maybe not five minutes.

Sawyer probably wasn't the type.

But, then, Isabel had been a people person. She'd known how to respond to people, she'd known how to work a crowd. All the things that Callie didn't have a clue about.

The voices were rising. Things were reaching a crescendo.

It was time to step up. Whether she liked it or not, it was time to take charge.

She pushed her way through the crowd around the desk and jumped up onto the reception area desk. "Is this the PA system?"

The clerk gave her a nod as she picked up the microphone and held it to her mouth. Adrenaline was starting to course through her system. All eyes were on her. She could do this. She pressed the button on the microphone and it let out a squeal from automatic feedback. Anyone who hadn't been listening before was certainly listening now.

"Hi, everyone. I'm sure you know I'm Callie Turner from the DPA. Let me bring you up to speed."

The anxiety in the room was palpable. The eyes staring at her were full of fear.

"You all know that we're dealing with two suspected cases of smallpox. That's the reason why the E.R. has been closed and we've enforced a quarantine. The samples have been collected and sent to the DPA lab for identification. The laboratory tests for smallpox are complicated and time-consuming. We should hear back in around forty-eight hours what type of virus it is— whether it's a type of pox or not—but it takes longer to identify what strain of virus it is. That can take anything up to seven days. So, until we know if it's a pox or not, we need to stay here. We need to try and contain this virus."

"I don't want to be in isolation," one of the men shouted.

"You're not," Callie said quickly. "You're quarantined—there's a difference. Isolation means separating people who are ill with a contagious disease from healthy people. The children who are affected have been isolated. Quarantine restricts the movement of people who have been exposed to someone or something, to see if they will become ill. That's what we're doing with all of you." Her hand stretched out across the room.

She could still feel the tension. Anxious glances being exchanged between staff and patients. She could see the questions forming on their lips. Best to keep going.

She tried to keep her voice calm. "The incubation period for smallpox is around twelve days but it can range from seven to seventeen days. Smallpox is spread person to person by droplet transmission. It can also be spread by contact with pustules or rash lesions or contaminated clothing or bedding.

"A person with smallpox is considered infectious when the rash appears, but at the moment we're going to consider any affected person infectious from the onset of fever. This should help us control any outbreak. It's important to remember that only close contacts—those who were within six or seven feet of the infectious person should be at risk."

She was talking too quickly, trying to put out too much information at once. She was hoping and praying that someone wouldn't pick up on the fact that they could be quarantined together for seventeen days.

"Should? What do you mean, 'should'? Don't you know?"

Callie took a deep breath. She didn't blame people for being angry. She would be angry too. But as she opened her mouth to speak, Sawyer got in there first. He'd appeared out of nowhere, stepping up alongside her, his hand closing over hers as he took the PA microphone from her.

"This isn't like some disaster movie, folks. A person with smallpox doesn't walk, coughing and spluttering, through a crowd and infect everyone around them. For a start, most people infected with smallpox don't cough anyway. And the last data available from the DPA shows that the average person affected can infect around five to seven people. And those would only be the close contacts around them. Let's not panic. Let's keep this in perspective."

She was watching him, her breath caught her in throat. He was doing what *she* should be doing. He was keeping calm and giving them clear and easy-to-understand information.

Part of her felt angry. And part of her felt relief.

She was out of her depth and she knew it.

The DPA was a big place. And she was a good doctor—when she was part of a team. But as a leader? Not so much.

Put her in a room with a pile of paperwork and she was the best. Methodical, good at interpreting the practical applications of a plan.

She could do the patient stuff—she could, obviously, or she wouldn't have made it through medical school or her residency. Actually, some of it she had loved. But she'd enjoyed the one-to-one patient contacts, patients a physician could take time with, understand their condition and give them long-term advice. Not the hurried, rushed, wide perspective of the DPA.

But, then, the DPA had been Isabel's dream, not hers. She'd never wanted this for herself.

And now? She was stuck with it.

"So, that's it folks. We'll let you know as soon as we hear back from the labs. In the meantime, we'll have arrangements in place to make everyone more comfortable with the facilities we have here." He raised his eyebrows at her. "It could be that in a few hours we move to somewhere more suitable?"

She nodded wordlessly. He must have known that Callum would already have put the wheels in motion to set up a category C facility for containment.

"In the meantime, follow the infection control procedures on the walls around you. Take a deep breath and show a little patience. We're all scared." He pointed at the figures lining the walls with their clipboards, "It's important we help these guys out. Tell them everything you know." He looked back at Callie. She was sure that right now she must resemble a deer caught in a set of headlights. "And if you have any questions, Dr. Turner is in charge. That's it for now."

He jumped off the table and headed back down the corridor.

The room was quieter now, the shouting had stopped. Her legs were trembling and she grabbed hold of a hand offered to her as she climbed down off the table. Heads were down, people working away, going about their business. One of the security guards was helping one of the nursing aides carry linen through to another room to help set up some beds.

Callie knew she couldn't leave this. She knew she

had to talk to him. Even though he was trying to put some space between them.

"Sawyer." She was breathless, running down the corridor after him. "I just wanted to say thank you. For back there."

His green eyes fixed on hers, just for a second, before they flitted away and he ran his fingers through that hair again. Her heart clenched, even though she couldn't understand why. He was exasperated with her. "That was a one-off, Callie. Don't count on me to help you again." He turned and strode back down the corridor, leaving her standing there.

Alone.

CHAPTER THREE

"You need to manage things better." He couldn't help it. There were probably a million other ways to put this more delicately, but Sawyer didn't have time to think about nicer words.

Her head shot upwards. There it was—that rabbit-in-the-headlights look again from her.

He hated it. Because it made his stomach churn. He didn't know whether to be irritated by it or whether he really wanted to go over and give her a quick hug.

"What on earth do you mean, *'manage things better'*?" She made quote marks in the air with her fingers as she repeated his words back to him. He could see the lines across her brow. She was tired and she was stressed. And he understood that. It was part and parcel of the job at the DPA.

He could feel his lips turn upwards. She looked even prettier when she was cross.

"What are you smirking at?" She stood up from behind the desk. A desk lost under a multitude of piles of papers—no doubt more copies of plans and protocols. A few sheets scattered as she stood.

His smile broadened. He could tell she really wanted to stop and pick them up.

She was in front of him now, her hands on her hips. "What?"

He liked that. Sometimes she just got straight to the point. No skirting around the edge of things.

He gestured to the door behind him. "You need to clarify some things about the vaccination. There are still a lot of questions out there."

She sighed and ran her fingers through the short side of her hair. "I know. I'll get to it. I've got a million and one things to deal with." Her eyes flickered in the direction of the hidden desk.

"Then delegate."

She started, as if the thought of actually delegating horrified her.

"But I'm responsible—"

"And you need to be visible. You need to be seen. You have to be on the floor—not stuck in some office. You can make your decisions out there, not from behind a desk."

He could see her brain ticking, thinking over his suggestions. Truth be told, she'd been delegating from the minute she'd walked in the door—just not the important stuff.

"And you need to do something about Alison."

Her eyes narrowed. "I thought you wanted to deal with Alison."

"And I have—we've had the discussion about the vaccine. She hasn't decided what to do yet, but I think she'll opt on the side of caution and say no."

"So what's the problem?" She'd started to walk back over to the desk.

"The problem is she's a nurse. She's stuck in a room at the bottom of the corridor. Isolated. Quarantined—"

"You know that's not the case."

He touched her shoulder. "But she doesn't. You need to tell people, explain to them what the difference is. You explained that to the masses—but you need didn't explain it to her. She's in there frightened and alone. You need to communicate better." He could feel her bristle under his touch. "Alison needs to do something. I understand you think she might have been exposed but you can't leave her sitting there for hours on end." He picked up a pile of papers from the desk. "Give her a list of phone calls to make for you. Let her do some of the specialized phone contact tracing."

"She can't do that. That's a special skill. You need of hours of training to do that properly," she snapped.

He could feel the frustration rising in his chest. "It's only a list of questions! She's an intelligent human being. Give her something to do. Something to take her mind off things."

He grabbed the first random thought that entered his head. "Let her organize the food, then! Something— anything—to stop her thinking that if she hadn't come to work this morning she wouldn't have risked the life of her baby."

He could see the realization fall on her face. And suddenly he understood.

She was a big-picture girl. The perfect person for public health. She didn't individualize, or personalize, the other side of the job. The things that affected normal people.

He took a deep breath. He wasn't trying to make this harder for her. He knew she'd been thrown in at the deep end.

Part of him wanted to offer to take over, even though he knew that would never be allowed to. And part of him still wanted to run for the hills.

He hated this. Everything about this situation grated on him. He'd thought he'd be safe.

He'd thought he'd distanced himself enough to never to be in a situation like this again. How often did an E.R. notify an outbreak on this scale? Rarely.

And this type of disease? Well, let's face it, not in the last thirty or forty years.

No matter what his brain told him, he would not allow himself to be dragged in. Even though he was right in the middle of everything he needed to keep some distance. He needed *not* to have responsibility for this outbreak.

She was hesitating. He could see it written all over her face. Then the decision was made. It was almost as if he could see a little light go on behind her eyes.

She looked him square in the eye. "You're right. I can give her something to do. Something that means she's not at risk to herself or anyone else around her." She picked up a list from her desk. "She can order the food supplies, linen supplies and any extra medical supplies that we might need. The food's turned into a bit of a nightmare in the last few hours." She picked up a hefty manual from her desk, ripped out a few sheets and attached them to a red clipboard. "This will tell her everything she needs to know about how to arrange the delivery of supplies that keeps all parties safe."

Her eyes swept around the room.

It was almost as if once she'd made a decision, that was it. She was ready. She was organized. The courage of her convictions took her forward. She could be great at this job, if only she had confidence in her abilities. And she would get that. It would just take a few years.

A few years that she would normally have had in the DPA, working with their most experienced doctors.

His thoughts went back to Callum and he glanced at his watch. "I need to make a phone call."

Her hand rested on his arm. The warmth of her fingers stopped him dead.

"I need you to do one more thing for me before you go."

She was looking at him with those big eyes. The ones he preferred not to have contact with. This was where his gut twisted and he wanted to say no. Say no to anything that would drag him further into this mess.

There was a new edge to her voice, a new determination. She handed him a file from the desk. "I need you to look over this with an independent eye. You've been out of the DPA long enough to make an assessment."

He was confused now. What was she talking about? Instinctively, his hand reached out for the file.

"You told me to delegate. Everyone thought the next smallpox outbreak would be deliberate—a terrorist act. Nothing we've seen here supports that. All the information from the parents and contacts would lead me to suggest this was a natural outbreak—however impossible or improbable that may be."

He was nodding slowly. It was one of the first things that Callum had asked him. It was one of the most immediate priorities for the DPA: to try and determine the source.

"I need you to look over the rest of the evidence the contact tracers have collected. I have to phone Evan Hunter in the next half-hour. It's my professional opinion that this isn't a terrorist act." Her voice was wavering slightly. This was one of the most crucial decisions she would make in her lead role for the DPA.

Everything she was saying made sense and he knew that she would have read and analyzed the evidence to the best of her abilities. But time was pressing. If there was any threat to the general population, they had to know now.

He understood what this meant to her. And he understood why she was asking him.

It wasn't just that he'd told her to delegate. It was that this could impact on everything. The actions and reactions the world would have to this outbreak.

She had to be right.

She had to be sure.

If Callum had been here, this would have been on his head. But even then, he would have had Callie to bat things back and forth with. To agree with his decision-making.

She didn't have that.

She didn't have anyone.

So she was asking the one person here who might have those skills.

He laid his hand over hers. "I'll make the phone call. It will take two minutes and then I'll close this office door and look over all this information. If I have even a shadow of a doubt, I'll let you know."

Her shoulders sagged just a little. As if she'd just managed to disperse a little of their weight. "Thank you," she said as she walked out the door.

Sawyer watched her leave, trying not to look at her rear view in the pink scrubs. He couldn't work out what was going on. One minute she was driving him crazy. The next?

He slumped back in the chair a little, the mound of paper in front of him looking less than enticing. His phone slipped from his pocket and clattered to the floor.

It was like an alarm clock going off in his head.

Violet. He really needed to contact Violet.

His sister worked at the DPA and must be going crazy. She would have heard his name bandied about by now and know that he must be in the middle of all this.

His phone had been switched to silent for the last few hours and he glanced at the screen and cringed. He'd known as soon as he'd called the DPA that his number would have been logged in their system.

It made sense that she'd tried to get in touch with him—after all, he'd changed his number numerous times in the last few years—only getting in touch when he could face it.

He really didn't want to know how many missed calls and text messages he'd had from her. It just made him feel even guiltier.

When his wife had died and he'd walked away from the DPA, he'd also more or less walked away from his family.

It had been the only way he could cope.

He couldn't bear to have any reminders of Helen, his wife. It had been just too much. He'd needed time. He'd needed space.

On occasion—when he'd felt guilty enough—he'd send Violet a text just to let her know that he was safe. Nothing more. Nothing less.

She deserved better and he knew that. He just hadn't been in a position to give it.

The one saving grace was that no one in the DPA knew they were related. She'd started just after he'd left. And the last thing any new doctor needed was to live in the shadow of the family black sheep.

He turned the phone over in his hands and looked at his watch. The mountain of paper on the desk seemed to have mysteriously multiplied in the last few minutes.

He would phone Violet. He would.

But right now time was critical. He had to do this first.

Callie was mad.

But she was trying not to show it.

Everything he'd said was right.

The doctor who was apparently bad-tempered and temperamental was making her feel as if she was the problem and not him.

The worst thing was he'd sounded clear-headed and rational. He was right, she did need to delegate. No matter how alien the concept seemed to her.

So she'd delegated the most obvious duty to him. Evan Hunter would have a fit.

But she was in charge here. Not him. And since Callum wasn't here, she had to rely on the one member of staff who had some experience in this area—whether Evan Hunter liked it or not.

"Callie?"

She'd reached the treatment room. One of the second-year residents was emptying the refrigerated container of vaccines.

"What is it?"

"How many of these do you want me to draw up?"

She shook her head. "None—yet." She glanced at the face of the resident, who was obviously worried about doing anything wrong. A few years ago that would have been her.

"Have you used the ring vaccination concept before?"

The resident shook her head.

In the midst of all this madness Callie had to remember she had a responsibility to teach. To help the staff around her learn their roles. To lead by example.

The words started repeating to a rhythm in her head.

"Ring vaccination controls an outbreak by vaccinating and monitoring a ring of people around each infected individual. The idea is to form a buffer of immune individuals to prevent the spread of the disease. It's a way of containment."

"And it works effectively?"

Callie gave a small smile. "We thought it did. Ring vaccination was held as essential in the eradication of smallpox. For the vast majority of people, getting the smallpox vaccine within three days of exposure will significantly lesson the severity of the symptoms."

"What about people who were vaccinated before against smallpox? Aren't they already protected?"

Callie shook her head. "It's a common misconception. Why do you ask?"

"One of the men in the waiting room said he'd had the vaccination as a child and he wouldn't need anything."

Callie smiled. "Last time ring vaccination was used for smallpox was in the late seventies. But if he was vaccinated then, he would only have had protection for between three and five years. There might still be some antibodies in his blood but we can't assume anything."

"Would we vaccinate him again?"

"It depends where he falls at risk. In the first instance, we vaccinate anyone who has been, or may have been, exposed to someone who has the infection."

"He was sitting next to the family in the waiting room."

Callie nodded. There was so much about this that wasn't written entirely in stone and open to interpretation. "Then we need to assess how much contact he had with the family—and for how long."

"And that's where all the guessing games start."

The deep voice at the door made her head jerk up. Sawyer was standing with her file in his hand. He walked over and held it out towards her. "You're right, Callie. It didn't take long to review the information." He shook his head. "There's absolutely nothing there to hint at anything other than a natural outbreak—the very thing the DPA declared could never happen."

The sense of relief that rushed over her body was instant. She'd been scared. Scared that she'd missed something—that she'd overlooked something important. Something her sister would never have done.

It was the first time today she actually felt as if she might be doing a good job.

She took the file from his hand. "I guess we don't know everything, then," she murmured.

He gave her a lazy smile and raised one eyebrow at her. "Really? You mean the DPA hasn't managed to find its way into every corner of the universe to see if there are any deadly diseases left?"

Her eyes were scanning the sheets in front of her. She shrugged. "It makes sense. The Keatings said that it was the first time the locals had come into contact with outsiders."

"First contact. Sounds much sexier than it should."

She raised her eyebrows at him. "Sounds like a whole can of worms."

The resident lowered her head and busied herself in the corner of the room. In some ways Callie wanted to do that too.

She wanted to take herself out of the range of Sawyer's impenetrable stare. It was making her hair stand on end and sending weird tingles down her spine.

She felt like a high-school teenager on prom night, not an experienced doctor in the midst of an emergency situation.

She picked up one of the vials on the countertop. "I guess I should lead by example."

He was at her side in an instant. "What do you mean?"

"If I'm going to recommend first-line vaccination, I guess I should go first."

"Are you sure about this?"

Callie almost laughed out loud. Was he joking? "Of course I'm not sure. But I've got to base this on the evidence that I've got, no matter how imperfect it is. If this is smallpox, I've a duty of care to protect others and contain the virus. You, me, the parents—anyone else assessed as 'at risk' should be vaccinated."

She picked up the diluent and delivered it swiftly into the container holding the dried vaccine. Her hands rolled the vial between her palms, watching the liquid oscillate back and forth.

"I think you should wait. I think we should have a definite diagnosis before we start vaccinating."

She nodded. In an ideal world that made sense. But this wasn't an ideal world. It was a completely imperfect situation. If she hesitated, she put people at risk.

This was her decision. The buck stopped with her.

"There are risks attached to any vaccine but this vaccine was widely used and we've got a lot of data on the issues raised. I've reviewed our medical notes. There's nothing in my history, your history or the parents' that would prevent vaccination. The only issue is Alison— and she's already told me she's decided against it."

There was an expression on his face she couldn't

fathom. Something flickering behind his eyes, as if the thoughts in his head were about to combust.

This man was almost unreadable.

Was he relieved or mad? Did he want Alison to have the vaccine and put her baby at risk? Or did he want her to take her chances without?

Obviously, she knew the outcome—but that didn't help here.

Had Sawyer's wife been in similar circumstances and avoided a vaccine because she had been pregnant? Or had she taken a vaccine—that was untried and un-tested on pregnant women—with devastating conse-quences?

It was almost as if he'd gone on autopilot. He washed his hands, lifted a syringe and needle and tipped up the vial, plunging the needle inside and extracting the vac-cine. "If this is what you want, let's do it."

She was stunned. She'd thought he was going to re-fuse—going to argue with her some more and storm off. This was the last thing she'd expected.

"Are you going to get vaccinated?"

He nodded almost imperceptibly. "Of course."

She tilted her head and raised her eyebrows at him, the question obvious.

"I'm working on the assumption you're going to say that only vaccinated personnel can work with the kids. These kids are mine. They're *my* patients. I won't let you keep me out. And if a vaccine is what it takes…" he shrugged "…so be it."

The words were stuck in her throat now.

The thing that seemed to pass her by. The people thing.

The thing she really wanted to concentrate on, but her

public health role wouldn't let her. She'd learned over the years just to lock it away in a corner of her mind.

But it was the thing that was on the forefront of *his* mind. And it was affecting his reactions. If only she could have the same freedom.

He was prepared to take a vaccine with known side-effects in order to keep looking after these children.

And no matter how hard she tried not to, she had to admire him for it.

There was only one thing she could do.

She turned her arm towards him. "Let's do it." Her voice sounded confident, the way she wanted to appear to the outside world. Her insides were currently mush.

His finger ran down the outside of her upper arm. Totally unexpected. The lightest of touches. She heard his intake of breath before he went back to standard technique and pinched her skin.

It was over in the blink of an eye. She never even felt the bifurcated needle penetrate her skin. It wasn't like a traditional shot and she felt the needle prick her skin a number of times in a few seconds before it was quickly removed and disposed of.

"You know this won't be pretty, don't you?"

She nodded, automatically reaching up and rubbing her arm. "I know what to expect. A red and itchy bump in a few days…" she rolled her eyes "…a delightful pus-filled blister in another week and then a scab."

She washed her hands at the sink as he drew up another dose of vaccine and handed it to her, pulling his scrub sleeve up above his shoulder. She could feel herself hesitate, taking in his defined deltoid and biceps muscles. Did Sawyer work out? He didn't seem the type.

"Something wrong?"

"What? No." She could feel the color flooding into

her cheeks. How embarrassing. He hadn't given her arm a second glance.

Concentrate. Focus. He was smirking at her again, almost as if he could see exactly what she was thinking.

She scowled, pinched his arm and injected him, delivering the vaccine in an instant. It was as quick as she could get this over and done with, so she could turn her back to dispose of the syringe.

"Ouch." He was rubbing his arm in mock horror. "It's all in the technique, you know."

"Yeah, yeah." She started washing her hands again. "You're not supposed to rub your arm, you know."

He shrugged. "Everyone does. It's an automatic response. Being a doctor doesn't make me any different." His arm was still exposed, and this time, instead of focusing on the muscle, her eyes focused on the skin.

It was full of little pock marks and lumps and bumps. The obvious flat scar from a BCG vaccination. He followed her eyes and gave her a grin. "A lifetime's work. Chicken pox as a child, then a whole career's worth of DPA vaccinations."

She pulled up her other sleeve. "Snap."

His finger touched her skin again and she felt herself suck in her breath as it ran over her BCG scar. He was standing just a little too close for comfort but seemed completely unaffected.

He turned and smiled at her. "At least you don't have chicken pox scars." Maybe it was the lazy way he said it or the way his smile seemed kind of sexy.

"Oh, I do. Just can't show them in public." She couldn't help it. The words were out before she had time to think about them. She was flirting. She was *flirting* with him. What was wrong with her?

That was the kind of response that her sister might

have given. The kind of response that had men eating out of the palm of her hand and following Isabel's butt with their eyes as she walked down the hallway.

But this was so *not* a Callie response.

What was she thinking of?

It wasn't that she was some shy, retiring virgin. She'd been on plenty of dates and had a number of relationships over the years. But she wasn't the type of girl who walked into a bar and flirted with a man. She was the kind of girl who met a man in a class or in a library, and went for a few quiet drinks before there was any touching, any kissing.

She wasn't used to being unnerved by a man. To find herself flustered and blushing around him. It made her cringe.

But Sawyer seemed immune. Maybe women flirted with him all the time? He just gave her a little wink and crossed the room. Now he was in midconversation with the second-year resident, explaining where some of the supplies were kept and how to access them.

He obviously didn't feel heat rising up the back of his neck to make him feel uncomfortable.

She took a deep breath and moved. Out to the madness of the corridor, where the incessant sound of phones ringing must be driving everyone mad.

She picked up the nearest one as she passed. The voice made her stop in her tracks.

"Callie? Is that you?"

Evan Hunter. It must be killing him to be stuck at Headquarters instead of being in the thick of things.

"Well?" His abrupt tone was hardly welcoming.

It was beginning to annoy her. Every phone call she'd had from this man had started with him snapping at her and shouting orders. Wasn't he supposed to be supporting her?

He knew she'd been flung in at the deep end.

"Hold on." She set down the phone, ignoring the expletives she could hear him yelling as she walked over to the whiteboard on the wall. The DPA team was well trained. Every piece of relevant information and the most up-to-date data was right in front of her. She didn't need to run around the department asking a barrage of questions.

She watched as a member of staff rubbed one number off the board and replaced it with another. The potential 'at risk' group was now at five. Not bad at all.

A list of queries had appeared around the containment facility. She would need to get onto them straight away.

The only glaring piece of information that was missing was around the plane. There was the number of passengers, with the number of contact details obtained. Three hundred passengers—with contact details for only seventy-six.

This was taking up too much of her team's time. They needed to deal with the issues around the containment facility. It was time to delegate.

She could feel her arm tremble slightly as she picked up the phone again. Isabel would have been fit for Evan Hunter. She would have chewed him up and spat him out. It was time to embrace some of her sister's personality traits.

"Evan?"

"What on earth were you doing? When I call I expect—"

She cut him off straight away. "What have I been doing? What have *I* been doing? I've just been getting my smallpox vaccination and I've just inoculated another member of staff. I've been assessing our most up-to-date information to determine whether or not this is a terrorist attack." She glanced at the clock. "Information I wasn't due to present to you for another eight minutes. And, incidentally, my professional opinion is that it's not.

"I've also been trying to keep the staff and patients here calm and informed about what's going on. I'm trying to find out how Callum is but no one will tell me anything. I'm having problems with the containment facility. We can't make all the contacts for the plane passengers." She was starting to count things off on her fingers.

"We're just about to vaccinate those exposed—but we have a pregnant nurse to consider. Oh, and Sawyer is driving me crazy." She took a deep breath. "So, how's your day going, Evan?" She couldn't help it. The more she spoke, the more she felt swamped, the more she felt angry that Callum wasn't at her side. The more she realized that Evan Hunter, boss or not, should be doing more to help her, not adding to the problems.

The silence at the end of the phone was deafening. Her heart rate quickened. Had she just got herself sacked?

No. How could he? Not when she was in the middle of all this.

She heard him clear his throat. "Point made."

She was shocked. "What?"

"Point made, Callie. What do you need?"

For a second she couldn't speak. *What did she need?* Apart from getting out of here?

"I need you to take over the plane contacts. We've got three hundred passengers and only contact details for seventy-six. I also need you to take over the viable threat assessment for these people as our details are sketchy. I'll get one of the contact tracers and epidemiologists to conference-call you." Isabel used to quote the English expression *"In for a penny, in for a pound"* before she took a risk. Somehow, it seemed apt.

"Fine. I can do that. Anything else?"

She felt like a girl in a fancy department store on a fifty percent sale day. But nothing else screamed out at her. "Can you magic me up some pediatric ICU facilities?"

"That might be a little tricky."

"Didn't think so. Never mind. I'll let you know if I need anything else. When can I expect to hear from the lab?"

"That's what I wanted to tell you."

Oops. She almost felt bad for being snarky with him.

"The samples have been received and are being processed. It's only been a couple of hours. In another ten we should be able to tell you which virus type it is. That will give us something to work with."

She nodded as she scribbled notes. "That's great."

"And, Callie?"

"Yes?" This was it. This was where he blasted her for the way she'd just spoken to him.

"Leave Sawyer to me. I'm going to try and find out where he's been and what he's been doing these last few years. Let him know who's in charge. Only use him if you have to. He's not part of the DPA anymore."

She could feel the steel in his words and instantly regretted her outburst that Sawyer was driving her crazy. "He's actually been quite helpful. He's just a little…" she struggled to think of the word "…inconsistent. One minute he's helping, the next he looks as if he could jump out the nearest window." She looked over at the window next to her. The sun was splitting the sky outside. She almost felt like jumping out the window herself and heading for the nearest beach. Chicago had good beaches, didn't it?

Her stomach rumbled loudly. What she wouldn't give for pizza right now.

Evan was still talking.

"Sorry, what?"

"I asked if you wanted another doctor sent in."

"No. Not right now. If things progress, then probably yes. But let's wait until we have the lab results. You're dealing with plane passengers and hopefully things are contained at our end."

Her brain started to whirr. She couldn't really understand why, in the midst of all this, part of his focus was on Sawyer. Surely Evan should just be grateful that she had any help at all? No matter how reluctant.

She rang off and stared at the phone. Her stomach rumbled again loudly. She didn't have time to figure that out right now.

Along with many other things, it would have to wait.

CHAPTER FOUR

"Sawyer? Are you in here?" Callie stuck her head around the door into the darkened room. It was three a.m. and she could make out a heap bundled against the far wall, lying on a gurney.

The heap moved and groaned at her. "What?" He sat up and rubbed his eyes.

"Oh, I'm sorry," she whispered, searching the room for any other sleeping bodies. "Have you just got your head down?"

He swung his legs off the gurney and stood up, swaying a little. She walked across the room and put her arm on his. "I'm sorry, Sawyer. I didn't realize you were sleeping."

"I wasn't," he snapped.

She smiled at him. "Yes, you obviously were."

"What's wrong? Did something happen to the kids?" It was almost as if his brain had just engaged.

She tightened her grip on his arm. "No. I'm sorry. Nothing's changed. The kids are still pretty sick. Laura, one of the DPA nurses, is in with them now. I've kept Alison away, just like you said. She's still down at the other end of the corridor in a room on her own." She held up a paper bag and waved it under his nose. "She's doing a great job, by the way. She got me banana and toffee muffins."

"Oh, okay." The words took a few seconds to sink in then he scowled at her. "What is it, then?"

"It's Max Simpson, the chief of staff. It's three a.m. and I've just realized I haven't seen him yet. I've been so busy with things down here."

She could see the realization appear in his eyes. He grimaced.

"What is it?"

"Yeah. I meant to speak to you about Max too. I sort of made an executive decision there."

"You did what?" She was on edge again. What had he done now? He'd already broken protocol once. Had he done it again?

He shook his head. "I'm sorry, Callie, I meant to talk to you earlier. Max is the reason I'm here."

"What are you talking about? I don't understand."

"Max has prostate cancer. He's undergoing chemotherapy—midway through a course. He's immuno-compromised. So I told him he can't be anywhere the possible threat of infection and he can't be near anyone we immunize—including us."

The words struck home. For a second she'd thought he was going to say something unreasonable—something to get her back up. Instead, Callie felt the tenseness ease out of her muscles. Another piece of the jigsaw.

"So, what? You're covering for him right now?"

She could see the hesitation on his face. "Yes, I guess I am. Max was a real hands-on sort of guy. He dropped out of his clinical commitments a couple of months ago and has just been doing a few days' office work a week. He wants to keep his hand in during his treatment but couldn't manage any more. I was only supposed to be here for two weeks, covering someone's vacation leave. But I met Max, he liked me and asked me to stay and cover his clinical work in the E.R. for a few months."

She was trying to read behind the lines. Trying to understand the things that he wasn't telling her. She couldn't work this guy out at all.

Matt Sawyer's reputation had preceded him. Apparently when his wife had died, he'd had the mother of all temper tantrums, telling everyone around him what he really thought of them. She could only imagine that Evan Hunter had been one of them.

But here he was describing how he was helping out a sick colleague. Someone he'd only met a few months ago.

Was it just everyone at the DPA he hated? Did he blame them for his wife's death?

She could see him searching her face. Was he worried that she would be unhappy for him not putting her in the picture before now? Or was he worried she would actually see his human side? The side he'd tried to hide from her when he'd said his help had been a one-off event.

She wrinkled her nose at him. It was late and she was getting tired. Her defenses were weakening as she approached that hideous hour in the middle of the night when her body was screaming for her bed.

"I don't get you, Matt Sawyer," she whispered.

"What don't you get?" He took a step closer. The lights in the room were still out and the only light was from the corridor outside, sending a warm, comfortable glow over them both. He'd changed into the regulation DPA pale pink scrubs. Pink on a man. Whose idea had that been? He made them look good, though. Kind of inviting.

He reached up and gave one of her wayward locks at little tug, a sexy smile crossing his face, "This hair of yours, it's driving me crazy. I keep wanting to grab a pair of scissors and lop this off."

Her hand reached up too, brushing the side of his face and touching his brown hair that was mussed up around his ears. "Likewise," she whispered.

For a few seconds neither of them spoke. Callie had no idea what she was doing. She was in the middle of the biggest potential outbreak of her career, in a strange city, with no real idea of what could happen next. There was nothing in the plan about this. There was nothing that told you what to do when your colleague was sick and you had to take over the management of a situation like this. She needed a friend. She needed someone to reach out to.

"I saw your hand shaking earlier. Are you scared, Dr. Turner?" His voice was low, barely above a whisper. No one else could possibly hear them.

"Scared?" she repeated. "Matt, I'm terrified." She felt a whoosh of air come out of her lungs. It was the first time she'd said the words out loud. She'd spent the last twelve hours thinking them but she couldn't have imagined actually saying them to someone. It was like laying herself bare. To a man she hardly knew. It had to be a recipe for disaster.

He raised one eyebrow. "Like I said earlier, we're all scared. There's not a person in this E.R. right now who wants to be here—except, of course, for a few DPA geeks. Most people would sell their right arm to get out of here." He touched the side of her arm, running the palm of his hand up and down it. "Fear of the unknown is one of the most terrifying fears that there is."

She nodded, knowing what he was saying was true. There was something soothing about his voice. Something reassuring.

Her hand touched the side of his cheek. He almost flinched. She could see it. But he stood firm, his pale green eyes fixed on hers. "I can't work you out, Matt Sawyer. You're supposed to be a bad boy—a rule-breaker. Mr. Nasty. But right now I'm seeing a whole other side to you."

He wrinkled his nose. "What's that smell?"

"What smell?" She sniffed the air around her. "I can't smell anything."

"It's weird. Like strawberries or fruit or something."

She smiled. It was proof that they were standing too close to one another. "It's raspberries. It's my shampoo."

He moved even closer, his nose brushing against the top of her head as he inhaled again. "Almost good enough to eat," he murmured.

She couldn't wrap her head around all this. Maybe it was the time of night and her befuddled brain. She'd heard that Sawyer had lost it after his wife had died, had finished treating the patients he'd had to, had roared at everyone and walked off the job. He'd refused to make contact with anyone after that.

But here he was. Obviously struggling. But here.

His hand reached up and tightened around hers. There was an edge to his gaze. A shield going up right before her eyes. "What do you want to know?"

"I don't *know* that I want to know anything. I guess I just want to find out for myself. If I'd listened to Evan Hunter, I wouldn't have spoken to you at all when I got here, but I like to go on instincts."

"And what are your instincts telling you, Callie Turner?"

Wow. What a question. Because right now her instincts were telling her she was acting like a seventeen-year-old girl rather than a twenty-nine-year-old woman.

He moved their hands from the side of his cheek to resting both of them on her breastbone. Could he feel her heart beating against the skin on his hand? A man who had seen her virtually naked a few hours before?

What was she thinking about? Outside, down at the desk, there were a million things that she should be doing. Being in here, with Matt Sawyer, wasn't on the list that she'd prepared earlier.

But the words came too easily, "My instincts are telling me that Callum Ferguson is one of the wisest men I've ever known. And if he had hope for you, then maybe I should too."

He was even closer now. She could feel his breath on her cheeks, warming her skin. He bent forward, his lips brushing the side of her ear. It felt like the most erotic touch she'd ever experienced. "What if I told you I'm still a bad boy? What if I told you I left my last two jobs in Alaska and Connecticut before they could fire me?"

And then it happened. Callie just let go. Just like she'd done on the phone earlier with Evan. She didn't think, she just acted. She spoke the words that came instantly into her brain. *What was happening to her?* "I'd say you found problems in the places you were working. I'd say you told them what was wrong and how to fix it. I'd say they probably didn't like it."

He tilted his head to one side, the lazy smile still fixed on his face. "I knew you were young. I thought you didn't know anything. I thought you only followed rules."

His words were supposed to be teasing but something else happened.

Something flooded through her veins. Adrenaline, laced with fear.

She shouldn't be doing this. She shouldn't be in here with him. It was compromising her ability to think straight.

He was right. Following rules was what she knew. Following rules was *safe*.

Last time she hadn't followed the rules it had ruined her life.

No. It had ruined her *sister's* life.

So, getting involved with a rule-breaker?

Not an option.

His phone buzzed, in that gentle, quiet way it did when it was switched to vibrate instead of ring. She sprang backwards. "I need to go, Matt." She pushed the door open, flooding the room with light.

"Wait!" He grabbed her arm as he glanced at his phone. "I'm guessing here as I'm not sure of the number but I think it's my sister. She's the only person I know who would be so persistent."

"Your sister?" The words cut through her like a knife. Her back-to-reality jolt was instant. "You have a sister?"

Something had just happened. And Sawyer didn't understand it. One minute they'd been almost nose to nose in the darkened room—as if something was about to happen. The next minute he had almost seen her building the wall around herself.

He had no idea what had made her just snap like that.

Miss Hoity-Toity had looked almost inviting a minute ago. For a second he'd almost thought about…

No. Not possible. He didn't think like that any more.

Well, not unless he was in a bar and halfway through a bottle.

But for a few seconds she'd looked vulnerable. She'd looked like someone who could do with a hug. And he wasn't the hugging type.

And that smell from her. The raspberry shampoo. More enticing than any perfume he'd ever smelt.

It was weird what confined spaces could do to a person.

She was still looking at him with those too-wide eyes. What was with her? What was the big deal?

"Yes, I've got a sister."

"I meant to ask you if there was anybody you wanted to notify that you had been quarantined. Haven't you told her what's happened?"

His eyes fixed on the floor. This wasn't going to be pretty. "My sister's called Violet. Violet Connelly." He waited for the penny to drop.

And it did.

"Violet Connelly's your sister?" Her voice rose, filling the quiet room.

He leaned against the doorjamb and folded his arms. He was well aware he was trying to look laid back, but he was feeling anything but. All of a sudden he was hit by a wave of emotions that he didn't want to deal with. He tried to focus on the face in front of him. "Yes. Why so surprised?"

"Violet Connelly is your sister?"

"You've already said that and I've already answered."

She wrinkled her nose. It made her look kind of cute. "Why hasn't she said anything? I've never heard her mention you and I've been at the DPA for the last three years."

"I'm the family black sheep." Explanations weren't really his thing. It seemed the easiest solution.

"Bull. Violet's not like that at all."

Okay. Maybe not.

"And why don't you have your sister's number in your phone?"

He shifted uncomfortably. "I've been out of touch for a little while."

"With your sister?" Her voice rose in pitch. "How can you be out of touch with your sister?" Little pink spots had appeared on her cheeks.

"She has a different name. How come?"

"So now you're getting personal?"

"Don't get smart, Sawyer. You've just told me a woman I've worked alongside for the last three years is your sister. Violet's a sweetheart and she's never mentioned you once. Why?"

He shrugged. He really didn't want to have this conversation. It was way too uncomfortable. And it was bringing up a whole load of guilt that he really didn't want to consider. "It's complicated."

Now she looked angry. That middle-of-the-night woman angry. Never a good sign. "Don't give me the *'it's complicated'* crap." She raised her fingers in the air again. "Tell me why on earth she would keep something like that secret? Maybe Evan Hunter was right—maybe we should be looking a little closer at you."

He could feel the pent-up anger build in his chest. His temper was about to flare. Here. In the middle of the hospital. In the middle of a crisis situation.

He turned and flipped on the light, walking over to the nearby sink and running the cold tap. He bent over and started splashing water on his face. How dared she?

That was almost an implication that he was involved in this crisis situation.

This woman didn't know him at all. Didn't know anything but hearsay and gossip. If she knew even the tiniest part of him she'd know he'd do anything to get out of here.

He could feel the pressure building in his chest. Wasn't it bad enough that she'd just reminded him how guilty he felt about pushing his family—and his sister—away? He felt as if a truckload of concrete had just been dumped on his head.

As if this situation wasn't already bad enough.

Now she was making him think about things he'd spent the last six years pushing away.

He grabbed some paper towels and dried his face. Breathed in through his nose and out through his mouth. The flare was reducing. He didn't feel the urge to hit a wall any more. He was trying to think reasonable, rational thoughts.

But Callie Turner was still there. Wondering what she'd just witnessed.

He turned to face her. "Try walking in Violet's shoes for a while, Callie. Her brother's reputation is in the doghouse and she's just about to start her residency at the DPA. You know how important that is so why would you do anything to spoil it?"

She took a deep breath. He'd looked so angry a second ago.

But no wonder. She'd said something completely unforgiveable. She'd more or less accused him of being responsible for the smallpox outbreak. And he obviously wasn't.

Callum had already told her how difficult this would be for Sawyer. He was the one person here with more experience than her. Whether she liked it or not, she needed him. The last thing she should be doing was insulting him.

And more to the point, he was right. She hadn't told anyone about Isabel. She couldn't have dealt with the reaction that she'd been in a car crash that had killed her sister—a sister who would have given anything to work at the DPA. She hadn't let anyone in on her secret. Why should Violet?

She was telling herself to be reasonable and rational.

But something was skewing her thought processes. He had a sister. And it had caught her unawares.

It seemed ridiculous. Half the world had a sister. But most of the time she was prepared. She was ready. This time she hadn't been.

It didn't help that Violet Connelly was one of the sweetest people she knew. Not unlike Isabel. The fist squeezed around her heart even tighter.

She met his gaze. His face was flushed; he was still holding back his anger.

She'd kept her family secret too. She hadn't done anything to spoil her job at the DPA. She hadn't gone to her interview and said, *Well, actually, this was my sister Isabel's dream and since I was driving the car that killed her I feel I owe it to her.*

She took a deep breath, "I guess I wouldn't do anything to spoil it," she murmured.

He moved closer to her, the edges of his hair now wet around his face. "Our mum got remarried when I was a teenager. Violet was still quite young—she changed her name to our stepfather's. I didn't."

She raised her eyebrows at him. "What? You mean you were a rebellious teenager, Sawyer?" Anything to lighten the mood, anything to ease the tension in the room that was still bubbling away in her stomach. Anything to release the squeezing around her heart.

He nodded slowly. Then something else jarred into her mind.

"Does Evan Hunter know Violet's your sister?" She'd spoken to him numerous times on the phone today. "It was Evan that wanted you checked out."

He rolled his eyes. "I know that. Evan and I go way back. I haven't had a chance to phone Violet yet. I meant to, I just got caught up in everything. She's texted me and called me. She must have heard my name mentioned at the DPA. I need to fill her in on the details."

"You mean she didn't know you were here?" She couldn't keep the shock out of her voice. Why on earth would his sister not know where was?

He hesitated and for a second looked kind of sheepish. For a man with a reputation as a bad boy it almost didn't fit.

"I kind of dropped off the radar."

No. She didn't get this. She didn't get this at all.

"What do you mean? I know you didn't tell anyone at the DPA where you were—in a way, I almost kind of get that. But your sister? Your own sister, Matt?"

Her voice was raised. She couldn't help it. He had a sister. He had options. Options she didn't have.

How on earth could he do that? How long had he been off the radar? Six years?

Six years of no contact? It was unthinkable.

Her voice was shaking. "How could you do that, Matt? You have a sister who clearly loves you. She must have been frantic with worry. She's still frantic with worry. Why would you do that to her? Why would you put her through that?"

There it was again. That action. The one he always

did when he was thinking of an answer. He ran his fingers through his hair. "It's not as bad as it sounds."

She stepped right up to him. "Really? How? How is it not as bad as it sounds? Explain to me, Matt."

She was mad. She could never have done that. Never have cut Isabel out of her life for six years. It was unthinkable.

Nearly as unthinkable as being responsible for her own sister's death.

"I texted her. Not often. Just every now and then to let her know I was safe."

"And that was supposed to be good enough?"

He flung his hands up in frustration and shouted, "You don't know, Callie. You don't know anything. That was as much as I could manage. I needed time. I needed space. I didn't want anything familiar around me. I wanted to get my head straight."

"For six years?" She was shouting back.

His lips tightened. She knew there were tears threatening to spill down her cheeks. She couldn't help it. What a waste. He'd dared to risk his relationship with his sister.

A relationship she'd give anything to have again. It made her hate him.

"Not everything in life is part of a plan, Callie. Maybe if you get some life experience, you'll find that out."

She felt as if he'd just punched her in the ribs.

He couldn't be more wrong if he'd tried.

But, right now, in the middle of the night, she was hardly going to fill in the blanks to a man she hardly knew.

It was time to get some perspective. He had no idea

how much those words had hurt. And she'd no intention of telling him.

Distance. That's what she needed.

Being in an enclosed space with Matt Sawyer was doing weird things to her. Being in an enforced quarantine for up to eighteen days would plain drive her crazy.

"Sawyer!"

The shout came from down the corridor, followed by the sound of thudding feet. They both sprang to the door at once, yanking it open and spilling out into the hallway.

"What is it?"

The nurse was red faced, gasping for breath. "There you are. I need help. Jack's struggling to breathe—he needs to be intubated. The spots must be causing his airway to swell." She glanced from one to the other. "Tell me we've got a pediatrician who can do this?"

Their eyes met.

They didn't have pediatric intensive care facilities. They were an ER—not a PICU. Their options were limited.

Sawyer grabbed a gown and a mask. "I'll do it." He started to run down the corridor before she could ask any questions. "Get me a portable ventilator," he shouted over his shoulder.

Her head flooded with thoughts. What did the plan say? Were there algorithms for intubating smallpox patients? Were there risks attached to ventilating this child and possibly allowing the spread of disease?

There was no time to think. There was only time to act.

Sawyer had already sprung into action.

And for once she agreed.

CHAPTER FIVE

EVERYTHING HAPPENED IN a blur. A portable ventilator seemed to appear out of thin air.

The fear that had been hanging around everyone, crystallizing in the air, was pushed to one side.

Jack's stats were poor, his lips tinged with blue, but his face was red with the strain of struggling for breath.

Intubating a child was never easy. Particularly a child who was panicking. Sawyer was at the bedside in a flash. "Give me some sedation."

The nurse next to him nodded, pulled up the agreed dose and handed him the syringe.

Sawyer leant over Jack. The panic flaring behind the little boy's eyes was obvious. Sawyer tapped his arm at the point where Jack's cannula was sited. "I know you're having trouble, little man. But I'm going to help you sort that out. I'm going to give you something to make you a little sleepy then put a tube down your throat to help you breathe. It will make things much better."

On a normal day he would have given a child some time to ask questions. Then again, on a normal day he wouldn't be doing this. He administered the drug quickly, waiting for Jack's muscles to relax.

A few seconds later his little body sagged and the whole team moved seamlessly. Sawyer positioned himself at the head of the bed. "Give me a straight-blade laryngoscope and the smallest ET tube you've got."

Callie pulled the light closer, trying to aid him as he slid the tube into place. It didn't help that it was the middle of the night and there was no natural light. It would be tricky to intubate a partially blocked airway, not something that she would ever wish to attempt. It had been a long time since she'd been in an emergency situation like this. DPA callouts usually involved febrile kids and adults and lots of sick bowls and emergency commodes.

On occasion, people got really sick and died. But Callie didn't usually get involved in that side of things. She was usually left to consider the big picture—the spread of disease.

Watching a little kid struggle for breath was something else entirely.

She gave a sigh of relief as Sawyer slid the tube into place and attached the ventilator. There was a murmur between him and nurse standing at the bedside as they set the machine. Callie frowned. Who was she? She didn't recognize her.

In fact, she didn't recognize half the people in this room. Was this what happened in the case of a medical emergency? Isolation procedures were ignored?

She squeezed her eyes shut as she tried to rationalize her thoughts. Isolation procedures weren't being ignored. Everyone in here had the regulation disposable gowns, masks and gloves in place. But there was a whole host of new people in this room—not just the restricted one or two.

One of the residents was talking in a low voice to the parents, trying to calm them. Another nurse was standing next to the half-pulled curtain next to Ben. She was leaning over him, obviously trying to distract him from the events surrounding him, telling him a long-winded version of the latest kids' movie.

Another guy came through the door. "You wanted a pediatrician? You've got one."

Callie's head shot up. "Where on earth did you come from?"

She couldn't see his face properly behind his fitted mask but his eyes flitted over to her and then instantly away. His priority was obviously the child, not the surrounding bureaucracy. "Upstairs," he said, as he walked over to the bed and started to fire questions at Sawyer, who turned to face him.

"Wish you'd got here five minutes ago," he said.

Callie was incredulous. "*Upstairs?* What do you mean, upstairs? This unit is closed. There's no one going out and no one coming in." Her hands were on her hips.

She was watching her whole world disintegrate around her. The first rule of quarantine: no one in, no one out. "Which door did you come through? Who let you through? Didn't you realize there was a quarantine in force down here? Do you know you've put yourself at risk by walking into this room?"

She was shouting. She couldn't help it. Next she would have infected people running down the streets and the media crucifying the DPA for not handling the outbreak appropriately. Evan Hunter would be on the phone telling her she was a failure.

"Callie." It was Sawyer. He was right in front of her, his pale green eyes visible above the mask. "Calm down. We put out a call for a pediatrician. We can't handle these kids ourselves."

"You did what?" She couldn't believe it. This was the

problem with delegating. Mistakes got made. People did things they shouldn't. People did things that put others at risk. "Who gave you the right to do that?"

"I did." Sawyer's voice was calm but firm. "Decisions like this get made all the time. I'm in charge of the clinical care of these patients. And, as much as I don't like to admit it, this is getting beyond my level of expertise." He nodded towards the pediatrician. "Dan's great. We discussed the risks a little earlier. He knows he'll need to be vaccinated."

"It's much more than that!" She exploded. She couldn't help it. "Once he's vaccinated he may be able to look after these children but it'll put him out of commission for the general hospital for nearly a month. There's no way a doctor exposed to the smallpox virus through vaccination can be near anyone who is immuno-compromised. "Did you even think about that, Sawyer? Did you even consider it? And it's not just him. Who are all these people?" Her hand swept around the room. "They'll all need to be vaccinated too!"

"Stop it." She could sense his gritted teeth beneath the mask. He leaned closer, "You're making a scene and, quite frankly, it's not helping. Do you really think you're telling me anything I don't know or haven't already discussed with Dan? Do you really think these people don't already know the risks attached to coming into this room?"

She could feel the tiny hairs stand up at the back of her neck—and not in a good way. But he wasn't finished. "The difference between you and me, Callie, is that I know when I'm beaten. I know when to look for other options—options not in the plan. It's time you learned some new skills. Not everything in life is down in black and white."

He turned and walked away from her, leaving her stunned. She watched the second hand tick around on the clock on the wall in front of her. Less than twenty minutes ago she'd almost been in a compromising position with him.

Then, in the blink of an eye, everything had changed.

He made her want to cry. He made her want to scream. He was truly and utterly driving her crazy. The tears had automatically pooled at the corners of her eyes.

And it wasn't just the fact he behaved like an insubordinate teenager. It wasn't just that standing near to him made her hair stand on end or that sometimes there was wisdom in his words, even though they weren't in the plan.

It was the fact that in the midst of all that she just didn't know what she thought of him. She didn't know how to *feel* around him.

She was focused. She was precise. She followed the plan. Most of the time she'd helped develop the plan. And back in Atlanta these had seemed smart, comprehensive plans. Back in Atlanta they had seemed to cover every eventuality.

But they didn't cover the Sawyer element.

Not at all. They didn't cover the get-under-your-skin clause.

A smell drifted past her nostrils. What was that? She glanced at her watch—it was nearly five in the morning. Where had the time gone?

"Pizza," came the shout from down the corridor. She walked quickly along the hallway. She had to get out of there. She didn't have any pediatric skills and Dan clearly had things under control.

She also needed a chance to regroup.

Twenty pizza boxes were being descended on from every angle. It was like a plague of locusts. Someone was reading the tops of the boxes, shouting out what was in each one. "Hawaiian. Ham and cheese. Vegetarian." Arms appeared from everywhere, grabbing at the outstretched boxes. "Tuna and pineapple? Who on earth ordered that?"

A smile broke over her face. Alison had taken her responsibilities very seriously earlier when Callie had asked her to organize food for the patients and staff.

She'd asked what Callie's favorites were and so far she'd magicked up banana and toffee muffins and her favorite pizza. She pushed her way to the front. "That's mine." She held out her hand for the box.

The guy behind the desk wrinkled his nose in disgust. "Take it," he said as he moved on to the one underneath.

She smiled and drifted off with her pizza box. She'd learned early on as a junior doctor that ordering takeout was a whole new skill. Order something simple that everyone liked and you would never see it. Sweet and sour chicken, pepperoni pizza, chicken tikka masala, all would disappear in a blink of an eye. Order something a little out the ordinary and no one would touch it with a bargepole.

Tuna and pineapple pizza was an acquired taste. Isabel had sworn by spinach and anchovies. Even the thought sent a horrible tremor down her spine and made a smile dance across her face.

Sometimes the memories were good. Sometimes the memories were fun.

The typical teenage fights over clothes and boys had almost been blotted from her mind. The competition between them in medical school continued to hover around her. Isabel always had to be first to see their exam results. To see if she'd beaten Callie. But it had been a pretty even split. Both of them had excelled in different areas. Callie in planning, anatomy and biochemistry and Isabel in epidemiology, diagnostics and patient care. If things had gone to plan, they could have been a dynamite team.

Callie leaned back in her chair, her appetite leaving her abruptly. It always happened like this.

She was fine, she was focused. Then it would hit her again—what she'd lost. Just tumbling out of nowhere, like a granite rock permanently pressing on her chest.

The grief counselor had told her she'd get over it. It would just take time. But every year—particularly if there was an event that Isabel had especially enjoyed—it just seemed to shadow her all the more.

She turned her head to the right. The pile of paperwork about the type C containment building. The place that was currently having power issues. Would Isabel really have handled all this better? Would Isabel have been better organized than she was?

Would she handle Sawyer better than she was?

Her leg started to itch again and her hand automatically went to her scrub trousers and started scratching. She didn't have time for this. She didn't have time to be morose. She had a containment facility to sort out and there was no time like the present. Why should city hall officials get to sleep when she couldn't? She took a bite of her pizza and lifted the phone.

The children were as settled as they could be. The parents had been calmed, and in the end Dan had decided to give Ben some sedation too. Nothing about this situation was ideal and the little guy had become hysterical when he'd realized there was a machine breathing for his brother.

Sawyer breathed a sigh of relief. His too-big scrub trousers seemed to have given up trying to stay in place, partly due to the missing elastic at the waist and partly due to being weighed down by the phone in his pocket.

What time was it in Atlanta? He looked at his watch and tried to count it out. But what did it matter? Violet had been trying to phone him for hours. Whether he liked it or not, it was time to call her back.

He lifted his hand. Then pressed it down again on the desk.

He couldn't remember the last time his hand had shaken like that.

Come on. This was easy. It was one phone call.

So, how come the voices in his head had to will him on?

He took another breath and lifted his hand again, trying to ignore the shake. His fingers slipped and he missed the buttons.

Darn it. What kind of a fool was he?

Three-year-old kids could dial a phone—why couldn't he?

Concentrate. Get this over with. It would only be a few minutes out of his life.

The first time would be the worst. Once he'd done it, the heavy weight pressing on his chest might finally lift and let him breathe again.

Stop thinking about it, you moron—just dial!

He pressed the buttons on the phone, praying it might automatically jump to voicemail.

He didn't even hear the first ring. "DPA. Can I help you?"

"Violet Connelly, please."

There was a few moments' silence as the call was connected. He resisted the huge temptation to hang up and hide.

Hang up and go and find a beer.

"Violet Connelly."

He could almost picture her in his mind, doing ten things at once with the phone perched between her shoulder and her ear. Even at this time in the morning she'd be multi-tasking.

"Hello?"

Patience had never been her strong suit.

"Hey, Violet." His voice cracked.

There was a loud crash. All he could imagine was that her chair had just landed on the floor. "Sawyer? Sawyer?"

He cringed, guilt flooding through him. The concern and anxiety in her voice was crystal clear. He should have texted her hours ago. Why hadn't he? Ten seconds. That's all it would have taken.

Scrub that. He should have phoned her six years ago. Not just send the odd random text from an occasional phone.

"Yeah, it's Sawyer."

Some not very ladylike words spilled down the phone. The concern had quickly been replaced by anger. "'Hey, Violet'? Is that the best you can do? Six years, Matt. *Six years!*"

"I know. I'm sorry but—"

"You're sorry? *You're sorry?* You've got to be joking. I've been trying to phone you for hours. *Hours.* You logged that call here hours ago, Matt. You must have known I would hear about it straight away. I've been trying to contact you ever since. I've been frantic."

"Violet, please—"

"Please? Please?" It was obvious she wasn't going to let him speak. Six years of worry and pent-up frustration were erupting all over him. "How do you think I feel? How do think it felt to know that after six years you phone the DPA and ask to speak to Callum Ferguson? *Callum Ferguson?* You must have known I would be here. You must have known the news would spread like wildfire. I don't care that it's about a smallpox outbreak. I don't care that it's the scariest outbreak we've ever dealt with. I want you to stop for five minutes and think about what that felt like for me."

Wow.

One thing was for sure, she'd been waiting to say that for a long time.

If Violet could see him now she would see that for the first time in years he was hanging his head in shame. "Give me a break, sis."

"*Give you a break?* Right now, I'd like to break every bone in your body."

Ouch. Harsh. And definitely not Violet's normal response. During the biggest potential outbreak in years, she'd just found her lost brother. She must be stressed up to her eyeballs. The added fact that no one knew he was her brother couldn't be helping—and she wasn't finished yet.

"Why haven't you answered my texts? Why haven't you answered my phone calls?" He could hear it now. The tiny waver in her voice. Violet never liked anyone to know when she was upset. He could almost picture the glimmer of tears in her eyes.

He sighed. "I've been busy, sis. I've got some really sick kids here." He leaned back against the wall, "Plus I've got an invasion of DPA faces that I'd hoped never to see again."

He stopped talking. He didn't need to say any more. Violet knew exactly how he felt about all this. He'd never actually said the words to her, but his sister knew him better than anyone.

"You can do this, Sawyer." Her voice was almost a whisper. A cheerleading call for him. After all this time she was still trying to instill confidence and strength into him.

She was the one person in the world who could chew him out one minute, then fight to the death for him a second later.

Family. He'd almost forgotten what it felt like.

"I'm just in the wrong place at the wrong time again, Violet. Story of my life."

Silence again. She realized the enormity of his words. The price he'd paid the last time had almost destroyed him.

"Are you safe? Did you put yourself at risk before you realized what it was?"

It was natural question—a sisterly question—but it still grated. Especially when he'd been part of the DPA. "I was in the same room as the kids, breathing the same air. I took precautions as soon as I had reason for concern, but they didn't have the appropriate masks. I had to send the other member of staff away—she's pregnant."

He heard Violet's sharp intake of breath. She knew exactly the impact that must have had on him.

"So, for a couple of hours it was just me treating the kids. You know how it is, Violet. That's the way it's got to be. I've had my smallpox vaccination. Now I just need to wait."

"I don't like this. I don't like any of this. I've waited months to hear from you again—eight measly texts in six years—and now this? All I've ever wanted to know is that you were safe, Sawyer, but when I finally hear from you, you're in the most dangerous place of all. It just doesn't seem real."

Sawyer felt himself bristle. He didn't want to get into this with Violet. He didn't want to answer a million questions about where he'd been or what he'd been doing. That was a conversation for another day—and maybe not even then.

And even though he could hear the note of desperation in her voice, he just couldn't go there.

"How's Callum? Have you heard if he's okay? I tried to call the hospital earlier, but they wouldn't tell me anything."

There was hesitation at the other end. She was obviously trying to decide what to tell him. "He's had a massive MI. They took him for angioplasty hours ago and apparently it went well."

There it was again. That tightening feeling around his chest. The way it always came when things were outside his control.

He hated the fact that even though he was a doctor he couldn't always help the people he loved.

He changed the subject.

"What do you know about Callie Turner? She seems a little out of her depth."

"You think?" Violet's answer was snappy, verging on indignant. She was obviously suffering from the same lack of sleep that he was. He was forgetting what time it was. "Callie's one of the best doctors I've worked with. She does everything to the letter. She's very focused, very ordered. Don't get in her way, Sawyer, she won't like it."

"Tell me something I don't know." In a way he was

surprised. Violet was always honest with him. She would tell him if she had any doubts about Callie. The fact that she hadn't mentioned even one was interesting. He decided to take a new tack. "What about her scars?"

"What scars? Callie has scars?"

She sounded genuinely surprised. Didn't the women in the DPA locker room look at each other? Maybe he should call them all on their observation skills.

"Yeah. A big one, snaking right down her leg. She didn't get it at work, then?"

"How come you've seen Callie's scars? Ah...the protective clothing. I get it. No, I had no idea Callie had a scar. She definitely didn't get it at work. She's never had any accidents here. It must be from years ago."

He leaned against the wall just outside the children's room again. All of a sudden he was embarrassed. He hadn't had a proper conversation with his sister in the last few years and he was asking her about other people? He should be ashamed of himself. He took a deep breath, "How are you, Violet? Are you okay?"

"How do you think I am? The biggest potential outbreak in who knows how long and, oh, yeah, my brother's in the middle of it. The DPA's in an uproar. Some rooms are deathly silent and in others you can't even hear yourself think. We've got another couple of outbreaks in other places but none like this." She lowered her voice, as if she was hiding her conversation from someone near her. "What do you think? Do you really think it's smallpox?"

He blew a stream of air out through his lips. "That's the million-dollar question. I'm sure it's a pox—and it definitely isn't chicken pox. But am I sure it's smallpox?" He shook his head. "I just don't know, sis. That's for the lab rats to tell us."

He heard her laugh at his affectionate name for his friends who worked down in the labs. "By the way, Frank says hello. He also cursed a little. He was just about to start his vacation when your lab samples arrived. He says you owe him and his wife a trip to Hawaii."

Memories started to come flooding back into Sawyer's mind. Memories he'd blocked out for a long time. He'd worked with Frank Palmer for six years. They were the same age and had got married around the same time. When Helen had died, he just hadn't been able to stay in touch. Everything was a permanent reminder.

Frank's wife Lucy was a petite, gorgeous blonde who had probably had her suitcase packed with a different bikini for every day of their vacation. She would have been *mad*.

Helen and Lucy had been good friends. They'd made plans together and enjoyed each other's company. Lucy had been heartbroken when Helen had died.

His heart gave a little squeeze. It wasn't just his sister he hadn't considered.

He hadn't considered other people. Other people who had been devastated by Helen's death. He'd been too busy focusing on his own grief to allow anyone else's to touch him.

"Tell Frank I'm sorry—no, tell Lucy I'm sorry." He hesitated for a second then asked, "Frank and Lucy—do they have any kids?"

It had been another of Helen and Lucy's grand plans, that they would all have kids at the same time. They'd always joked that their imaginary offspring could be prom king and queen together.

He heard Violet take a deep breath and her voice had a new edge to it, a harsher edge. "You've been away too long, Sawyer. Frank and Lucy lost their daughter last year to stillbirth. It was an extremely traumatic time—Lucy nearly died and had to have a hysterectomy. They can't have any more children."

He felt as if someone had just twisted a knife in his guts. For a few fleeting seconds he'd been jealous. Jealous that Frank still had Lucy. That he still had a future with his wife.

Violet's words sent chills across his body. It just showed you—you never knew. You never knew the minute when things could come crashing down all around you.

And now he was feeling something else. Disgust with himself. He hadn't been there to support his friends in their time of need. People who had reached out to him when he'd been at his lowest ebb.

It didn't matter that he'd walked away and ignored everyone. He could still remember every card, every phone call, every email, every handshake.

Helen would have been livid with him. He could almost hear her reading him the Riot Act.

Touching reality again was making him realize that her death hadn't affected only him. It had affected everyone around them.

Some of the contact tracers in the team could barely look at him today.

And it wasn't a reflection on them. It was a reflection on *him*.

They had no idea how he would react to them. How he would react if they brought up the past and expressed their sympathies about Helen—even after all this time

Violet cleared her throat at the end of the line and he snapped back to attention. "I take it you're still flying under the radar in there? They haven't made the connection between us?" he asked.

"No. No one knows." He heard her breathe a sigh of relief. "Or if anybody knows, they're not saying anything. Evan Hunter's walking around here like a bear with a sore head. I've spent the last few hours trying to avoid him. He didn't take it well that you're involved in this."

Sawyer couldn't help the smile that automatically spread across his face. "He'll get over it," he murmured. He looked at his watch. "Hate to say it, sis, but I need to go. I might have a chance to get my head down for a couple of hours. One of the pediatricians has just arrived to share the responsibility of the kids. We've just had to intubate one of them. This might be the only chance I get to sleep in a while."

"Okay, Sawyer. Stay safe and keep an eye on Callie. She has lots of good qualities. And keep your phone switched on. If I call and you don't answer…"

"I get it, sis. Keep your head down and stay out of Evan Hunter's way. He'll find something else to gripe about soon."

He stared at the phone as he heard her hang up, puzzled by her parting shot about Callie. It was almost like a little beacon, glowing orange in the dark sea. She knew exactly how to play him. Some things never changed.

CHAPTER SIX

VIOLET HAD ONLY just replaced the receiver when Evan Hunter came stomping across the room, shouting orders as he went. They might be an hour ahead of Chicago but hadn't anyone told him it was six o'clock in the morning and most of the staff had been up all night?

"Somebody get that man a coffee," she grumbled as she slid her chair under the desk and pulled up the screen she'd been reviewing. It was a distribution model of the potential spread of the smallpox virus. They'd started working on this while they had still been trying to determine if the passengers on the plane had been exposed or not.

"Violet! *Violet!*"

Rats. It was almost as if he had an internal radar and could hear her thoughts.

"What?" She turned to face him as he hovered above her, obviously irritated by her lack of instant response. "What's happened?"

"Where have you been? I've been looking for you?"

Darn it. She'd only ducked out for five minutes to speak to Matt. How on earth could he have known that?

There was only way to shut him up. "Ladies' room." She gave him a sarcastic smile. That was all the information he would need.

He scowled at her. "I need you to get some background on Matt Sawyer for me. Find out where he's been for the last six years. Find out how he managed to end up in an E.R. in Chicago."

She was stunned. It was the last thing she had been expecting. A few hours ago it had been a whole hullaballoo about a graph of the potential spread of smallpox. And, well, yes, she could almost understand it. That was just the kind of thing he wanted to appear instantly before his eyes. Stuff the grunt work. He practically expected people to work at the speed of light. It wouldn't be the first time she'd told him in no uncertain terms that data needed to be checked and rechecked, assimilated and analyzed beyond any shadow of a doubt.

But this? Asking her to investigate her own brother?

It was totally out of left field. A complete bolt from the blue.

Anyone else might have been intimidated by his stance, leaning over her. But Violet wasn't. She'd been this close to Evan before. About six months ago after a work night out.

The medic and her boss. Never a good idea.

Too bad she couldn't shift the inappropriate memories out of her head, which came up at the most inopportune moments.

"Violet? Did you hear me?"

She snapped back to attention. Back to reality. Sawyer and Evan Hunter had never got on. She'd no idea why and she didn't really care. Just as well she'd never told her boss that Sawyer was her brother.

She stared at him, unfazed by his annoyed face. Violet didn't do well on lack of sleep. It was the standing family joke that everyone should stay out of her way if she'd had a bad night on call as a resident. Her patience had just flown out of the window.

"Why on earth do you want me to check up on Sawyer? Shouldn't we be focusing on the real issue—the potential smallpox outbreak? I thought you wanted a complete rundown on the potential spread? That's what I've been working on for the last few hours and I'm not finished yet."

Evan leaned closer. "Don't you dare tell me what to do right now. I'm the team leader around here. I decide what happens. Sawyer is irresponsible and reckless. He's the last person we can trust. And a few hours ago he phoned in the biggest threat to this country's health in years. Am I suspicious? Absolutely I am! Now…" he pointed at the computer "…find out where he's been and what he's been doing. I want to know now!"

He swept into the office next to her, slamming the door behind him as if he could knock it from its hinges.

Violet sagged back down into her seat. She didn't need to do what he asked. She'd been doing it for the last six years and had found nothing. *Nada.*

Apart from a few cursory texts since his wife's funeral and his departure from the DPA, she knew nothing.

His texts had only ever told her that he was safe. Nothing else. Not where he was or what he was doing.

The hard fact was that if she wanted to know where Sawyer had been she would have to ask him. And right now she had a distribution model to finish.

She stared at the slammed door. Violet was used to prioritizing her own workload.

She set her jaw.

Evan Hunter could wait.

* * *

He watched the walls shake around the door he had just slammed. What on earth was wrong with him?

Evan felt sick. He had potentially one of the most well-publicized outbreaks in the DPA's history to handle and at the heart of it all was a man he hated. A man he didn't trust.

And he was taking it out on the people around him—he was taking it out on Violet.

The last thing he should be doing.

The press was all over this. The media room at the DPA was currently packed out, with the phones ringing constantly. He could handle stress. It wasn't the first time he'd handled a major outbreak.

What he couldn't handle were his reactions to Violet.

Those were the things he couldn't control.

He was going to have to do something about it—and fast.

"Callie, phone."

Callie looked up from where she was standing, talking to Sawyer. The plans for the containment facility were almost complete. The nurse dangled the phone from her hand. "It's the lab."

Callie and Sawyer moved in unison, diving for the phone at the same time.

Their hands clashed and Callie shot him a dirty look and shoved him out of her way. "Callie Turner."

"It's Evan."

She really couldn't face any niceties. Her brain could only fix on one thing—and from the expression on Sawyer's face he felt the same way.

"What is it? What has Frank found?" Sawyer flinched next to her at the sound of Frank's name. What was that all about? Frank had worked at the DPA for-ever. They must know each other.

She could hear the deep intake of breath at the end of the phone. "Electron microscopy revealed a brick-shaped virus. It's definitely an orthopox."

Callie felt her insides twist. She knew better than to say the next words. But she couldn't help it—it was automatic. "He's sure?"

Beside her she saw Sawyer drop his head into his hands. He knew exactly what was being said.

"He's sure."

She touched his arm and met his pale green eyes, giving him a silent nod. Sawyer let loose a string of expletives. The lab was only confirming what they'd all suspected. It was the first step in trying to classify the disease. It just made it all seem a little too real.

It was time to get down to business. "How long be-fore he can be more specific?"

"He's still running the PCR. You know how this is—we could have something for you in twenty-four hours or it could take up to seven days. Direct fluorescent antigen testing has ruled out varicella. Tell Sawyer he was right—it's definitely not chicken pox." She heard Evan sigh. Those words must have been painful for him. "Your next stage is the move to the containment type C facility. Are you ready for that?"

Callie looked at the whiteboard on the wall next to her. Every detail was clearly displayed. Her team was good. "The power company's just been in touch to let us know the power has been reconnected. We're just wait-ing to hear back from the chief of police about closing the highway and getting the police escort. Once that's in order we'll be ready to move."

"Keep me posted. I'll be in touch if we have any more news."

Callie stood in a daze for a few seconds, the phone dangling from her hand. She was trying to assimilate the information she'd just been given. A warm hand closed over hers and replaced the receiver.

They didn't speak. For once it seemed that their minds were working in unison.

Callie looked around at her bustling colleagues. Someone was going to have to tell them. Someone was going to have to confirm that this was a real and credible threat. It wasn't just a suspicion any more. They'd moved a stage beyond that now.

And it was her job.

Her job to ensure the safety of her team under these confirmed conditions.

Her job to keep the staff informed.

Her job to be responsible for the patients who were—most likely—infected with smallpox.

Her job to help prevent the spread of the disease.

It was almost overwhelming. Could she really do all this?

Sawyer was watching her. He could see the tiny flare of panic in her eyes. And as much as this was the worst possible news, he knew it was time to step up.

They were close together, low enough for their voices not to be heard.

"What exactly did Evan say?"

"It's definitely an orthopox." The anxiety in her voice was palpable. But a little smile appeared on her face. "And Evan said to tell you that you were right—it's definitely not chicken pox. They've ruled it out."

He pulled back a little. "Evan Hunter said that?"

She nodded. "I think he was more or less pushed into a corner on that one." Her eyes swept the room, trepidation returning to them. "I need to tell the team. We have to move to the containment facility."

If only she could see what he did. At times she had a little-girl look about her, as if she was about to be swept away by a tidal wave. As if the situation and events were totally out of her control. But these were tiny, fleeting glimmers that disappeared in an instant.

Then she would tilt her chin and act exactly the way she should. Just like she was doing now.

She was pushing aside her own fears and focusing on the details of the job. Just like a good doctor should.

They were close together again. Hiding away from the rest of the world. Her eyes were much bluer this close up. Last time they'd been like this had been in a darkened room and he hadn't really had a chance to appreciate her finer features.

She was lucky. No lines marring her complexion, only some dark circles under her eyes. Her gaze met his and her brow wrinkled. "Can I do this, Matt?"

Matt. Hardly anyone called him that. Just the way she said the word took him by surprise. He was so used to being called by his surname that it actually made him stop for a moment. He reached out and took her hand. She didn't flinch, didn't pull away. She just inched a little closer.

He saw the glimmer of fear register in her eyes. Her tongue peeked out and ran along her dry lips, moistening them and leaving them glistening.

He was fixated. He couldn't look away.

He bent down, his lips brushing the side of her cheek.

"Of course you can do this, Callie. This is what you trained for."

If he turned his head just slightly his lips would be on hers. It was the most inappropriate, most inopportune moment. But Sawyer didn't care.

For the first time in a long time he was finally starting to feel again.

And everything else just paled in comparison.

He was getting another waft of that raspberry shampoo.

But then she moved, lowering her face beneath his and resting her hands on his shoulders. There was something else in her expression. It was almost as if she was taking a minute—as if she wanted to tell him something. And it was clear she had no idea about the thoughts currently circulating in his head.

He tried to focus. To take his gaze off her pink lips. She was close enough that he could smell the mints she'd been eating.

They couldn't stay like this. Any minute now someone in the E.R. would notice they were closer than normal.

He had to get some perspective before he did something he might regret.

He jerked back. "How long until we find out the diagnosis?"

If she noticed him pulling away she didn't react. "Evan wasn't sure. Anything from between another twenty-four hours up to seven days. But at the moment we still need to tell everyone the quarantine will last for seventeen days."

"Seven days is a long time to wait for a diagnosis."

She nodded and turned away from him. Focusing on work, getting back to the job. Staring up at the whiteboard. "I guess we'd better start vaccinating again. Everyone going to the type C unit needs to be vaccinated beforehand."

She was right. She was being professional. Her mind was focused on the job. Just where his should be.

He nodded and said the words he was supposed to. "Let's get to work."

How on earth was he going to manage in an enclosed space with her for the next seventeen days?

CHAPTER SEVEN

"Wow! How DID they manage this in such a short space of time?"

Callie peered out of the transport-vehicle window as they approached the containment facility. It was more than impressive. A bright white building sitting in the middle of an industrial site.

It was almost the regulations personified.

A single building located at least one hundred yards from any other occupied facility. Non-shared air-conditioning, heating and adequate ventilation systems. Single rooms with negative air pressure. Advanced medical and laboratory systems. Dependable communication systems and controllable access.

Then, more than the obligatory one hundred yards away, another type R facility to host everyone who'd been exposed, vaccinated and hadn't developed any symptoms. All the patients who'd been exposed in the E.R. could now be safely housed and monitored for the next two weeks.

Sawyer pressed his face up against the window next to her. The slow-moving convoy had taken nearly forty minutes to get here. It had been a surreal experience. But, then again, it had been years since anything like this had happened. The fact that the ambulance transport crews were kitted out in masks, gloves, gowns and shoe covers probably hadn't helped. Particularly with the amount of news crews that surrounded the hospital.

Callie found that incredible. Who, in their right mind, news crews or not, would want to be that close to a possible smallpox outbreak? If she'd been any other kind of doctor she would have headed to the city limits as quickly as she could.

Callie shuddered at the thought of the news headlines that evening. The pictures of the crew transporting the 'infected' patients could be terrifying to the general public. She could only hope that Evan Hunter would be in charge of damage control.

"I guess it must have been something else. A school? Some kind of lab? A warehouse?" Sawyer wrinkled his nose, as if he was aware that none of those things really fitted. "Did Callum leave you any notes?"

Callie rummaged through the pile of papers on her lap. "I've been so busy sorting out the problems—getting the electricity and water turned on, medical supplies delivered—that I didn't really think about it. He just told me he'd identified 'suitable premises.' Ah, here it is." She dragged a pale cream piece of paper from the bottom of the pile.

"What's wrong?"

Her eyes were still scanning the page and what she was reading was obviously translating straight to her face. "It's just a little odd." She lifted her head and stared at the building again, "It was a research facility."

"What's odd about that?"

"It's apparently been here for the last hundred years." A strange sensation swept over her. "Do you think they used it for the last smallpox outbreak?"

"Now, there's a creepy thought."

They pulled up outside the buildings and both heads turned to look again. Sawyer opened the door and jumped down, holding out his hand to help Callie. She left her papers on her seat and jumped out with him.

They stood next to each other, hands on their hips, trying to work out what was going on. "It looks brand-new," Callie muttered.

"It certainly does. Maybe it's just had a coat of paint?"

He stepped forward and touched the exterior wall. "It's certainly had new windows and doors."

Callie nodded. "And a new ventilation system." She gave a nod to the system that was clearly venting all its air outside through the designated HEPA filters. "They couldn't possibly have had that last time round. It must have been used recently."

She turned around as the rest of the transport started to pull up behind them. "Let's take a look inside."

Sawyer matched her step for step as they strode through the building. Everything about it was perfect. A laboratory, newly refurbished patient rooms and clinical treatment rooms. Then a whole separate building that fitted with type R requirements, with single bedrooms and bathrooms where all the people under the containment could be housed, with extra facilities available for them all. Kitchens, sitting rooms, children's playrooms, even a cinema room, it was extraordinary.

All with the proper ventilation systems to prevent the spread of infection.

Callie ran her fingers along the wall in the one of the corridors. She didn't feel uneasy. This place didn't have a bad feeling attached to it, but there was a certain air of mystery. "If these walls could talk, what would they tell us?"

Sawyer turned to face her, "What do you mean?"

She pointed to the nearest room. "This almost seems too good to be true. This place has obviously been in use recently—though we did have to get the water and electricity switched back on. They haven't managed to do all this in twenty-four hours. I wonder what kind of research they did here?"

Sawyer pushed open the nearest room—full of state-of-the-art monitoring and ventilation equipment. "Does it really matter? We've got good facilities here." He nodded as Dan, the pediatrician, appeared at his back, entering the room to make sure it had everything he needed for the children.

A smile appeared across Dan's face. "These are the latest ventilators. I've been trying to get Chicago General to buy some. They cost serious money. They'll be perfect for the kids. But here's hoping I only need one." He gave a nod to Callie. "I don't know how you managed it but this is perfect."

That strange feeling spread again. "I don't know how I managed it either," she said quietly. Everything seemed to have miraculously fallen into place. Maybe her rant at Evan Hunter had worked. Someone in the DPA had excelled themselves here.

Sawyer placed a hand on Dan's shoulder. "How do you want to set things up? Do you want to have Jack and Ben in separate rooms? We've got the negative air pressure facilities here, we can use them."

He was obviously just trying to give Dan his place. As the only pediatrician, the care and responsibility of the two boys fell to him. It didn't make sense to bring in any other doctors. And although he wasn't a pediatrician Sawyer had already volunteered to assist with the care of Jack and Ben. Since he'd done the initial diagnosis he seemed reluctant to let them go. But he was quite happy to take instructions from Dan.

Dan shook his head. "Actually, no, I want to keep them together. They've been equally exposed anyway. Separating them at this time isn't going to benefit either of them. Unless you can tell me something different?"

Callie shook her head.

Sawyer cut in. "I'm with you, Dan. In that case, for the sake of the two of them, it's better they stay together. This place would be terrifying for a six- or seven-year-old on their own. There is no viable clinical or psychological reason to keep them apart. They're brothers. They're meant to be together. Let's not add to the stress."

Callie could feel her heart flutter in her chest. He couldn't possibly know or understand what those words would mean to her. It was just the fact that somebody, somewhere had even the slightest inkling about the connection between siblings. The reassurance of being together, no matter how unscientific. And the possible benefits for the boys.

She'd heard miraculous stories before about premature twins being reunited in the same special-care cot and the baby that had been expected to die had made an unlikely recovery.

She herself had been badly injured in the car accident, almost unconscious. But when it had become apparent that Isabel was going to die, an experienced nurse had insisted her trolley be pulled in next to her sister's. Then she'd lifted Isabel's hand to let Callie hold it as her sister's life had slipped away.

It had been the worst moment in Callie's life. If she hadn't been going straight to Theatre, they would have had to sedate her.

But now, with the benefit of hindsight, it was one of her most precious and treasured memories. She'd been able to say things to Isabel that she might never otherwise have had the chance to say. Even though she realized Isabel had probably not heard her, it had still given her comfort. It had also meant the world to her parents, who hadn't been able to make it to the hospital in time to see their daughter before she'd died.

So Sawyer's words and understanding meant more to her than she could ever possibly reveal.

Dan and Sawyer were already striding down the corridor, organizing the transfers from the ambulances. Staff were streaming past, carrying boxes that were systematically being unpacked into cupboards.

Callie walked back out and watched the rest of the people being shown into the other building, carrying their belongings with them. One of the planners came up and handed her a large plan of the building, complete with names assigned to every room. "Thought you'd need this, Callie."

She nodded as she looked over the plan, a smile crossing her face when she assimilated the sleeping arrangements. "We don't seem to have adequate laundry facilities." She lifted her head to the planner, who consulted his list and shook his head. "We need to get right on that. In the case of smallpox, laundry can be a risk. It can carry contaminated fluids. We need to make arrangements for the laundry to be put in biohazard bags and autoclaved." The planner scribbled furiously then walked away.

She felt Sawyer's hand on her shoulder. "Our home for the next, what, seventeen days?"

"Sixteen," she said firmly. "We've already done the

first day." She gave a little smile. "Think you can stand me for that long?"

"I might be forced to give you a haircut."

"Ditto."

He jerked back a little. "Isn't that some crazy quote from a romance movie?"

"I don't know. I don't watch romance movies. I'm more an action girl myself."

"Really?" There was distinct tone of disbelief in his voice.

"Yeah."

He shook his head. "Just when I think I know you, even a little, you say something to surprise me."

"That I like action movies? If that surprises you, you've led a pretty sheltered life." She realized the stupidity of her words as soon as they left her mouth. But it was too late. They were out there.

Sawyer didn't react. He just pulled out some equipment from the back of one of the ambulances and gave her a weak smile on the way past.

She was cringing inside. A man whose wife had died on a DPA mission had obviously never led a sheltered life. How could she possibly last another sixteen days around him without making an idiot of herself?

He turned back to face her, his expression unreadable. "What about Alison? Did everything work out okay?"

So it was back to business. A few seconds of personal chat that she'd just ruined. She'd only herself to blame. She forced a smile onto her face. "I think in a few hours we'll all wish we were Alison."

"How come?"

"We couldn't bring her here because we couldn't vaccinate her. The next option in the plan is to isolate the person at home. But Alison didn't want to take the risk of being isolated at home in case she put her family at risk."

Sawyer nodded. He would know that being isolated at home would be the logical answer but not entirely practical. "So you had to think outside the plan? Interesting." He folded his arms across his chest. "I bet that gave you a spasm. So what's happened to her?" The grin that had vanished a few minutes ago had reappeared. Callie resisted the temptation of rising to the bait.

"It seems that somebody in the DPA budget office was in a nice mood. They've rented out an entire boutique hotel for the next fortnight until we're sure she's symptom-free. Alison will be living in the lap of luxury."

Sawyer's response was instant. He shook his head. "Maybe to you or me. But not to her. Alison dotes on her kids. It will drive her crazy not to be with them for two weeks."

Callie tried not to grimace. She'd been thinking of the gorgeous surroundings, fabulous food, luxurious bedding and unlimited TV channels. She really hadn't thought much past the idea of ordering room service every night.

"I guess not," she murmured, as she followed him down the corridor as he dumped some more supplies in the treatment room.

"Let's grab our stuff and dump it in our rooms." They walked back outside and Sawyer lifted her rucksack and suit carrier from one of the vans. "Did you really travel this light? Or do you have a giant suitcase hidden somewhere?"

She laughed. "I do have a suitcase, but it's a carry-on." She looked around her, "I've no idea where it is, though. What about you?"

Sawyer lifted a polythene bag. "My worldly goods."

"You're joking, right?"

He shook his head. "I came to work to do a twelve-hour shift. I didn't realize I should have packed for a fortnight."

"Wow. We're really going to have to get you some clothes, aren't we?" She started to laugh. "What about all your hair products? Won't they need a suitcase all of their own?"

"Cheeky!" She ducked as he flung his bag at her head. The contents spilled on the ground. Another pair of Converses, a T-shirt, a pair of ripped jeans, a pair of boxers and a bunched up pair of socks. She raised her eyebrows as she stuffed the contents back in the bag and lifted up one shoe. "Two pairs?"

He shrugged. "That's the good pair. The scruffy ones are work shoes." She smiled at the kicked-in shoes she held in her hands. She wouldn't even have worn them to paint a fence—and these were the good ones. "Nothing else?"

"What? I wear scrubs at work all day. What else do I need?"

"I hate to think. You got anything to sleep in?"

"What kind of a question is that?"

"The kind of question from a woman who's sharing an apartment space, kitchen and bathroom with you."

Ever since she'd looked at the plan she'd felt nervous. Excited nervous, not scared nervous. Wondering what his reaction would be to the sleeping arrangements.

"Why aren't I sharing with Dan? Wouldn't that have made more sense?"

She nodded as they headed over to the building. "It

does—and he's sharing with us too, along with one of the other DPA doctors. Four people per apartment. But I guess they figured you'd be doing the opposite shifts from Dan. Doesn't make sense for you to be working at the same time."

"Callie, Sawyer!"

They turned their heads as one of the nurses shouted over to them.

"We need you in the treatment facility. There's a few patients with symptoms that need checking out."

They looked at each other and swiftly dumped their bags at the entrance.

"Guess we can do this later," Callie said flatly.

His gaze met hers. "I guess we can."

There was something in the way he said it. The tone of his voice. The way his eyes held contact with hers. The way there was a hint of smile on his face. It sent a weird tingle down her spine.

All of a sudden that excited nervousness didn't seem so odd after all.

Callie looked down at her map as they walked along the corridor. "Next left," she said.

It was late and they were both tired. Checking over a few symptoms had taken a lot longer than expected.

Sawyer pushed open the plain white door with the number seven on the front. It opened into a large sitting room with white walls and red carpet and a sofa. It was much bigger than she'd expected. An open-plan kitchen stood at one end of the room with a door to another corridor at the bottom.

Callie was a little shocked. It was much better than she had expected. "I thought it would be like student accommodation." She gave a little shrug, "You know, kind of drab and definitely tiny." She pressed her hand down on the comfortable sofa with matching cushions. "I guess not. Who do you think stayed here?"

"Who cares?" Sawyer had made his way to the pristine white kitchen and started to rummage through a cardboard box sitting on one of the worktops. "Wonder where this came from? Gotta love those planners. I'm starving." He emptied the contents onto the surface— milk, bread, butter, cereal. Callie automatically opened the door to the fridge and started depositing the perishable items inside.

"Yes!" He punched his hand in the air as if he'd just won an award.

"What is it?"

"My favorites." He pulled out a packet of chocolate cookies and ripped it open. "I didn't realize how hungry I was." He tilted his head at her as the cookie disappeared in two bites. "Who sorted all this stuff out? Was it Alison?" He looked back in the box. "Because I swear, if I find a tuna pizza in here I'll—"

"You'll what?" She swatted his arm. She almost felt relieved. He was back to his relaxed self again. The way she preferred him. The way he was when he didn't feel as if he had the weight of the world on his shoulders. Along with two very sick kids.

He squinted. "It's a bit bright in here, isn't it?"

Her eyes swept around the unexplored apartment again. It was clear neither of their other colleagues had found their way here yet. She nodded and flicked the overhead light back off, plunging them back into darkness. She walked over and pulled the curtain at the window, which looked onto the rest of the industrial site. Dim light flooded through the kitchen. The moon was high in the dark sky outside and the external lights surrounding the buildings let a little more light into the room.

It was nice. Kind of private.

Sawyer flicked the switch on the kettle. "A coffee pot and some decent beans obviously weren't on the inventory."

"And that'll be my fault, will it?" In the dim light Sawyer didn't seem anywhere as near as intimidating as before.

Maybe that was what he needed. To be out of the hospital environment and the things he was obviously struggling with. Maybe this—an environment like someone's home—made him feel more chilled. More easy to be around.

Or maybe she was remembering the last time they'd been in a darkened room together. Because she was feeling herself drawn towards him, her feet on autopilot.

She was up close, just under his chin. He turned back round and gave a little start at her close proximity. Was she reading this all wrong?

But from the lazy smile that came across his face she obviously wasn't.

He leaned one elbow on the counter top. "Did I say it was your fault?" He was so close that his breath warmed her cheeks.

"You didn't have to, but it always seems that way."

He lifted his hand and rested it gently on her hip. "Maybe you're just a little too uptight. Maybe you need to stop following the rule book all the time." He moved forward in the darkness, his lips brushing against her ear. "Maybe—just maybe—you need to learn to relax a little."

It was the way he said it. His tone of voice. She hadn't read anything wrong.

She was reading everything perfectly. He thought she couldn't throw the rule book away? Even for a second?

Under normal circumstances she would have been horrified. But nothing about this was normal. And nothing about how she felt drawn to this man was normal.

Maybe for just five minutes she could follow her own rules. Not the ones that felt safe.

She looked at him steadily in the dim light. "Maybe. I was just thinking the same thing about you. Maybe you need to learn to relax too," she whispered.

For a second nothing happened. Her breath felt caught in her chest. Her skin prickled. What would he do?

It was almost as if she could see him thinking, weighing up things in his mind. Had she just made a huge mistake? The wait was killing her.

Then she felt it—a warm hand slipping into hers. It electrified her skin. He pulled her over towards the sofa and sat. He tugged her down next to him, the moonlight spilling over them both.

Maybe she should feel a little intimidated by how close they were. If she leaned forward right now she could brush her nose against his. But she didn't feel intimidated at all. She didn't feel they were close enough.

In the dim moonlight and up this close she had her best-ever view of his pale green eyes. She'd seen a previous stone that color once in a tiny boutique jeweler. It was called paraiba tourmaline and she'd never seen one again. Which was a pity because it was the exact color of his eyes. And she could see the little lines all around the corners of his eyes. Were they laughter lines? Or were they from the permanent frown that he usually saved for her?

His shaggy brown hair didn't annoy her nearly so

much when she had a close-up view. She kind of liked it. In fact, for a split second she could see her fingers running through it in the midst of…

She shook that thought from her mind, squeezing her eyes shut for a second. *Wow. Where had that come from?*

But she didn't feel embarrassed. She didn't feel awkward. The heat emanating from his body was warming hers. And she was enjoying it. No matter how crazy that was.

When had been the last time she'd been in this position? This close to a man? It must have been over a year ago.

Harry. Like all the others, he hadn't worked out either. It wasn't that there had been anything wrong with him. He had been kind, handsome, considerate. Just what any girl would want. But she just hadn't connected with him. Hadn't been able to let herself go enough to plan ahead for a future with him in it. Because that would have meant letting him in. Telling him everything he'd needed to know. And she hadn't been there yet.

She hadn't been ready to share.

So what was so different about Sawyer?

Was it that he challenged her to let the rule book go? Was it that he pushed her to do better?

Or was it that he'd lived through the pain of loss himself? Maybe he would understand in a way that no one else could? Maybe that was the truth of why she was drawn to him—a fellow lost soul.

He moved. The shadows had gone from his eyes and there was no barrier between them—no shutters.

Callie's stomach was in a little knot. Was he finally

letting down his guard? Would he actually talk to her about what had happened?

His hand came down on her the side of her leg. His warm hand instantly connected, shooting warmth through her thin scrub trousers.

"So, Callie, are you going to tell me?"

She turned to face him. His hand was still on her leg but now she'd angled her body around to face his so they were almost nose to nose.

"About what happened. To your leg."

This was it the moment she should pull away. The time for her to retreat into herself and hide away from the rest of the world.

She'd done it before. It was automatic. It was so easy.

Her hands moved, up around his neck.

She was about to take the biggest step she'd ever taken.

"Not now. Maybe later."

Four words. That was all.

But it felt like a giant leap forward.

It was the first time she'd ever even considered telling someone about what had happened.

He could never know the strength that had taken.

She was sure she started to hold her breath. She believe how distracted she was right now. She was sure he must think her a little crazy.

But she didn't have time to think of any of these things.

Because she was kissing Sawyer.

CHAPTER EIGHT

CALLIE WASN'T QUITE sure who made the first move. She didn't think it was her, but then again she didn't think it was him. It was almost as if they read each other's minds and moved simultaneously.

There was no light-hearted kissing. No nibbling. Nothing gentle. Nothing delicate.

From the second their lips locked there were no holds barred. His lips devoured hers, fully, passionately without a moment's hesitation. And she liked it.

She could feel the scrape of his emerging bristles on his chin against her skin, abrading it as they kissed. Their teeth clashed and they both ignored it, his hand pressing firmly on her back to bring her even closer.

She wanted to run her hands over his body, across his chest and down his back. Everything about her was acting on instinct. The one thing she wasn't used to.

His kisses moved. Down her neck, along her throat. Then he groaned and shifted position, pushing her onto her back on the sofa and slowly moving on top of her. He pressed her arms above her head, straddling her body, and starting work on her neck again.

She was gasping now, willing him to go lower. Itching to let her hands feel his skin under her palms.

She wrenched one of her hands free and grabbed

hold of his hair, pulling his head back up towards her and capturing his lips again. She loved the feel of them. She loved the way he kissed her.

If this was what kissing a bad boy was like, she should have done it years ago.

She moved her head, kissing down his neck and releasing her other hand to slide it around his back. She was pulling him closer, working her hands under his scrub top, dancing her fingers up and down his spine.

She heard him groan and felt his muscles flex beneath her fingers. Somehow knowing she had some control made her feel bolder. She wanted to feel his skin against hers, she wanted to *see* his skin. She pulled at his scrub top, tugging it upwards until he'd no choice but to stop kissing her for a second and pull it over his head.

There. Just what she wanted. Sawyer, bare-chested.

She ran her fingers across the scattered dark hairs on his chest, wishing they were tickling her bare skin. But he hadn't moved quite as quickly as she had. His fingers were just edging beneath her top. Her back arched automatically towards him, willing him on.

He gave her that lazy smile. *Did this man know just how sexy he was?* Then he bent and whispered in her ear. "Have a little patience, Callie."

Patience. The last thing on her mind right now.

His voice was rugged, husky. A perfect voice for the middle of the night in a darkened room in a place that belonged to neither of them. It seemed all the more wicked. All the more illicit.

He started tugging her top over her head. His eyes widened at the pink satin push-up bra he revealed. Callie was a girl who loved her fancy matching underwear, no matter what clothes she was wearing on top. *Thank heavens for small mercies.* Just wait until he reached the thong.

He didn't hesitate for a second. His gaze was fixed on her breasts enclosed in the pink satin. "So you have a thing for pale colors and matching sets? Last time I saw you half-dressed it was in lilac."

His voice was lower. Growling. And it turned her on a lot. "I have lots of matching sets." She raised her eyebrows and gave him a calculating smile. "What's your favorite color?"

"Red," he groaned, as his palms skirted the outside of the bra cups. Her breasts seemed to be swelling at his touch. But the appreciation of her underwear was momentary. Sawyer cut to the chase—his patience obviously as limited as hers. He reached behind her back and released the clasp, her bra flung aside a moment later, releasing her breasts into his clutches. As his teeth brushed against her peaked nipple she could begin to feel the throb between her legs.

"Or maybe emerald green." He tweaked, licked and blew his hot breath across her as she moaned beneath him. Her hands kept trying to move, to make further contact with his skin, to get between them and reach down below. But he kept moving, changing position and diverting her attention.

This man had talent in the diverting attention stakes.

Her legs automatically widened and he moved from straddling her to bringing his legs between her thighs. Again she acted on instinct, raising her hips and tilting her pelvis towards him. Thin scrub trousers couldn't disguise what lay beneath and she gave a little gasp.

His hand slid beneath her scrub trousers, sliding first across her pelvis then down along her thigh, his fingers tracing the line of her scar. But she didn't flinch, she didn't jerk the way she had when some other lover had touched it. This felt easy, this felt natural. His hand ran back up the inside of her leg, sending a rush of blood to her groin, working his way around her buttocks and smiling as he played with her thong. He gave a little tug and there was an instant ping, along with a loosening sensation. Thirty dollars gone in one tug. She could almost visualize the thin gossamer straps breaking. It only excited her more.

His fingers crept back around to the front, coming into contact with her pubic curls. She moaned and opened her legs, willing his fingers closer, and her frustration built.

The scrub trousers were annoying her now. She didn't want any barrier between them. She didn't want anything between them at all. She moved his arms out of the way to give her a clear path to where she wanted to go.

She pushed her hand down the front of his scrub trousers, ignoring his boxers and sliding right inside. She could feel his back arch and she wrapped her hand around him. Finally. Just what she wanted.

His mouth was moving lower now, his fingers still dancing a fine tune as she moaned in response. This bad boy certainly knew how to play her.

"Anyone home?" The door of the apartment slammed loudly.

They froze. For a few seconds neither of them moved.

Dan. It was Dan. The bright light flicked on, sending illumination over their bare skin. Sending them both into instant panic.

Sawyer pushed himself up, pulling his hand out of Callie's scrub trousers and starting to stand. Callie's head jerked from side to side, trying to find where Sawyer had flung her bra.

That was as far as they got.

Dan had obviously walked the few steps into the apartment and his jaw dropped.

Callie could have died.

She didn't even have time to cover her breasts—her scrub top had been flung far behind in her in the midst of passion. Sawyer let out an expletive and stepped in front of her. "Give us a second, will you, Dan?"

Dan gulped. "Sure." The color spread rapidly up his cheeks as he walked back outside in stunned silence.

Sawyer closed the apartment door and leaned against it.

Callie felt the tears rapidly building in her eyes. She wanted to die of embarrassment. She felt like some teenager caught in a compromising position.

The silence in the room was deafening. She moved quickly, threading her arms back through her bra, fastening it and pulling the crumpled scrub top over her head.

Dan's face was haunting her. He'd seen her almost naked. A guy she hardly knew.

Sawyer was still standing with his back against the door, his eyes not meeting hers. The obvious bulge was still apparent in his thin scrub trousers. And the irony of it hit her. *Another guy she hardly knew.*

This wasn't her. She didn't act like this. She sometimes didn't even kiss on the first date.

But Sawyer had literally been by her side since she'd arrived in Chicago and the attraction had been instant. Instant but ignored.

This was the worse possible time for her. She needed to be a leader—someone that people could respect and respond to. What if Dan told the others what he'd just seen? That the doctor in charge of the potential small-pox outbreak had been lying half-naked on the sofa with a guy she'd just met?

What if he told them that her mind certainly wasn't on the job? That she was focusing on something else entirely?

She squeezed her eyes shut and tried to push the hor-rible thoughts from her mind. Could this be any worse?

Yes, it could.

Sawyer still couldn't look her in the eye. He hadn't even moved to pull his scrub top back on. He was just leaning against the door, his eyes fixed on the window straight ahead.

What was worse than getting caught in a compro-mising position with the bad boy?

Getting ignored by the man who'd just kissed you as if his life depended on it.

"Are you ready?" His voice startled her. It was almost a growl. Almost as if he thought this was all her fault.

It made her bristle. It made her defensive. It hurt.

She had to work with this man. She had to *live* with this man for the next two weeks. It would be so easy to hide her scarlet cheeks, put her head down and walk out of this room. But she couldn't. Not like this.

"I'll be ready to go when you can look me in the eye, Matt."

His head shot up. He flinched. It was so unfair that he was still standing there, bare-chested, right before her eyes. Men had it easy. He looked startled by the use of his first name—she'd only ever called him that a few times.

Or was he just surprised she'd immediately called him on his reaction?

"Let's not get into this now." He turned his back on her, picked up his scrub top, clenching it in his fingers, and put his hand on the door.

"Why not?" She couldn't think straight. Not after what had just happened.

"What?" He was beginning to look annoyed.

"Why not get into it now?" She gestured towards the door. "I'm really not looking forward to going out there and facing Dan. I don't even want to think about how I'm going to have to appeal to his better nature not to tell everyone about this." She shook her head. "My guess is that the last thing he'll want to do is share an apartment with us. Who would? We've just behaved like a pair of hormone-crazed teenagers."

She stepped forward and put her hand on his chest and he visibly flinched again. *Actions spoke louder than words.* It told her everything she needed to know.

"We have to work together, Matt. We've been stuck together in close proximity, under pressure, for the last two days. I guess we're just going to have to chalk this up to experience."

Her heart was thudding against her chest. She had no idea if she'd just played him right. She was trying to remain detached. She was trying to be rational. But she didn't feel that way.

In truth, she was mortified.

Hot and heavy after a first kiss, after only a couple of days.

She didn't need to justify herself. She didn't need to explain herself. But she just couldn't let him think that was her normal behavior.

"I guess there's a first time for everything." She kept her voice as steady as she could. He'd finally raised his eyes to meet hers but the shutters were well and truly down again. "It's probably best for both our sakes, and for the people we're responsible for, that there isn't a repeat performance."

His face remained blank. As if he was listening to her words but not really hearing them.

"If you will let me pass, I'll go and face the music with Dan."

He stepped out of her way, remaining silent.

She opened the door and stepped out into the corridor. His silence was angering her now. First he wouldn't look at her. Now he wasn't talking to her.

She turned her head to the side, praying he wouldn't see the tears glistening in her eyes. "Maybe you'd better try and sort out other sleeping arrangements. This situation is untenable."

On the outside Sawyer was frozen to the spot, but on the inside he was a bubbling cauldron, full of sulfur and about to explode.

Dan had appeared at the worst possible time—that much was obvious.

And Callie was right. They both had to pray that he would keep things to himself; otherwise Callie's authority could disappear in the blink of an eye. And in a situation like this that could be disastrous.

He knew that she'd been hurt by his lack of response but the truth was that she was right, he couldn't look her in the eye. And after what they'd just shared Callie would have wanted some kind of sign. A sign as to whether this had been just a one-off mistake or if it could lead somewhere.

And the truth was he just didn't know.

Every nerve ending in his body was on fire. Every place that she'd touched his skin seemed to burn. She'd been so willing, so responsive. If Dan hadn't appeared, chances were nothing would have stopped them.

And how would he have felt then?

Feel.

That was the problem.

Sawyer had been down this road before. Meet a woman in a bar, exchange small talk, have meaningless sex, sneak out before morning.

But all of a sudden the road had changed direction.

No, scrap that, this was an entirely new road.

In the space of a couple of days this woman had started to get under his skin. To invade his senses. To make him feel things that he hadn't felt since he'd first met Helen.

And it felt like a betrayal. It didn't matter that Helen had been dead for six years. It didn't matter that she would have never have wanted him to lead this closed-off life. His impersonation of the walking dead was growing stale, even for him.

But on any of his chance encounters before, he'd never *felt* anything. Apart from the obvious. He'd just been going through the motions. Making sure everything still worked.

This was different. This was nothing like that.

From the moment Callie Turner had appeared on his radar everything had turned upside down.

At first he'd thought he was annoyed because Callum was sick, then he'd thought it was because she was inexperienced. Or struggling. Or getting things wrong. Or all of the above.

But the truth was he was looking for a reason—any reason—not to like Callie Turner.

He was fighting the way he was drawn to her—was curious about her and wanted to know more.

The sight of her getting changed into her scrubs. The scar on her leg. The almost kiss in the treatment room.

The way he'd felt as soon as his lips had touched hers. The way she'd reacted to his touch. The feel of her skin next to his. The arch of her back. The tilt of her pelvis. The small groan she'd made at the back of her throat.

All of it driving him crazy. All of it making him act on instinct. Something he hadn't allowed to happen in a long time.

How could he have gotten into this? How could he have ended up in a specialist containment unit for a seemingly extinct disease? All of this was so unreal. This had bad movie written all over it.

Wrong place, wrong time.

The words danced around his brain again. He'd first thought them when he'd raised the alarm about the apparent smallpox cases. The words had been so in tune with how he had been feeling. He couldn't wait to get out of Chicago General. He couldn't wait to get away from the whole situation.

But now the words made him feel uncomfortable. He still didn't want to do any of the infectious disease stuff. But his Hippocratic oath had him firmly by the short and curlies. He had to stay here and help look after these people. He had to work with the team from the DPA. He had a responsibility. To them. To the patients. To the staff. To Callie…

Everything came back to her. No matter where his head drifted off to, she was always the thing he came back to. Like an anchor point.

He could almost see the picture of Helen that still sat on his desk at home. Her smiling face, dark hair and dark eyes. Home? When was the last time he'd gone home? When was the last time it had felt like home?

He sagged against the wall again. Everything was bubbling to the surface, thanks to the way he was feeling towards Callie, and he just couldn't deal with this— not on top of the DPA issue all over again.

Did she even realize how hard this was for him? To be amongst these people again? To be amongst the people that reminded him at every glance of how much he'd failed his wife?

What kind of a husband couldn't save his wife? Maybe for a regular guy that could be acceptable. But he was a doctor. And his wife had died from a medical complaint. One that, under normal circumstances, could have been treated and her life saved.

For a few hours with Helen he'd felt as if they had been trapped on a runaway train.

They hadn't got to experience the joy of a positive pregnancy test. They hadn't got to celebrate their child's arrival, planned or not. He felt cheated out of so many experiences—all because they'd been in the wrong place at the wrong time.

Worst of all, he didn't know who to be angry at most. Himself? The DPA? Evan Hunter? Helen?

It had been Evan who had sent Helen into the field, not him. Even though she hadn't been feeling one hundred percent. None of them had had any suspicion she might be pregnant—not even Helen. But their baby had decided to defy the odds of their contraceptive of choice. And by the time they'd known, it had been too late.

A ruptured ectopic pregnancy in the middle of nowhere. There had only been one possible outcome.

He had to get past this. He had to move on. Everything about this situation was wrong.

He couldn't begin to work out his feelings towards his past and the guilt he felt, in this new situation and his pull towards Callie. He felt pressured. Callie was pressured. It wasn't the right time or the right place. He had to step back. He had to step away.

And from the hurt look in Callie's eyes, he'd already done that. Whether he'd planned to or not.

He could hear mumbled voices through the door. They sent a cool breeze dancing over his skin, covering his chest and arms in goose-bumps. He grabbed his scrub top and pulled it over his head.

He had to go out there. He had to act as if nothing had happened. He had to try and help Callie save face, because if word of this ever got back to Evan Hunter...

He had no intention of being around to face the fall-out.

He glanced at his watch. Forty-eight hours. That was how long he'd lasted when a beautiful woman had been dangled under his nose.

The pull was just too strong.

But everything about this was wrong. They would be together for the next fourteen days. Fourteen days and nights with Callie Turner.

And he'd just made it all worse.

His hand hesitated on the door handle.

Because now he knew how her skin felt. Now he knew how she reacted to his touch. Before he could only have imagined. And that could have kept him safe. That could have kept him on a reasonably even keel.

But now...

He closed his eyes. And it was Helen's face he saw. Helen's eyes. Helen's smile. The instant image made him jump.

The sear in his chest was instant. Like his heart was being twisted inside his ribcage. He couldn't do this. He couldn't do any of this.

Callie was a career girl. He used to be the same.

But now he was a getting-by kind of guy. In two weeks' time, for the second time in his career, he would walk away from the constraints of the DPA. And nothing would give him greater pleasure.

No. He could do this. He could keep his head down. He could stay out of her way. He could work the opposite shift from her. He could make sure they were never alone together. He could make sure that opportunity didn't knock again.

Because that would keep him safe.

Because he wasn't entirely sure how he would react.

He straightened his shoulders and walked out into the corridor.

It was empty. Callie and Dan were gone.

CHAPTER NINE

EVAN WAS IMPATIENT. The computer graphics filled the wide screen on the wall, mapping the potential spread across the world, along with the corresponding time-scale. It was hours and hours of hard work and dedication. Every eye in the place was fixed on the simulation. The color-coded icons were blinking at him, the red ones demanding his full attention.

He turned round and folded his arms across his chest. Violet was wearing red today too. Almost as if she was marking a claim on the piece of work she'd just created. A fitted, knee-length red dress with a black belt capturing her waist. It was an unusual color for her to wear and he was surprised by how much it suited her. Her blonde hair sat on her shoulders and she peered through matching red-rimmed glasses. It was almost as if she was trying to divert his attention…

Then it struck him—she was.

His mind drifted back to a few months ago and a blurry night with drinks after work. She'd been wearing red then too. And he'd definitely been distracted. He felt the fire burn in his belly that she might have been thinking about that while getting dressed that morning and had deliberately chosen her outfit accordingly. His own thoughts made him feel distinctly uncomfortable and, consequently, irritable.

"Where's the stuff on Sawyer?" he snapped.

"What?" Delicate lines creased her forehead. She looked at him as if he was talking a foreign language.

"You know what," he accused. This was all becoming more and more obvious. "I asked you to do a background check on Sawyer. Find out where he's been and what he's been doing. I asked you more than two days ago. Where is it?"

She waved her hand in at him irritation. "Earth to Evan. I've been kind of busy on the save-the-planet-from-smallpox stuff."

He pulled his shoulders back in shock. Cheeky. Insolent. Not the way that Violet Connelly ever spoke to anyone—least of all him, her boss. She was really pushing him. And it didn't help that every time she came into his field of vision his eyes fixed on her lips.

Lips of which he'd already had experience.

He could see some ears pricking up around them, People craning their necks above their partitions to see how he was going to react.

Did anyone here know what had happened between them?

He had to make sure there were no suspicions. He couldn't let anyone think he would give Violet preferential treatment.

He placed a hand on her desk and leaned forward, drawing his head level with hers. Up close and personal she was a tiny little thing. His hands could probably span her waist. He could see her nibbling her bottom lip as if she was nervous. And she probably was with his big frame towering over her.

He pulled back a little and kept his voice calm. It

wasn't his job to entertain the crowds—they had enough work to be getting on with. "Dr. Connelly, I gave you a specific task to do a number of days ago. I expect you to have completed it." He caught the glimmer in her eye. It definitely wasn't fear. It was much more like rebellion!

"I've been busy." The words were firm, even if he could see the slight tremble in her hand as she picked up a pen.

"You're telling me that in the last two days you've found out nothing about Matt Sawyer? Nothing?" His voice was steadily rising now, despite his best intentions.

Was he imagining it or had she just pouted her lips at him? This woman was going to drive him crazy.

She shrugged her shoulders. "Oh, I've looked. But there's nothing to find. I've no idea what Matt Sawyer's been doing or where he's been." She raised one eyebrow at him and tilted her chin. "Why don't you ask him?"

She was baiting him. In front of a room full of colleagues. The hairs were standing on end at the back of his neck. It was all he could do not to growl at her.

"You've got two hours, Violet. Two hours to find out exactly what I requested on Matt Sawyer. If you don't deliver, I'm taking it to the director."

He turned on his heel and walked out of the room. The pen still dangling from Violet's fingers.

"Still nothing?"

The DPA guy shook his head as Sawyer leaned against the wall. It had been three days and they still had no word on the classification of the disease. They were still stuck in the no-man's land of a "brick-shaped orthopox", which told them something but pretty much told them nothing at the same time.

Sawyer had been doing his best impression of the invisible man. And it made him feel lousy.

When Callie worked days, he worked nights. When Callie was in the apartment, he was out, finding any excuse to be somewhere else. There had been a few awkward moments, a few "almost" bumps in the corridor, resulting in both of them jumping and staring at walls and floors instead of the person right before their eyes. A huge amount of avoidance tactics on his part.

He was beginning to find it almost comedic. The number of times he'd heard her voice behind a door he had been about to open, only to swerve and end up in a place he really didn't want to be, having conversations with people he barely knew.

On the other hand, yesterday he'd found himself in the children's playroom, leading the Portuguese soccer team on a quest for worldwide domination against the children in the US soccer team. It had been game controllers at dawn. But he'd had to let them win, even though he'd suspected they were playing dirty.

There were five kids, aside from Ben and Jack, in the containment facility, of varying ages and nationalities. None seem to have had any side-effects from the vaccine. And the minor ailments that had brought them into the E.R. in the first place had all been resolved. It was amazing what the threat of an infectious disease could do.

But spending time with the children had been fun. They were treating everything like a vacation. They could watch want they wanted on cable, play a mountain of console games and pretty much eat whatever they liked. He'd made a mental note that the children's playroom was now going to be his number-one place to go to avoid Callie.

Today had been torture. The trouble with a containment facility was that no matter how hard you tried to find somewhere else to sleep there really wasn't anywhere else to go so he had to stick to the apartment he'd been allocated.

The aroma of coffee had drifted under his door around lunchtime. He was supposed to be sleeping, but he'd only dozed on and off for a few hours. The temptation to get out of bed with his nose leading him directly to the coffee pot had been huge, but then he'd heard her voice. Callie was obviously in the kitchen, grabbing a bite to eat. And the last thing he wanted to do in his sleep-deprived state was run into her.

She was already destroying the few hours' sleep he was actually getting by invading his dreams. Sometimes happy, sometimes angry, but always in state of undress. Funny, that. It was taking him back to his teenage years.

And that probably wasn't a place he wanted to go. Violet had enough blackmail material on his misspent youth to last a lifetime.

The trouble with avoiding Callie was being out of the loop of information. She was the focal point around here—all paths led to Callie and if he wasn't communicating with her, he didn't always know exactly what was going on.

He had been sure that the DPA would have had a more definitive diagnosis by now. Frank Palmer would be working flat out. It didn't matter that he knew it could take up to seven days. He wanted to know *now*.

One of the nurses came and touched his shoulder. "Can you take a look at Mrs. Keating, Ben and Jack's mum? She's not feeling too good."

His stomach plummeted. It was the one thing they had all been waiting for—someone else to show signs of infection. He picked up Jill Keating's notes and started walking across the corridor. The thick bundle was packed full of assessments and observation notes. For a woman with no significant disease history it was surprising how quickly notes filled up in an isolation facility.

"What's she complaining of?" he asked the nurse.

There was another person that was having trouble looking at him.

But for an entirely different reason. The nurse's eyes would be full of unspoken worries and unanswered questions. Things that nobody wanted to say out loud right now.

Everyone was dreading someone showing signs of infection. It would give them all the confirmation of the infectious disease without the laboratory diagnosis.

"She has a low-grade temperature and a headache. Her pulse is fine and her blood pressure only slightly raised. But she's vomited twice."

Mrs. Keating was lying in bed in the darkened room. It had taken her more than forty-eight hours to finally leave the room that her children were in and have some rest. The woman was probably exhausted and that could explain the headache and the slight rise in blood pressure. But the temperature and vomiting?

He pulled on the protective clothing, regulation mask and gloves and pushed open the door. "Hi, Jill. It's Dr. Sawyer. Want to tell me how you're doing?"

She averted her eyes straight away as the light from the corridor spilled into the room. It sent an instant chill down his spine. "Wake Callie," he whispered over his shoulder to the nurse.

He spent the next twenty minutes examining Jill. She was definitely exhausted. And despite being surrounded by food and drink she was showing clinical signs of dehydration. The black circles under her eyes were huge and she vomited into a sick bowl again during his examination.

Callie was standing at the window in the corridor, looking anxiously through the glass. He'd signaled to her to wait outside.

She moved to the door as he came back outside and waited impatiently while he discarded his protective clothing.

"Well? What do you think?"

He started scribbling some notes on Jill's prescription chart. "I'm sorry that I woke you, Callie."

"Why? Is she okay?"

He nodded. "I can't say for certain but I suspect she is in the throes of her first-ever migraine. The only thing that doesn't really fit is the low-grade pyrexia. But everything else makes me think it's a migraine. And after the stress she's been under I wouldn't be surprised. I'm going to give her an injection then sit here and wait until her symptoms subside."

"And will they?"

He shrugged his shoulders. "I certainly hope so. This is a wait-and-see option. We need to give it a little time. An hour or so."

"Call me if there's any change."

He nodded. Disappointed. He'd half expected her to wait with him. This could be crucial in determining the nature of this disease. But it obviously wasn't to be. She couldn't get away from him fast enough.

And he couldn't really blame her.

Or maybe she was just showing faith in his competence as a doctor?

Whatever it was, he was just going to have to get

over it. But his stomach was gnawing at the memory of how much he'd missed those eyes in the last few days.

His nose picked up the smell of toasted bagels. It was time to follow his stomach. This could be a long wait.

An hour later Jill was in a deep sleep. The migraine relief seemed to have worked well and Sawyer was breathing a sigh of relief. He'd checked on the boys—both Jack and Ben were stable and showing no obvious signs of improvement or deterioration. It was four a.m. That horrible point of the night when nausea abounded and sleep seemed so far away.

He looked around. One of the nurses touched his shoulder. "Go and have some coffee, Sawyer, you look like crap."

"Thanks for that."

She smiled at him. "Oh, you're welcome. I'll page you if I need you—but I doubt it."

He headed down the darkened corridor. There was definitely a pot of coffee on the go somewhere. The smell seemed to be drifting towards him and making him follow it like the children had followed the pied piper. And he could hear some background noise.

He reached one of larger communal kitchens. The coffee pot was just on the boil. Just the way he liked it. Straight, black and hot.

He poured a cup and headed towards the noise. The kids must have left the TV on in the cinema room. It was something sappy. He slumped into one of the seats. If he just sat down for five minutes and drank this coffee, he would be fine. The caffeine would hit his system and keep him awake for the last few hours.

Five minutes.

"What are you doing here?"

He jumped. The voice cut through the darkness and he spilled hot coffee all down the front of his scrub trousers. "Hey!" He rubbed frantically at the stain, lifting the wet trousers from his groin area—some things just shouldn't get burned.

Callie appeared at his side and peered at the spreading stain. "You klutz." She started to snigger. That crazy middle-of-the-night kind of laugh that night shift staff got and couldn't stop.

Sawyer sighed and set down his half-filled coffee cup. "I came down here for a coffee to help me stay awake and wondered what the noise was. What are you doing here?"

"I couldn't get back to sleep."

"So you came down here, rather than sit up with me next to the patients?" It sounded almost accusing and he didn't mean it to come out that way but in the middle of the night social niceties disappeared.

"I guess I didn't want to sit next to you, Sawyer."

Yip. It worked both ways. Night shift certainly did away with the social niceties.

He didn't want to get into this. Not here. Not now. He glanced at the big screen. "You told me you were an action girl, not a chick-flick girl. What happened?"

Their eyes turned in unison at the screen as the hero's eyes followed the heroine, staring at her unashamedly.

Even in the dark Callie's cheeks looked a little flushed. Maybe it was the intimacy of the scene. Not intimate in that sense. But intimate in the fact it was the first time the audience could see how smitten the hero was with the girl of his dreams.

And he could relate.

Here, in the middle of a darkened room, in the midst of an outbreak, Sawyer could totally relate.

He could see Callie's long eyelashes, the blue of her eyes dimmed by the light. But the flickering screen highlighted her cheekbones, showing the beautiful structure and lines of her face. He couldn't take his eyes off her.

Her eyes met his. "I am an action girl. But I was too late this time. It seems the kids are action fans too—and they all have DVD players in their rooms." Her voice was quiet, almost whispered. It made him naturally lean towards her to hear what she was saying above the background noise of the movie.

"I'm an action girl" were the words playing around in his mind.

She held up another DVD and tilted her head to the side, revealing the long line of her neck.

His hand went automatically to her waist and she didn't flinch, didn't move. Her arm stayed half in the air, still holding up the DVD, almost as if she was frozen.

Sawyer stepped forward, the full length of his body next to hers. He forgot about the damp coffee stain on his scrubs. This was where he should apologize. This was where he should tell her he was having trouble getting his head around all this.

This was where he should tell her about Helen. About the fight with Evan and the consequences. This was where he should clear the air.

Because if he didn't, he'd never move on.

But he didn't do any of those things.

He just kissed her.

His hands captured her head, winding his fingers through her hair and anchoring her in position.

But he didn't kiss her like he had before.

This time he was gentle. This time he was slow. This

time he wanted her to know that he meant it. It wasn't just a reaction. It wasn't just a physical thing.

This was him, Matt Sawyer, wanting to make a connection with her, Callie Turner.

So he started on her lips. Brushing his against hers then moving along her jaw and down her neck.

He was just working his way back up the other side of her neck when Callie's hands connected with his shoulders, pushing him back firmly.

"No, Sawyer. Stop it."

He was stunned and immediately stepped away.

Even in the dark he could see tears on her cheeks. "I can't do this. This isn't me. And I know you don't mean it. I can't do what we did a few days ago and then just walk away. You need to leave me alone." She started walking towards the door. Away from him. "Just leave me, Sawyer. Leave me alone."

"Callie, wait—" But his words were lost because she'd almost bolted out the door. He stared down at his hands. The hands that had just touched her. That hands that still wanted to be touching her.

He didn't blame her. His earlier actions had been pretty much unforgiveable. But the pull towards her was real. And it wasn't going to go away any time soon.

He sagged back down into one of the chairs. There was no point in going after her right now.

He needed the proper time and space to talk to her.

His eyes went back to the screen flickering in the darkness. They'd reached the point in the movie where the heroine was telling the hero she was marrying someone else.

Kind of ironic really.

Callie flew along the corridor as if she were being chased by swarm of angry bees. He'd kissed her again. And she'd been so close to responding to him. So close.

But she couldn't let that happen again. She couldn't be caught in a compromising position with Sawyer. She had to keep her mind on the job.

That was the rational part of her brain talking.

Her heart was saying something else entirely.

She couldn't let him touch her again. She couldn't let him evoke those feelings in her again, only to walk away without a single glance.

She wasn't built that way. She couldn't deal with things like that.

Isabel had been entirely different. *Isabel* would have been the one kissing Sawyer and walking away without a second thought. She had always been in control.

Not like *her*.

History had taught her that she hated things she couldn't control. And there were lots of elements of this spinning out of her control, without adding her feelings for Sawyer into the mix.

When were these feelings ever going to go away? She'd thought working at the DPA where she and Isabel had planned to be would have given her some comfort. But in the end it hadn't.

The guilt she felt about her sister still gnawed away at her. She constantly compared herself to Isabel, without ever really meaning to.

Even with the men she'd dated she'd kept her sister at the forefront of her mind. Would Isabel have approved? Would she have liked this one? Would she have thought that one good enough?

But with Sawyer it was different. She didn't even want to give them space together in the same thought. Why was that?

If Sawyer had met Isabel, would he have been attracted to her instead of Callie?

That thought made her feel physically sick. She felt a horrible creeping sensation over her skin, along with a realization of her continued exasperation with herself.

When would this go away? When would she feel as if she was living her own life and not doing penance for the loss of her sister's?

Everything in her work and personal life was so mixed up right now. And being stuck in an enclosed space with Sawyer wasn't helping.

Yesterday she'd spent time fretting over the plan. While all her instincts had told her that keeping the brothers together was ultimately the right decision, the truth was that the plan told her otherwise.

She'd spent a few hours weighing up the pros and cons of insisting the plan be followed before finally deciding to let it go. The only thing was, unease still gripped her. Gnawed away at her stomach and kept her awake at night.

Plans were evidence based. Plans had been researched within an inch of their lives. How would she defend her decision if challenged from above?

Sawyer had whispered to her to relax and stop following the plans a few nights ago and the truth was it hadn't been nearly as scary as she'd thought.

Just like making the decision about the brothers.

Her phone buzzed in her pocket and she pressed the answer button straight away. It was five in the morning so it had to be the DPA.

"Callie? How are you? How are you holding up?" Her footsteps froze.

"Callum?"

"Who else would call you at this time in the morning?"

Relief flooded through her and the tears that had just vanished came spilling down her cheeks again.

Callum. Her port in a storm. The one person she actually *did* want to talk to.

"You don't know how happy I am to hear your voice. How are you, Callum?"

She heard the hearty laugh she was so used to. The familiar sound made her miss him all the more.

"I'm fine. You were right—it was an MI. They whipped me down to the angio lab and inserted a stent. Missed most of the last few days because of the drugs. But I'm feeling great today."

She leaned against the wall, sliding down onto her haunches. "If you're feeling great, why are you phoning me at five in the morning? Shouldn't you be resting?"

"Resting's for amateurs. Couldn't sleep and no one at the DPA will tell me anything useful. I blackmailed one of the nurses into letting me use her phone. It's been five days and I should have been officially discharged by now. Funny thing is, my doc won't discharge me to the containment unit."

She shook her head at his tenacity. She wouldn't put it above Callum to try and discharge himself straight to the containment unit. "You phoned the DPA?"

"Of course I did. I wanted to know how my favorite doctor was getting on."

She felt warmth spread across her chest. "I bet you say that to all the girls." It was so good to hear his voice. She'd heard about the stent but no one would actually say if they'd spoken to him. This made all the difference. She smiled. "And anyway who is your favorite doctor—me or Sawyer?"

He paused. Obviously deciding what to say next. "Yeah, Sawyer. Well, he used to be my favorite but you've taken over from him now. How are you getting on with him, Callie?"

His voice sounded a little strained. And the realization hit her. That's why he was phoning. That's why he was trying to get to the containment unit. He was worried.

"Ask me something else."

"Oh, I see. It's like that."

That was Callum. He knew her too well. She couldn't lie to him and try and dress this up but she didn't want to add to his stress. "Yes, it is. Ask me about the small-pox."

She heard the sigh at the end of the phone. "I'm assuming you don't have a definitive diagnosis yet."

"You're assuming right. We know it's an orthopox and we know it's definitely not chicken pox. We've vaccinated all those exposed and moved to the containment facility. What was this place, by the way? I'm assuming you know."

He cleared his throat. "It's just a little place that was on the back burner."

"What does that mean? The building is old, but the facilities are state-of-the-art." Her curiosity was piqued now—no matter what the time.

"How are the patients?"

She gave half a smile. An obvious deflection. He knew it. And she knew it. Whatever this building had been, he'd no intention of telling her. "We've got two sick little boys—one ventilated. And we're monitoring symptoms in everyone else. Had a bit of a scare with the boy's mother but it turned out to be nothing. Oh, that reminds me. We had someone we couldn't vaccinate. A nurse who is eighteen weeks pregnant. She's currently holed up for a fortnight in an exclusive Chicago hotel."

"Oh, no." Callum's silence was ominous. She'd expected him to say something else or to ask more questions.

"Callum?"

"How's Sawyer? Was he okay about that? How did he deal with the pregnant nurse?"

She shifted her weight from one leg to the other. What could she say? That initially he had freaked out? But he'd managed to contain how he'd been feeling and had done the job? It was truthful, but was probably too near to the bone. "He was fine. I know that his pregnant wife died on a DPA mission but no one really knows the details. Want to fill me in?"

His answer was brusque. "Not really. Is he following protocol?"

"Ours or his?"

"So it's like that. I might have guessed. Sawyer's never going to change." Even though he sounded a little exasperated, Callie could almost see the smile on his face as he said the words.

"If you tell me about him, Callum, maybe I'll understand him a little better. Maybe it will help us work together."

She could almost hear his brain ticking over at the end of the phone. "Are you having major problems with him? Professional problems?"

How did she answer that question? Because, like it or not, the professional problems were minor. It was the personal problems that were the real issue.

Callum had never been slow off the mark. He was a man who could always read between the lines.

"It sounds as if it's not up to me to tell you, Callie. It would be better coming from him." Words of wisdom from a man who was obviously seeing things much more clearly than she was. "Maybe I should give Sawyer a ring. Have you got his number? Did he ever change it?"

"Maybe you should relax. Maybe you should follow the post-MI protocol like a good patient."

"Give me his number."

"No."

"Dr. Turner, I asked for his number." His voice was rising now and he was obviously getting agitated. He only ever called her Dr. Turner when he was trying to tell her off. It made her smile.

"I'm hanging up now, Callum."

"Don't you dare!"

"Take care now."

She was smiling but still close to the floor on her haunches. Her legs were beginning to cramp.

She stood up and arched her back, trying to release the tension. Her head was beginning to thump, probably from lack of sleep and all the stress she was under. Nothing to do with Sawyer.

Nothing at all...

Sawyer was lying on his bed, trying to get some sleep. He glanced at his watch for the tenth time. The sun was streaming through the windows. Seemed like no one had thought of blackout blinds for this place.

He picked up his phone and pressed in Violet's number. His guilt was starting to kick in now. He should have phoned her earlier. His excuses were weak—even he knew that.

She picked up straight away and let out a big sigh. "Perfect timing, bruv."

He sat up in bed. The chance of sleep was long gone. "What's up?"

He heard her slow intake of breath. "I've got Evan Hunter breathing down my neck. He wanted me to check up on you—find out what you've been doing these last few years."

"Well, I'll make it easy for you. I don't want you to be next on Evan Hunter's hit list. Check out Borneo, Alaska and Connecticut."

"What?" He could almost hear the wheels spinning in her brain at the eclectic mix of places he'd been in the last six years.

"There's nothing sinister to find, Violet. You know that."

Her answer was instant. "I know that, Matt."

"What's Evan's problem? No—scratch that. I know what his problem is—me. But what exactly does he think he's going to find?"

Violet sounded annoyed. "I have no idea. He threatened to report me to the director if I didn't get back to him with a report in two hours."

"What? He asked you do to a report in the middle of the night?"

"Well, not exactly. He first asked me to do it five days ago. Then he gave me the two-hour time limit three days ago."

"And you still haven't done it?"

He could hear the casualness in her voice. "Yeah, well, I didn't really think he'd complain about me to the director. He was just growling at me. Trying to show me who's boss. Now you've given me the heads up I'll at least go and give him that to chew over. It should be enough to finally satisfy him you're not involved in this." He could hear the hesitation in her voice. "How are you, Sawyer? Is everything okay? Any other symptoms?"

"Not yet. We had a little scare earlier but it's fine. I'm fine." He paused. "Well, actually, I'm not fine."

There was a long significant pause at the end of the phone and he knew why. He'd never discussed anything with his sister before. He avoided personal issues at all costs.

"What's wrong?" Her voice was quiet, almost afraid to ask the question.

"It's Callie."

"Is something wrong with Callie? Does she have symptoms?" It was only natural for her to jump to the most obvious conclusion.

"No. It's not that. I kissed her."

"You did what?"

Well, that had got her attention. Other than their last conversation, he couldn't remember the last time Violet had ever shouted at him. But, then again, she was also defying Evan Hunter left, right and center, which was also unheard of. It seemed his sister had turned into a whole new person over the last six years. All while he'd been hiding in the outer parts of the planet.

"I kissed her." He flopped back down on the bed. The words seemed so much worse now he'd finally said them.

But they felt so much better. It was nice to finally offload.

"Why on earth did you kiss Callie Turner?" her voice hissed down the phone. She was obviously trying to keep anyone from hearing.

Sawyer felt like a teenager. Why did any guy kiss a pretty girl? "Because I wanted to. And I think she wanted me to."

"You mean she didn't slap your face?"

"Not quite."

Violet was obviously a bit stunned. "So, what's the problem?" She hesitated a second. "I mean, this isn't the first time you've kissed someone since Helen, is it?"

He let out a snort of laughter. "I think I can safely say no to that. But this is different."

"Different how?"

She'd put him on the spot now and he didn't quite know how to answer. "Different because I don't want to hurt her. But there's a definite attraction between us. And I know she feels it too."

"Has an alien inhabited your body?"

"What do you mean?"

"I mean that for the first time in years you're talking to me about your feelings. Since when have you done that?"

He couldn't answer.

"Okay, brother, I'm only going to say one thing. I like Callie. I mean, I *really* like her."

"Well, I think I like her too." There. He'd admitted it. To someone other than himself.

"Then don't mess this up. Don't hurt her." The words were blunt and straight to the point. Violet had never been one to mess around with how she felt.

"Can't you give me something else? Can't you tell me to handle this? You know her better than I do." He was beginning to sound desperate, but right now he didn't care.

"Really? Well, here's the clincher—I haven't been in a lip-lock with her, Matt. And I'm sorry but you don't reach the grand old age of thirty-six and ask your sister for dating advice. That ship sailed a long time ago, buddy. Probably around the time you told everyone about my high-school crush."

He cringed but it brought a smile to his face. He'd

made a poster and stuck it up outside the school. Violet had locked herself in her room and hadn't spoken to him for days. She still hadn't got over it.

"So, no advice, then?"

"Absolutely not. Not on your love life anyway. Just stay safe, brother. And phone me if there's any problem. Any *work*-related problem."

"What about Evan?"

Her voice had a hard edge to it now. "Leave me to worry about him. I'm hoping I'll be out of his hair soon enough." She hung up before Sawyer had a chance to ask her what she meant.

He stared at the ceiling. Potential smallpox day five. Great.

CHAPTER TEN

"WAKE UP, SAWYER."

One of the nurses stood above him. Liz? Julie? He really couldn't remember. He sat bolt upright in the bed, not even thinking about hiding himself.

She turned sideways. "Cover yourself up, boy. And get dressed. Some guy from the DPA wants to talk to either you or Callie, and I can't find her."

Sawyer pulled the sheet half across his body, lifting a crumpled pair of scrubs from the floor and tugging them on. He smirked as the nurse rolled her eyes and handed him the matching top.

He let out a laugh as she walked to the door then stopped and threw him a can of deodorant. Then something registered with him. "What do you mean, you can't find Callie? Where can she be?"

The nurse shrugged. "I just know the guy said he had to speak to either one of you. He's been holding for a few minutes because I tried to find Callie first. When I couldn't, he said to wake you."

"Where's the phone?"

"At the nurses' station."

He jogged along the corridor. His brain was in overdrive. It was day seven. This had to be a diagnosis. But where on earth was Callie?

He picked up the phone. "Frank?"

"Finally. Sleeping beauty wakes up."

"Have you got something?"

"Is this Frank? Is this the man who is supposed to be in Hawaii with his devoted and gorgeous wife, who'd bought eight different bikinis for our long-awaited vacation?"

Seven days. He'd waited seven days for this. "Frank?" He couldn't hide the impatient tone in his voice.

"It's monkeypox."

"What?" Sawyer was stunned. He'd never seen monkeypox before. It had never really been on his radar.

Frank seemed to know exactly what to say. "You'll need to examine the boys again for bites, scratches and abrasions. Monkeypox usually only occurs in Western or Central Africa but strangely enough the last known case was in the U.S. in 2003, caused by prairie dogs."

"What?" Nothing about this made sense. His brain couldn't process what he was hearing.

"Monkeypox can be spread by squirrels, dogs, rats, mice and rabbits. That's why your boy had swollen glands. It's one of main differences in symptoms between smallpox and monkeypox."

Sawyer ran his hand through his hair. Where was Callie? He had to talk to her about this straight away. Things were starting to register in his brain. Should he have guessed this? He hadn't given too much thought to the swollen lymph glands—even though they were unusual in smallpox. He'd just assumed it was a viral response.

"What are our options?"

Frank cleared his throat. "None, really. No known treatment. It's less severe than smallpox and the smallpox vaccine can lessen the symptoms. But it can still be fatal—monkeypox can have a one to ten percent mortality rate. All the smallpox infection controls should remain in place."

They spoke for a few more minutes then Sawyer replaced the receiver. "Wow." He leaned against the wall.

His head was spinning. His eyes swept across the room. Everyone was going about their business quietly and efficiently. What effect would this news have on the people here?

In a way it was a relief to finally have a diagnosis but with no known treatment it still made things difficult. He racked his brain, trying to remember what he could about monkeypox. It wasn't much.

He only hoped there was a plan.

Had he just thought that? Him, Sawyer, wondering if there was a plan?

Callie was obviously rubbing off on him.

Callie—where was she?

He started walking along the corridor, stopping people on the way past. "Have you seen Callie? Do you know where Callie is?" Time after time his colleagues just shook their heads.

Finally, one of the contact tracers furrowed his brow. "I saw her go down there a little while ago." He pointed down one of the long corridors.

Sawyer strode along. He couldn't remember this part of the building on the plan. It was well away from the small labs and isolation ward. He reached a double door at the end of the corridor and pushed it open.

It took his breath away.

The tiny little room was extraordinary. A small stained-glass window was set into the facing wall, with the sun streaming through causing a kaleidoscope of colors across the white walls. It was like a magical light show.

Callie hadn't even heard him enter. She was sitting on one of the wooden pews near the altar at the front. There was no particular religion celebrated here. It was one of those non-denominational rooms that could be used by anyone.

A quiet place. For contemplation.

He walked along the carpeted aisle and sat down next to her. She jerked, conscious of no longer being alone, and opened her eyes. He slid along a little. She was sitting directly in the stream of coloured light. Her face and skin were lit up like a rainbow. It was dazzling. He'd never wanted to reach out and touch anyone more than he did right now.

Papers were scattered all around the floor at her feet.

"What do you want, Sawyer?" She sounded weary, exhausted. The relief that had instantly flooded him when he'd heard the diagnosis disappeared. All of a sudden he could hear the countdown in his head. Now they had a definitive diagnosis, it was another step closer to getting out of there.

It was a step closer to getting away from the dreaded DPA. It was also a step closer to getting away from Callie.

And he wasn't prepared for the way that made him feel.

"Sawyer?"

He was still looking at her pale skin bathed in myriad colors. It was taking his breath away. As were the feelings sweeping over him.

He took a breath. "We have a diagnosis. It's monkeypox."

"Monkeypox?" Her voice rose automatically then she looked around her, as if conscious she shouldn't shout in a place of worship. She fell to her knees on the paper-strewn floor where papers had been tossed in all directions.

He joined her. "Do you think there's something about monkeypox in here?"

She nodded. "There is. It isn't much, just some basic information and guidelines." Her head shot back up, "Who did you speak to?"

"Frank. And before you ask, he was positive. He said you could call him back. He'll stay at the lab until he gets a chance to speak to you."

"Here it is!" She pulled a few crumpled pieces of paper from the floor. Her eyes started racing across the text. She was mumbling under her breath, "Same transmission precautions, slightly shorter incubation period." Her eyes lit up. "I'm not entirely sure—I'll need to check—but I think this is good news for Alison. It seems to be a larger droplet infection. There's a good chance she won't have been infected."

He nodded. "Actually, it still has a seventeen-day incubation period. She'll need to wait a little longer before she can go home."

Callie nodded but the smile reached all the way up to her eyes. "It's something. I was dreading a smallpox diagnosis."

"Me too." He looked around him. "How did you find this place?"

She let out a little laugh. "Curiosity got the better of me. It wasn't marked on the plans and I wanted to find out what was down here." She put her hands out. "Once I'd found this place I wanted to keep this little piece of paradise to myself."

"I don't blame you." His eyes met hers. He didn't want to fight. He didn't want a confrontation. Both of them knew they needed to talk. But this just wasn't the right time or place.

She looked down at the mess she'd made on the floor. A bright red folder had been pushed under one of the pews. "I came here to escape. To get out of the rat race." She edged the folder with her foot. "I had a bit of a disagreement with the plan. It sort of ended up all over the place."

He folded his arms and gave her a lopsided grin. "Shock, horror. Callie Turner threw the plan away?"

"I guess I did." She was biting her lip as she stared at the scattered papers. Didn't she know how much that distracted him?

He rested back against the wooden pew. Not exactly designed for comfort. Any minute now Callie would be off, her brain kicking into gear and taking off at full speed. He could picture her talking nineteen to the dozen and shouting instructions to everyone.

That's why he kind of liked this place.

"How long have you had this hidden gem?"

She arched her eyebrow at him and had the good grace to look embarrassed. "A few days. Right after we bumped into each other in the kids' cinema room. I needed somewhere I could have a little space."

"From me?" He didn't want her to say yes. He *really* didn't want her to say yes. But somehow it was more important that she was honest with him than that his feelings were hurt.

She sighed. "From you, from me, from everything." She threw up her hands but her voice was remarkably steady. "I had to sort a few things out in my head." She gave him a sad sort of smile. "I spoke to Callum. He wanted to call you—to interfere—but I wouldn't let him."

It was probably the first time in his life that he didn't automatically jump to his own defense. He didn't need to. He knew exactly what she would have said to Callum and exactly what he would have said in response.

"So, is he going to kick my ass?"

She let out a little snigger.

"Just as well I changed my number, then." He turned to face her. "Seriously, is he well enough to call?"

She nodded.

"Do you mind if I call him and tell him about the monkeypox? It might be the only thing that distracts him from tearing me off a strip or two."

"I think that would be fine." She stood up, her feet brushing against her paperwork. She looked a little lost. "I'll come back for this later. I still haven't really figured out if this is the place for me. I need to do a little more thinking."

"The place for you?" He looked around him in confusion. "A chapel?"

She shook her head slowly and took a deep breath. "No. The DPA."

There it was, he thought. The thing that was bothering her most. Him kissing her had only been a distraction.

And it was obviously the first time she'd said it out loud.

The underlying issue was still there. She was uncomfortable. She wasn't truly happy in her work—he knew it and she knew it. He'd known it right from the beginning. So he wasn't the main cause of her problems, only an antagonist.

"You're doing a good job, Callie." It seemed important to tell her. It seemed important to rally her confidence.

"You think so?" She'd reached the door now and turned back to face him.

He nodded. "I do. And don't think about things too long, Callie. Take it from someone who knows. Sometimes while you're doing all that thinking, life passes you by."

She pulled her shoulders back as if she was a little startled by his words. Her hand wavered on the door-handle and then she came back and sat down beside him again.

It didn't matter that she had other things to do. Other news to spread. Other plans to follow. Sometimes you just had to act on instinct. To take the moment before it passed.

"Is that what happened to you, Sawyer? Life has just passed you by?"

He froze, lowering his eyes and taking a few breaths. Her hand crept over and held his, interlocking their fingers.

He nodded, still looking at the floor. "I've lost six years," he whispered "being angry at everyone and everything."

His gaze rose again and fixed on the wall in front of him, staring at the beautiful light streaming through the stained-glass window. She squeezed his hand. Sometimes it was better to say nothing. Sometimes it was better just to give someone the time to say what they needed. Sometimes the best gift to give to someone was just to listen.

It struck her like gold. This was part of what she wanted to do. Not just for Sawyer but for her patients too.

"I was angry with Evan for sending her into the field. I was angry with myself for not knowing my wife was pregnant. I was angry with Helen for not realizing she was pregnant."

He turned to face her. His eyes were wet with tears and he wrinkled his brow. "I was angry that the plan didn't have any contingencies for things like this—a member of staff needing surgical intervention in the middle of nowhere."

He took a deep breath. "But most of all I was angry at myself for not being able to save her. I was her husband. I should have been able to save her…"

She let his voice tail off. She wanted to put her arms around him. She wanted to hug him as tightly as she could.

But there was a balance here that could so easily be tipped. He'd shared something with her that she doubted he'd shared before. What did that mean?

It seemed almost like a step towards her. But she couldn't be sure. And was she ready to take a step like that while she still had demons of her own?

Something twisted inside her. Could she talk about Isabel? Was she ready to share? She was still faltering. She still had to step out of Isabel's shadow before she could do anything else. Too much was happening all at once, so where did Sawyer fit into this equation?

She rubbed her hand over the top of his. Words seemed so futile now but she had to say something so she kept it simple. "Thank you for sharing, Sawyer. I know it was hard. And I'm glad you did." Her words were whispered and he gave her a little smile.

"I think it's time you went outside and faced the masses. Better share the good news and tell them what they need to know."

She nodded and slowly stood up. He needed some time. He needed some space. She could appreciate that.

And if she really cared about him, she had to give it.

"Come out when you're ready." She gave him a little nod and walked out.

Sawyer leaned back against the pew. In a matter of minutes it would be chaos out there again. Everyone would have questions and be looking for answers. The people currently quarantined would need up-to-date information. They would need to know what would happen next. Everything would have to be reassessed, re-evaluated, reconfigured.

As soon as the door closed behind her, Sawyer felt the air in the room become still. He didn't feel any urge to hurry after her. It would all still be out there in a few minutes—or a few hours. It was truly peaceful in here. No outside noises and far enough away from the clinical areas and staff to shield it from any external influences. Not even the noise of the birds tweeting outside.

He sat there for the longest time watching the colorful reflections from the stained-glass window dance on the wall to his right.

He looked at the scattered pieces of the plan around his feet.

Plans. He'd spent so long hating plans and everything about them. Blaming them and the DPA for the part they'd played in Helen's death.

It didn't matter that he was supposedly an intelligent, rational man. Nothing about his wife's death had seemed rational to him.

It had all seemed so random.

The DPA planned for every eventuality—or so he'd thought. But it hadn't planned for that. It hadn't planned for his wife to collapse with an ectopic pregnancy in the middle of nowhere and too far away for any emergency treatment.

And it had made him mad.

It had made him behave in a way that would have embarrassed Helen. He had questioned everything. He had torn up plans and set them on fire. He'd refused to follow any of the protocols that the DPA had set. And then he'd walked away from it all.

He'd walked away because he hadn't wanted to deal with anything.

He couldn't possibly believe that they'd just been unlucky. That Helen's death had simply come down to dumb, rotten luck.

He'd tried to forget everything and push everyone away.

But now it was time to stop all that. It was time to open his eyes.

It was time to remember—both the good and the bad.

And he remembered. He remembered everything about his wife that he'd loved.

And for the first time in a long time he took joy in remembering.

The dark shade of her hair, the chocolate color of her eyes. The fact that every item in her wardrobe had been a variation of a shade of blue. Her collection of bells that had sat on the window ledge in their bedroom. The smell of her favorite perfume, which she'd worn every single day. The candles she'd lit around her bath at night. The grey and blue felt hat she'd worn in winter that he'd always said made her look one hundred and five.

All the things that he'd been terrified to forget. Once—just once—he'd forgotten who her favorite author had been. It had sent an irrational, horrible fear through his entire body. How could he forget something about his darling Helen? Those books were still sitting on her bedside cabinet.

So he'd made lists and chanted things over and over in his bed at night. He hadn't been able to stand the thought of her fading from his memory. That the love that he'd felt for her would ever die.

He remembered their first date at the movies, their first kiss, their first fight and their first home. Their wedding day. Their wedding night.

And the way he'd held her on that last, horrible day when they'd both known she was going to die.

That nothing could save her. Even though he kept telling her she'd be fine.

The way she'd felt in his arms as he'd felt the life slowly drain from her body.

The way she'd told him she'd love him forever. And to live a good life.

Here, in this special place, it felt right. It felt right to remember her. It felt like a celebration.

Of life.

Of love.

Of forgiveness.

A single tear rolled down his cheek. He'd cried an ocean's worth of tears but now it was time for the last one.

Now it was time to let go.

Now it was time to live his life.

CHAPTER ELEVEN

THE ALARM STARTED sounding sharply. Sawyer and Dan were on their feet almost simultaneously. Even though the ventilator was breathing for Jack, his blood results had shown that his organs were starting to fail.

"Cardiac arrest. He's in V-fib."

Sawyer was almost through the door before one of the nurses blocked his path. "Gown!" she shouted.

Dan hadn't been so forgetful and already had a gown half on and his mask in place. Sawyer hated this. What was the point? How effective were the masks really? How much protection did the gown really offer? Wouldn't it make more sense just to get in and defibrillate him?

He hauled the gown and mask on and entered the room just as Dan placed the paddles on the boy's chest. "Clear!"

Jack's little body arched and all eyes fixed on the monitor.

Still VF.

Callie ran into the room, her gown barely covering her shoulders. "No!" she gasped, and ran to the other side of the room.

It was then Sawyer heard the high-pitched squeal. The squeal of a little boy watching people attempt to resuscitate his brother and not having a clue what was going on. He cursed and pulled the curtain between the beds. Why hadn't he realized? Why hadn't he even thought of that?

But Callie had. She had her arm around Ben's shoulders and was whispering to him through her mask. Her face was mainly hidden but he could still see her eyes. And there were tears in them.

Dan was moving quickly, seamlessly, shouting instructions to the surrounding staff. Jack's mother and father appeared at the window, horrified at what was happening to their son.

Jill Keating promptly dissolved into a fit of tears, her legs giving way beneath her.

They started CPR, a nurse with a knee on the bed using one hand on Jack's small chest. Regular, rhythmic beats. It was painful to watch.

The ventilator had been unhooked. Another doctor was bagging Jack down the tube already in place.

Drugs were pushed through Jack's IV. Anything to try and restart his heart.

"Everyone stop a second!" Dan shouted.

Callie's head shot up, a look of horror on her face. She moved from Ben's bed over to where Sawyer was standing. "You can't stop!" she shouted. "Don't you dare stop!"

A hand tapped Violet on the shoulder. "You've to go the boardroom."

Her head shot up. "What for? I'm in the middle of something right now. Can't it wait?"

Maisey shook her head. "I seriously doubt it."

Violet spun around in her chair. Maisey's voice didn't sound too good. "What do you mean?" She had a horrible feeling in the pit of her stomach.

"I'm sorry, Violet."

Violet reached out and grabbed her sleeve as she tried

to walk away. "What do you mean, you're sorry? Why have I to go the boardroom?"

Maisey couldn't look her in the eye. "It's the director. Along with Evan Hunter. I think Evan's complained about the deadline you didn't meet—the report he's been waiting four days for."

Violet's heart started to thud in her chest. "But that's what I'm working on." She held up the crumpled piece of paper.

Maisey shook her head. "I'm sorry, Violet. The director said he wanted to see you straight away."

Violet stood up, trying to ignore the tremor in her legs.

Rats. She'd known she was treading on thin ice when she hadn't had the report ready for Evan on time.

The truth was she had been hoping he would forget all about it now they had a final diagnosis of monkeypox. Sawyer should be the last thing on his mind right now.

She scrabbled around her desk for the report she'd been writing. Not only was it very late, she'd also left the details scarce. It would hardly placate the director.

Was he about to fire her?

Was she about to get fired because she'd tried to cover for her brother?

Her heart pounded as she crossed the department on her way to the boardroom. At this rate she would be sick all over the director's shoes.

The boardroom—where all official business was carried out.

One thing was sure—if she was going down, she was taking Evan Hunter with her. Let Evan see what the director thought about the boss cavorting with his staff.

All heads turned towards her. Callie's heart was racing, sweat lashing off her brow and running down her back.

Sawyer stepped into her line of vision, blocking the view of Jack and the rest of the staff. It took her a second to focus.

"Callie. Calm down."

Her skin was prickling. The scar on her leg itching like crazy. Her head flicking back between Ben's fearful face on the bed behind her and Sawyer's wide frame standing in front of her.

Everything seemed to be spiraling out of her control. She didn't feel in charge any more. "We can't stop. We can't. It's not been long enough." She was shaking her head. This wasn't even her area of expertise. What did she know about resuscitating a child? The last time she'd been involved in a pediatric resuscitation she'd been a first-year resident. It had made her realize that pediatrics wasn't for her.

"Callie." His hands were firmly on her shoulders now. "Step away from this. It's under control."

That's when she lost it even more. "You think this is under control? Under control? How? How is this under control? Is this part of the plan?"

She moved closer to Sawyer and hissed in his ear, "If Jack's about to die, you need to tell his family. You need to give them a chance to say goodbye." Her eyes drifted back to the bed behind her. "You need to give Ben a chance to say goodbye. He should get to hold his brother's hand."

She was feeling frantic. She couldn't let this happen. It didn't matter that she wasn't a pediatrician. She was the doctor in charge of this outbreak so, at the end of the day, everyone should be doing what she told them.

Sawyer reached up and stroked her cheek. The action took her by surprise. It brought her instantly back to the here and now. "Callie, Dan's not stopping. He's only waiting for a few seconds to recheck the cardiac monitor—to see if Jack's heart rhythm has changed. Think, Callie. We always do this at arrests. Don't we?"

His voice was quiet, only loud enough for her to hear. Not that the rest of the staff were bothering. Most were still round Jack's bed, assisting with the arrest. Another nurse had appeared at Ben's side and was sitting with her arm around him, talking in his ear.

Ben.

He was terrified. He was crying. He was asking the nurse questions. Callie felt herself start to shake.

"We've got a rhythm!"

Both their heads turned towards the shout. Dan had just defibrillated Jack's little chest again and the monitor had given a little blip. Dan started shouting more instructions for different drugs. The room was a hive of activity. IV's were being hung and Mr. and Mrs. Keating had been gowned up and were being shown into the room.

Callie was trembling. She couldn't stop herself.

Then a warm hand slipped into hers and pulled her out of the room, walking her along the corridor and sitting her down in an easy chair. A cold drink was pressed into her hands and Sawyer sat in the chair opposite her.

He didn't say a word. He just sat.

The cold juice slid down her throat. The intense itch in her leg increased. She was clawing at her leg and couldn't stop. He bent over, his hand capturing hers and stopping her scratching. His head was underneath hers and he looked up at her. "Want to tell me what just happened in there?"

She felt her throat constrict. "I don't think I can."

He sat back in his chair. She could tell he was contemplating what to do next. What on earth must he be thinking of her?

His gaze was steady. It felt as if he was looking deep inside her. Somewhere she didn't want him to go. "It's time, Callie. Tell me about your scar."

She took a sharp breath. How did he know? *How did he know there was a connection?*

She laid her palm flat on her thigh. The desire to scratch was overwhelming. but she knew it was all psychological. No matter how hard she scratched, it wouldn't stop the itch. She'd just end up breaking her skin and drawing blood.

"I was in a car accident." She didn't know where the words had come from. It almost felt as if someone else had said them. But it was definitely her voice.

"How long ago?" It was a measured question. A prompt. It was almost as if he knew she just couldn't come out and tell him everything at once—it would be too painful.

"I was twenty-three."

"Were you badly injured?"

She took a deep breath. Although the scar was a permanent reminder, for the most part Callie had pushed all memories of her injuries aside.

Physical injuries could heal. Psychological injuries not so much.

"I had a fractured femur and tib and fib. Fractured ribs too."

"Wow. You must have had to take some time out of medical school."

"Only a few weeks. I became their first official on-line student. They recorded lectures for me and sent me notes. I did my assignments online for a couple of months."

It almost gave the game away and she could see the

calculating expression on his face. Her professors had gone above and beyond their responsibilities and he had to be wondering why. Most medical schools would have told a seriously injured student to take time off, recuperate and come back the following year.

His gaze remained steady. It was obvious that he'd figured things out. "Who else was in the car, Callie?"

She was instantly on the defensive. "What makes you think someone else was in the car?"

"Who else was in the car, Callie?"

He'd just repeated the question. There was no fooling Sawyer.

Her throat was instantly dry again and her voice cracked. "My sister, Isabel."

He moved forward and took her hands again. "Isabel. What a beautiful name. Tell me about your sister, Callie." Again he was surprising her. He wasn't hitting her with a barrage of questions, he was just giving her an open invitation to talk.

"I can't," she whispered, as a single tear slid down her cheek. This was just too hard.

He reached up and caught it in his fingertips. "Yes, you can."

Everything had just changed color for Sawyer. He already knew her sister must be dead. The look on her face had said it all and the hairs currently standing on end at the back of his neck agreed.

He could see how much she was struggling. He could tell she wanted to run from the room like a frightened rabbit. She'd barely been able to get the words out.

A sister. Callie had a sister. Or she'd *had* a sister.

Now he understood her reaction when she'd heard about Violet. Now he understood why she'd been so angry with him. If she'd lost a sister and felt as if he'd abandoned his…well, her reaction was entirely normal.

"Isabel was a year older than me. She was at medical school too. She wanted to work at the DPA."

"Did you?" Things were starting to fall into place for him. This was behind the reaction in the chapel earlier. This was why she wasn't sure of herself.

She hesitated. "I…I didn't know what I wanted to do."

"Was Isabel injured in the car accident?"

Callie couldn't speak now. She just nodded. The tears were spilling down her face. Her hands were icy, almost as if she was in shock. He rubbed them gently, trying to encourage the blood flow and get some heat into them again.

It was obvious that Callie didn't talk about this to people. Violet hadn't heard a single thing about this—he suspected that no one at the DPA knew. Hadn't anyone ever asked her about her scar?

It was one of the first things he'd noticed about her.

It was time to ask the ultimate question. He had to give her a chance to let go. "Did she die?"

And that's when the sobs were let loose. Big, loud gasping sobs. The kind where you couldn't catch your breath before the next one took over your body.

He knew how that felt. He'd been there too.

He moved, sitting on the arm of the easy chair, wrapping his arm around her shoulders and letting her rest her head on his shoulder as she cried. It was the most natural thing to do.

Grief was all-consuming.

"There was a nurse and she knew Isabel was going to die. My parents hadn't got there yet. They were about to take me to Theatre but she wouldn't let them. She pulled me over to Isabel and put her hand in mine. It was the best and worst moment of my life. She knew how important it was. And I never even got to thank her. Everything just turned into a blur after that. My parents arrived and…"

"That's why you wanted the boys to hold hands. Now I get it," he murmured. It all made sense now. The look of terror on her face, her reactions. They were all the actions of someone who had walked in those shoes. Only someone who'd had that experience could truly know what it all meant and how important the smallest thing could be.

Her voice tailed off. She couldn't talk any more. He lifted a damp lock of her hair and dropped a kiss on her forehead. "I understand, Callie. I understand better than you could ever know."

"How can you?" she whispered. Her whole body was shaking. "We were fighting. I've never told anyone this but Isabel and I were fighting. A car came round the corner on the wrong side of the road and I didn't have time to react. I didn't have time to react because I was distracted. I was trying to stop Isabel from getting her own way yet again."

He could see the pain written across her face. And more than anything he wanted to take it away.

The feelings almost overwhelmed him. It had been so long since he'd felt like this that he almost didn't recognize it. That intensity. That urge to protect.

The feelings of love.

Sawyer sucked in his breath. The pain spread across his chest. His heart thudded, his muscles tensed.

Every one of his senses was hyper-aware. He could hear her panting breaths, feel the dampness of her tears between his fingertips. He could smell the aroma of her raspberry shampoo and remember the taste of her on his lips.

And he could see her. All of her. Her bedraggled hair, damp around her forehead. The little lines etched around her clear blue eyes. The pink tinge of her cheeks. The dark red of her lips.

Her pink scrub top clung to her, outlining her firm breasts and the curve of her waist. The matching trousers hugged her hips and thighs. Her bright pink casual shoes cushioned her feet, with one dangling from her silver-starred toes.

All of this made up the picture of the woman that he loved.

The realization made him want to run. Made him want to escape for a few minutes to sort his head out and realign his senses.

But he couldn't leave. He could never leave her like this. His hand rubbed her back and he tried to keep his eyes off her silver-starred toes and the pictures they were conjuring up in his mind.

"All siblings fight, Callie. That's normal. That's what being a brother or sister is all about. You were just unlucky."

She shook her head. "But it didn't feel like that." She pressed a hand to her chest. "Isabel had always been really competitive. Medical school was just making her worse." Her eyes turned to meet his. "Of course, her fellow students would never have said that. They all embraced that kind of lifestyle. As if everything was a race, every mark a victory. But she carried it home with her. And it made being her sister tough." Her voice cracked and sobs racked her shoulders once again.

Sawyer pulled her close. She was consumed with guilt. That much was obvious. Not just because she'd been driving the car but because of how she'd been feeling towards her sister.

"Callie, I know. I understand. Violet was the good girl in the family. The one who always looked perfect in pictures. Sometimes I even hated her."

"You did?" Her eyes widened, her expression was one of surprise.

"Of course I did—she's my sister. Family's like that. You can't love or hate anyone more than your immediate family. No one else generates the same emotional energy. The same tug. Even in love." He gave her a smile.

"I walked away a few years ago. If I'd stayed near my family they would never have allowed me to live the way I have. The first thing Violet did when I phoned her was chew me out. Just wait till I see her. There won't be anything left for you."

"For me?" The tone in her voice changed. Her gaze fixed on his.

He bent his face to hers, taking in her trembling lips. Right now he didn't care about the monkeypox. He didn't care about the quarantine and vaccinations. And he certainly didn't care about the plans.

All he cared about was the woman in front of him.

It didn't matter how long he'd known her. It didn't matter how much they'd have to work through. All that mattered now was that he wanted a chance with her.

A chance to see where life could take them.

"Callie, what would it take to make you happy?"

She shook her head. "What do you mean?"

He knelt down in front of her. "I want you to stop thinking about anyone else. Stop thinking about the situation we're in with work. Stop thinking about responsibilities. Stop thinking about what anyone else thinks about you." He clasped both her hands in his.

"I've spent the last six years in a fog, Callie, and being around you has finally woken me up."

He looked around the plain white room they were in. "I can see the color in things again. I can see light again. And it's all because of you."

She took a deep breath and drew back a little. She looked scared. Not of him—but of what he was saying.

"But we're not a good match, Sawyer. We're nothing alike. Even Callum said we're like oil and water."

Sawyer smiled. Trust Callum to see things long before anyone else could.

"And opposites attract, Callie." He drew her closer and whispered in her ear, "And in case you haven't noticed, I'm really attracted to you."

"Ditto," she whispered.

Their eyes met. They were reliving the conversation in the kids' cinema room.

"Callie, do you really want to be part of the DPA?"

"What?" She looked shocked.

He held his hands out. "This, Callie, all this. Is this really what you want? Because I can see you're a good doctor but I have to keep convincing you of that." He laid his palm on her chest above her heart, "And if you don't feel it in here, I wonder if you're doing the job of your heart or if you're just doing your duty to your sister."

All of a sudden she couldn't meet his all-too-perceptive gaze.

He put a finger under her chin and gently made her look at him. "Sometimes you need someone else to put things into perspective for you. Callie, I see a beautiful woman who is a great doctor but who is clearly in the wrong job. Was it in your heart to come to the DPA? Or did you come because that was the path that Isabel had mapped out for you both?"

"We wanted to work together. It was our dream."

"Both your dreams? Or only hers?"

"Don't say that. I don't like the way you make that sound. It was our plan." Her eyes drifted away from his and became fixed on the blank wall. "When you don't follow the plan, things go wrong. That's what happened that night. I took a different road—I was just so sick of Isabel being in charge all the time. Planning what we were doing every second of every day. Even down to what we ate."

Her shoulders started to shake again, her widened eyes turning back to meet his. "Don't you see what happened? When you stick to the plan, things go fine. But when you don't...that's when things go wrong. We would never have been on that road if I hadn't fought with Isabel. If I'd just gone along with what she'd wanted, everything would have been fine."

"You don't know that. You *can't* know that." He touched her cheek. "And would you have liked this job any more if Isabel was working next to you? Or would you still hate it just as much but do a better job at hiding it—all to keep her happy? To stick to the plan?"

She opened her mouth to speak but Sawyer wasn't finished. "Sticking to the plan doesn't always work. Helen and I stuck to the plan. The plan didn't cover what to do in a surgical emergency with no equipment in the middle of nowhere. Because that's all it was—a plan. Nothing more, nothing less. Just another tool to have in your box. Life has a funny way of making its own plan, no matter what's down in black and white."

"And if you don't like it?"

"That's the beauty of having a plan, Callie. Knowing when to use it and knowing when to drop it." He crouched down in front of her, "Thinking of Isabel, does it still hurt?"

She hesitated. "Yes." Her voice was barely audible.

"Callie, if Isabel were here right now, what would she say to you?"

Callie shifted in her seat. "She'd tell me to get my act together." She looked Sawyer in the eye, "She'd tell me not to get distracted by other people. She'd tell me not to waste the last nine years of my career by throwing away my role in the DPA now." Was she trying to convince him or her?

"And if she could see you now—if she could feel how you felt every day at work? Do you honestly think that's what she'd say?"

Callie sighed and he could see light dawn across her face. She was finally going to stop giving the answers she was expected to give. "No. She'd give me a boot up the ass and ask me why I hadn't said something sooner."

He smiled at her. "I think I would have liked Isabel."

She buried her head in her hands. "What will my parents think if I tell them I don't want to do this any more? They'll be so disappointed." Her voice drifted off and he could see pain flit across her eyes again.

"Callie, they've lost one daughter. They've gone through the worst pain imaginable. All they could want for you is to be happy."

He put his hand back on her heart. "Think of me as your own Aladdin's genie. I'm going to grant you a wish. And I'll do everything in my power to make it happen. What is it that you want, Callie?"

She was looking into his eyes, searching his face. He could tell she was terrified of revealing what she really wanted. He prayed he wasn't making her take a step too far.

But this felt right. It wasn't just him who needed to

move on—it was her too. And they could do it together. Because nothing else could feel as good a fit as they did.

She sat for a few minutes. He could hear her deep breaths. He didn't want to push her any more. He knew how he would have reacted if someone had tried to push him too hard a few years ago.

She needed to be ready. She needed to be sure.

She lifted her eyes and they took on a determined edge. This was the Callie Turner who'd swept into his E.R. and told him she was in charge. This was the Callie Turner who'd made the decision to start vaccinating. This was the Callie Turner who hadn't blinked an eye at him watching her change her clothing. "I want more than one wish."

He felt relief wash over him. "Cheat. I'll give you two." His heart was thudding in his chest. He could only hope where this might go. "The first for work, the second for life." He felt his lips turning upwards, praying he wasn't reading her wrong.

She sucked in a breath and held it for a few seconds.

"The first for work," she repeated.

He nodded.

"I want to leave the DPA." As she said the words her shoulders immediately relaxed. It was almost as if someone had released the pressure in her and it had escaped. "I want to leave the DPA." She repeated the words again, this time more determinedly, with a smile starting to form on her lips.

The smile progressed, reaching across her face until her eyes started to light up. "I want to retrain. I want to work in family practice."

"You do?" He couldn't have picked that lottery ball if he'd tried.

She nodded. "I do." Those words sounded ominous. She met his eyes again and laughed.

"And your second wish?"

She stood up and pulled him up next to her. "This could be a difficult one."

Sawyer felt his heart plummet. "How so?"

She wrapped one arm around his waist. "I'm going to need some help while I retrain. I'm going to need some support."

He could see where this was going. "And where do you think you could get that support?"

"I'm kind of hoping I can rely on a friend."

"A friend?" His voice rose.

She stood on tiptoe and murmured in his ear. "It would have to be a special kind of friend. One who doesn't mind helping me study." She dropped a little kiss on his ear. "One who could make dinner and tidy up after himself because I'm going to be really busy."

He nodded. "Really busy. And where do you think you could find someone to meet all these demands?"

She ran her fingers down his chest. "I'm kind of hoping my genie can arrange it."

"Oh, you are?" He pulled her closer. She molded her body to his and wrapped her arms around his neck.

He got a waft of her raspberry shampoo. This was going to drive him crazy. Hopefully for the next fifty years.

She pulled back a little. "Come to think of it, most genies grant three wishes. I guess mine kind of short-changed me."

"Why, what would be your third wish?"

She stood on tiptoe again and whispered in his ear, with a sparkle in her eyes and a pink tinge to her cheeks.

"Now, that I *can* make happen straight away."

And he took her by the hand and led her down the corridor.

EPILOGUE

IT WAS A perfect day.

The deep blue water was lapping up onto Osterman beach. Callie wiggled her feet and felt the sand shift under her toes. The ocean breeze blew her hair around her face, one side catching more of the breeze than the other. She grabbed a few strands and tucked them behind her ear.

The white canopy above her swayed in the wind, shading the guests from the early morning sun. She sighed and relaxed back into her white canvas chair and closed her eyes.

There hadn't been time for much sleep last night. Sawyer had just arrived back from his latest conference for the DPA and had been anxious to show her how much he had missed her. His new role as a DPA lecturer had been a surprise for them both. But he'd embraced it with more enthusiasm and vigor than he'd apparently possessed in years.

She could hear the ripple of voices around her. The ceremony was due to start in few minutes. There was a thud as Sawyer flopped into the chair next to her.

"How are you doing, beautiful?" He leaned over and dropped a kiss on her lips. She caught a whiff of his aftershave and touched his newly bare jaw.

"You've shaved. I was kind of liking the jungle warrior look." His hair was still slightly damp from his shower and she pushed it back from his eyes. "Next thing, you'll be having a haircut. Then I *really* won't recognize you."

He gave her a cheeky smile. "Never gonna happen."

She kept her hand on his face as she ran her eyes up and down his body. He was wearing a pale blue shirt with the sleeves rolled up and white cotton chinos. She stared down at his feet, at his toes pushing the sand around like her own.

"What happened to the shoes I bought you?"

He let out a laugh. "I decided to go native." He held out his hands at the beautiful scenery, "Somehow I don't think anyone will notice."

His phone buzzed and he pulled it from his pocket, a smile instantly appearing on his face. He handed the phone over. It was a text message with a photo of Jack and Ben, complete with Stetsons, on vacation in Texas. Jill had added the words "*With thanks to you both. xx.*" Jack still looked a little frail and both boys still had pockmarks on their arms.

Callie sighed. "They look so much happier. I'm so glad they're doing well."

The music started and they both stood, turning to watch Alison, her husband and three kids walk down the sandy aisle between the chairs. Jonas, her eight-month-old, was held in her arms. He was wearing a white and blue sailor suit and hat and was chewing on his thumb.

He was older than the average baby who was christened, but Alison had wanted to wait until she could arrange something special. This was truly a baby to celebrate.

Callie felt a surge of warmth in her chest. He was the picture of health. It had been great relief to everyone that Alison had never shown any symptoms of monkeypox.

"Can we have the godparents, please?"

She felt a sharp nudge as Sawyer stood and held out his hand towards her. "Shall we?"

She slid her hand into his. It still gave her the same little tingle along her spine that it had all those months ago when they'd met.

Time had flown past. She'd handed in her resignation to the DPA and had started to retrain for family practice. From the first day and hour that she'd started, she'd known she'd made the right decision.

Family practice was so much broader than any other specialty. She got to see a little of everything and she loved it—from young people to old, from runny noses to lumps and bumps. More than anything she got to spend more time with her patients and follow through on their care. It was a better fit than she could ever have imagined.

She smiled and straightened her flowery summer dress before joining the family at the front.

The ceremony was over quickly. The family gave thanks and Jonas was officially named, with Callie and Sawyer the proud godparents.

Just when she thought it was time to head for the buffet lunch, Alison turned to face her friends and colleagues. "If you'll just give me a few more minutes." She waited for people to settle back into their seats.

She smiled at Sawyer and Callie. "Most of you will know how I met Jonas's godparents. And I'm delighted that they agreed to take the role today and join us in this beautiful location."

She paused, before giving Callie a knowing smile. "And it seems such a waste to let this be over so quickly." Then, in the blink of an eye, she sat back down.

Callie was stunned. Had she missed something? What had just happened? Was that it? Were they supposed to head off to the beautifully decorated buffet tables for lunch?

A glass was pressed into her hand, the cold condensation quickly capturing her attention. Sawyer was grinning at her. She took a quick sip. Champagne with a strawberry at the bottom. Delicious.

She watched as waiters appeared and passed glasses to all the guests. How nice. Had Sawyer arranged this to drink a toast to the baby?

He straightened up and cleared his throat. "I'm sorry for stealing Alison's thunder, but she gave me a severe talking to a few weeks ago." He gave her a little nod. "About not wasting time."

Callie felt her heart start to flutter in her chest. *No.* He couldn't be.

But he was. He'd dropped to one knee.

"Callie Turner, I've only known you for twelve months. And it's official—you drive me crazy."

The guests started to laugh.

"I've never met anyone who can burn mac n' cheese like you can. Or who can take up an entire closet with shoes."

She felt herself blush. Maybe she had gone a little overboard in making him build her a special shoes closet, particularly when she wasn't wearing any right now.

"But what I've realized in this life is that when you find someone who makes your heart sing like you do, who makes you think about everything that you do, and who you don't want to spend a day without, then you should never let them go." His pale green eyes met hers and she could see his sincerity.

"Callie, when I met you I thought I was in the wrong place at the wrong time. I couldn't believe I was so unlucky to come across an infectious disease and be stuck in the middle of it all again." He shook his head. "I didn't know how wrong I was."

"I'd been stuck in the wrong place and the wrong time for the last six years. This time—for once in my life—I was in the right place at the right time. Because it's where I met you."

The crowd gave a little sigh.

"Callie, the whole world knows that I love you. I want you to be the first thing I see every morning and the last thing I see every night. Would you do me the honour of becoming my wife?"

He'd opened a small box and a beautiful solitaire diamond glistened in the sun.

She couldn't speak. She couldn't say anything. She was too stunned.

Sawyer, the man who couldn't plan anything, had completely and utterly sideswiped her.

"I can read your mind, I know this isn't in the plan, honey, but do you think you can say something? I'm getting a cramp down here." Beads of sweat were breaking out on his forehead.

He was nervous.

For the first time since she'd known him Sawyer was nervous. It was kind of cute. But she didn't want to prolong his agony. She didn't want to panic the man she loved.

And she didn't want to give him a chance to change his mind.

She bent down and didn't hesitate. "How about a yes," she whispered.

"Yes!"

He swept his arms around her waist and swung her round.

She was laughing and he was squeezing the breath out of her with his enthusiastic grip. "Wait a minute, there's one condition."

He settled her feet back on the sand and slid the diamond ring onto her finger. "Anything, honey, you name it. Your wish is my command." He gave her a low bow.

She smiled. Plans could work both ways. "Well..." she ran her finger down his cheek "...since you made such good plans for today, I'm thinking that maybe you should be in charge of the wedding plans too."

His face dropped instantly then he tried to recover with a nervous smile. "If that's what you want, honey."

She reached up for him again and planted her lips on his. "Perfect."

* * * * *

ABOUT THAT NIGHT...

BY
SCARLET WILSON

MILLS & BOON®

First published in Great Britain 2013
by Mills & Boon, an imprint of Harlequin (UK) Limited.
Harlequin (UK) Limited, Eton House, 18-24 Paradise Road,
Richmond, Surrey TW9 1SR

© Scarlet Wilson 2013

ISBN: 978 0 263 89906 1

Harlequin (UK) policy is to use papers that are natural, renewable and recyclable products and made from wood grown in sustainable forests. The logging and manufacturing process conform to the legal environmental regulations of the country of origin.

Printed and bound in Spain
by Blackprint CPI, Barcelona

Dear Reader

This is the second story in my duet, *Rebels with a Cause*, set around my Disease Prevention Agency. This story looks at another aspect of the DPA and their international role in the fight against polio—a disease that is the subject of a global eradication programme.

Violet Connelly has her own reasons for wanting to be part of the programme. After hiding away for the last three years at a desk job, she feels the time is right to get back out there. Evan Hunter isn't so sure. He's already worked with Violet in the DPA and knows she's hiding something. But is here, the heart of Africa, the place to find out what's been stopping her from forming relationships with those around her and, more importantly, him?

There are some serious issues at the centre of this story. Stillbirth is a very sensitive issue—particularly for Violet, as her circumstances mean she hasn't shared with her family what has happened to her. And Evan already has issues with Violet's brother.

The bad blood between Evan and Sawyer is one of the key linking elements of these stories. Evan was in charge of the mission where Sawyer's wife died. Neither of them has ever spoken about it, but now, with Violet at the heart of things, it's time for them to resolve their issues.

Because—as we all know in the world of Mills & Boon®—everyone deserves a Happy Ever After!

Please feel free to contact me via my website and let me know what you think of these stories: www.scarlet-wilson.com. I love to hear from readers!

Scarlet

In my late teens and early twenties I had the most fabulous group of friends. We've all grown older, maybe a little wiser, and families and continents keep us apart.

So, to the nights in the Metro, Sullivans, Club de Mar and Ayr Beach Promenade with Julie Paton, Gillian Lapsley, Joyce Kane, Jaki Lynch, Shona Kennedy and Marianne Stevenson. I've never laughed so much. Whose turn is it to drive?

And to @stephenfry, @justinpollard and the lovely elves at QI who gave me sleeping sickness just when I needed it!

CHAPTER ONE

VIOLET WAS SHAKING in her shoes—literally.

The walk to the director's office had never seemed so long. On every one of the thirty steps her legs felt more like jelly and her brain like laundry on a permanent spin cycle.

Her hand gripped the piece of paper in her hand tightly—the only evidence that she'd actually done any of the work she was supposed to have completed days ago. The three sentences didn't exactly help her defense.

But inside her, next to her churning stomach, rage was building. Rage against Evan Hunter, her boss.

It was his fault she was in this situation.

He'd asked her to find out background information on her brother, Matt Sawyer, who'd been at the heart of the most prolific outbreak in the history of the Disease Prevention Agency. Granted he hadn't known Matt was her brother, but that did nothing to quell the anger in her belly.

She'd used her other work as an excuse not to comply with Evan's request. Plotting the potential spread of the suspected smallpox virus was surely more important than finding out about the ex-DPA doctor who'd made the preliminary diagnosis. Too bad Evan didn't feel that way.

Her legs trembled as she reached the door.

Stay calm, she repeated in her head. Erupting in front of the director would do nothing to help her cause.

But there was a surprise. Evan's broad shoulders immediately towered over her. It seemed like he was waiting for the director too.

There he was. Blocking her way to the boardroom. His arms were folded across his chest. In another world she might have found him attractive.

In fact, a few months ago and after a couple of glasses of wine, she *had* found him attractive and had ended up locked in a heated embrace that neither of them had admitted to or acted on again.

Evan could certainly turn heads. His tall frame and broad shoulders, combined with his dark brown hair and blue eyes, attracted female attention wherever he went.

To say nothing of the sexy three-day stubble currently on his chin.

Too bad he was about to be her executioner.

So why did he look a little twitchy?

"What are you doing here?"

She jerked at the tone in his voice. "I could ask the same of you. The director sent for me."

"He did?" Evan looked surprised. Surely he'd initiated this by complaining about her?

"Why do you think we're here?"

Evan's eyes met hers. They were steady, uncompromising. "I can only guess it's about the report I sent him."

She could feel her stomach turn over. "What report was that?"

"The one about Matt Sawyer—you know? The one I asked you to write days ago." He shot her a steely glare. "It seemed a remarkable coincidence that a former DPA employee was around when a provisional smallpox diagnosis was made." It was almost as if he was trying to bait her.

"What's the supposed to mean?" The words were out before she could stop herself.

"Oh, come on, Violet." His words were frustrated. "You must appreciate that the chances of smallpox occurring naturally are virtually impossible. All situations in our current plan are around a terrorist attack. What are the chances of a former DPA employee being around when it happens? You were asked to compile a report of Matt Sawyer's recent history. It was essential that we found out exactly where Matt Sawyer had been and who he'd been consorting with."

Violet couldn't hold her tongue any longer. "Consorting with? You've got to be joking, Evan."

But he continued as if she hadn't spoken. "You ignored my requests for information—even after I gave you a warning. That information could have meant the difference between preventing a terrorist attack and putting more lives at risk. You still haven't handed over any information on Matt Sawyer. What exactly have you been doing with your time, Violet?"

The rage that had been simmering beneath the surface was threatening to erupt. Idiot. The man was clearly an idiot. And the implication in his words meant she couldn't think straight any more.

"You honestly thought that Sawyer was a terrorist? That idea actually crossed your tiny, warped mind? You have absolutely no idea what you're talking about. How dare you?" Her voice was rising in crescendo and in pitch.

Evan towered over her. He was furious. "How dare I? I was the lead on this investigation. It was up to me to cover every eventuality—including the possibility of terrorism. How dare *you*, Violet? How dare you obstruct me?"

But Violet wasn't even listening to the words he was saying. She was still stuck on the ridiculous thought that her brother was even remotely connected with this. "I can't believe you thought Sawyer was a terrorist. I can't believe you considered he'd have anything to do with the outbreak. The last thing Sawyer wanted was to be involved with the DPA again. I've never heard anything so ridiculous in my life."

Evan stepped closer. A dark expression swept across his face. "What is it with you and Sawyer, anyway? How do you even know him? He left long before you even got here." His face was only inches from hers. "Why should you have any loyalty to him? What was he—your lover?"

What kind of a question was that? And what was it to him, anyway? Was he jealous?

"What?" The red mist was descending. She couldn't even see his scrunched-up angry face any more. "He's my brother, you idiot!"

There was a hiss. A sharp intake of breath. Evan jerked back as if she'd just delivered an electric shock.

"Your brother?" His voice was barely audible and he looked horrified. "But how can he be your brother?"

Her heart was thudding against her chest wall. Oh, no. She'd just revealed the secret that she'd kept for the past three years.

She couldn't think of anything sensible or rational to say. But, then, Evan had just asked a pretty stupid question. "The same way anyone can be someone's brother," she murmured.

But that clearly wasn't enough for Evan. He hadn't finished with her.

"Sawyer is your brother?" His voice had started to rise.

She nodded. But it obviously wasn't sinking in for him.

"Sawyer is your brother? How can that be possible? You have different names—and you're not married."

Her brain was starting to work in another direction. She had deliberately kept this a secret. Could it be considered fraud? There hadn't been anywhere on her application form to state if family members worked at the DPA. But, then, there would have been an expectation of disclosure. Would she get in trouble for this?

She took a deep breath. "Yes, Matt Sawyer is my brother. I'm well aware that he left here under a cloud and thought it best not to mention our connection. We have different surnames because our mother remarried when I was young. I took my stepfather's surname— Matt didn't."

She held the crumpled piece of paper up in her hand, trying to ignore the fact that it was shaking. "As I'm sure you were aware, Matt hasn't made much contact over the past few years. He struggled with Helen's death. I've never known where he's been working. It turns out he's been in Borneo, Alaska and Connecticut." She hesitated. Should she say any more? "And I never found that out for myself. I've been trying to find out where my brother's been for years. Matt told me and I checked the details."

Evan erupted. "Why on earth didn't you tell me he was your brother? I asked you to investigate him and you said nothing! You had a conflict of interest that you should have declared. Of all the unprofessional—"

Violet flinched and stepped forward instantly, her face inches from his. "Unprofessional? Well, let's talk about unprofessional behavior, shall we? Because I'm not the only one to indulge in that. I'm not the only one keeping secrets around here."

"Ahem."

The loud noise of someone clearing their throat made them both jump.

The director was standing behind them both with a pile of papers in his arms, looking less than impressed. He pushed open the door to the boardroom. "Let's take this inside, please, and stop entertaining the masses." How much had he heard?

Violet's jaw dropped and her head shot round to the office space where just about every member of staff was standing on their feet, their heads above their cubicle walls, staring at her and Evan.

How long had they been like this? And why hadn't she noticed? She felt heat flood into her cheeks and hurried into the boardroom behind the director.

She couldn't breathe. She couldn't think. All the nerves that she'd felt a few minutes ago on the walk to the boardroom instantly returned.

The director seemed cool and unfazed. He walked around the desk and sat down in his chair. He placed his paperwork in front of him and gestured to the chairs on the other side of the desk. "Take a seat please. Violet, Evan."

What was that paperwork? Was that the HR documentation he needed to fire her?

She swallowed. A tennis ball was sitting in her throat. *Just get this over with.*

There was a few minutes' silence as the director looked at the paperwork in front of him. It was agonizing. The wait seemed to stretch on and on for ever. She couldn't stand it.

Evan obviously couldn't either. "Director, if you'll just let me explain—"

The director held up one hand. "Enough."

Evan tried to speak again, his face flushed. "But—"

"From both of you." The director's voice cut him dead. He pulled some papers out from the file in front of him.

Violet felt her chest tightening and she struggled to breathe. Was this it? Was she about to get fired?

The director looked her in the eye. He had pale grey eyes. She'd never really noticed before. She'd always been too busy keeping her head down and stopping herself being noticed.

"Dr. Connelly."

She gulped. He was addressing her formally. This couldn't be good.

He sighed. "Putting aside what I just witnessed outside, I actually came here today to let you know that your transfer request has been approved."

"What?"

"What?"

Their voices rang out simultaneously, as if neither of them could really believe their ears.

He folded his hands in front of him. "But with hindsight it seems as if there are a number of issues we need to address here today."

"Transfer request? What transfer request?"

Evan's head was spinning. He'd had no idea why he'd been called to the boardroom. He'd assumed it was regarding the missing report. The report on her brother.

Now it seemed as if the director hadn't even noticed the report *was* missing.

The director shot him another steely glare. He obviously didn't like to be interrupted. "Dr. Connelly had requested to be transferred to the emergency operations center and join the stop transmission of polio program."

His brain whirred. Violet Connelly had been driving him crazy for months. Ever since they'd kissed on that night out and both of them had pretended it hadn't happened.

But the issues in the past few days had been serious. Serious enough for him to consider reporting her. No matter what their history was. As team leader he had a responsibility to ensure everyone pulled their weight.

Since when had Violet wanted to do field work? And why had she never mentioned it?

"I had no idea. She obviously didn't see fit to mention it to me." The hard edge in his voice was crystal clear and he could hear the way his words must sound to her—cold.

Did that hide the fact he couldn't explain how he was feeling?

Was Violet leaving because of him? Was she leaving because of their mistaken, fumbled kiss?

And why did the thought of not seeing her any more drive him just as crazy as working with her every day?

He watched as she seemed to sag into her chair. As if all the tension had just left her body. Disbelief was written all over her face.

"Really? You've approved my transfer? When can I start? Where am I going? What will my role be?" It was obvious her mouth was running away with her and her brain had gone into overdrive.

Meanwhile, he was still getting over the shock that he wouldn't be seeing Violet anymore. It almost squeezed the air from his lungs.

"Hold on." The director raised his hands. "I think there are bigger issues here." He looked between the two of them and leaned back in his chair. "I have to say that I'm disappointed in you both." Evan felt his heart sink like a stone. This couldn't be good.

"Evan, I'm surprised that Dr. Connelly didn't tell you about her application to transfer. As her line manager I would have expected you both to have discussed this." The implication was clear. Why couldn't Violet speak to him? He kind of wondered that himself. Was he really so unapproachable?

"And Dr. Connelly…" He turned his head back to Violet. "Unlike Dr. Hunter, I don't really care that Matt Sawyer is your brother. I can't think why you thought it necessary to hide that, but I'm very happy with the work your brother has done over the past few days for us. And I'll be keen to work with him again in the future." He tapped his pen against the desk, as if he was contemplating what to say next.

"It's my opinion that your reaction to Dr. Hunter was unreasonable. He was just exploring every angle regarding the possibility of a smallpox outbreak. We would have checked up on anyone who reported a suspected outbreak, no matter who they were. But what's clear to me is that Dr. Hunter didn't explain his rationale for his request very well. But then again, why should he? He was in charge of the team."

Evan had no idea where this was going. He could see Violet struggling to swallow. She was finding this as difficult as he was. One second he'd thought the director was going to come down on Violet, and the next second he thought his own head was going to be on the chopping block.

Something struck him. *Was.* The director had said he *was* in charge of the team. Oh, no.

Violet's face had fallen again. And he hated it when she looked like that. One minute she was getting her dream transfer the next she was thinking she was being given her marching orders.

"What's most clear to me here is that the two of you need to learn to work together as a team. I don't care what your personal issues are. What I do care about is how the staff at the DPA work together. It's one of the most vital components of our jobs." His eyes narrowed, "And the display I've just witnessed gives me great concern."

He turned on Evan. "You're one of my most experienced and senior doctors. I would expect better from you. The exchange outside seemed unprofessional."

This was it. He was going to be fired.

Unprofessional.

The word that he and Violet had just flung at each other. Hearing it come from the director's mouth was an entirely different matter.

It was the most offensive word you could say to a doctor. Particularly when it hit home.

"You are two of the best clinically competent doctors that I have and it's time to put your skills to good use. So I've come to a decision. Violet, you will be joining the polio team in Nigeria. I've already approved the transfer. They are on the final push to try and stop the spread of polio. Your field assignment will last three months and you'll be leaving in a week. Start packing."

Evan swallowed nervously as the director turned to face him. "Evan, I think it's time for a change of scene for you. And maybe a change of climate. I'm happy with the way you handled the potential outbreak. I'm

even happier that it turned out to be monkeypox instead of smallpox, but I think it's time you learned a
different skill set.

"I've had no complaints about you—no complaints
at all. I am conscious, though, that working in the same
area of the DPA can make a doctor complacent. I need
adaptable team leaders who can work anywhere, covering every eventuality. You need to work on your interpersonal skills. Specifically, your interpersonal skills
with Violet."

He tilted his head to one side, almost as if he was lost
in thought for a moment. "I think, at times, you can be
a little hard on your team." A smile drifted across his
face, "A little too alpha. I need a team leader for the
polio program at short notice and was struggling to find
someone appropriate—someone who could take care of
the strategic work alongside the clinical. It seems like
I've just found him."

"Me?" Evan could hardly get the word out. This
couldn't be happening. This was like a bad movie.

The director nodded. "That's why I was late for our
meeting. I was taking a call from Africa. One of our
team leaders needs to get back home in a hurry—his
father has been taken seriously ill. I'm sure you understand." The words hung in the air—along with the
implication.

What a terrible position. There was no way Evan
could say no now.

The director gave him a little nod. "You'll be assigned to work with a national counterpart. The
Healthly World Federation and Global Children's Support Organization are our partners in this area. You'll
have to plan, implement, roll out and monitor the program in your designated area.

"You'll have to manage a team of civilians and train them to help administer the program." He almost gave a little smile. "That will take all your people powers. You'll have to learn to be flexible, working under difficult conditions with people from different cultures." He gave a curt nod. "It could be the making of you, Evan."

The director was moving now, picking up his paperwork. He glanced from one to the other. "Maybe three months in a hot climate will help you two sort out your differences."

The realization of what was about to happen hit him like a boulder on the head. "We're going together? To Nigeria? I'm going to be *Dr. Connelly's* team leader?"

He couldn't possibly mean that. From the little Evan knew about the polio program it worked across a number of countries. Surely, the director didn't plan on sending them together on the same field assignment?

"Of course. This is perfect. Hard work in an area uncluttered by other distractions. The two of you are there to represent the clinical expertise of the DPA, so I expect you to iron out any personal issues. Both of you report to Dr. Sanday tomorrow morning. He'll give you all the background information and travel arrangements that you need."

"But what about here? What about infectious diseases?"

The director gave him a wry smile. "Donovan's served his time well. I think he's ready to take the next step—a more strategic direction. It will stretch him, do him good—just like it will you."

And then he was gone.

Violet sat in the chair, unmoving. Evan could almost sense she didn't want to meet his gaze.

There was so much going on in his head right now.

And most of it concerned her. She was shifting constantly in his mind. Violet, Sawyer's sister. Violet, his colleague who'd ignored his instructions. Violet, the woman he'd kissed a few months ago. Violet, the woman who'd asked for a transfer without talking to him first.

Violet, the woman he was going to spend the next three months with—in close proximity.

Was that better or worse than her leaving? Right now he didn't know.

It didn't help matters that he was being replaced by a guy he considered a cocky upstart.

"Are you going to say something?" She'd rested her elbow on the desk and was leaning her head on her hand. She looked exhausted.

Then again, she'd barely slept in the past few days. None of them had, thanks to the crisis.

Her eyes were closed. For the first time he noticed she had little dark circles under them. They marred her usually perfect complexion. Her blond hair was swept back with a clip but little strands had escaped around her face. Even in a state of exhaustion Violet Connelly was a thing of beauty.

But her beauty couldn't distract him from the thoughts rattling around in his brain.

"Why didn't you tell me about Sawyer? No. Why didn't you tell *anyone* that he's your brother? Are you ashamed of him?"

Her eyes shot open, sparks of fury shooting in his direction. She opened her mouth to speak then pressed her lips together firmly for a few seconds, obviously having second thoughts. Maybe she'd been outspoken enough for one day. She bent forward, putting her head on the desk in exasperation.

"You do that to me," she mumbled.

He was thrown. "What?"

She lifted her head, so he could only see one pale green eye. "You make me mad at the drop of a hat. It irritates me. And I'm just too exhausted to fight with you."

He nodded slowly. This wasn't exactly where he thought this conversation would go.

"Of course I'm not ashamed of my brother. I love him dearly. But he's had issues. He needed time. He needed space. Ever heard of the expression *'If you love someone let them go'*? That's Sawyer. The past six years have been hard." Her pale green eyes looked off to the side and she nodded slowly. "But I think he's on his way back."

Wow. Nothing like getting to the heart of the matter. But he didn't have time to think about what she'd said because she wasn't finished.

"But I don't know where you fit into this picture."

"What do you mean?" Her conversation seemed to jump all over the place. What was going on in her mind? Was this lack of sleep?

She folded her arms across her chest and straightened herself in the chair.

"I know you had issues with my brother but I don't know what they were. Sawyer never told me. Will you?"

Now, there was a question. The words hung in the air. Could he really put into words the complexity of what had happened between him and Sawyer and how he felt? He almost didn't know where to start. And did he really want to have this conversation with a woman he would spend the next three months with? The answer was easy.

"Probably not."

She sucked in a deep breath. "Well, where does that leave us?"

"What do you mean?"

"Does your irrational hatred of my brother extend to me too?"

He swallowed, not really sure how to answer. The truth of the matter was that it did change how he perceived her. His bias against Sawyer was already affecting how he felt about her. Would she exhibit the same traits as her brother? Would she walk out on a mission when it was at its most vital stage?

He set his lips in a firm line but he couldn't look at her and his voice was low. "You know I don't hate you, Violet." His brain was painting pictures. Pictures of Violet in that red dress she'd been wearing a few days ago with a thick black belt cinching her waist. He was sure she'd worn it to distract him from the fact she hadn't produced the report. And she had been right to, because it had worked.

Her eyes drifted off to one side. "I thought I was going to get fired."

He nodded slowly. "Me too."

Her green eyes met his. "I don't want to get fired," she said steadily. "I love my job."

"I don't want to get fired either. My job's the best thing in my life right now."

Why had he said that?

That was far too personal. And Evan tried not to mix his personal life and with his working life. Or, at least, not usually.

"So I guess we both have to make the best of the situation."

She didn't acknowledge his words. Instead, she

pulled out a flower-covered notebook and started scribbling.

"What are you doing?"

"I need to make plans. I need to make arrangements for my apartment. The electricity, the rent, the mail…" Her voice tailed off.

The enormity of the upheaval started to hit him too. He'd need to make similar plans—all in the space of a week. To say nothing of the handover he'd have to give to Donovan about running the team here. The next week would be a nightmare.

Violet was scribbling again. It was almost as if he wasn't there. He watched her as her hand flew over the page. Her hair was falling over her face. His fingers itched to reach out and tuck it behind her ear. Why on earth did he think like this around her?

"Any chance of a copy of your list? It will save me doing mine."

She raised her head and the sides of her mouth turned up. "Not a hope." She stood up and walked toward the door. "I'm going to start going over my files, see what work I need to hand over to someone else."

"Violet?"

She stopped, her hand on the doorhandle. "What?"

He couldn't help it. He had to ask. Did she have the same kind of traits that he'd seen in her brother? He needed to know. The next three months were going to be a strain. Ever since that kiss he'd spent the past few months avoiding being in close proximity to her.

They'd never spoken about it. Never mentioned it. A drunken fumble on a work night out that no one knew about.

He had no idea how she felt about it.

More importantly, he'd no idea how *he* felt about it.

He'd woken up the next morning with the strangest feeling in his stomach. Part dread, part excitement. He was her boss. He should never have gone near her. It compromised their working relationship.

And now it seemed as if she was prepared to hold it over his head. That made Violet dangerous. That made Violet a threat.

"When the director interrupted us you were saying something about me being unprofessional. You were implying that because of the kiss. You thought you were about to be fired. Were you going to try and get me fired too? Would you do that, Violet?"

Her eyes met his and he saw a little flash of fire. She didn't hesitate for a second. "In a heartbeat."

She pushed open the door and walked out, leaving Evan wondering what he'd got himself into.

CHAPTER TWO

THE HEAT HIT her as soon as they stepped off the plane. It was like stepping into a fan-heated oven.

How on earth could she function in this for the next three months? Would she ever get used to it?

The sweat was already starting to run in rivulets down her back and catch in her bra strap. She rummaged in her bag and pulled out a travel-sized antiperspirant spray. "I'm heading to the ladies' room. Can you watch for my bag? It's lime-green."

Evan nodded and dropped his rucksack onto the floor beside the luggage carousel. Great. A twelve-hour flight from Atlanta to Lagos, Nigeria, and he still wasn't speaking to her.

Not that she cared. But it was unnerving to sit next to someone for that long without exchanging a single word.

She splashed some water on her face and pulled a ponytail band from her bag, sweeping her sticky hair from the back of her neck. She pulled off her white top and sprayed liberally before swapping it for a purple one in her rucksack. It was a little crumpled but it would have to do.

Was Evan planning on speaking to her any time soon? And what did he have to be so mad about, anyway? She'd only told him the truth. And if he couldn't handle the truth…

She heard the squeak of luggage being wheeled past the doorway. People were obviously leaving so the baggage must have arrived.

She picked up her bag and headed back outside, just in time to see Evan drag her lime-green suitcase from the carousel.

It landed with a thump at her feet. "What on earth have you got in here? Did you pack the entire contents of your apartment? I've never seen a suitcase that size in my life. As for the weight, how on earth did you get it down your stairs?"

She watched as he pulled another suitcase—this time with one hand—from the carousel. It was a medium-sized navy blue case. She couldn't help the smile that flickered across her lips.

She tilted her head up at him. "Oh, so now you're talking to me, are you?" She pulled the handle up on the side of her case and tilted it onto its wheels. The initial tug was tough but once the case picked up a little momentum, it sailed along behind her.

"Do you remember the name of the person we're meeting?" She walked in the direction of the exit.

Evan was matching her stride for stride, holding his case easily in his hand—he had no need for wheels. He pulled a piece of paper from his top pocket. "Someone called Amos should be waiting for us outside Arrivals with a car. They said under no circumstances should we get in a local taxi." His eyes fell on her suitcase again. "Though at this rate we'll probably need an eighteen-wheeler to move that. What do you have in there?"

Violet rolled her eyes. "Just everything a girl could

need. Hold up a sec," she said, as one of the customs officers gestured toward her.

Two hours later they finally made it to the exit.

"Of all the ridiculous, over-packed, stupid items to have in your suitcase—"

"Oh, drop it, Evan. I'm too hot and tired to listen to your whining." She nodded in the direction of a man with a board showing their names in his hand. He looked as if he was wilting.

"Hi," she said. "Amos? I'm Violet Connelly and this is Evan Hunter. Sorry we took so long."

The man's brow furrowed. "Was there a problem with the officials? I hope not."

Evan let out a snort. "The only problems were the ones that she caused. Probably by trying to transport the equivalent of an elephant in her luggage."

"An elephant? I don't understand."

Violet placed her hand over his. "Dr. Hunter is being sarcastic. The officials searched my luggage and removed certain items."

"Items? What items?"

Violet shook her head. "Nothing important. Some U.S. candy. Some electrical items. Nothing I can't live without."

Evan was obviously becoming impatient. The two-hour-long inspection of Violet's luggage must have been the final straw for him. "Do you have a car?"

Amos nodded. "The minibus is parked outside. I'll take you to the Healthy World Federation building and give you some safety instructions. Stay next to me, please, as we leave the building. Some of the local taxis will try and encourage you to go with them."

He grabbed hold of the handle of Violet's case and stopped dead, obviously unprepared for the weight. He

struggled to give her a smile as he dragged it along behind him. Within a few minutes they were outside the
terminal building and were immediately accosted by a
whole host of taxi drivers.

"Stay close!" shouted Amos as they pushed their way
through. Evan's hand appeared from nowhere and rested
gently at her waist, guiding her through the shouting
faces until they reached the car park.

"How far to the city?"

The long flight, followed by the search at customs,
had taken their toll. Violet was ready to collapse in a
heap. "Around fifty minutes. We're just going to the
outskirts. It's a relatively safe area. Don't worry."

He opened the back door of the minibus and nodded to Evan. "Give us a hand with this, please." Evan
grabbed the other side of the case and between them
they tossed it into the back of the minivan. Maybe a
big suitcase hadn't been such a good idea after all. But
at the time she'd been packing everything had seemed
like an essential.

The journey flew past. Violet could barely keep her
eyes open as they sped through the city suburbs. It was
immediately apparent that poverty was an issue—just
like in so many other cities throughout the world.

She felt a sharp nudge on the ribs. "Wake up, Violet, we're here."

Her eyes shot open. When had she fallen asleep? The
last thing she remembered was staring out the window
at a group of children playing football in the street.

Somehow she'd fallen asleep with her head on Evan's
shoulder, and the heat from his body in the air-conditioned van had been comforting. She pulled herself up
straight and rubbed at her cheek. Great. She could feel
the creases of his shirt embedded in her face.

She looked out the window as Amos opened the door and let the heat flood inside again.

She'd had a little handheld, battery-powered fan in her suitcase. Too bad she hadn't thought to put it in her hand luggage.

She jumped down onto the street and immediately pulled her sunglasses down from her forehead. She glanced at her watch. It was still set to Atlanta time. Lagos was only five hours ahead, but the jump between time zones had totally disorientated her. It felt as if it should be the middle of the night.

Amos hauled her case up the front steps of the building and pushed open the glass doors. Air-conditioning again. Bliss.

A woman in traditional dress met them at reception. "Dr. Hunter? Dr. Connelly? Welcome to headquarters." She gestured toward the rear of the building. "If you want to head to the lifts, I'll give you a key to your rooms. You'll have a chance to freshen up, but we need you back down here later to meet the members of your team and have a safety briefing."

"No problem." Evan obviously wasn't suffering from the same travel effects that she was. Right now she just wanted to lie down on some cool cotton sheets.

Evan glanced at the number of the key and pocketed it. Both of them stood for a few more seconds, waiting for the second key to appear.

It didn't.

The lady looked back up. "Oh, didn't someone explain? We're a little short of space. You'll be bunking up together. That won't be a problem, will it?"

Her manner was so relaxed it almost disarmed Violet. What Violet really wanted to do was scream and shout and stamp her feet on the floor. Her patience and fatigue was at an all-time low.

"No problem at all." Evan's cool voice cut through the strop she was currently throwing in her head and he headed off toward the lift.

She bit her tongue and tugged her case after him, struggling to pull it over the seam between the floor and elevator door. Evan's hand slid over hers and he gave it a final tug, sending her hurtling backward into the lift. She landed against the back wall with a thud.

"Thanks." She couldn't hide her sarcastic tone and wasn't even going to try.

"My pleasure." She could hear the edge of amusement in his voice and she really wasn't in the mood at all.

He pressed a button and the elevator slid smoothly upward, opening onto a brightly lit corridor with a procession of identical brown doors.

"Can you manage?"

"Of course." She tugged her case with both hands, smiling as his foot came into contact with one of the wheels. It really did feel as if she had a dead body inside.

He flinched. "We're in here." He slid the card into the door and pushed it open, revealing a regular-sized room with a large white bed.

One large white bed.

Silence.

Who would react first?

It was Violet. It was the final straw.

"You have got to be joking!"

Evan's eyes swept the room, obviously looking for somewhere else to sleep. No stowaway bed. No pull-down couch.

One bed. Or nothing.

Violet stomped over to the bathroom and stuck her head inside. Clean. Functional. White bath and a separate shower.

"What are you looking for, a secret bed?"

His voice made her jump, his warm breath tickling the hairs at the back of her neck. She spun round. "Don't do that!"

He smiled and it caught her unawares. The sun was streaming through the window, lighting up his face. When had been the last time she'd seen him smile? She couldn't remember.

One thing was for sure. Evan Hunter should smile more often.

There were little lines around his blue eyes but they didn't detract from how handsome he was. They only added character. And he was so close she could see little flecks of gold in them.

She was so tired right now. All she wanted to do was lean forward, bury her head in his firm chest and go to sleep. The bed in the middle of the room was practically shouting her name. But there was no way they could share a bed.

Especially after what had happened a few months ago.

The kiss had been steamy enough. But the two of them in a bed?

No. The picture that was conjuring up in her brain was too much. This fatigue was stopping any rational thoughts whatsoever.

Evan folded his arms across his chest.

"I don't know about you, Violet, but I have no intention of sleeping on the floor."

He was right. She knew he was right.

She glanced around at the floor. There wasn't even as much as a rug to lie on.

Sharing a room in close proximity to Evan would be hard enough. But sharing a bed? It didn't even bear thinking about.

There was a small table and chairs in front of the window in the room.

"How about we sleep in shifts?" She moved quickly, crossing the room in strides and jumping onto the bed. "I'll go first."

Her head sank instantly into the pillow. Perfect. She didn't care what he thought. She needed to get some sleep. Now.

Evan sat down on one of the chairs, leaning forward and pulling a thick wad of papers from the zipped pocket in his case. His eyes ran over her body as she shuffled her shoes off and kicked them to the floor. Was he looking at her curves? Was he thinking about the last time he'd had his hands on her body?

That sent a whole new sensation prickling across her skin.

"Cranky when you're tired, aren't you? Fine. You sleep. I'll read. I'll wake you up in a few hours, in time for the briefing. Okay?"

"Okay," she said instantly. There was no way she was getting off this comfortable bed.

How bad could this be? Maybe in a few hours they would be able to find someone else to share with?

Her eyes flickered shut.

She and Evan Hunter in a shared room.

Not the best start to her new life. Three years ago she'd originally applied to be part of this program but circumstances had changed and the thought of mainstream clinical work—potentially with lots of children—had been too difficult for her.

It hadn't helped that her grieving brother hadn't been in touch. Neither were her parents. They still hadn't recovered from the loss of their daughter-in-law and first grandchild some years earlier. Telling them about her own circumstances would only have added to their pain. And they hadn't needed that.

So she'd gone through everything herself.

Oh, she'd had some good friends who'd been there for her but it wasn't the same as family, no matter how much she tried to spin it in her mind.

But life had come full circle. Time was supposed to be a great healer.

Maybe it was. Maybe it wasn't.

She was ready for a change. She was a doctor. She'd spent the past three years in the epidemiology and planning department of the DPA.

It had been fine—for a desk job. But Violet was a people person.

The conflict—and incursion—with Evan Hunter had given her the impetus she needed to apply for a transfer. She wanted to have contact with patients again. She wanted to help people. She wanted to make a difference.

And out here, in Nigeria, she could certainly help to make a difference with the polio program.

It was time to get back out into the real world. And you didn't get much more real than the heart of Africa.

She had her mind set on this. Getting involved again. Having contact with families. Having contact with mothers. Having contact with children. Having contact with babies.

Evan Hunter was nothing more than an inconvenience.

A handsome inconvenience.

She had work to do here, and he'd better not get in her way.

She snuggled further into the pillow and prayed she didn't snore.

Evan gave her shoulder a little shake again, raising his voice just a little. "Violet. Violet. It's time to wake up. We've got the briefing in half an hour."

She stirred and mumbled something. It almost felt unfair to wake her. She was much nicer while she slept.

Less distracting. Less confrontational. Less a reminder of her brother.

He still hadn't got over that. Matt Sawyer's sister. Wow. He hadn't seen that one coming. Not by a long shot.

She was mumbling again. She'd spent the past few hours doing that. Talking in her sleep. It was kind of cute. Not that he thought Violet was cute.

Not at all.

Plus, he didn't have a single clue what she'd been saying. At one point it had almost sounded like someone's name.

Her eyes flickered open and took a few moments to focus. At the exact moment a drip from his still-wet hair landed on her nose. He'd taken the opportunity to shower while she'd been sleeping and hadn't got round to rubbing his hair with a towel.

"Eeeewwww!" She sat up sharply, her hand automatically rubbing her nose.

"Sorry."

She glanced at her watch then screwed up her nose. "What time is it here? I'm still on Atlanta time."

"It's nearly six o'clock. You'd better get ready. I thought you might want to shower."

She pushed herself up the bed. "Have you left any hot water?"

He shrugged. "You know what they say—if you're not fast, you're last."

A pillow sailed from the bed and caught him on the side of his head. "Hey!"

Her head turned to the side, taking in the table where he'd been sitting. The papers and documentation had spilled over onto the other chair and across half the floor.

"Did you kill half a tree while I was sleeping?" She walked over and picked up some of the paperwork. "Do we really need to read all this?"

He shook his head. "You don't. I do. You only need to read around half."

She seemed to gulp. "Wow."

She gave her eyes a little rub. "I think I will shower." She tipped her case over and opened it up.

She hadn't been joking. She really did have everything—despite having had some things removed at the airport. But what was more interesting was how everything was packed. Rolled-up tiny items, all in blocks of color. Nothing like the flat-folded items in his case. She even had her toiletries stuffed into her shoes.

She unrolled a light yellow dress, some white underwear and pulled some shampoo from a shoe. "I'll only be five minutes."

And she was. Her hair was still wet but pulled back into a braid that fell straight down her back.

It really was disarming how pretty she could look without even trying.

She picked up a notebook with purple flowers on the front. He squinted. "Are those violets?"

She nodded and smiled. "I have a whole boxful of these at home. Pretty, aren't they? At least no one can steal my signature notebook." The smile reached all the way up to her eyes.

It was nice to see a genuine smile. The past few weeks she'd had a permanent scowl on her face. But maybe that was especially for him. He liked her better this way.

"Did you buy them?"

"No. Sawyer did."

How to break a moment. It was like someone had just thrown a bucket of ice over him.

He just couldn't get past the connection.

He'd been the team leader. The one responsible for all members of staff.

And Sawyer's wife, Helen, had died on that mission. Stuck out in the middle of nowhere with an ectopic pregnancy. By the time they'd recognized what was wrong it had been too late for her.

He blamed Sawyer. He must have known his wife was pregnant and yet he had let her go on that mission.

But Evan also had reason to blame himself, and six years on he still couldn't get the guilt out of his head. Six years on he still hadn't managed to shake the feeling that he was living a life his colleague wasn't. It didn't seem fair. It wasn't as if he was short of offers. Sure, he dated. But the first time he even felt a flicker of something toward the woman of the moment, they had to go. Because why should he get to live, love and procreate when his colleague didn't?

The sensation of guilt was a hideous, never-ending

cycle. Sometimes it faded a little, only to flicker back into life as soon as something sparked a memory.

Violet was ready now, her eyes quizzical as if she had been reading his secret thoughts, her hand on the doorhandle. "Let's go," she said quietly.

He followed her to the elevators and down to the conference room. It was impressive. One wall was covered in maps of the states of Nigeria. Another had organizational charts of the team members. Another had immunization targets and notifications.

Everything they needed was right before their eyes.

"Welcome, Evan. Welcome, Violet. I'm Frank Barns, director of DPA's Nigeria office." He gestured to the walls. "Welcome to the operations center."

He shook their hands and led them over to the nearest wall where the maps were displayed. "I finished a briefing for the other new staff earlier. You've probably realized we're at a real tipping point with polio eradication. If immunity is not raised in the three remaining countries to levels necessary to stop poliovirus transmission, then polio eradication will fail. Nigeria is the only polio-endemic country remaining in Africa. There are several high-risk states and I've decided to send you to Natumba state. We've had sixty-two cases of wild poliovirus this year—more than half of them notified from Natumba. One third of all children there remain under-immunized."

He gave them a little nod of his head. "You'll have your work cut out for you there. The DPA works in conjunction with The Global Children's Support Organization and the Healthy World Federation. But there are several issues for our workers." His expression was deadly serious. "There have been bomb threats, killings and kidnappings. We have to make security a priority for our staff. You don't go anywhere unescorted. While in Lagos you stay with a local guide, and the same applies when you reach Natumba."

Evan could see Violet's face pale. Was she frightened? Maybe she hadn't been expecting this. He moved next to her and placed his hand over hers. Frank was still talking, outlining the things they should or shouldn't do. He almost expected Violet to snatch her hand away. But she didn't.

Instead she twined her fingers with his, while keeping her breathing slow and steady. She was scared.

And it scared him too. He was going to be team leader again. He was going to be out in the field, with a whole host of unknowns. A whole host of things he might not be able to predict or control.

What if something happened to one of his team again?

The guilt had almost destroyed him last time. What if something happened to Violet? It almost didn't bear thinking about.

He pressed his fingers closer to hers and gave her a little smile while Frank continued with the briefing.

He would keep her safe. He had to.

He couldn't think beyond that.

"Wow. What did you think of all that?"

It was an hour later and they were sitting in the dining room in the HWF building.

"So much for having a last supper before starting on the job." She glanced around at her surroundings. They'd been advised not to leave the building at night, and neither of them had wanted to ignore the security brief.

"It's probably for the best. We've got an early start tomorrow with the flight to Natumba."

He was pushing his food around the plate, his mind obviously on other things.

"So, how do you feel about it?" She felt as if something was caught in her throat. Would he feel the same way she did? Sick with nerves? She hadn't expected this. She hadn't planned for it.

His eyes met hers. And she could almost see the shutters go down. It was apparent he wasn't going to tell her how he was feeling about it all. After all, he hadn't even wanted to come here, had he? He'd been more or less pushed into this.

She'd chosen to come here. She should have been better prepared for what she was getting into. The briefing today had knocked her for six. Would she even sleep tonight?

Sleep. That other issue.

"Did you manage to get the sleeping arrangements sorted out?" Evan had said he would try and talk to someone about finding another room.

He looked up from his plate, a smile dancing across his lips. "Yes and no."

"What does that mean?"

"It means I've got us some extra pillows."

"And what are they for?"

"To put down the middle of the bed." She almost dropped her fork. They were still sleeping in the same bed? Oh, no.

Her skin was starting to tingle. The hairs on her arms were standing on end. Sharing a bed with Evan Hunter? Pillows or not, she wouldn't sleep a wink.

"You okay with that?"

He seemed so cool. So calm and collected. His mind was obviously focused on the job and not doing a merry dance around the thoughts of a heated kiss a few months ago.

Not the way hers was.

"I'm fine with that." She put her fork down. "I've had enough. I think I want to get to bed early."

She'd said the words. She hadn't meant them to come out sounding like that. Sounding as if she was hinting at something. She wanted to die of embarrassment and felt the rush of blood to her cheeks.

Evan kept his eyes fixed on his dinner plate. He handed over the key to the room. "I'll let you go on ahead. I've got some things to work out with Frank. We'll probably be talking late into the night. Leave the door on the latch. I promise I won't wake you when I come up."

She nodded and just about grabbed the key from his hand, thankful that he seemed to have missed the implication of her words. "Good night, then." She sped off to the room. The sooner she had her head under the covers the better.

This was going to be a long night.

Evan watched her retreating back. In the artificially lit room he could see her silhouette through her thin yellow dress, showing the curve of her bottom and hips. He did his best to look away.

This was all going to end in disaster.

He'd lied. He didn't have to see Frank about anything. He'd been given all the information he could possibly need.

The worst thing was that he'd left all the paperwork

in the room. He was going to have to hang around and kill time with nothing to do.

It had seemed easier to make something up. To let her slip away and get to the room without him pretending not to watch her every move.

Leave the door on the latch. He cringed at his words. It was like something an old married couple would say to each other. Where had that come from?

Everything about this situation was just too uncomfortable.

He'd caught a waft of her floral perfume the other day and it had invaded his senses, instantly taking him back to that night in the bar.

The night when Violet had drunk too many glasses of wine and had virtually propositioned him in the corridor leading to the back exit. The night when he'd had too many whiskies and had no resistance to her in her red dress and spiked heels, her hair all mussed up on her head.

The feel of her hungry lips on his had made him forget where they were and the consequences of his actions.

By the time someone had interrupted them, he'd practically had her dress up around her waist.

Hardly the ideal position for a DPA team leader and a member of his staff.

And the next day it had been as if nothing had ever happened. He sometimes wondered if Violet even remembered the incident.

Surely she hadn't been that drunk? Because that thought made him sick to his stomach. That would mean he'd taken advantage of her. Something he would never do.

But in the meantime her floral scent lingered around him.

How could he sleep in a room tonight with that aroma and all it conjured up in his mind?

There was no question about it.

Violet Connelly was going to drive him crazy.

CHAPTER THREE

THE LIGHT AIRCRAFT touched down in a cloud of dust.

"We're here." Violet pressed her nose up against the glass window, trying to take in the wide landscape ahead of her.

Natumba state covered more than eighteen thousand square kilometers, and they'd landed in the northern-most tip, at the three local government areas most affected by polio. Only a few days ago there had been another two diagnoses of wild poliovirus.

Part of her was relieved they weren't going to be based in the capital, Natumba. There was another team already based there.

But the wide open landscape and vast terrain made her realize the huge task they were undertaking and the number of miles they'd need to cover. All in the blistering heat.

There were a few figures dressed in white next to the landing strip, along with a whole host of multi-terrain vehicles—some looking a little worse for wear.

"That must be Dr. Yusif. He said he would meet us here and take us to the campsite."

"I didn't expect it to be so green. I expected it to look more barren."

Evan turned as he unloaded their bags and all the

supplies from the plane. "Natumba is quite an agricul-
tural state—they produce a lot of groundnuts. The land
is supposed to be well cultivated and irrigated."

"And the villages?" She left the question hanging in
the air between them.

Both of them had read as much as they could about
the surrounding area. Only half of the population in
the area had access to portable water and appropriate
sanitation. Health care was limited and the education
system in a state of neglect.

Although the government had launched national
campaigns to raise awareness about polio, the reality
was the message wasn't reaching the villagers.

"Nigeria isn't all savannah. The far south has a tropical rainforest climate and good rainfall. There are also
areas of saltwater swamp and mangroves. The border
with Cameroon has highlands and a rich rainforest. It's
not the dry desert wasteland that some people expect."

Dr. Yusif was striding across the ground to meet
them. He was dressed in a white shirt and trousers with
a white *kufi* cap on his head. "Welcome, welcome." His
smile reached from ear to ear. "I'm so glad to see you."
He shook hands with them both and guided them over
to the vehicles. "Grab your bags and let's get on the
move. It will be too hot to travel if we don't start now."

"How far away is the campsite?" Violet asked as
she slid into the backseat of the four wheel drive. The
upholstery of the seats were ripped and scorched by
the sun. She pulled her skirt down to stop her skin
from sticking to the surface. It must be around one
hundred degrees in here, nothing like the comfortable,
air-conditioned vehicles they'd had in the city, or that
she took for granted back home.

"It's only around an hour, but the roads can be rough. Hold on to your hat!"

Evan slid in next to her and they listened as Dr. Yusif filled them in on some of the background to where they'd be working. Violet clung onto the grab handle on the roof as the car pitched over the uneven terrain—anything to stop her sliding across the seat and landing in Evan's lap.

He was managing to look as cool and calm as ever. How did he do it? The sweat was already starting to trickle down her spine and she was wishing she had pulled her hair off her collar with an elastic band.

Dr. Yusif seemed to talk constantly. It seemed that he'd been here, without support, for some time and was relieved that they'd arrived. He was moving on to another area and would introduce them to the team covering the three local areas, which Evan would be leading.

Every now and then he turned and spoke to the driver of the car in another language. "What language is that you're speaking?" Violet queried.

"It's Hausa, the native language around these parts. Don't worry. You'll be assigned a local guide who'll be able to interpret for you. And it might surprise you, but some of the villagers speak English. It's one of the official languages of Nigeria. You'll get along fine here."

The countryside sped past. They passed some smaller villages, where people were working in the fields, and had to pull over as some livestock were driven along the road toward them.

Violet was feeling nervous.

This was what she'd wanted—a complete change of scenery. A chance to do the job she'd initially set out to do. A chance to test herself again—to get in among real live people and see if she could make a difference to their health and future prospects. A chance to get away from Evan Hunter.

The past few weeks had been a terrible strain. Working with Evan had been hard enough after their passionate interlude. But seeing his reactions to her brother's involvement in the potential smallpox outbreak had made her throw all rational thought out the window.

She'd thought that by applying for a transfer she'd not only get a new start for herself but also a new start away from him.

But the director had obviously had other ideas.

Being trapped in a room with him last night had been more than a little strange. Of course she'd heard him come into the room.

Her heartbeat had quickened as she'd heard the rustle of his clothes. Willing herself not to imagine what lay beneath.

She'd been very conscious of her own breathing, trying not to let it change to keep up the pretense of being asleep when the mattress had sunk as he'd sat down on the edge of the bed. Then there had been the careful placement of pillows between them.

All the while her mind had been throwing them back off the wall on the other side of the room.

But why did she feel like this? She didn't want to like him. She didn't want to find him attractive. It was so much easier when they were arguing and scowling at each other. But this man had crept under her skin in so many different ways that she didn't even want to think about.

All from that one kiss.

Why had neither of them ever acknowledged it? A relationship would have been frowned on by bosses at the DPA. Particularly if things had gone on a downward spiral and affected the work of the team.

But more importantly, for Violet, it was easier to pretend it had never happened. Because then she would have to deal with how it, and he, had made her feel. And she wasn't ready for that, not then and not now.

She wasn't ready for anything other than the job. Thinking about a man would bring a whole host of other emotions to the surface. She was only ready to take baby steps.

Only her first baby steps had been like stepping onto the moon. A giant leap for mankind and a giant leap for Violet.

Working at the DPA had sheltered her for a while. It had almost made her feel safe. Watching the crops and dust speed past was exciting—her first visit to Africa. But it was just so, so different from being based in the DPA at Atlanta.

Could she really handle this? Or was it all just a step too far?

The car jolted to a halt outside a makeshift building. This was obviously the village. Most of it was in a state of disrepair. There was a huge variety of structures from thatched-roof huts to wooden buildings, from brick buildings to some traditionally built *husa* houses.

Her eyes were drawn immediately to the overhead water tank at the edge of the village. At least this village had one. From what she'd learned, access to improved water and sanitation was a daily challenge for most Nigerians, particularly in the rural north of the country where less than half the population had access to safe drinking water and adequate sanitation.

She jumped out and followed Evan into the building. Although the surroundings were poor, the equipment almost made her do a double-take. Two computers sat on a bench—where the generator was she'd no idea. Her eyes widened at the sight of some mobile phones and GPS monitors sitting on another bench, alongside vaccine transporters and fridges into which the vaccines were already being unpacked.

There was whole host of people to meet. Some of the village leaders, some health staff, community outreach workers, midwives and members of another voluntary organization involved in water aid.

But most importantly, outside stood a row of women with their children. Violet cringed with embarrassment as her case thudded from the back of the car. Three months' worth of clothes and a whole pile of other things now seemed extravagant and ridiculous.

It didn't matter that she also had a whole host of medical supplies in her case. The size and weight of her lime-green case now seemed like a beacon of excess. She wanted to send it straight back home.

Evan's much smaller, navy blue case seemed much more appropriate. Something else to hold against him.

Dr. Yusif was still fussing around them, probably relieved that there were finally some colleagues to hand over to. "Your accommodation is over there. I'll get your luggage taken over. Would you like to go and freshen up?"

Violet followed where his finger was pointing at a solid brown building just a few hundred yards away.

"Separate rooms?" she asked. It was the first thing that sprang to mind.

"What?" He looked confused then started laughing. "Of course. There are single rooms for all of our staff. They are small and pretty basic, a single bed with mosquito net, a chest of drawers—" his eyes danced over her bulging case "—and some toilet facilities, but I'm sure you'll be comfortable."

"I'm sure we will be." She was relieved. Being stuck in a room at night with Evan had unsettled her, and she had no idea if that would be expected in their field assignments too. Thankfully not.

She glanced at her watch, unsure what to do first. She nodded at the people outside. "Want me to get straight to work?"

Dr. Yusif looked a little taken aback. "Don't you and Dr. Hunter want to take some time to settle in? I've got a whole host of things to hand over to Dr. Hunter before I leave—it will probably take the rest of the day."

Violet shrugged. She wasn't there to be a team leader. She was there to be doctor. And there was no time like the present.

Dr. Yusif's hand touched her skin. "You do realize you won't just get to administer polio vaccine straight away? Most of these people are here because their children are sick." He lowered his voice. "This is where it gets really difficult. People come because you're a doctor, not because of the vaccine. If you start to treat every problem, you'll never get the job done that you're here for."

Violet looked at the anxious faces. She could already tell where she would fall down in this job. She couldn't just administer vaccine. She had to look at the whole health of a person, how they lived, their home and their facilities, in order to give them the best advice possible. It was the heart of public health.

"Well, let's just get me started in the meantime. We can reassess how things are going in a few days. Can you pair me up with an interpreter?"

Dr. Yusif nodded quickly and gestured to a young

woman dressed in bright clothing to come over. "Ola-bisi, come over here please."

The woman hurried over, her bright orange and red skirts sweeping along the floor. "Dr. Connelly wants to start straight away. Can you interpret for her, please, and show her around the clinic?"

Evan touched her shoulder. "Are you sure about this?"

He was leaning over her, watching her again with those blue eyes. He was close enough to see the gold flecks.

He couldn't possibly know. He couldn't possibly know how hard these first few steps would be.

Should she tell him?

Of course not. That would be another fault. Another black mark against her name. She'd already kept one secret from him. What would he say if he found out there were two?

He would undoubtedly question her suitability for the job.

But she wanted this. She *needed* this.

Even though it would inevitably break her heart.

It was time to move on.

She turned to face him and met his gaze. "I think it's for the best. If I can get started straight away it will help build some relationships with the villagers."

She could almost hear his brain tick, trying to decide if it was the best thing to do. "I'll come and find you in an hour, okay?"

She nodded and smiled. "That's fine. If there's anyone needing immunization I can do that as I go."

"You're happy with the protocol for recording?"

"It seems straightforward enough. I'll give you a yell if I run into any problems."

He seemed to hesitate, as if he wanted to say something else, but she didn't wait to find out. She walked to the doorway. Olabisi was already talking to some of the mothers waiting outside, forming them into two separate queues.

"Ah, Dr. Violet." She pointed to the queue on her left. "This one is yours, all these mothers understand English. The other queue is mine. These villagers only speak Hausa. We should be able to get through more this way. Okay?"

Violet smiled. Olabisi was already looking like a professional rather than a local volunteer with rudimentary training. She could learn a lot from these people.

She turned to the first woman in the queue, who was clutching a baby in one arm and holding the hand of another small child with one limb showing clear signs of atrophy. Already they were too late. This child had already been affected by polio.

She gestured with her hand. "Please come in. I'm Dr. Violet."

The afternoon flew past. Polio had blighted this community. Most villagers had probably never even realized they'd been affected. Ninety percent of sufferers had no symptoms.

But then there were the few poor souls—children and adults alike—where the virus had entered their central nervous system and destroyed their motor neurons, leading to muscle weakness and acute flaccid paralysis.

And with the poor sanitation in the village it was no wonder that polio was still spreading.

In the space of a few hours, Violet had delivered and recorded more than forty doses of oral polio vaccine, along with dressing wounds, listening to chests and dealing with a large number of cases of malaria and diarrhea in young children.

But then everything changed.

Then she was faced with a baby.

A really sick baby.

Even before she touched him she could tell instantly how unwell he was.

And she did the worst thing possible. She hesitated.

A horrible sense of dread was sweeping over her. If she could run outside and be sick right now she would. Her mouth felt as dry as a stick as she approached the woman clutching the tiny bundle in her arms.

The words almost stuck in the throat. How awful. How ridiculous. This was exactly why she'd come here. There was no way she could let her nerves get the better of her now.

But this was harder than she'd thought.

This was the first time she'd been in contact with a real, live sick child since her daughter had died.

Her arms trembled as she held them out. "Can I see him, please?"

The mother nodded, burst into tears and handed him over.

Violet held the little bundle in her arms. Aware of the sensations sweeping over her and trying to push them all aside. Trying to keep her "doctor head" in focus. He was seriously underweight, his skin wrinkled with no fatty tissue underneath. According to his mother, after a bout of diarrhea he hadn't been able to eat anything in the last week. It was clear he was severely dehydrated.

Back home a child like this would be rushed into Pediatric Intensive Care, with a central line inserted and IV fluids delivered in a systematic manner to stop overload leading to organ failure. Here, Violet had none of those facilities.

She sat quietly, gently rocking the little boy backward and forward in her arms. Taking a few moments just to gather her thoughts. His eyes were too glazed to focus properly—a clear sign of his ill health.

She spoke quietly to Olabisi. "Do we have any oral rehydration salt sachets?"

Olabisi shook her head. "We go through them so quickly. The Global Children's Support Organization supply us regularly but we're not due another delivery for a couple of days."

Violet nodded. This little boy didn't have a couple of days. He might only have a few hours. She lifted her head. "Could you go and find my case please? Open it up, you'll find some sachets near the back. Bring them to me."

Olabisi bobbed her head and left the room quickly. The sense of dread was leaving Violet. This was a baby who needed comfort. Something else was sweeping over her now.

She felt her lips turn upward and she did the most natural thing in the world to her. Violet started to sing. This little boy needed more than comfort. He needed all the medical care in the world. Children died every day from gastroenteritis and diarrhea, all because of a lack of clean water, sugar and salts. What a difference a little medicine could make. A few sachets could put this little boy on the road to recovery again.

Back in the U.S. some doctors would have given specific instructions to parents to make a suitable solution themselves. But it was a dangerous balance. Too much sugar or salt could upset the child's system. And out here it was wiser to use the ready-prepared solutions.

Violet watched his dark brown eyes while she continued to sing. It would be helpful if there were some antibiotics available too. She'd need to check with Evan if they had their own supplies and could dispense them.

Olabisi gave a shout and the mother stepped outside the room. Violet already knew that Olabisi would be explaining how to use the medicine. The young woman's knowledge and expertise were impressive.

She was left alone with the baby.

For a second it scared her. This was a really sick little baby. But she was a doctor, she should be used to sick kids.

Only right now she didn't feel like a doctor.

Right now she felt like a mother.

A mother whose heart had been wrenched out.

Her little girl hadn't felt like this. A little bundle of bones.

Her baby had been tiny, well formed and perfect.

Except for the fact she hadn't been breathing.

Violet had been building herself up to this, knowing that at some point she would hold a living, breathing baby in her arms and it would bring back a whole host of bad memories.

But this was different.

And it didn't make her feel the way she'd thought it would.

She didn't want to weep and wail about her own loss. About the lack of rhyme or reason to her perfect daughter being stillborn.

She wanted to weep and wail for *this* baby. For this little boy. For the fact that a few hours of simple medicine could make the difference between life and death for him.

For the fact she *could* do something for this little

boy when she hadn't been able to do anything for her own daughter.

And she knew it. She knew it straight away.

She had made the right decision coming here. Evan or no Evan.

Why had she waited so long to do this? Maybe she should have done this straight away, not waited three years until she felt as if her heart had healed.

Maybe if she'd done this sooner she could have moved on with her life, rather than hiding away at a desk job in the DPA.

That first instant, before she'd held him, had been the worst. That had been the moment when she'd thought she would rather do anything else in the world than this. But everyone had experiences like this. The first time doing anything was always the toughest. But always the most worthwhile because it set the scene for what came next.

She cradled the little bundle in her arms. Olabisi arrived a few minutes later with the mother clutching a bottle of the electrolyte mixture, and Violet handed him over with a few extra words.

And then she sat in the fading light in the medical center, watching the mother feeding her child. Knowing that every weak suck and mouthful gave this child another chance at life.

Grateful that someone had a chance to save their child—even if it wasn't her.

Evan stood in the dying light, watching Violet with the baby in her arms. The handover from Dr. Yusif had taken much longer than expected and he'd gone to the accommodation, expecting to find Violet there.

Instead, he found Olabisi rummaging through Violet's lime-green case for some rehydration sachets. She'd quickly explained what she was doing and he'd followed her back to the clinic, waiting outside while she demonstrated to the mother how to use them.

He was feeling overwhelmed. It wasn't that he felt incapable. He was more than capable of doing this job.

It was just that it was so different from what he'd been used to. He hadn't even really had time to get his head around the fact he was coming to work in Africa for three months before their plane had touched the ground.

This time last week he'd been in the director's office, thinking he was kissing his job and Violet goodbye. This time last week he'd gone to a bar for a drink on the way home, trying to sort out in his head how he could be in Violet's company for the next three months. By the time he'd reached his apartment he had been sure he could keep this entirely professional. It had only taken him a few phone calls to sort out the arrangements for his apartment. No family, no girlfriend to placate, no pets to rehouse. It was kind of sad really, and made him realize how alone he was.

Would anyone miss him while he was gone? His group of male friends had disintegrated in the past few years. Some had moved away as their careers had progressed or splintered in other directions, others had settled down and had families of their own. In the end he'd only had to call a few to let them know he would be gone for a few months and ask them to keep an eye on his place.

So now there was just him and Violet on the outskirts of three local government areas in Nigeria for the next three months.

The "entirely professional" part had worked until

he'd seen her at the airport, with her crumpled white shirt, floral skirt and bare legs. From there on out he'd been fighting a losing battle.

Violet was clearly off-limits. If she'd been interested she would have let him know months ago, after their kiss.

But clearly she wasn't.

And since he was obviously on the director's radar, the last thing he needed was to pay undue attention to another member of staff. Nothing like signing your own death warrant.

So why did watching Violet singing to a sick baby in the dark send a whole host of weird sensations creeping down his spine?

Was it the way she was looking at the baby? The way she seemed to want to soothe it? The gentle way she stroked the side of his face?

Or was it the fact she was so at ease, so comfortable in this strange environment? An environment in which he'd just spent the past few hours wondering how he could keep her safe?

He pressed back against the wall. The heat had dissipated a little now. Would it be cool enough to sleep?

Who was he kidding?

Sleep? With Violet Connelly and her sweet lullabies in the room next door?

Not a chance.

CHAPTER FOUR

"Do you feel up to this?"

The sun had barely risen above the horizon and breakfast was still settling in her stomach at this unearthly hour.

"Of course I am. It's why we're here, isn't it?" She didn't mean to sound tetchy but she couldn't help it.

Evan's eyebrows rose slightly and he handed her one of the GPS transmitters. He sighed. "I still can't believe we can get equipment like this to work out here and some families don't have access to running water. It seems almost absurd."

She nodded. "I know. I'm having trouble making sense of things here. I had another two children at the clinic yesterday affected by polio and their mothers still refused to get their younger siblings immunized. It didn't matter what I said to them."

Evan finished stowing the rest of the vaccines in the carriers. "They were from the village we're going to this morning?"

Violet nodded. "Olibasi claims most of the children in that village aren't immunized against polio. It's swept through the village twice already. Some of the older adults are virtually paralyzed, but they still won't immunize their children."

His hand came over and rested on her forearm. She tried to ignore the warm sensation that trickled up her arm. "Dr. Yusif left me some notes on that village. They were part of a previous testing trial for another drug for meningitis. Eleven of the children died and many others suffered injuries. Some are blind, some deaf, some kids have brain damage and some liver damage. Is it any wonder the villagers are suspicious? If you were a parent in that village, wouldn't you refuse any other drug offered by strangers?"

Violet felt a tightness spreading across her chest. He'd asked her how she'd feel if she were a parent.

He couldn't possibly know how those words went straight to her heart.

She would have done anything possible to save her child. No matter what that meant. Putting herself into the shoes of these villagers wasn't as difficult for her as Evan might think. Would she have allowed her daughter to be vaccinated by something that might have caused harm?

Absolutely not. Not question about it.

She could almost hear the fear from the villagers. Understand their protectiveness toward their children.

Evan was watching her closely. Waiting to see what her reaction would be.

"I think I would refuse anything that I thought would cause harm to my child." She turned her face away and started searching through her bags, anything to take her away from his close scrutiny. "Here, this is the pictorial flipbook that Olibasi has been using. It's got pictures and health information on health hygiene and sanitation on caring for a baby, as well as information on polio. Gentle persuasion might be the route we have to take, instead of going in with all guns blazing."

Evan smiled at her. The early-morning sun was sending warm orange tones sweeping across the pale earth surrounding them. Why did it make him seem almost… inviting? The midday heat had proved too oppressive for them to work in this last week, so they'd decided to make an early start the norm. But making an early start meant sharing beautiful sunrises with a totally unsuitable man.

Evan had been wrong six months ago and he was still wrong now.

She sucked in a little air. *One step at a time.*

She wasn't ready to consider a relationship of any sort right now—particularly with a man who'd had suspicions about her brother, no matter how good he looked at this time in the morning.

So why did she sometimes feel as if he was sensing the same electricity as she was? The same strange pull?

Was it all in her head? Was the pull just a figment of her imagination? Because in moments like this it felt very real.

His voice cut through her thoughts. "Olibasi is quite an ambassador, isn't she? I'm impressed."

She *was* imagining it. His train of thought was heading in an entirely different direction from hers.

Violet tried to keep the sadness from her tone. "She's fabulous. At another time, in another place she could probably have a whole different career. It's hard to believe she's only had four years of formal education—it's the same for most women her age. Most of what she's learned has been self-taught."

"Want to secretly train her to be a doctor or a nurse?"

Violet sighed. "I wish I could. I just think of the opportunities I had back home. All because I had a good education. It just seems so unfair that most young girls don't have much formal education." She gestured toward the book. "It's why this works so well. It's difficult to judge someone's level of literacy. And if someone can't read well there's no point in giving them leaflets."

Evan loaded their final supplies into the truck. "From what I've heard, radio is the most popular media in Nigeria. It's ideal for getting the message out to communities, particularly if people are less able to read."

"I've noticed it playing while we've been in the villages. It's like a constant backdrop. Aren't they doing the national campaign for polio via radio?"

He nodded and opened the front door of the truck. "Life expectancy around here is forty-seven years. Thirty percent below the world average. In the U.S. it's seventy-eight. Doesn't it make you feel as if there's a really good reason to be here? To do the work that we're doing?" His eyes looked off into the distance for a second then he jumped up into the truck. "Are you ready? We're picking Olibasi up *en route*."

For a second she was mesmerized by the look on his face. Slowly but surely this man was getting under her skin. It didn't matter what the history was with her brother. It didn't matter that they'd shared a kiss. Evan Hunter was essentially a good man. And it was something that she occasionally forgot in among all her mixed-up feelings about him. Maybe it was time to just focus on that?

He leaned over as she stood at the side of the truck and flicked the switch on her mobile emitter, which was attached to her waistband. The movement was so quick, so unexpected that his warm fingers touching her flesh made her jump.

"Oops, sorry." He pulled his hand back. "We need to keep these switched on. The software has been specially designed to track the daily progress of vaccinators, uploading their routes to the server. It generates maps showing which areas have been covered and highlighting areas of risk."

She slid into the truck next to him, trying to ignore the sensations creeping over her skin. "Like I said, I can't believe that GPS and smartphones work and the water supplies don't."

He started the engine and they set off down the gravel track. "Let's just try and do the best in the situation that we're in. We'll be there in around an hour."

He had his mirrored sunglasses on and a white shirt with the top few buttons unfastened. She could see several light brown hairs curling through the opening.

Nope. It wasn't helping. Even in profile he still looked like a movie star. This was going to be a long day.

The "good man" thoughts were being wiped out in her brain.

Work. She had to focus on work. "How did things go yesterday?"

"It was good. There was a volunteer community mobilizer network targeting caregivers who refused vaccination and children who'd been missed. It was a shame really, lots of kids had missed vaccinations just because they'd been in playgrounds, out in the fields or visiting friends the last time the team was there. They visited eighty households yesterday and immunized one hundred and ninety-three children. Essentially all these children need to be vaccinated four times to be fully protected."

"Wow." Violet leaned back against the burst upholstery. She gave Evan a sidelong smile. "Think we'll match that target today?"

"If only..." His voice sounded wistful. "I've got to just look at the big picture. They tell us if we can get at least one dose of vaccine into the kids who've not been vaccinated, it should give fifty percent of the recipients immunity to the three types of polio. That's got to be worth the trip." He pulled over at the side of the road to let Olibasi join them.

"Violet! You wore the clothes!" She smiled as she jumped in next to them.

Violet shifted in her seat and tugged at the bright pink loose clothing. The longer she was here, the more she realized how unsuitable her normal clothing was. All her white T-shirts were covered in dust, as were her khaki trousers and long skirts. She seemed to trail dust wherever she went. Water was a precious commodity and washing machines weren't exactly available.

Olibasi had arrived with a bag for her the other day containing some more traditional and practical clothing. *Buba* loose-style shirts and *iro* wrap-around skirts. She'd hinted that it might be useful if Violet tried some of the more traditional dress while they were visiting the village today. And even though she wasn't used to the bright colors, already she felt more comfortable.

But the loose clothing still hadn't stopped Evan from touching the bare skin at her waist when he'd flicked the switch on the transmitter. Maybe she should try wearing one of the NASA-style spacesuits they wore in the infectious disease labs at the DPA? It might be the only thing to stop the sensations currently zipping through her skin.

Evan leaned over and switched on the radio. "Relax, ladies. If the road ahead is clear, we'll be there in under an hour."

Evan was trying his best not to stare at Violet's new

clothes. Whilst they were much looser than the clothing she normally wore, the vibrant colors suited her and
brightened up her skin tone. In a way it was sexier than
her usual khaki trousers and white shirt approach—
even though it hid the curve of her hips and breasts.

His hands gripped the wheel tighter. *Where had that
come from?*

Why was it that every time he thought he'd managed
to shoehorn Violet back into the "colleague only" category, his brain liked to throw a wrench into the works?
It wasn't as if he didn't have enough work today. He
could spend every waking hour planning and organizing their schedules for vaccinations over the next three
months.

But every now and then, with one little random
glance at Violet, an errant thought would enter his head
and he would find that she was first and foremost in
his brain.

It was beyond frustrating. Nothing was happening
here.

Because Violet seemed oblivious. Sure, sometimes
she reacted to his touch but most of the time it didn't
seem in a good way.

Most of the time she was totally focused on her
work—just like he should be.

Except he couldn't. Not while he was around her.

He still couldn't get over Violet's connection to Sawyer. And it smarted that she'd kept it quiet. What other
secrets was Violet keeping?

The director had been wrong. They weren't learning
to work together as a team out here. They were learning to tiptoe around each other as if they were in some
skillful dance. Trying to avoid being alone together.
Trying to avoid an accidental brush of arms or legs.

Trying to avoid the fleeting eye contact that seemed to stop them both dead and make them oblivious to their surroundings.

So, no, nothing was happening here. Not at all.

Evan focused on the road ahead. Two months, three weeks. That's how much longer he had to last.

No time at all.

"Evan, are you okay in there?"

Violet rattled the wooden door to the makeshift toilet. They'd been working in the villages for hours, but on the way back the truck had got a flat. Evan had changed the bigger-than-average tire, but not before the jack had moved, causing the truck to split the skin on his forearm. "Can I do anything to help you?"

She opened the door just an inch, catching sight of his bare flesh and pulling back just a little. But her curiosity got the better of her. His dust-ridden white shirt lay in a heap on the floor, some blood staining the sleeve.

She edged her head back a little, running her eyes over his wide muscular back. Yup. If he was movie-star material in profile, he was definite movie-star material bare-chested. All defined muscle with not an ounce of fat. It automatically made her suck in her stomach. And made her skin tingle when she realized she'd actually shared a bed with this body.

Was Evan a surfer? Because that's what the defined tone and lines of his body told her. He had a curved scar on his shoulder blade. Flat and well healed. It had obviously been there for years. Where had he got that?

"Seen enough?" The grumpy voice made her jump and she felt her cheeks flush a little at being caught staring.

She straightened her shoulders. "I came to see if

I could give you a hand. Do you need stitches? Can I clean your wound for you?" He still hadn't turned around and she was feeling bolder. "Here, let me have a look."

He'd spent the past twenty minutes driving with a blood-soaked rag wrapped around his arm. There was no telling how much dust and grit must be in the wound, and she wanted to inspect it.

There was only a faint trickle of water at the sink. Preservation of water was a must in the village, with their only supply coming from a special tank. Violet screwed up her face when she caught sight of the wound. It was longer and deeper than she'd expected. She caught his wrist in her hands as she leaned forward, trying to ignore the fact his bare chest was only inches away from her. Trying to stop herself from looking.

"I'm sure there's some iodine in the store. I'll go and get some."

He tutted. "Don't fuss, Violet."

She peered at the wound, which was still dotted with little specks of grit. "If I stitch it like this you'll end up with an infection."

"You won't need to stitch it."

"Excuse me?" She lifted her head and raised her eyebrows at him. "I'm the doctor and you're the patient. And just so we're clear—I'll be stitching your wound."

"Oh, it's like that, is it?" There was something different. A different inflection in his voice, a different tone. More humor. A little teasing even.

Her eyes met his.

She and Evan Hunter. Bare-chested in a confined environment. She could see every light brown curly hair on his wide chest. She could see the flecks in his blue eyes again—she was *that* close.

It was tempting. It was *so* tempting.

Her brain spun back to six months before and the feel of his hands on her skin, his lips on her neck. The way that she'd felt that night when she'd finally let go—even if it had just been for a few seconds. She felt herself flush again.

He blinked, but his eyes didn't move. They were still there. Still staring right at her. All she could hear right now was the sound of his breathing. She could see the rise and fall of his chest in her peripheral vision.

But she couldn't pull her eyes away from his.

This really was too close for comfort.

Something was happening. Something was happening right before his eyes. Violet seemed to stop in her tracks. Her pupils had dilated and her cheeks flushed. The air around them seemed to close in.

She couldn't be thinking the same things that he was, surely? Violet didn't think about him like that, did she? Not since that night when she'd had a few glasses of wine.

What was the story with Violet Connelly?

There didn't seem to be a man in her life. In fact, in the three years she'd been at the DPA he couldn't remember ever hearing Violet refer to a boyfriend or partner.

From his casual enquiries he knew she lived alone.

But why? Why was a knockout like Violet unattached?

She might be prickly around him, but she was warm and gregarious around others. She was well liked. He couldn't imagine she was short of offers, so why didn't she pursue them?

Because right now, in this confined environment, he was looking for an excuse not to act.

In fact, he *needed* an excuse not to act.

It would be so, so easy to lean forward and kiss those plump lips. In fact, he'd been waiting to do it for six months. Six long, long months.

But there had never been a sign, never been even a flicker from Violet. And yet here she was standing in front of him, her pale green eyes almost obliterated by those dilated pupils and her tongue running along her lips. It was enough to drive a man crazy.

Sawyer's sister.

Did he care? Did he really care? His animosity toward Sawyer had burned away at him for years. But Violet affected him in a totally different way. Besides, right now he couldn't think straight. Not when she was biting her lip like that. He took a tiny step forward. His body was starting to react an entirely male way.

She was going to report you for inappropriate behavior. She almost did report you to the director.

What if he was reading this all wrong?

There, that did it.

It stopped him in his tracks. If he kissed her now, what would the consequences be? Would he be accused of seducing her? Of taking advantage of a member of staff? That would be unthinkable.

He stepped back, putting some distance between them.

Violet started. Her eyes widened then she lowered her head.

She *had* expected him to act. She had expected him to kiss her. There was no misreading the confused expression on her face.

"I'll go and get the iodine," she mumbled as she headed out the door.

He shifted uncomfortably. While his body might think he was having a totally normal reaction, his head was telling him differently. Thank goodness she hadn't noticed. It made him feel like some horny teenage boy.

He pulled open the door of the room. Violet and himself in a confined space would have to be avoided at all costs. Not when it caused reactions like this.

She appeared a few seconds later carrying the iodine, some lidocaine and a sterile suturing kit. The flush was gone from her cheeks and her demeanor was entirely professional. "It would probably be best if you sat down while I stitched your arm."

The words sounded a little strained, and definitely formal.

He nodded and sat down at one of the tables while she opened the kit and cleaned his arm, removing all the little pieces of grit before she injected him with some lidocaine to numb the wound. Eleven deftly placed stitches later she placed a non-adhesive dressing over the wound. "Let me know if you have any signs of infection."

She gathered up the waste and disposed of it. "Need anything else?" The question was an entirely innocent one, but it instantly conjured things up in his mind.

This would have to stop, he couldn't continue like this.

She was frozen on her way to the door, looking at him again. Was she thinking about his possible answers to the question?

"Violet? Are you there?"

Their heads turned as one of the other team members appeared in the doorway.

"Yes, I'm here. What is it?"

"There's a call on the satellite phone for you. I think it's your brother."

There. That would do it.

Nothing like slicing the tension in the air with a knife. Nothing like turning the sizzle of electricity into a damp squib.

He could see her bristle. Obviously anticipating his reaction.

She looked a little surprised.

"That's great, thanks. I'll be right there."

Then she walked out the room without a second glance.

CHAPTER FIVE

"WHAT ARE YOU doing in Nigeria, Violet? And when were you planning on telling me?"

Violet sighed and sat down in the nearest seat. This time two weeks ago she would have sold her soul to hear her brother's voice. But right now, when her brain was mush and her body was reacting to things she couldn't seem to control, it really was the last thing she needed.

What had just happened between her and Evan?

"Get off my back. I'd applied for a transfer and the director granted it. We needed to leave at short notice because there were problems in the team. And how was I supposed to get in touch? You were still in the middle of the monkeypox fiasco." She paused, then added, "It's not like keeping in touch has been your priority in the past few years." It was a cheap blow, but she was hoping he'd missed her *faux pas*.

"We? Who is we?" Nope. He'd picked up on it straight away.

She could almost hear the drum roll. "Evan Hunter got transferred too. He's in Nigeria with me." She moved the satellite phone away from her ear. But it didn't matter, the noise reverberated around the room. She'd expected expletives, what she got was deep, hearty laughter.

"Matt? What are you laughing about? Why do you find it funny?"

"I can't believe for a minute he'd request to go to Nigeria! Evan—Mr. Keep-everything-in-order Hunter. He'll hate the chaos out there."

She felt her hackles rise. "He's actually doing okay. The polio program needed a team leader and the director thought Evan might benefit from a change."

"And how would you know this?"

His retort was immediate. And she knew she'd slipped up. There was no way she should know that—no way she should have heard the director telling Evan that. She tried to turn the conversation around. "How did you find out I was here, anyway?"

"The director. He's been speaking to me every day. Trying to persuade me that there is a role for me at the DPA. But I'm still undecided."

"Really?" It was first good news she'd heard. Sawyer had been so set against the DPA when his wife had died. But the past few weeks' experience had obviously changed his perspective. Things must be changing for him. She smiled. "Is someone helping you make this decision? A certain blonde someone?"

"Sis..." He sighed. "Give it up."

"What's happening with you and Callie? Are you seeing her? Remember, I warned you. I like Callie a lot." She felt her stomach clench a little. Her brother had been distraught when his wife had died on a mission with him and Evan. After six years, meeting Callie had finally put a little joy into his voice again. She really didn't want him to screw this up.

"Callie is good. No, scratch that. Callie is *great*." She could almost see the grin on his face, "We're going to take things slowly, but I like that. I like *her*."

"Should I buy my wedding hat?"

He hesitated and her heart leaped. *Matt, really, thinking about that again?* "I'm taking it slowly—remember? But maybe you'll need one in the future." He changed the subject quickly. "How are you getting on with Evan? Is he treating you okay?"

How did she answer that? That he was keeping her mind from the job and could potentially lead her astray? That she felt as if her skin was on fire every time he brushed against her? That she could have almost put money on the fact he'd been about to kiss her and then he'd stopped? That she didn't feel ready for any of this?

"He's a good team leader," she said quietly.

"What? Tell me you didn't just say that?"

She straightened in her chair. What did he mean? Did he still hold a grudge because Evan had been team leader when his wife had died? Was there always going to be this animosity between them?

"Listen, Sawyer, I know you probably don't rate him. And I wasn't there all those years ago, so I don't know what happened between you. But Evan seems to be a good team leader. He's diligent. He's professional. He's organized."

"Whoa, sis, stop right there. You sound like you're giving me a reference for a business partner, not telling me how the person you've traveled with to the other side of the world is treating you."

"Oh." She pressed her lips together to stop herself from putting her foot in it any further.

But Sawyer hadn't finished. "I know we've never spoken about this, but I want to make sure he's treating you okay. Evan and I—there isn't a lot of love lost between us. My wife died—I was upset. My behavior could have been better. A lot has gone down between us in the past and none of it has ever really been resolved. I'm not sure what his take is on everything, but I don't really care. What I care about is my sister. Are you okay, sis?"

She held her tongue. How long had she waited to hear those words? What wouldn't she have given to hear those words three years ago, when she'd felt all alone in the world with a baby to bury?

She blinked back the tears. Thank goodness Sawyer wasn't here, looking into her eyes. He would know straight away that she was hiding something. And she couldn't have that conversation with him yet. Maybe never.

Things had been so bad back then. Her mom and stepdad and been devastated when Matt's wife had died from an ectopic pregnancy. Their daughter-in-law and potential grandchild wiped out in one fell swoop. Not to mention a son who had then shut himself off from the world and disappeared. They hadn't coped. They hadn't coped at all.

So when she herself had fallen pregnant unexpectedly, she had felt as if she couldn't tell them. They would have worried themselves sick. Particularly when they found out she'd chosen to go it alone. Her relationship with Blane had been serious but they had both been so focused on their careers, his in business and hers in medicine, that a baby had never been part of that equation. It had been no surprise when he'd walked away.

So she'd decided to wait. To wait until she had a brand-new granddaughter to present to them. They might be a little shocked, but the arrival of a new grandchild would overcome all of that.

They would have been delighted.

If only it had all worked out that way.

Instead, she'd been left alone with only a few close friends for comfort. She couldn't tell them—no matter how much she needed them. It would have broken their hearts all over again. They were frail enough as it was.

And now she was here. Three years on. Trying to move on with her life.

First steps. She was still taking the first steps.

"I'm fine, Sawyer. I'll keep in touch, okay?" There was so much they probably had to say to each other, but now just wasn't the time. She hung up the phone quickly before he had a chance to say anything else.

It only took her a few moments to get outside. Tears were threatening to spill down her cheeks. She had to get a hold of herself. It was time to move on.

Across on the other side of the village she could see a small gathering of people. Maybe some new arrivals? There seemed to be a few new families in the village every day. She picked up one of the flipbooks about the vaccine.

It was time to get back to work. And there was no time like the present.

"Evan, can you come and look at a child for me, please?"

He pulled himself away from the computer-generated program that was running, plotting where they still needed to vaccinate.

"Sure. What's up?" He stood up from the chair and cricked his back. He'd been sitting too long and was getting stiff. It was time to do some leg work.

"One of the children we vaccinated yesterday isn't looking too well. Can you come and see him?"

He nodded and grabbed his stethoscope and small bag. The mother was in one of the rooms with Olibasi, the small child clutched in her arms. Tears were streaming down her face and she was talking frantically.

Evan walked over quickly and held his hands out for the baby. "What's wrong, Olibasi?"

Olibasi hesitated, her face serious. "This is Nkoyo. I'll need to translate as she doesn't speak any English. She says her son has become unwell since receiving his first vaccine yesterday. She thinks it's given him polio."

Evan raised his head quickly. "How old is her son?"

The little boy in his lap was obviously underweight and underdeveloped. Vaccine-associated paralytic polio was rare, but the risk in immuno-deficient children was around seven thousand times higher. A major concern about the oral polio vaccine was its known ability to revert to a form that could cause neurological infection and paralysis—but not this quickly.

"He's one year."

Evan took in a sharp breath. The baby looked around seven months and didn't appear to be meeting his developmental milestones. He couldn't sit or grasp with his hands. His temperature was low and his abdomen distended. His skin was dry and peeling and his hair thin and discolored. His arms and legs were extremely thin. His head was rolling from side to side and he was limp in Evan's arms.

He quickly sounded the child's chest. "Check with his mum—he was okay yesterday? He didn't feel cold? His belly wasn't distended like this?"

His brain was working frantically. Whatever was wrong with this child was serious. Olibasi was talking in a low voice to the mother. She was shaking her head.

"I think he's been unwell for a longer than a day. His abdomen has been distended for a while and he's had chronic diarrhea. He hasn't been eating."

Evan took a deep breath. "Has his mother stopped breastfeeding him recently?"

Olibasi turned back to the mother. "Yes, she has. The family don't have much food. She says she wasn't producing enough milk."

"Who gave the baby the vaccine?"

"One of the community mobilizers."

"And they're not from this village? Have you ever seen this baby before?"

Olibasi shook her head. "They're from an outlying village. This is the first time they've come here."

Evan ran his finger over the child's skin again. He was sure he knew what was wrong. But how he explained it to the mother would be most important. The last thing he wanted to do was make her feel responsible.

He cleared his throat. "Tell her it's definitely not the vaccine. It couldn't cause effects like this so quickly. Vaccine-associated paralytic polio is very rare—about one case per seven hundred and fifty thousand vaccine recipients. And it's more likely to occur in adults than in children."

Olibasi took a few moments to translate to the mother. "She wants to know what's wrong with her son."

Evan gave her his best reassuring smile and tried to tread carefully. "I think her son is suffering from a type of protein-energy malnutrition called kwashiorkor. It develops in babies who've been weaned from breast milk and who often suffer from other conditions like chronic diarrhea. It causes stunted growth and wasting of muscle and tissue." He reached over and put his hand on Olibasi's arm. "Be careful how you translate. This condition hasn't appeared overnight. Do you think the vaccine gave her an excuse to bring her baby to the village?"

Olibasi's eyes darkened and she gave just the slightest nod of her head. "Give me a few moments to speak with her."

Evan kept the little boy in his arms and went to the supply closet. This was the first real case of malnutrition he'd seen since he'd got here. And it was heartbreaking. Back home this child would have bloods taken and be admitted to hospital and given intravenous fluids or tube-fed if required. But out here the options were distinctly limited.

He found some first-line electrolyte solutions and some supplements. It felt inadequate but was the best he could do. "Ask her if she's willing to stay in the village for a few days. Tell her it's really important." There was a real chance that the little boy would be left with an inability to absorb nutrients properly through his intestines, so it was essential that they monitor him in some way.

Olibasi took the sachets from his hands. "I'll do my best to persuade her. I'm sure I can find somewhere for them to sleep. Do you want to see him again?"

Evan nodded. "Every day for the next few days. We need to see if he starts to improve." He handed the little boy back to his mother.

Olibasi slid her arm around the woman's shoulder and led her outside. Evan picked up a file and started to scribble some notes. It didn't matter that they were there to administer the polio vaccine. It didn't matter that they really shouldn't get involved in all the general medical problems of the villagers.

What mattered most was building rapport with these people. Building an element of trust. There was enough miscommunication about the polio vaccine already. How else could a woman in an outlying village know about vaccine-associated polio paralysis?

It was the age-old problem. Nothing spread quicker than a bad news story.

If word had got out that the polio vaccination had caused that child's illness it would be a disaster. It didn't matter that it had nothing to do with it. It was what the villagers believed that mattered. And Evan could only do his best to try and contain the situation and get the little boy on the road to recovery.

"You did good."

He jumped. Violet was standing in the doorway, her figure silhouetted against the ebbing sun.

He stood up and walked over to her. "You were listening?"

She gave him a little smile. "I was coming to see you. When I saw you were consulting with a patient I decided to wait. It was nice getting to see you play doctor."

He folded his arms and leaned against the doorjamb. "Play doctor. That's what it feels like." His eyes fixed out on the setting sun in front of them. "I understand why we're here—I really do. And I understand the rationale about not getting caught up in other issues. Not to lose sight of our task." He flung up his hands in exasperation.

"But how can we realistically do that? The polio work has to come hand in hand with the welfare of these people. I can't ignore malnutrition—even if I don't have the right tools to prevent it. I can't ignore malaria—even if I have to beg another agency for mosquito nets. And I can't ignore the sanitation problems. Because they are connected to everything else." He shook his head. "But

I feel like there will never be enough supplies or equipment to do the job we really need to do."

He looked down at Violet. She was watching him carefully and he knew instantly that she understood. She understood his frustration about all the things that were outside their control. She understood that he was going to spend the rest of the night worrying about that little boy and whether he would make it through till morning.

And he didn't need to say any more. Because Violet just moved. And it happened naturally.

She shifted her feet and leaned against him, making it seem like the most natural thing in the world to rest his arm around her shoulder.

She rested her head against his chest. Could she hear the beating of his heart?

Her voice was quiet. "The things we can't control will always be the hardest. Particularly when we can't even understand some of them."

There was something else. Something he hadn't heard before.

For the first time he felt as if he'd picked away at one of Violet's unending layers. She wasn't just talking about here and their situation. Yes, it was part of it, but she was also talking about something else.

It was so calm, so peaceful right now. And he didn't want to destroy this. He didn't want to destroy this moment. It would be so easy to ask her if something was bothering her. It would be so easy to pry. But he didn't want to take a chisel and chip away at her layers. He didn't want to back her into a corner. He had to let her unpeel her layers herself.

Maybe he'd never reach the center of Violet Connelly. But it might be nice to wait around and see.

He chose his words carefully. "Maybe we're not

meant to understand everything, Violet. Maybe we're not here to change the world. Maybe we're just meant to learn how to live through it."

She gave a quiet murmur and lifted her hand and placed it on his chest.

And the two of them stood, watching the sun set over the wide landscape in front of them.

CHAPTER SIX

THE MEETING ROOM was crowded. Evan's meticulous planning for the polio campaign was going well. The huge map on the wall and the corresponding graph with the number of vaccines delivered was impressive by anybody's standards.

But it wasn't good enough for Evan. And Violet wasn't surprised.

He clapped his hands together to draw the chattering crowd to attention. "Thanks for coming, everyone. I wanted to look at a few ways we can improve the total uptake of the polio vaccine and give added protection to the people of Natumba."

He pointed to a certain area on the map on the wall. "There are a few villages where there is a high rate of refusal." He nodded to one of the community volunteers. "I've arranged a series of meetings between the volunteers, ourselves and some of the village elders. We need to work in partnership with these people if we want to make any lasting improvements."

Violet heard the mutterings around her. Lots of attempts had been made in the past to try and increase the uptake of polio in these villages but Evan's persistence might pay off. He'd spent time in these villages in the past few weeks, taking time to get to know the elders and some of the health issues facing the inhabitants. He was slowly but surely gaining their trust and that had to help.

He pointed to another area on the map. "We still haven't made much headway mapping the Fulani nomadic routes. Most of the Fulani people haven't been vaccinated and they have a high rate of individuals affected by polio. It's always difficult to try and target a group of people who are constantly on the move. But we've had some news that they are about to arrive in our local area and we want to be ready."

He nodded to one of the Healthy World Federation members of staff in the room. "Dr. Brasi will be leading the team this week that will be attempting to make contact with the Fulani people and vaccinate them."

Violet smiled. It all made sense. Evan was being methodical and consistent in his approaches. The number of people vaccinated was rising every day. Surely they would meet the targets they had been given?

"And finally..." He paused, his eyes meeting Violet's for a second. She felt her heart flutter a little. They hadn't been alone together since that night when they'd watched the sunset. Once the sky had darkened he'd given her hand a little squeeze and walked her to her room.

Her heart had sunk a little when she'd realized he wasn't going to attempt to kiss her. Then she'd lain awake wondering why she wanted him to kiss her. Nothing made sense to her anymore. Her head kept telling her she wasn't ready for any of that kind of thing, but her body was reacting differently.

He gave her a little smile. "One of the areas we need to improve on is new births. Newborns need to be tracked and immunized through the midwife service scheme, with oral polio vaccine being placed in delivery rooms to ensure administration of a dose at birth. We need to strengthen links with traditional birth attendants and traditional leaders." He paused for a moment. "And I'm going to ask Dr. Connelly to lead on this."

What?

Her smile froze in place. Why hadn't he talked to her about this beforehand? He gave her a little nod and continued talking, totally unaware of what he'd just unleashed.

Violet couldn't move. Her brain was mush. Her heartbeat was quickening in her chest—and not in a good way. She felt sick.

He had no idea. He had no idea at all at what he was asking of her.

But, then, how could he? Because she hadn't told him what had happened to her. He couldn't possibly know that the last time she'd been in a delivery room had been the worst day of her life.

The day she had welcomed her daughter into the world and then bid her farewell.

How on earth could she cope with being in that environment every day?

She took a deep breath.

She was a doctor. This was her job. She had wanted to come here—she wanted to move on.

It had been three years, and a birthing room here would be nothing like a delivery room back home. How could it evoke the same memories and experiences?

All she was being asked to do was set up links with local midwives and birth attendants. She wasn't being asked to *be* in the delivery rooms.

But that thought didn't stop her thudding heart. She wasn't stupid. She'd done her research before she'd arrived in Nigeria.

The stillbirth rate in Nigeria was one of the highest in the world, with half occurring while the woman was in labor. It was inevitable that she would come across one at some point in the three months that she was here.

Evan was still talking. And people were listening. He was captivating his audience with his enthusiasm and passion for the tasks ahead. Heads were nodding all around them and people were shouting out suggestions and ideas.

Would she be able to face the challenges ahead with the same enthusiasm and passion?

Her eyes fixed on her hands. It was easier than looking at Evan. Most of her nails were broken and her skin was starting to tan lightly in spite of the sunblock she was constantly applying. Back home she'd had her nails manicured every month. But the truth was she didn't even miss it.

While the lifestyle out here was tough—no hot running showers, no wide array of facilities, no hair salons, no easy transport—the experience she was gaining was far outweighing the negatives. Even working with Evan wasn't as bad as she'd feared.

Why had she wanted to get away from him so badly? Was it really because of the issues with her brother? Or was it the fact that she didn't want to face up to how she felt about him?

Whatever it was, she didn't have brain space for it right now. Getting through the work with the midwives would be a tough enough challenge.

And one that would take up all her emotional energy and spirit.

He'd noticed it. Even though she didn't realize.

But, then, he noticed everything about her.

That fleeting moment, that wave of fear that had seemed to pass over her eyes.

What did it mean? Or had he just imagined it?

He couldn't trust anything he felt around Violet Connelly. His instincts seemed to be completely wrong around her. She messed with his mind. Ten minutes in Violet's company and all rational thought went out the window.

He'd thought she'd be happy that he'd assigned her a specific task she could get her teeth into. Something she could lead and tackle on her own. Giving her the midwifery role had seemed to make sense.

He'd been watching her. She was wonderful around babies and children. She seemed to come into her own. She excelled at dealing with them. This job should have been perfect for her.

So why the fear in her eyes?

But something else was bothering him. Something else was eating at his stomach.

Was that really the reason he'd given her this task?

Or had he just wanted to avoid it himself?

Evan had no reason to avoid children or babies. But he did have a reason to avoid pregnant women.

Helen. Sawyer's wife.

She'd died of an ectopic pregnancy. No one had known she was pregnant. Not Sawyer, and apparently not Helen.

And seeing pregnant women immediately brought Helen to mind.

It hadn't been as though she'd looked pregnant—not as if a glance at a pregnant woman reminded him directly of Helen.

No, it just reminded him of what *should* have been Helen.

And that's what made him sick to his stomach.

He'd spent the past few years thinking that Sawyer must have known his wife was pregnant. They both must have known and kept it secret, otherwise Helen would never have been allowed to go on the mission in the first place.

But that was an excuse. And it was a poor excuse.

It was so easy to push the blame onto Sawyer and not to take any responsibility himself. But he had been the team leader. He had been the one responsible for the health and wellbeing of everyone in his team. And Helen had told him she wasn't feeling one hundred percent.

It had been a fleeting comment. An unremarkable conversation. And if Evan hadn't been so caught up in the details of the mission he might have stopped for a minute to consider what she'd said.

He could have asked her a few questions about what was wrong, and to specify exactly how she was feeling. And he knew, deep down, that at some point there was a tiny chance he might have asked her if there was a possibility she was pregnant.

And even though Helen hadn't known herself, it might have given her pause to stop and think and consider the possibility. It might have made her stop for a second and do a pregnancy test.

Bottom line. It might have saved her life.

The ectopic pregnancy had been a horrible inevitability for Helen. But where it occurred wasn't.

If she'd been in Atlanta when she'd had the symptoms, she would have gone to the nearest hospital and undergone surgery. And lived.

But none of that had happened. And the sight of Helen lying in her husband's arms, with the life slow-ing but surely seeping out of her, had haunted Evan for the past six years.

He had been the team leader. Helen had been his responsibility.

He'd never shared this with anyone. And he never would. Least of all with a member of Sawyer's family.

He watched as the team assembled around him, Violet among them, talking quietly with some of the voluntary workers.

Another team he was responsible for. Another team whose lives were in his hands.

He could do this. He could. He just had to focus and keep his mind on the job.

He had to keep his eyes and ears open to the health and wellbeing of his team. Which meant he had to get to the bottom of what was wrong with Violet. She was his responsibility—whether she liked it or not. And he couldn't ignore the fact that something could be going on with her. He wouldn't be able to live with himself if he missed something in a team member again.

He watched for a few seconds. Violet was fidgeting with her flower-covered notebook, picking away at the edges as she spoke to someone. Every few moments she would bite her lip. She put her notebook down and her fingers went automatically first to her ear then to a strand of hair that she wound round and round one of her fingers.

The person she was talking to seemed oblivious to Violet's nerves. They were talking quickly, gesturing with their hands, only taking notice of her occasional nods.

Was that how he'd been with Helen? So wrapped up in other things that he hadn't looked at what had been right in front of him, or listened to her words?

It made him feel sick to his stomach.

Violet looked over and for a second those pale green eyes met his. Every muscle in his body tightened but she instantly averted her gaze, reluctant to let him read anything at all.

It only made him more determined.

He couldn't decide if he'd given her the midwifery role because he wanted to avoid it himself or whether he'd given it to her to show how much he valued her as a part of the team. But that was irrelevant.

What was important was what happened next. What *he* did next.

And that was the one thing that he could control.

CHAPTER SEVEN

EVAN WAS IN a good place. They'd immunized over one hundred people today, the majority of them children.

It was a good outcome for the team, giving them the boost that they'd needed. The past few days had been tough on them. Several visits to villages had been unproductive, with hours spent going from house to house, even though most people were still refusing to be vaccinated. It was heartbreaking. All around them there were signs of the destructiveness of polio and its lasting effects. Some elderly villagers, struggling for every breath, their chest muscles virtually paralyzed by polio. The first sign of an infection would wipe them out.

Children of various ages with one weak, wasted limb affecting their mobility—and parents still wouldn't immunize their other children.

It didn't help that the one thing he'd dreaded had finally happened. One of the few families that had been vaccinated had actually given vaccine-associated paralytic polio to one of their distant adult cousins. It was a rare complication, usually caused by an adult changing the nappy of a recently vaccinated child and picking up the disease due to poor hand washing. But it was a blow the team didn't need.

Evan felt as if he were banging his head on a brick wall. Things had to be better than this.

And now they were here. This village had welcomed them with open arms. People had queued for hours to be vaccinated, bringing family members of all ages. And the community workers had come back with a list of houses to visit where people were unable to come to the clinic but still wanted to be vaccinated.

It didn't matter that it was more time-consuming and difficult. Evan didn't care. He would happily walk around every home in the village individually if that's what it took to get everyone vaccinated.

Time was marching on. It had been a long day— they'd been here nearly ten hours and they still had an hour's drive back home.

He approached one of the final houses, a lightweight structure made of a mixture of wood, bricks and mud. Jaja, his community worker, gave him a smile as they approached the house. "This lady has four children she wants vaccinated. She would have come to the clinic but one of her sons, Dumkata, has been very sick these past few days."

Jaja pushed opened the door to the house and engaged in a long conversation with the mother, who seemed more than happy to see them.

But Evan's eyes were drawn to the corner of the room, where a small boy was lying on a makeshift bed. His siblings were playing around him and he seemed oblivious to the noise in the room. Evan's instincts were automatic and he went to the bed of the sickly child.

"Hi, there, Dumkata."

The dark eyes flickered open at the sound of the foreign voice. The little boy's hands automatically started scratching at his skin, as if he had an uncontrollable itch. It was almost as if Evan's voice had broken him out of the half-slumber he'd been in.

Evan turned to face Jaja. "Can you ask the mother if she minds if I take a look at her son?"

Jaja answered quickly. "She was just asking me the same thing. She knows you're only here to give the vaccinations and didn't want to take up your time."

"It's no problem. I'm happy to look at him. Can you organize the polio vaccination for the rest of the family, Jaja?"

The community worker nodded and pulled out the vaccine carrier and flip book to explain things to the family.

Evan touched Dumkata's forehead. It was just as he'd expected. Burning hot. He pulled his medical bag over and took out the tympanic thermometer. It beeped within a few seconds. It indicated that the boy had a temperature.

He pulled out his stethoscope to sound the little boy's chest. Dumkata barely responded, he still seemed fixated on the itch in his skin. "Can you ask the mother what he's been complaining of?"

Jaja took a few moments to reply. "She says he's had a terrible headache for the past few days and his joints are painful and sore. Dumkata is usually running about constantly. She says this is not like him."

Evan nodded and gestured to Jaja. "Could you help me sit him up for a moment, please?"

Something was setting off alarm bells in Evan's head. He had the strangest feeling, and experience told him to go with his instincts.

He spent some time examining Dumkata's skin. There were a few angry marks—just like bee stings— along with a rash that was difficult to see on Dumkata's dark skin and some swelling in the subcutaneous tissues.

He pressed his fingers gently around Dumkata's neck and groin, checking the lymph glands and finding them enlarged. It was clear that some type of infection was circulating around the child's body.

"Can you go and find Violet for me, please? I'd like to have a chat with her."

Jaja nodded and slipped out of the door. Violet had been working in the village today too but their paths had barely crossed. They'd mapped out the village and decided on separate routes to try and cover the majority of people who had requested to be seen. It made more sense for them to split up than work together.

It also prevented any awkward conversations or, more likely, awkward silences.

It was almost as if she was deliberately avoiding him. She'd never complained about working with the midwives and birth attendants. She'd just put her head down and got on with the job.

But he hadn't forgotten the look in her eyes. Or the way she'd realized that he'd noticed. At some point they were going to have to have that conversation. If he'd learned anything these past few years it was he needed to be sure about the welfare of his team.

The little form moved on the bed in front of him. He tried to focus on the matter at hand. The niggling feeling he had in his gut about this little boy.

Violet appeared in the doorway. "Evan? You were looking for me?"

Pretty as a picture—even after ten hours on the job. She was wearing another of Olibasi's outfits, this time in pale pink instead of the brighter colours. Her blond hair was swept up in a clip and her normally pale skin was starting to tan slightly.

Olibasi had been right about the effect of wearing local clothes. Violet seemed to be widely accepted wherever they went. Some reports on previous villages had been a little alarming. But in the past few weeks Violet seemed to be getting good results. The uptake of the polio vaccine was rising in places where it had previously stalled.

It didn't make sense that it was all down to the type of clothes that the doctor wore. Violet's quiet, easy nature and never-ending patience was obviously a major factor. But the fact she wore the clothes so well wouldn't exactly be a hindrance. He tried to keep the smile from his face.

"Thanks, Violet. I know we're just about to finish up but I wondered if you'd mind brainstorming with me for a minute."

She looked a little surprised but took it in her stride. "No problem." She crossed the room and kneeled down next to him at the side of the bed. "Who do we have here?"

"This is Dumkata—he's seven. According to his mom he's usually the life and soul of the party, but he's been unwell these past few days. He has a temperature, a headache, sore joints with some noticeable swelling, some bites and swollen lymph glands." He caught Dumkata's hand as it started to scratch again. "He also seems to have an irritating itch."

Violet nodded. "Well, it could be whole host of things with those symptoms. What's worrying you most?"

Evan scratched his chin. "Probably the bites." He turned to face her. "Probably my gut instinct." He shook his head. "I'm just not happy."

She nodded. "Then let's be methodical about this. Is anything springing to mind?"

She bent over Dumkata and started examining his skin. The rash was difficult to determine but was widespread across his skin. It appeared mainly to be speading out from the two bite marks on his skin. "Does the mom know what caused these bites? Is there something in particular we should be considering?"

Evan wrinkled his nose. "Probably. It's frustrating. Back home we've got everything to hand. Out here it's much more difficult."

Violet gave him a little smile. She understood completely. Back at the DPA they had a computer program for everything. Every tiny sign or symptom all calculated and computed to tell you any possibilities and what to look for next. She pulled a tiny pocketbook from under her traditional skirt. "Want a look at this?"

It was a copy of a tropical disease handbook—ten years old and obviously well worn. She'd had it since she'd been a student and had hardly looked at it in recent years. But it had been a last-minute addition to her suitcase.

As Evan turned the pages, one fell out in his hands. "Sorry," she muttered. "I'm sure I've got some sticky tape somewhere."

Jaja walked over to them. "The mother has no idea what the bites are. Her son was playing out near the fields a few days ago. He came home with the bites. She hasn't seen them before and Dumkata just said they were bee stings."

Evan's head shot up. It was almost as if a little light had just gone on in his head. He started muttering and flicking through Violet's book, "Fields...flies..." His eyes met hers.

"What about tsetse flies? What about the first signs of sleeping sickness?"

"Really? I thought that had almost disappeared?"

Evan pulled out his PDA and looked up some files. He frowned. "Only two cases reported in Nigeria last year. Could it really be something like that?"

Violet shook her head. "You'll have to remind me about it. I can't remember that much."

His eyes scanned between the screen and the book he held in his hands. "African trypanosomiasis is a vector-borne parasitic disease, known as sleeping sickness. The parasites are transmitted to humans by the bite of the tsetse fly. Most common in areas of fishing, animal husbandry or—" he lifted his eyes to meet hers "—agriculture."

"What do the flies look like?"

He shook his head. "There aren't any pictures. It just says they are about the same size as bees and quite aggressive."

Violet looked over at the mother. Jaja was doing his best to relay their conversation to her and the distress on her face was visible. She rushed over and put her arm around her child.

"Help my baby."

Violet could feel her stomach muscles clench at her reaction. The instant fear that something could happen to her child—something completely out of her control.

She took a slow breath. "We need to stay focused. Does it list the signs and symptoms?" She lowered her voice slightly. "How serious is it? Do we have anything to treat it?"

Evan's eyes were still flickering back and forth between the book and the screen. "The signs and symptoms are compatible with the first stage. The temperature, itching, joint pains and headaches. They are all signs that the trypanosomes are multiplying in the subcutaneous tissues. It's called the haemolymphatic phase."

Violet could almost feel her own skin start to itch at the thought of parasites circulating around the little boy's body. It was horrible.

She tried to pull her doctor's head back into focus. She was finding it so hard not to look at Dumkata's mother and see the pain and fear in her eyes. Even though this was an entirely different situation from her own she wanted to reach out and tell her that she understood. That she knew the fear of the unknown, the protectiveness she was feeling and the helplessness at things being out of her control.

"How do we diagnose this?"

"We need to take a blood test. It used to be really difficult to diagnose because the number of parasites in the blood can be low and they need to be separated from the red blood cells." He pointed to something on the screen. "There's a pan-African campaign on the eradication of trypanosomosis. Let me see if can get some more details." He pulled out his satellite phone and pressed in a number as he headed toward the doorway. "Give me a few minutes."

Violet nodded as she watched him leave. "Jaja, can you come and sit with us? I'd like you to translate for me, please."

Violet's eyes flickered over the screen as she picked up some more details. She finally had the courage to meet Dumkata's mother's eyes. "Tell her we need to make a diagnosis and Dr. Hunter is just finding out the best way to do that." She watched as Jaja rapidly translated. "Tell her we think that if it is sleeping sickness, then it's been caught at an early stage—a stage that can be treated."

Within a few seconds she could see the relief as the woman relaxed her shoulders and shot some rapid questions at Jaja. He gave her a few answers, obviously trying to reassure her, then turned back to Violet. "She wants to know how long it takes and what the treatment is."

Violet nodded. It's the kind of thing she'd want to know too. Evan appeared back in the doorway. He gave her a wide smile—obviously good news. His broad shoulders filled the door way and the tired look that had haunted him for the past few days had disappeared.

The African sun was agreeing with him. His skin had already been a light golden-brown that was deepening with every day. It only succeeded in making his teeth look whiter than ever and his blue eyes more prominent. His brown hair was lightening in the sun, giving the ends blond tips. She couldn't have achieved that look even if she'd spent ten hours in the hair salon. Her hair was becoming more brittle day by day. The leave-in conditioner she was using every other day in an attempt to waylay the damage made her hair feel slimy. Hardly a good look, by anybody's standards. Why did men have things so much easier?

She was still struggling with the task he'd given her last week. Not that she wanted anyone to know that.

By anyone else's standards she was doing fine. She'd reached out to the midwives in the neighboring villages and arranged to spend time with them all.

But a few had made it clear she'd need to see them on their own terms. Which was likely to mean in the middle of someone's home or the local birthing room.

All things that made her bristle with nerves and won-der if she could manage this.

Having Evan here today had been a welcome break from her other work. Even though they hadn't been working side by side today it was almost a comfort to have him around. To know that another doctor had her back in case they got into any difficulties.

It gave her even more of a buzz to know that he'd wanted her opinion—had valued her opinion on a case. He had confidence in her abilities, even if she some-times doubted them.

Evan crossed the room toward them. "The news is good. All I need to do today is take a blood sample. It used to be difficult to separate the parasites from the blood cells but we're in luck. Some Swedish scientists have developed a microfluidic device that separates the parasites from the blood cells using their shape, because parasites and red blood cells are very difficult to sepa-rate by size. It's being trialed in one of the local labs and they're going to arrange to pick up our sample." He placed his hand on Dumkata's mother's shoulders. "We should have the results very soon."

Jaja was speaking quickly, translating everything that Evan had said. She asked another question and he turned back to Evan. "And the treatment?"

Evan nodded. "We'll need to do one other test if the blood test is positive—a lumbar puncture. Tell her we'll take a little sample of Dumkata's spinal fluid. It gives a clear indication of what stage the disease is at. We sus-pect it's in the first stage and if that's confirmed, the treatment is relatively simple, a drug—pentamidine, which is supplied free of charge by the Healthy World Federation."

He waited a few minutes for Jaja to relay the news.

Dumkata's mother seemed satisfied with the answers but Violet stood up in front of him.

"It all seems too good to be true. What happens if the disease is further on than we expect?"

Evan frowned and lowered his voice. "I'm pretty sure it's not. We're lucky they are trialing the new diagnosis system here. It should give a much more accurate result."

Violet raised her eyebrow. He still hadn't really answered her question, and it was the second time she'd asked. It was as if he were playing a careful game of dodgeball with her. She looked over her shoulder. Dumkata's mother couldn't hear them speak right now.

"I can't remember, but is sleeping sickness fatal if it's not diagnosed early enough?"

His eyes fixed on hers and he gave a little sigh. "Well, yes, it can be. The second stage isn't too pleasant. The parasites cross the blood-brain barrier and infect the central nervous system. It causes neurological damage, bringing confusion, sensory disturbances, poor co-ordination and disturbance of the sleep cycle—it's what gave the disease its name." His eyes drifted over to the other side of the room to the little figure huddled up in the bedclothes. "At that stage, it can be fatal."

She reached over and touched his arm, trying to ignore the way the hairs on her own arm reacted. "But we're not at that stage, are we?" She gave his arm a little tug to move outside. "How do you feel about doing the lumbar puncture? Are you happy to do it? I can do it if you want. I have to put my hands up and admit it's been a little while since I've done one."

He shook his head, his eyes fixed on the fact she still had her hand on his arm. She hadn't really wanted to move it but the intensity of his gaze made her pull her hand away.

"No, it's fine, Violet. I cover on a regular basis on a pediatric unit. I'm happy to do the lumbar puncture."

She tried not to let the sense of relief she felt show. "You do? Why have you never mentioned it?"

He sighed, his eyes on her face. "We don't exactly have these social conversations, do we?"

She felt her face flush. He wasn't saying the words but he didn't have to. She was always quick to rebuff any of Evan's attempts at small talk. It was her own small measure of self-protection. The less she knew about him, the less she could feel.

But she was moving on. She was attempting to feel in control again.

He was still staring at her and she felt very self-conscious under his gaze. She couldn't imagine how she looked after ten hours in the claustrophobic heat. She probably looked like the equivalent of a well-cooked sausage. Hardly an attractive prospect.

But the timing felt right. The way Evan was looking at her was speaking volumes to her. She glanced over her shoulder. And it was just them. No one else was around.

She took a step forward. It was tiny—literally just a few inches. But it felt like jumping off the edge of a cliff.

She put her hand back on his arm, well aware of the way it would make heat run up her arm and her skin tingle. She was ready for it. She was prepared for it.

"Maybe it's time to start." She hesitated for a moment. If she waited to see how he would react she might never continue. "So, why do you cover in a pediatric unit, Evan?"

She held her breath and watched as his pupils dilated

ever so slightly, and he leaned toward her, closing the space between them.

"So, we're going to have those kinds of conversations?" It was a simple enough sentence. But it meant much more than those few words.

She took a deep breath. "I think we should try."

There. She'd said it. She'd taken that giant step. What did it really mean?

Evan was as cool as a cucumber. His eyes were steady. If he stayed still much longer she would start to count the flecks in his eyes.

He blinked and straightened his shoulders.

"I trained in pediatrics before I joined the DPA. My friend Tyler is a doctor at the Memorial Hospital in Atlanta. He's had skin cancer these past few months and needed surgery and treatment. I've been covering some of his shifts."

"As well as working at the DPA?" She was surprised. To be truthful, it was the last thing she'd expected. Why did she always think the worst of him? It was hardly fair. She was trying to hide the fact that her skin had just prickled when he'd said the name. Atlanta Memorial. The same hospital where she'd had her daughter. It was almost as if just when she'd decided to move forward, reminders kept popping up everywhere.

He shrugged. "He's my friend. His job's important to him. It felt good to work with kids again—to keep my clinical skills up to date. I'm not the bear you think I am, Violet. There's nothing like working with kids to bring you back down to earth."

Her throat felt dry, her mouth parched. She ran her tongue along her lips. The world seemed to have gone quiet around them. All her focus was on Evan and the diminishing space between them. It was all that seemed important right now.

"I don't think you're a bear, Evan," she whispered.

His hand rested on her hip. "So what *do* you think of me, Violet? Because I really don't have a clue. I can't read you at all."

His face was only a few inches a way from hers. She could sense the sizzle in the air. And for the first time it didn't frighten her at all.

The edges of her mouth turned upward. "I'm still trying to figure that out." She lifted her hand and placed it on his chest, feeling the rise and fall of his breathing. She couldn't take her eyes off his. It was if he was hypnotizing her, drawing her in.

His voice was deep, husky. She could tell he was as affected by this as she was. "I've kissed you before, Violet. And you've never mentioned it since then. Do you even remember it?"

A whole host of prickling sensations swept over her skin. Did she remember it? Was he crazy?

"I remember every second."

His finger touched the side of her face. "Even though you were drinking?"

"Even though I was drinking." She tilted her head toward his hand, willing him to touch her some more.

This was a totally different experience from the last time. There was no alcohol to make her bold, to make her act out of character and be swept up in the moment.

She couldn't use alcohol as excuse for her behavior here.

He bent a little lower. She could feel his warm breath on her forehead, a smile dancing across his lips. "I'm going to kiss you now, Violet. Because I can't stop myself. Are you okay with that?"

She couldn't wait a second longer. She slid both palms up his chest, wrapping her hands around his neck and pulling him closer. "I think I can live with that."

And then his lips touched hers. Gently at first, a sweet and tender kiss. It was perfect. It was inviting. It made her want more.

She didn't feel threatened. She didn't feel scared. All she wanted to do was kiss him some more.

She took the final step, closing that last inch between them. Her body pressing up close to his.

She could feel his body awakening, just as she could feel her own doing the same thing. Their kiss deepened, his tongue gently probing into her mouth, willing her to separate her lips and give in to his demands. Her fingers slid through his short hair. Nothing had ever felt this good. Not even that last kiss.

This was better. This was more real. Every part of her body was awakened. Reacting to his touch and his responses. Everything about this felt good and so right.

His hands slid around her hips and cupped her bottom, pressing her even closer to him. Even though they were still kissing she could feel herself smile at his natural response. It made her feel in control. It gave her confidence.

His mouth pulled away from hers, moving along her chin and down her neck. This wasn't enough. This could never be enough. She wanted more and she wanted it now.

She could almost feel her heart rate quicken and her breathing change, her body preparing her for something else.

Something she hadn't even considered.

"Evan?" she murmured.

"Yeah?" His head was still down at the side of her neck.

"How long will it take us to get back?" She held her breath.

He straightened up immediately, his pupils dilating even further. He looked at her carefully, as if he was considering the implication of the question. His scrutiny made her lower her eyes. She was beginning to feel a little embarrassed. Her emotions and desire were clearly on display. What if he didn't feel the same?

He curled his finger under her chin, lifting her head back up to meet his. He was smiling at her. That lazy, sexy smile that drove her crazy. Most of the time he didn't realize he was doing it. But right now he was concentrating it on her, with full effect.

And the effect was dazzling.

He bent forward and whispered in her ear, his free hand capturing hers and intertwining their fingers, "Dr. Connelly, are you suggesting what I think you're suggesting? Because if you are, I'm about to hire a helicopter to get us back in two minutes flat."

Every hair on her body stood on end. His voice was so darned sexy. She smiled to taunt him a little more. "Make no mistake about what I'm suggesting, Dr. Hunter, and a helicopter is definitely required."

He gave her one final kiss on the tip of her nose then pulled back. "Let's finish our work here."

It brought her to her senses. Evan disappeared back inside the house. But she stayed outside. The sun was starting to set.

She should be feeling nervous. She should be feeling scared. The last time she'd had sex she'd been pregnant and still in a relationship with Blane. Evan would be the first person she'd slept with since the death of her daughter.

She lifted the hand that had held his and touched it with the other hand. She could still feel the warmth in her palm from where his fingers had intertwined with hers.

She wasn't scared. She wasn't. She was ready. And if he didn't reappear soon, she might drag him out of that house like a cavewoman.

Evan appeared at her shoulder. "I've got the blood sample. Jaja will meet me back here the day after tomorrow. We should have the results by then and be ready to do the lumbar puncture." He watched her for a second, obviously worried that the past few minutes had changed her mind. "Violet?"

He held out his hand toward her.

She didn't hesitate. "Let's see how fast you can drive." She slid her hand into his and pulled him off toward the truck.

CHAPTER EIGHT

THE JOURNEY SEEMED so long. Olibasi seemed oblivious to the sexual tension in the air and chattered away merrily about some of the families that they'd come into contact with that day.

Violet fixed a smile on her face, nodding at the appropriate times, all the while aware of the fact that Evan kept giving her sidelong glances. The tension was killing her.

When they finally reached the drop-off point for Olibasi and she slid out of the truck, the sigh of relief from the two of them was obvious.

They waited for a few seconds as Olibasi gathered up her colored skirts, gave them a cheerful wave and walked back to her village.

Their own was only ten minutes away.

"Well?" Evan raised his eyebrows at her, his voice laden with innuendo. "Have you changed your mind? Have you come to your senses?" Although his eyes were twinkling, she could almost hear the wariness in his voice—as if he was expecting her to run in the other direction.

She slid across the seat and put her hand on his firm thigh. "I can't tell you much about my senses right now, they seem to be going haywire."

It was almost as if she'd lit a match under him. He hit the gas pedal with a thud and the truck sprang forward instantly.

She moved her fingers in small circles over his thigh. He gave a little groan. "Not wise, Violet. Not wise at all."

"Really? Why ever not?" She was enjoying teasing him. She was enjoying feeling in control.

He lifted one hand from the wheel and pressed it down firmly on top of hers. Stopping her fingers in their tracks. "Five minutes," he growled.

She shuffled her shoulder closer to his. "Seems like an awful long time."

"Violet." He gave her a sidelong glance. "You're driving me crazy."

She felt something wash over her. A real feeling of contentment, a moment of pleasure. "Good, it's about time."

"What do you mean?"

"Working with you for the past six months has been an absolute nightmare."

His mouth quirked into a smile. "I'm hoping that's a good nightmare and not a bad."

She lifted her hand and touched the side of his cheek. It felt nice to finally touch him. She couldn't pretend she hadn't thought about it. She couldn't pretend that she hadn't done it in her dreams often enough. "It's been a torturous nightmare."

"You've still not told me if that's good or bad. And this from the woman with the slinkiest red dress in the world."

She felt her cheeks flush a little. He'd remembered. In the midst of the smallpox crisis he'd remembered her dress. "That was a distraction technique," she admitted.

"Well, it worked. Like a charm."

The truck ground to a halt outside their accommodation. Evan was out of the truck in an instant, pulling her door open and holding his hands out to capture her waist and lift her to the ground. He held her tightly for a few seconds. "Last chance, Violet."

She shook her head. "I don't need it."

There were a few people still around, still working and coming in and out of the clinic building next door. Evan murmured responses to their greetings as he pulled her along behind him. Pausing for a second, he ducked into one of the supply closets.

"What are you doing?" Violet hissed. She could feel the tension building inside her. There were several people around, all looking as if they might try to engage her in conversation at any moment. Talking was the last thing she wanted to do right now.

"Nothing." Evan came back outside, his hand stuffed inside his pocket. "Let's go."

"Evan, can you—?"

"Later." He dismissed the person holding a clipboard with a wave of his hand.

Violet suppressed a smirk. Evan never usually did things like that. Did he realize he'd probably just set tongues wagging?

But his strides were getting longer as they headed into the accommodation. More determined. He stopped as they walked in the main entrance, turning to face her. "Your room or mine?"

She pretended to think about it, putting her finger on her chin. "Hmm, decisions, decisions."

But Evan had obviously run out of patience. "Dammit. Mine is closer."

He pushed open a wooden door near them and pulled

her into his room, thudding the door closed and sliding the bolt.

There was no time to look around at his room. No small talk. No hesitant moves. Violet found herself pressed up against the door. "So, where were we?" He had that sexy smile and lowered eyelids look. The one that drove her secretly crazy.

She slid her hands around his neck and stood on tiptoe, which allowed her to place some kisses on his neck. "I think we were right about here."

His hands settled on her hips, his full weight pressing against her. "So what's changed, Violet? What's changed for us?"

Was this a conversation she really wanted to have? Or did she just want to lose herself in the heat of the moment, because that's how good things felt right now?

"Apart from the increased dose of chemistry?"

She concentrated on Evan, running her hands across the broad planes of his shoulders. She'd spent the past few months watching these shoulders from the other side of the room. Willing herself to forget what they'd felt like under her hands. Trying to erase all those thoughts from her head.

Because remembering had just made her want it all again.

And now she finally had it.

"Violet?" He wasn't going to give this up. He wanted to pursue why nothing had ever happened between them. Why, after they'd kissed, the next time she'd seen him she hadn't even looked him in the eye.

Her hands slid down the sides of his defined waist. She would have to ask him later whether he was a surfer. Maybe she'd do that when she'd finally got him naked.

Her hands inched lower, moving across his stomach,

making the muscles twitch because he knew the inevitability of where she was heading.

He grabbed one hand and pinned it against the door, above her head. "Violet? Distraction techniques again?" He was teasing her, but she could see the questions in his eyes.

Was he afraid? Afraid that she was doing something she might regret and it could come back to bite him? Because she'd threaten to expose him a few weeks ago to the director? And it didn't matter that she hadn't meant it. He thought she did.

She bit her lip and looked him in the eye. Her other hand hesitated over the button of his chinos. "I wasn't ready."

It was as much as she could say. And it sounded so simple. Something that could easily be brushed over.

Because, right now, with her hormones swarming all over the place, the last thing she wanted to talk about was the stillbirth.

The last thing she wanted to acknowledge was the fact she'd had no sexual contact since it had happened. Just one passionate kiss with *him*.

She didn't need him to psychoanalyze her to death. She needed him to sleep with her. She needed him to fulfill the unspoken promise he'd made when he'd kissed her and sparked a fire she hadn't felt in three years.

She saw something flicker across his eyes. He was contemplating stopping what they were doing. He was considering pulling back. *No!*

His hand had inched upward from her waist toward her breast. But it had stopped midway. "And are you ready now?" He looked as if it was taking all his self-control not to move.

"I'm ready." She flicked the button open on his chinos. *Distraction techniques? You bet ya.*

He let out a hiss as she slid her hand inside. "You'd better mean this, lady, because there's no turning back."

"I've no intention of turning back." She could feel the adrenaline coursing through her veins. This feeling might not last but she fully intended to embrace it while it was there. She hadn't let herself feel like this six months ago. She hadn't let herself let go.

Now it was time.

She smiled at him. "I take it this means you like me a little?"

He raised his eyebrows, "You can take it that means I like you a lot."

And the chemistry between them was leading her by the hand.

The air in the room was stifling. Claustrophobic. Or maybe it was their chemistry?

It was dusk; the early evening sun was vanishing, causing the dim room to be filled with occasional dark orange rays.

Something was making her want to get naked very quickly. And he obviously had the same idea because Evan started walking backward, pulling her toward the single bed. His fingers started tugging at her *buba* top, lifting the bottom and dragging it over her head. It hit the floor and he stopped for a second, taking in the sight of her pink-satin-covered breasts.

What was wrong? Didn't he think they were big enough? Was he disappointed by what he was seeing? How much could he actually see in this light?

Then a sexy smile appeared on his face, and his hands reached up and cupped her breasts. "You're beautiful, Violet. I've never got to tell you that before."

A wave of relief swept over her. But he wasn't finished. His hands pulled down her long skirt, leaving her in her pink satin underwear. She felt herself pulling her stomach in. Would he notice? She had a few stretch marks from when she'd been pregnant. And her stomach was gently curved. Nothing in the world would ever change that.

And she wouldn't want to.

But she couldn't take the questions right now—not when she was feeling so ready to take the next step.

Evan seemed to have missed her stomach. His eyes were fixed firmly on her legs. "Why am I the only one undressed here?" she said out loud.

She stepped forward, pushing him back to the edge of the bed and slowly starting to undo the buttons on his cotton shirt. He watched her, unmoving, taking a sharp intake of breath as she reached the last button and slid the shirt off his shoulders, bringing both her palms around and running them up and down his chest.

She was taking her time over this—she'd waited too long not to enjoy it.

The scattered dark curly hairs on his chest tingled against the palms of her hands. His nipples tightened and she loved the effect she was having on his body. She pushed him back on the bed and sat astride him. "How about you take something else off for me? It's a little hot in here, don't you think?"

She was making a rocking motion, feeling the hardness of him underneath her. It felt so good.

Evan took a few seconds to push his chinos down over his hips, kicking his shoes off and grabbing her hips.

There was very little between them now. And she couldn't wait for the inevitable.

Then something struck her and she froze. Why

hadn't she thought of that earlier? They were out in the middle of nowhere. This could ruin everything.

"What is it? What's wrong?" Evan's brow was wrinkled. "Violet?"

She thudded her hands down on his chest in frustration. "I'm not on the Pill. And I don't have anything with me."

His eyes twinkled. "That's why I'm the team leader around here. I plan ahead." He reached down and grabbed his trousers, pulling out a strip of foil packets that unraveled and almost reached the floor.

"Condoms? You brought condoms with you?"

He shook his head. "What did you think I was getting out of the store? I didn't plan *that* far ahead."

Of course. It was one of the standard supplies they had in abundance. To prevent sexually transmitted diseases and unwanted pregnancies. She'd been so wrapped up in the polio work she'd forgotten about them.

She reached over and grabbed the strip. "Just how many did you plan on using?"

He grabbed her around the waist and flipped her over so she was lying on the bed beneath him. "It's the one thing we have plenty of around here." The strip was still dangling from her hand and he flicked it with his fingers. "These are all for you and me, baby. However long it takes."

She ran her hands up his chest again. "That sounds good to me. Now, where were we?"

"Right around here." He slid his hands over her breasts, releasing them from the confines of the satin cups. Her eyes fell on her dark pink nipples just as his head came down and captured one.

His tongue teased her as she writhed beneath him, his hand slid inside her underwear, teasing her some more. All of a sudden her underwear was too much. It was getting in her way.

His way and hers.

"I think we're a little overdressed," she whispered in his ear. "It's time to get back to basics."

"Your wish is my command." He smiled as he snapped the clasp at her back and slid her panties down over her thighs. His boxers landed in a heap on the floor.

"Now, what exactly did you have in mind?"

Perfect. Just what she wanted to hear. She pulled his head down next to her mouth and started whispering in his ear again.

He raised his head. There was a wicked glint in his eyes. "Really?"

She nodded. "Really."

"Then let's get to work." His lips covered hers and she closed her eyes and let her previously secret dreams become a reality.

Evan should have felt on top of the world. The woman who had got under his skin months ago had finally ended up in his arms.

This was the point at which he should be walking around with a smile reaching from ear to ear.

But no matter how hard he tried, he couldn't keep a smile on his face.

Violet was currently his favorite person in the whole wide world. Here, in Africa, it was easy to push aside the issues he'd had with her brother.

It was easy to try and forget the way he'd felt.

But the gnawing ache in his stomach wouldn't leave him. Every touch of Violet's fair skin, every little smile from her seemed to send him hurtling into a vortex of guilt.

Violet was slowly but surely beginning to trust him. And that's what worried him most.

He was trying to forget the fact that he occasionally saw something fleeting in her gaze. Because right now he was praying it wasn't related to him.

He'd known from the minute he'd kissed her six months ago that he wanted to go further. This should be his perfect scenario. Out in the middle of nowhere, working on a task they both believed in, with no outside influences.

So why couldn't he sleep at night?

Why was the sight of Violet lying in his arms racking him with guilt?

Because deep down he knew he was going to have that conversation with her at some point.

He couldn't live with himself otherwise.

He was going to have to tell her his fears about Helen's death. That if he'd been more in tune with his team, he could have prevented it.

That would shatter anything that was building between them stone cold dead.

And the last thing he wanted to do right now was spoil it.

But it was eating away at him every day. He couldn't enjoy himself with Violet. He couldn't embrace the relationship the way he should because of the thought of what he had to do.

How would she feel about him then?

He didn't even want to think about that. He was acting like a coward. And that was one thing Evan Hunter definitely was not.

Two weeks had passed.

Two weeks of long days and even longer nights. He wasn't even attempting to hide to anyone that he and

Violet were an item. Neither of them was waking up early in the morning to creep back to their own room. Violet sat beside him at most of the briefings, letting their hands brush and giving him little smiles.

She wasn't outwardly affectionate. That just wasn't Violet. But she wasn't employing any of her past avoidance tactics.

And it felt good. Or it would feel good if he could let it.

She was still a little closed off. She'd let him know very little about her past. He naturally didn't ask her about Sawyer. But she seemed quite private, only mentioning a couple of close friends and nothing about any past relationships.

If he could get his head round his own problems, he might eventually delve a little deeper. He stared down at her face. She was lying tucked under his arm, one hand on his chest. Her naked breasts were rising and falling peacefully as she slept. Her blond hair was fanned over his shoulder. And she looked so peaceful. So calm.

He really didn't want to do anything to wreck it.

There was gentle knock at the door. "Evan? I need to speak to you a minute, please."

He was instantly wide awake. No one had ever disturbed him at night before. It must be something serious.

He slid his arm out from under Violet and grabbed the nearest shirt and trousers he could find. He opened the door and took a step outside into the hall.

Ben, one of the Healthy World Federation members of the team, looked worried.

"What's wrong? Has something happened?"

He nodded. "We've had some news. There's been a report of an attempted kidnapping of a health worker in the next state. All organizations are currently reviewing the safety of their staff. You're wanted on the phone."

Evan felt his heart rate quicken. They'd been briefed about the dangers before they'd arrived. But so far nothing untoward had affected them.

He walked into the control room and took the satellite phone.

"It's Evan Hunter, what can I do for you?"

He listened for a few minutes, making notes and asking questions. "Where, exactly? Do you know who was responsible? Is there any indication that the trouble will spread? What about the safety of my team? No, no. There have been no signs of trouble locally. How often will this be reviewed? And the other team, have they been safely withdrawn? Yes, yes, I understand. Please keep me updated. Thanks."

He replaced the phone and stared at the wall in front of him. He hated to think that any health staff or community workers were at risk. Even though there was no immediate risk to his staff, the thought of anyone being harmed or in danger made him feel sick to his stomach.

Helen had been a friend—a colleague. And even six years on he hadn't learned to live with that guilt.

Was that the reason he'd never managed to form a decent relationship? It wasn't as if he hadn't tried. But six years was a long time to never manage more than a few dates at a time. To always wonder if he deserved to be living the life that one of his colleagues wasn't.

But what if something happened to Violet? He couldn't stand that. It didn't even bear thinking about.

Ben touched his shoulder. "What did they say?"

Evan shook his head. "I'll need to give a briefing to the staff later. The other team has been withdrawn. Shots were fired and attempts were made to kidnap one of the doctors. It was in the next state, but they're not sure if the conflict could spill over. We've got to be very cautious in the next few days. We need to make sure we know where everyone is, at all times."

He pointed to the equipment lying on the table next to them. "Everyone has got to wear one of the GPS transmitters. Usually only one of the team members needs one, but we're going to have to review that situation and make it clear."

Ben nodded. "Whatever you think is best, Evan."

Evan walked over the wall and looked at the maps. "We're going to change our pattern over the next few days. Leave the villages nearest the border. We'll concentrate on those closest to us, until we're sure the situation is under control."

His brain was whirring. It didn't matter that it was the middle of the night. He was instantly awake and there was no way he could go back to sleep now.

It was one of the joys of being a doctor. That instant adrenaline buzz in the middle of the night that kept you awake, even when your body was telling you it wanted to be tucked up in bed. It happened frequently as an intern, and constantly as you progressed up the scale.

His eyes focused on the wall. Was there anything else he could do? How else could he ensure the safety of his staff? Nothing else seemed to be jumping out at him. It was the best he could do for now. What he really wanted to do was ship Violet out on the nearest plane, sending her back to Atlanta, out of harm's way.

But there was no way she would let him do that.

So he was just going to have to try and make things as safe as he could.

Because losing Violet just wasn't an option.

CHAPTER NINE

VIOLET THUDDED DOWN at the table. "What are you eating?" Her eyes were sparkling and her face flushed. Just the way she looked when was happy, or excited, or when they…

No. He had to stop thinking like that every time he was around Violet. It was becoming addictive.

He concentrated on the matter at hand. "Stew." He held up a forkful. It looked a little unconventional but the smell was great. "Where have you been?"

"On the phone." She grabbed a fork and scooped up a bit of his stew. "Yum."

"On the phone with who?"

The smile stayed fixed on her face. "Sawyer."

He winced. Sawyer again. The man was haunting his every move. For someone who had barely made contact with his sister—only the occasional call or text— for the past six years, he seemed to have renewed their connection with vigor. "What did he want this time?" He couldn't hide the tone of his voice. He would prefer never to hear Sawyer's name again.

Violet put the fork back on the table. He'd seen the flash in her eyes at his wince. She seemed to be taking her time before replying. Her cool green eyes met his. "Things are going well. The director has asked Matt to come back. He hasn't decided yet, but he'll need to make his mind up soon because Callie's handed in her notice."

Evan was shocked. Callie Turner was one of the most dependable doctors he'd worked with at the DPA. He couldn't believe she would want to leave. What had Sawyer done to upset her? It was instant—the thought that Sawyer must have something to do with this. Callie had always seemed happy at the DPA.

His stomach churned at the thought of having to work with Sawyer again every day. The thought of having a constant reminder of something he was doing his best to forget.

"What position has the director offered him?"

He was irritated. The director had shipped him off to the middle of nowhere and it sounded as if he was offering Matt Sawyer a tailor-made position.

Why couldn't Violet be someone else's sister?

Her voice remained steady but he could see something else going on behind her eyes. She shrugged her shoulders, "Consultancy. Lecturing. Whatever he'll agree to. Sounds like the director just wants to get him back on board."

She glared at him. "Why do you always automatically go against my brother? Callie and Sawyer are together. I didn't know this before, but Callie never wanted to work at the DPA. She had a sister who died in a car accident. They were going to work at the DPA together. I worked with Callie for three years and never knew that." She glared at Evan again. "Sawyer connected with Callie. He's given her the confidence to go after what she really wants—family practice."

"Callie Turner? Family practice?" He couldn't believe his ears.

"Yes, that's what she wants." Violet's voice had a

determined edge to it. She was getting annoyed with him, but he couldn't help his responses.

Or maybe he didn't want to. This Sawyer thing was always going to hang over their heads. It was always going to be the monkey on his back.

The thought repeated itself in his head again. *Why couldn't Violet be someone else's sister?*

It was beginning to eat away at him. It was beginning to find its way into all the good times he was having with Violet. Hanging over his head, waiting to crash down on top of them.

"And what does Sawyer get out of this?" It was still there. The hostility in his voice. Undisguised.

The expression on Violet's face changed. She looked off to the side. "A chance to be happy. A chance to have a life again." She sighed. "Everyone deserves a happy-ever-after, Evan. Even my brother."

She was mad. The words were gentle, but he could see the glint in her eye. Why did he do it? Why couldn't he just smile and nod glibly when she mentioned her brother?

Why couldn't he just forget about Sawyer and the fact he got all uptight every time he heard the name? Every time he remembered the circumstances they'd been in.

Every time he felt the guilt wash over him again.

But Violet had obviously reached the point of no return. "Enough is enough, Evan. I asked Sawyer about you, you know."

Evan felt his heart jump in his chest. "What? Why did you do that?"

"Because I want to bang your heads together. Neither of you will tell me what the issue is between you. Neither of you will really tell me what happened out there."

She steadied her gaze and lowered her voice. "This can't go on, Evan. How can we have anything together when you seem to hate someone I love so much?"

She was right. He knew she was right. His animosity toward her brother was killing this relationship stone dead.

But what if he told her the truth? Surely that would just give them the same fate? "What did he say?" he mumbled.

"He said Helen died and he was angry. He said you both have some—" she held her fingers up "—unresolved issues."

Unresolved issues. Well, that was one way to put it.

This was conversation he couldn't have. This was a conversation he wasn't ready for. He stood up, pushing his chair away, and walked from the dining room, out into the early evening sun.

Violet's footsteps hurried out behind him. "What? What just happened? I don't get this. Will you tell me what went on?"

"Just leave it, Violet."

"No!" She was shouting now. "I won't leave it! Why won't anyone talk about this? What happened out there? You know what? Helen was my sister-in-law and I loved her. She was perfect for Sawyer and made him very happy. I thought he was set for life. I thought they would grow old together. And then this…" She flung her arms wide.

"This happens and everyone comes back close-lipped. My brother barely functioning. Well, you know what, Mr. Team Leader? I've had enough. Helen was my family and I have a right to know what happened out there." She poked a finger into his chest. "And I mean besides the fact that she had an ectopic pregnancy and died. I want to know the other stuff—the stuff that you and my brother won't talk about."

Evan couldn't listen anymore. Everything was building up inside him like a tidal wave. Every pent-up emotion, feeling and load of guilt that he'd ever experienced.

It was too late. He couldn't hold on to this any longer.

"He must have known! Sawyer must have known Helen was pregnant! He let her go out there and put herself at risk!" He was shouting now but he couldn't help it.

Violet's face paled. She looked shocked. "What? Why on earth would you think that? That's ridiculous."

"Really? This is Sawyer and Helen we're talking about here. I've never seen a couple so connected. So in tune with each other. How could he possibly not have known?"

Violet shook her head fiercely. "Are you crazy? Helen didn't even know—and if she didn't know, how could Sawyer?"

Evan crossed his arms across his chest. "I don't believe that. I've *never* believed that."

Violet started to get angry. "What do you mean, you never believed that? You think my brother and his wife deliberately put the mission in jeopardy? Helen knew she was pregnant but didn't tell anyone because she didn't want to be taken off the duty rota?"

When Violet put it into words it sounded ridiculous. But, then, he'd never been able to think rationally about any of this.

"Well, she and Sawyer never wanted to be apart. Would that really be such a leap of faith?"

Violet was furious. "Of course it would." She nearly spat the words at him. "This is Helen you're talking about, Evan. Did you really know her at all? How can you even think that?"

His mind started to spin. Why had he said anything at all? He should have kept his mouth shut. This couldn't end well.

Violet folded her arms across her chest. "Evan, do you keep a note of when I have my period?"

"What? Don't be ridiculous." The question caught him sideways. He knew exactly what she was implying.

"Why is that ridiculous? We've been sleeping together for a few weeks now. You mean you aren't marking it on the calendar? Why not? You obviously expected my brother to."

"Of course I didn't!" he snapped.

"But, in essence, that's what you're saying. That my brother should have noticed that his wife had missed her period. They were both busy professional people. But you expected them to be counting up the days?" She shook her head. "I don't know anything about my sister-in-law's cycle. It wasn't the kind of conversation we used to have. But what if Helen had irregular periods? How could either of them have known she was pregnant? She would only have been two or three weeks late. Maybe she didn't even think she was late at all. Or maybe, with all the planning for the mission, it just hadn't crossed their minds."

Her voice tailed off. She was right. He had known Helen. He'd known her well and respected her. She would never have deliberately lied. Even to be with her beloved Sawyer. Deep down he'd always known that.

But that threw all his beliefs out of the window.

No, that threw all his *excuses* out of the window.

Finally, he had to stop blaming Sawyer. He had to stop pushing the blame onto someone other than himself.

He slid down the wall and put his head in his hands.

"Evan?"

He could hear that Violet was confused. He could hear by the tone of her voice. The way it had quieted. The way her anger had quickly dissipated.

He felt her hand on his wrist. She was kneeling down next to him. "Evan, what is it? What's wrong?"

Violet started babbling. Filling the air around about them. "No one knew, Evan. No one knew that Helen was pregnant. It was horrible. And I'm sure it must have destroyed you all. Knowing that if you'd been back home, chances are that Helen would have been fine. But it was one of those things you couldn't have known. It was one of things that no one could have predicted."

Her words cut him to the bone. She had no idea what she was saying to him. Her warm fingers were wrapped around his wrist. Her other hand was on the top of his knee. He had to tell her.

He couldn't keep quiet anymore. The guilt was going to eat him alive.

But telling her would destroy any chance of them having a relationship. Any chance at all. How could she have a relationship with the man responsible for her sister-in-law's death? The man who could have made a difference?

Things could be so different for Violet's family. Sawyer would still have Helen. Violet wouldn't have experienced an estranged relationship with her brother for the past six years. She wouldn't have had sleepless nights and days fraught with worry.

All because of him. All because he should have paid attention. All because he should have uttered a few words, asked a simple question.

It could have made the whole world of difference.

If only he'd done it.

He raised his eyes to meet hers. This was the most painful thing he would ever have to do. "I knew."

"What?"

This thing with her brother was never going to go away and she was getting tired of it. She was getting tired of pretending not to be relieved she finally knew where her brother was and what he was doing.

Her heart was singing for her brother right now. He'd finally met someone to put a little light into his life and she was very happy for him. What's more, he'd met someone she liked and respected. She couldn't have wished for anything more.

Except for Evan.

She'd finally moved on. She'd finally taken the step of having a relationship again. And for the most part, it was good. No, it was great.

Her stomach flipped every time she saw him, every time he looked at her. His smile made her think impure thoughts. His touch drove her wild.

And for the first time in a long time she felt good. Good about herself. Good about the world around her.

Hopeful.

Hopeful that there was still a life out there worth living.

It didn't matter that this thing with Evan might not last. It didn't matter that chances were they were using each other as a distraction while they were in Africa.

So, why this? Why now?

She just didn't get it. She didn't get the animosity he felt toward her brother. She didn't get any of this.

Her skin prickled. The hairs on her arms stood upright. There was something about what he'd just said. The way he'd just said it.

"What do you mean, Evan? What do you mean, you knew? Knew what?"

She could feel herself instantly building a wall around herself. Her self-protection mechanism was kicking in. Telling her to run. Telling her this couldn't be good.

His eyes were hidden under his heavy eyelids. Struggling to look at her.

She couldn't breathe. She couldn't swallow.

"About Helen." His voice was so low, so husky. He struggled to get those two words out.

A horrible sensation went down her spine. She instantly pulled her hands back, drawing away from him. "You knew what about Helen?" The thoughts were starting to form in her brain. She was trying to rationalize what she'd heard. "You knew she was pregnant?" No. He couldn't have. It wasn't possible.

He shook his head.

"Evan. Look at me." She couldn't stand the way he couldn't look her in the eye. This wasn't the man she knew. Evan Hunter didn't shy away from anything. So why couldn't he lift his head from his hands to look at her?

The frustration was overwhelming her. She reached over and yanked at one of his hands. "Look at me!"

He raised his eyes. They were laden with regret and guilt. What had he done? Had there been some cover-up at the DPA? Was that why no one was talking?

She couldn't bear the thought of that.

"Helen. She told me she wasn't feeling one hundred percent."

"What?"

He stopped to swallow. "While we were getting ready for the mission. I was packing up equipment and checking the inventory. She told she wasn't feeling great."

"And what?"

He shook his head. "That's just it—and nothing. I wasn't paying attention. I had too much on my mind. I didn't think anything else about it."

"Let me get this straight. A team member tells you they aren't feeling great before you leave and you didn't ask them anything else."

The words were obviously sticking in his throat. He nodded. He ran his hand through his hair. One of Evan's signs of frustration.

"What else did she say?"

"Nothing. She said nothing." He squeezed his eyes shut. "But I should have asked her. I know I should have asked her. If I'd stopped for a second, if I'd thought about it. Helen never complained. It was unusual. I should have asked her to think about it. Why she was feeling unwell. What exactly was wrong." He was wringing his hands together now.

Violet was running through things in her head. "What difference do you think that would have made? Helen didn't know she was pregnant. She'd already reported as fit for duty. She hadn't even told Sawyer she didn't feel well."

"Don't you think I know that?" His voice carried across the compound. "She didn't tell anyone! Anyone apart from me! And I did nothing!"

Violet flinched back as he shouted. This was turning into a living, breathing nightmare. He stood up and started pacing around, his feet kicking up the dust around them. She shook her head. Her brain was spinning. She couldn't understand all this.

"What difference do you think you could have made, Evan?"

He stopped pacing. "What?" His head was shaking, ever so slightly.

"She mentioned, in passing, that she didn't feel great. How could you, by asking her questions, have made a difference? I don't get it."

His face was becoming redder and redder by the second. In her heart she would have loved it if anything in the world could have made a difference to her sister-in-law's outcome but the reality seemed very different.

He held up his hands in frustration. "I should have stopped. I should have paid attention. I should have asked her if there was any possibility she was pregnant!"

"Why would you ask her that? Why would you even think that?"

"Because if maybe I'd considered it a possibility, she might have considered it a possibility!"

The words hung in the air between them. There was so much on the line here. He was exposing everything about himself to her. He was exposing his failings. His failings as a team leader and as a person. What man ever wanted to do that?

She tried to push her family loyalties aside but could feel herself torn. Was there even a shred of possibility that could be true? Would Helen really have stopped to think she might be pregnant if Evan had asked her a few more questions?

She needed to step back. She needed to step out of this situation. She needed time to think.

She lifted her head. It was hard to look at him right now. There was too much conflict here. The rational part of her brain came into play. "Did you ever stop to think that if you'd asked Helen if she could be pregnant, she might have thought you were being sexist? She wouldn't have thanked you for asking that question, Evan. If you knew Helen as well as I did, you would know she might even have been angry with you."

His voice was quiet. "She might also still be alive." He let out the biggest sigh. "An angry Helen I could have lived with. It's the dead Helen I can't take."

Everything was silent round about them. There was no one else around, it was just her and him.

In the heart of Africa even the insects seemed to have become quiet.

Tears prickled in Violet's eyes. The horrible realization that Evan might be right. If he'd asked Helen if she could be pregnant, would she have checked the calendar? Would she have stopped for a minute to consider it?

Might it have saved her life?

There were so many ifs and buts. There was nothing definite here. Just a world full of possibilities.

Possibilities that neither of them would ever know about, because the time had passed.

It was over. There was no time machine. There was no way to turn back the clock. How many other people felt like that? How many mothers whose child's hands had slipped from theirs moments before a car had appeared? How many doctors who had sent a patient home, only for them to come back later and die?

And for her, how many women who couldn't remember the last time they felt their baby move?

A never-ending list. A whole world of don't-knows. A whole lifetime of what-ifs.

Evan turned to face her, his hands hanging by his sides. Even with his large, broad frame he looked broken. "How can I live with this, Violet? How can I live with knowing if I'd done a better job Helen might still be here?"

She couldn't speak. She couldn't find the words she should be saying to comfort him, to reassure him that it wasn't his fault. That it hadn't been his responsibility.

It would be so easy to apportion him the blame. But, then, that's what he'd done to her brother. He spent the past six years blaming her brother for this. Thinking that he'd known about his wife's condition and had let her go on the mission with them.

He'd turned his anger on her brother rather than on himself.

How wrong. How unfair. As if Sawyer didn't have enough to live with.

Now he was blaming himself. Finally.

And in her heart of hearts she wanted to blame him too.

But she understood better than anyone what it was like to feel saddled with blame. Every moment in the last three years she'd wondered if she'd done something wrong. Something that had affected her pregnancy and stolen the life of her baby.

She'd interrogated her life to the point of not being able to move forward. Every thing that had crossed her lips during her pregnancy, every tiny twinge, every action she'd taken, every time she hadn't slept well or felt grumpy.

Anything that she could have changed that would have let her baby live.

Let her baby be born the living, breathing daughter she'd dreamed of.

But she'd had to let it all go.

Because no matter what she analyzed it didn't change the outcome.

It didn't change the results of the autopsy by the

medical examiner. It didn't give her a reason for her daughter's death.

Because there had been no reason. Or none that could be found.

And no matter how hard it was, putting it behind her was the only way to start to move on.

Sometimes there just was no one to blame.

Her throat was dry. The dust in the air around her was stifling, or maybe that was just how she was feeling, as if the whole world was closing in on her again.

She tried to find some words. It didn't matter how much of a struggle it was to say them.

"You have to realize that Helen was a professional. You have to realize she was responsible for her own well-being. You have to let it go." Her voice was breaking now.

"But how? How can I let it go?" He reached toward her hand. She didn't want him to touch her. She wanted him to leave her alone. "Can you forgive me?"

His eyes were pleading with her. She could see how much this had destroyed him. She could see how much this had been eating away at him.

But she was so mixed up right now. Feelings of guilt and responsibility were rushing to the surface and she didn't feel equipped to deal with them.

There was no one out here to talk to. No one who understood.

She couldn't deal with his feelings as well as her own.

She felt as if she'd just jumped back a dozen steps.

She needed time. She needed space.

She raised her eyes to meet his. "It's not my forgiveness you need, Evan. It's your own."

And she turned and walked away before he could see her tears start to fall.

CHAPTER TEN

Violet looked around the village they'd just been arrived at. It was the third one they'd visited that day. She was trying to ensure all the local midwives were enrolled in the midwife service scheme and the oral polio vaccine pre-placed in delivery rooms to ensure administration immediately following birth.

She'd barely been in Evan's company since that fateful night two weeks ago. She just couldn't find the time and space to deal with him.

Because he'd brought so much to the surface again she was finding this task harder than she'd first thought. She was feeling raw and exposed.

And dodging Evan Hunter had become her number one priority.

She looked around. This was one of the bigger villages, with over two thousand residents and a mixture of midwives and traditional birth attendants. The birth rate was high, as very little form of contraception was used in the village and some of the expectant mothers from neighboring villages even came here to give birth.

Violet could hear some noise coming from the delivery room that was used in the village. She walked over hesitantly, unwilling to disturb the midwife if she was dealing with an expectant mother. Many of the births were attended by female family friends as well as the midwife or birth attendant, so Violet's presence might be considered intrusive.

As she approached the doorway the first thing she noticed was that, apart from Urbi, the midwife, only one other person was with the expectant mother. She was obviously in hard labor and her moans could be heard from the road, but what Violet hadn't heard was the fact she was also weeping quietly.

A horrible sense of dread came over her straight away.

Urbi looked up. She was using a traditional midwife's Pinard to listen to the baby's heart and waved her hand at Violet to come inside.

"Ah, Dr. Violet. Can you listen for me?"

Violet tried her best to remain calm. "Is there a problem? Where are the rest of the family?"

Urbi shook her head. "I sent them away. Hasana has been in labor for more than twelve hours. I haven't been able to hear the baby's heartbeat for the last hour."

No. Violet felt a shiver go down her spine. She wanted to turn and run away. She wasn't specially trained in obstetrics. Her fundamental knowledge was basic at best. How much use could she really be?

But the look on poor Hasana's face was desperate. And Violet's heart went out to her. She would be hoping, praying that Urbi had made a mistake. With every breath she would be willing that Violet would be the person to find her child's heartbeat.

The coiled-up feeling in Violet's stomach made her feel sick. She had to do her duty as a doctor. This birthing room wasn't equipped with the latest technology. There was no sonogram. No fetal Doppler, no fetal monitor. The only piece of equipment was the Pinard horn, the most fundamental listening device to detect a baby's heart.

Violet took a deep breath. There was no running away from this. She couldn't find any suitable excuse not to do the task she'd been asked to. As a doctor, she had a duty of care. "Is there any possibility that the baby has turned into an awkward position?"

Urbi had her hands on the mother's stomach. Her eyes were sad. She was one of the most experienced midwives that Violet had met since she'd arrived in Natumba state.

Violet was grasping at straws here and she knew it.

But she knew this situation better than anyone. She'd had the experience of being that mother. It took all her strength and self-resolve not to run and hide away in a corner. She really didn't know if she could go through this again.

Urbi spoke a few words in Hausa to the expectant mother. She looked back at Violet. "She felt her baby move last night when her labor started. The movement continued for the first few hours. There's been nothing since."

Violet pulled her ordinary stethoscope from her bag. She already knew this would be a futile exercise. "Let me try both of these," she said, taking the Pinard from Urbi's hands.

Hasana was tightly grasping the midwife's hand as Violet placed her hands on her stomach. The tightness of the grasp turned her knuckles pale.

Violet felt Hasana's tight abdomen first to determine the position of the baby. She'd used to do this to herself on a regular basis. It felt good to know which way her baby was lying at different points in the day.

Once she'd determined the baby's position she placed

her stethoscope on the abdomen at the point where she should be able to hear a heartbeat. Her chest felt tight. She could feel Hasana's anxious eyes burning a hole into the side of her head.

"Has Hasana got any other children? Does she have any medical conditions?" The questions were rudimentary. They weren't going to change the outcome. But Violet felt she had to go through all the steps methodically.

Urbi shook her head. "This is her first. She has no medical conditions. There have been no problems during the pregnancy."

Something twisted in Violet's gut. It could be her they were talking about. No past history. No previous births or complications. A textbook pregnancy. No signs or cause for alarm.

She took the stethoscope from her ears and switched to the Pinard. She waited as Hasana was struck by another contraction and once it subsided she placed the Pinard on Hasana's abdomen in the hope something might have changed.

She was met with deathly silence.

Her eyes met Urbi's. "What have you told her? Does she understand English?"

Urbi shook her head. "Only a little. I will translate for you, Dr. Violet. I have already told her that I couldn't hear the baby's heartbeat. That was when I sent the family away. She knows I was just asking you to check again—to confirm what I suspected."

Violet nodded. Her brain was having flashbacks. Her own delivery room couldn't have been more different from this birthing room in Africa. Hers had been white, bright and modern with all the technology in the world. That hadn't made a bit of difference to her baby.

The gel being squirted on her stomach. The Doppler

unable to find a heartbeat. The change of position. The blank looks on the faces of the delivery room staff— aware that she was a physician and would know exactly what they were doing.

Finally, her obstetrician speaking to her in low, gentle words. The progression of labor. The pain and frustration of knowing that there wouldn't be a euphoric and happy moment at the end. Her mind filling with the preparations she'd made at home. A bassinet, a stroller, a car seat and drawer after drawer of tiny little clothes.

The bright, colorful letters spelling out the name she'd chosen for her daughter on the nursery door. How could she go back home to all that without her daughter?

She lifted her eyes to meet the dark eyes of Hasana. She had a job to do here. And as much as it pained her, because she understood, she realized she might be the best person to do this job.

She took a deep breath and reached out for Hasana's free hand. She shook her head and spoke slowly. "I'm so sorry, Hasana, but I can't find a heartbeat for your child. Your baby isn't moving. I think your baby is going to be born asleep."

She hated the word *stillbirth*.

She couldn't explain why. It just sounded so cold. So distant.

For some reason, to her, a baby being born asleep sounded easier. Even though she knew the reality was that nothing could make it easier. She wasn't going to keep talking. She wasn't going to bombard Hasana with anything else.

She wasn't going to tell her she couldn't give her a reason why this had happened to her baby. She wasn't going to tell her there was no reason that she couldn't have a healthy child in the future.

Because right now this was all about this baby. Hasana still had at least an hour of labor to go through.

A first labor. A long labor. And what should have been labor of love had turned into a labor of sorrow. And in that moment Violet knew. She wasn't going to go anywhere. She was going to stay right here and hold Hasana's hand. It was one thing she was absolutely sure of.

Urbi translated her words. Another labor pain gripped Hasana's body, the tightening of her abdomen apparent. But her sobs were reaching far and beyond the labor pain. The noises she was making sounded like her very heart had been ripped out of her body. Her friend kept her arm wrapped around Hasana's shoulders, holding her close and letting her sob. Silent tears dripped down her cheeks as she tried to be strong for her friend.

Violet put her hand on top of Urbi's. "If it's all right with you, I'll stay. I've got some experience in this. I'll help you."

Urbi nodded her head. "Thank you, Dr. Violet." Her dark eyes watched her carefully. "Most people want to leave the birthing room when they know there isn't going to be a joyous celebration at the other end."

Violet could feel the tears pooling in her eyes. She had to stay strong. She had to stay professional. It was the best way she could support Hasana. "Every baby's birth should be celebrated, Urbi, no matter what the outcome."

Urbi's head tilted to one side, her years of experience very evident. It was almost as if she was reading Violet like an open book. Instantly understanding all the secrets she'd kept hidden away for the past three years. She wrapped her hand tightly around Violet's and gave it a little squeeze. "You are a good woman, Dr. Violet. May the Lord bless you."

There was a loud noise outside. Indistinguishable.

Urbi started. She spoke rapidly to Hasana then turned to Violet. "Let me go and check what that was."

She disappeared in a sweep of skirts, the dust clouding around her. Violet peeked out of the door in curiosity. Had a car backfired?

She could see people coming out of the houses surrounding them, all walking in the direction of the noise. Men were shouting at their families to stay inside. Urbi was nowhere in sight.

A horrible sensation started to sweep over her, a real prickling of unease.

She ducked her head back inside, holding Hasana's hand through another contraction. She pulled a pair of gloves from her bag and signaled to Hasana. "Can I check?"

The language barrier appeared to have disappeared. She knew exactly what Violet wanted to do. Violet did an internal examination and found Hasana was fully dilated. Any time now the baby's head would start crowning.

She pulled her hand back just as her brain realized what the noise outside was. Hasana let out a little shriek.

Gunfire. That was definitely gunfire.

Panic. She instantly felt sick. Adrenaline started coursing through her veins. The fight-or-flight response had never been so obvious.

In the distance she could hear voices shouting, followed by gunfire. What on earth were they in the middle of?

Hasana's female companion darted outside. Where was she going? Was she leaving them?

Violet tried to remain focused. She had to make a decision in the next few seconds. Hasana might be able to move in the next few minutes, but once she started crowning it would be virtually impossible.

She had no information to go on. How on earth could she assess their safety, their risk? And where on earth would they go?

Her heart thudded in her chest. For the first time in two weeks she wished Evan was by her side. She didn't feel strong. She didn't feel ready to deal with anything like this.

The voices were louder now. Fear started to grip her chest. There had been reports about attempted kidnappings, bomb threats and health staff being slain.

All their intelligence had told them it was in the next state. There had been nothing to indicate any trouble at all near here.

But could she wait and take that chance?

What would Evan do?

Hasana's friend reappeared. She tugged at Violet's arm. "Go. Now. They are looking for you."

It was like all her worst fears realized. Her head went from one woman in the throes of labor to the other tugging her arm and pleading with her to leave.

"What about the rest of the team?" She might be the only doctor, but there had been four other community workers with her today. Where would they go?

Now she knew.

Now she understood what it felt like to have responsibility for the health and wellbeing of team members. Who to leave at risk—the staff or the patients? How on earth could someone make a decision like that?

"The villagers will hide them." It made sense. The community workers were all from surrounding areas and all had dark skin and wore traditional dress. As long as their equipment was hidden they could easily blend in. Her blond hair and pale skin would make her stand out like a sore thumb. It would put everyone at risk.

Hasana managed to stand up and gripped her other arm. "I need you. Please." For a woman who couldn't speak or understand much English, her words were crystal clear.

She'd never felt so conflicted. Evan had given them all clear directions if they encountered any hostility. *Don't hesitate. Get out.*

But her Hippocratic oath was bouncing around in her head. She had a duty of care to Hasana. She had to help her.

And Evan wasn't here. No matter how much she wanted him to be.

She darted around the room, picking up the few things she thought she might need. Bags, gloves, the polio supplies to hide and a few blankets. Her brain was frantically trying to formulate a plan. The truck. Evan had said always to head toward the truck. It was their guarantee of getting out. Their safe passage back to camp.

But the noises sounded as if they were coming from that direction—the compound where they had left the truck.

Then she heard it. A loud, screaming woman's voice. Urbi. And straight away she knew why. She was making as much noise as she could. Obviously to try and warn Violet to get out.

Her voice was up against another, a male voice shouting back. Their dialogue was a mixture of English and Hausa. "The doctor left this morning," Urbi was shrieking.

Violet headed for the door, dropping the things that she held haphazardly in her arms. "Leave them," Hasana's friend hissed as she scrambled about the floor, grabbing what she could.

Her bag. Her satellite phone. But she had no time. The voices were only a few houses away.

Violet slipped her arm around Hasana's waist, ducking her head, and they made their way as quickly as they could between the houses. She had no idea where she was going. All she knew was that she couldn't head toward the truck.

A figure stepped out in front of them, causing her to gasp in alarm.

The dark-skinned Fulani man in traditional dress silently pointed his finger in one direction. She'd vaccinated his children earlier.

She nodded in acknowledgment and hurried in the direction he pointed. It only took a few seconds to realize he was sending them out of the village and into the nearby hardwood forest. Plenty of cover for both of them.

They stopped for a few minutes as Hasana was gripped by another labor pain. She held on to a nearby tree trunk until she'd breathed her way through it. The voices were coming nearer. Closing in on them.

It was the most terrified Violet had ever been. She didn't know if she was more scared for Hasana or for herself. What would they do to Hasana if they caught her with the doctor? Would it actually be safer to leave Hasana behind?

No.

Hasana needed her right now. And she couldn't imagine abandoning her—not even for a second.

They stumbled through the forest, moving away

from the thinner trees on the outskirts and into the darker depths. She felt herself drop something again as she held on tightly to Hasana, helping support her, but didn't dare look back to see what it was. They pressed on into the forest.

Violet kept glancing over her shoulder, praying that no one had noticed them and no one was following. She couldn't hear the voices anymore or the gunfire. That had to be a good sign.

She urged Hasana on. What she really wanted right now was her satellite phone. If she'd had it she could have phoned Evan and he could have arranged to get them out of here and get some support for Hasana.

In her head she could see it lying on the floor of the birthing room. Going back for it might have cost them their lives. No phone was worth that.

Hasana crouched down, her labor obviously progressing. They were near a mound of dark moss. Violet spread a blanket across it and urged Hasana to sit down. She pulled some gloves from her pocket and checked her again.

But she didn't need to. Hasana's baby was almost crowning.

Violet raised her eyes skyward and started some silent prayers. Please don't let them be found—they couldn't move now.

Please don't let there be any birth complications. It was too late to save the baby. But Hasana's life could still be at stake here. Hemorrhage, abruption, there could be whole host of delivery complications that could risk Hasana's life. And she was hardly equipped to deal with them.

She gestured at Hasana, signaling when to push and when to relax. Hasana's sobs grew louder. She didn't have her friend's hand to hold any more. She didn't have anyone other than Violet to support her. And they both knew what would happen next.

Evan was staring at the calendar, counting the number of days until they could head back to Atlanta.

What on earth would he say to the director once he got there? The polio program was likely to be a success. But his teamwork? His professionalism? His relationship with Violet?

Strike one. Strike two. Strike Three. Out.

It didn't bear thinking about.

Violet had barely spoken to him for the past two weeks.

And he couldn't blame her.

It didn't matter that her last words had been about forgiving himself. She couldn't really have meant that. Not after what he'd told her.

It was no wonder she didn't want to be around him. He didn't want to be around him either.

He knew that she'd spoken to her brother a few times in the past two weeks. Had she told Sawyer what had happened between them? Would her brother be waiting at Atlanta airport with a baseball bat? That was all he needed.

He'd told Violet that they had *unresolved issues*. And he was right. They did.

Violet had told him he needed to forgive himself. And he was sorting all that out in his head—truly, he was.

But in order to fully be at peace with himself, the one thing he was absolutely sure about was that he was going to have to speak to Sawyer.

He didn't want to do it over the phone. He could

have used the opportunity in the past few weeks when Sawyer had phoned to speak to Violet. But this was too big for Evan. Too important. He needed to do it face-to-face.

The way he should have done six years earlier, before Matt Sawyer had disappeared.

And he had to take whatever Sawyer dished out because Violet was right about one thing. He couldn't live like this forever.

The phone next to him started ringing. He reached over and grabbed it. "Evan Hunter."

It was a hysterical babble. Not a single word made sense. It took him a few seconds for his brain to recognize the voice. "Jaja? Jaja, is that you?"

He stood up, the tone of his voice causing everyone around the room to stop dead.

"What is it, Jaja? Slow down, I can't make you out."

He gestured to one of the other team members. "Pull up the GPS signal."

He had six separate teams in different areas today, all working on the polio program. Where was Jaja working?

"What do you mean, gunfire? Who was firing? Where is the staff? Is any of the staff at risk? Are you safe?"

He was firing questions at Jaja and he knew he should take a deep breath and keep calm. The connection was terrible. He could hardly make out a single word. All he could gather was that there had been trouble in the village, shooting, and Jaja had barely made it to the truck in time to get out.

He started looking frantically at the papers on his desk, all describing the latest events in the neighboring state. There had been nothing about Natumba state.

Nothing at all. He'd been advised to continue working. Had he just put his staff at risk? Had he sent them to an area where they could have been kidnapped? Or worse?

The bounty on a healthcare worker's head was huge.

The thought made him feel physically sick.

His brain was in overdrive. "What village, Jaja? Say it again. What village?"

He shouted the name across the room to the worker on the GPS system. "Who do we have there?"

Silence. The staff were waiting. Waiting to hear who was at risk.

The tension was almost palpable. Everyone seemed to be holding their breath.

The man sitting at the screen pulled up a table, covering the intensive GPS tracking system they used. His face paled. He rattled off the names—four community workers, Jaja among them. Then he hesitated and turned to face Evan. "And Violet." His voice was almost a whisper. Everyone knew about their relationship.

Evan could hear a roaring in his ears. His worst dream had just been realized. For a second time stood still. He felt as if he were in one of those slow-motion movie scenes. This couldn't be happening.

His legs moved automatically over to the screen. "Do you have the signals?" Beside him a hand picked up the phone, reporting back to headquarters, while another voice started shouting about pulling a team together.

The screen operator nodded, focusing the map on the village. From an aerial view there were five signals. One was moving away rapidly—Jaja.

Three others were unmoving, one slightly outside the village limits.

One of the local staff moved up next to his elbow. "The workers will be hiding. The villagers will have taken them somewhere. Somewhere they won't be recognized."

"Where's this? Where is this area?"

Evan's finger was stabbing at the screen. This whole exercise was futile. Even though the workers all wore the GPS trackers, it only showed their positions. They didn't show a heartbeat. Didn't tell him if they were dead or alive. Didn't tell him if they were injured. Didn't tell him if they were safe or in danger.

And right now that was all he cared about.

The screen operator pulled up satellite images of the area surrounding the village. His face screwed up a little. "That looks like the outskirts, leading into the forest."

A forest. Cover. It could mean only one thing.

Evan felt a pull at his heart. "Violet. That's got to be Violet."

There was only one person who would need to head into the forest during conflict. One person who would be easy to spot in the village. He only prayed that Violet had headed into the forest of her own volition and not under duress.

The thought that entered his mind horrified him.

He pressed the phone next to his ear. "Come back here, Jaja. Right now. Don't stop. I need you to tell me everything you know." He turned to someone else. "How far away is that village?"

One of the staff members signaled him and said, "Headquarters say you've to stay put. You've not to go to the village under any circumstances. They will try and find out more intel for us. In the meantime, all staff are to start packing. It's likely they'll pull us all out."

Most of the faces in the room had paled. Imminent

danger. That was the message from headquarters. They all knew what that meant.

You cleared out. You didn't go back for team members. This wasn't the military.

Evan let out a roar. His hand cleared the nearby desk of everything that was stacked on it. Several staff jumped out of their seats.

"I will not leave without Violet!" His voice filled the room, echoing in every corner.

He stormed out of the office into the corridor, his head pounding. *No. No.*

He couldn't lose another team member. He couldn't live with himself.

Not Violet. Not the one person in this world he couldn't live without.

It didn't matter if she hated him. It didn't matter if she never forgave him. He could live with that. He could survive. As long as he knew that Violet was somewhere else in the world and safe.

That was all he could think about. That was all he could focus on.

Luke, one of the team members, approached him. "I've got the other truck ready. We'll be ready to go in five minutes. We can meet Jaja *en route*. We can stop and get the intel we need from him before we get to the village."

"What?" He tried to focus. Tried to see beyond the rage that was currently invading his head. He couldn't believe his ears. Everyone had just been told to get ready to leave. The instruction had been clear. Everyone was to pack up and wait for the evacuation.

It didn't matter to the haphazard plan that was currently igniting in his brain. He couldn't ever ask any member of his team to do what he was about to do.

He could never let anyone risk their life for him, or for Violet. It was too much. Too much to ask of anyone.

He caught the dark arm next to him. "No, Luke. I can't ask you to do that. I won't ask you to do that. Pack up. Supervise the rest of the team. Wait for the call from Headquarters about the evacuation."

Luke shook his head ever so slightly. There was no emotion in his voice. "You didn't ask, Evan. You wouldn't ask. But I won't leave. I was in the military. I'm the right hand that you need. Now, let's go get Violet."

Evan couldn't breathe. There was an iron fist gripped around his heart. He couldn't let Luke do this with him. There was no way he'd be leaving without Violet, but the thought that another human being would knowingly walk into something they might not get back out of—for him, for Violet—was too much of a struggle.

His team leader instincts were screaming at him to keep everyone safe. He'd spent the past six years whispering that mantra to himself, ever since Helen's death. Team safety meant everything to him. Sometimes to the detriment of the role of the DPA. Evan would never let team safety be compromised again.

This went against everything he believed in. It went against everything he lived for.

How could he accept help? Pictures of Helen's weak body being held by her husband haunted his mind. His brain couldn't even comprehend the risk.

He shouted some instructions to the other members of staff—to communicate with the villagers, to leave supplies of everything, to pack only essentials, to keep in constant contact with headquarters.

People were rushing past him. "Do you have a portable version of that?" He pointed to the GPS mapping system.

The analyst nodded and pulled a laptop out of the wall. "It's fully charged. Press this and this. Refresh every five minutes."

They were all the instructions he needed.

He strode back out toward the truck. Luke had positioned himself directly in front of it. Directly in Evan's path. His large frame was blocking out the sunlight. "Ready?"

Evan hesitated. He was team leader. He should order Luke to pack and leave. But something was stopping him. Something was making him take stock.

And this wasn't about Violet.

This was about all the things in life that couldn't be controlled. That *he* couldn't control. No matter how hard that was to accept.

Luke was making his own decision. A grown-up, adult decision to accompany a member of staff on a mission they might not return from. A mission to retrieve their colleagues.

He was an adult with his own free mind. Evan knew that if someone had told him he couldn't try and rescue Violet, he wouldn't have listened. Not for a heartbeat.

Why should Luke be any different? As a military man he probably understood the risks better than Evan ever could. But he was still here.

And in that instant Evan understood.

Understood that he had to accept the things he couldn't control. He had to let Luke make his own decision. He wasn't responsible for everything around him.

He was team leader. Not a ruler. Not a military commander.

He was one man. And there was only so much he

could control. So much he could be in charge of. No matter how much he hated it.

And right now all of his thoughts were on Violet.

He extended his hand toward Luke. "Thank you. Thank you for your help."

Luke shook his hand swiftly. "Let's go."

They'd been in the forest for just over an hour now. Violet tucked her watch back into her pocket.

She had no idea what was going on in the village right now. Was everyone safe? She couldn't bear the thought that anyone from the village had been injured trying to protect and hide her and her team.

Urbi. What would have they done with her? Someone must have told them the midwife had been working with the American doctor. Would she be safe?

What about the men who had come into the village? Were they still there, waiting for her to reappear? Had they been able to identify her team among the villagers?

She didn't even know what the men looked like. How many had there been? She'd only heard one voice. She'd heard the gunfire and the shrieks. Then the whispers that they were looking for her and wanted to kidnap her.

It was terrifying.

It didn't matter that she'd had safety briefings. She hadn't really believed they would be at risk. There had been no trouble in that area before and the truth was she'd always felt safe with the people in Natumba.

She hated that this had happened. She hated that this could put the polio program in jeopardy.

And she hated what this might be doing to Evan.

If it was possible, her blood would be running cold right now. He would be frantic—and in that state of mind there was possibility that he wouldn't act rationally.

Evan could put himself in danger—for her, and for the rest of the team, and she couldn't stand the thought of that.

She already knew that losing another team member was his greatest fear. She couldn't imagine the agony he was going through right now.

And he was the one person she wanted to talk to. It seemed almost ridiculous that she'd spent the past two weeks avoiding him. At any point she could have sat down with him and talked things out.

But no. She'd been too stubborn.

Her brain had still been mulling over what he'd told her. It had stung initially. That tiny second of deliberating whether he'd actually been to blame for Helen's death.

Of course he hadn't been. It was ridiculous.

But what was really obvious was that Evan had a way to go before he was ready to move on. She'd been deadly serious when she'd told him the first person he needed to forgive was himself.

She knew a lot about that.

She'd had a mountain to climb in order to forgive herself over her daughter's death. There was no blame to apportion and sometimes that made it all the harder to move on. To take the step forward to a new life.

She really didn't think she could handle someone else's unjustified guilt when she'd just managed to walk away from her own.

There was a rustle of leaves right next to them. She jumped and Hasana's eyes widened. She was in the grips of another labour pain—they were coming much quicker now—and she looked as if she wanted to cry out.

Hasana grabbed a piece of dry bark and pushed it between her teeth.

Violet felt as if she couldn't breathe because even taking a breath made a little noise that someone might hear. That could reveal their position.

She put her fingers silently to her lips, praying that Hasana wouldn't let a noise escape.

The leaves rustled again and Violet strained her ears. She couldn't hear footsteps. She couldn't hear voices. And somehow she didn't think these men would come through the forest quietly if they were looking for her.

The rustle continued. Then a small reptilian head appeared, followed by a body slithering along the ground.

A snake. The rustle had been a snake.

Violet didn't know whether to let out a sigh of relief or not. Was that type of snake poisonous?

She pointed with her finger and Hasana shook her head, gripping the tree bark with her teeth. A snake was the last thing on her mind right now.

Violet watched as the snake seemed to look in their direction once then slithered off without another glance.

Maybe bringing Hasana into the forest hadn't been such a good idea.

She waited for a few more seconds, listening for any other noises. But there were none.

She placed her hands on Hasana's belly. The baby was in the correct position. Its head had engaged and the labor seemed to be proceeding well. The baby was a good size. Maybe too big for a first-time mother?

Violet hoped not. She didn't have access to a theatre if an emergency Caesarean section was needed. She didn't even have access to a set of forceps if the baby's head became stuck on the way down.

Hasana was going to have to do all this on her own.

She checked the position of the baby again. The head was crowning. It was time for Hasana to push.

Something washed over her. She was about to face her greatest fear all over again. Only this time the pain wouldn't be hers, it would be someone else's. She had to be strong. She had to be strong for Hasana.

She had to push all her thoughts and fears aside. She had to get through this.

Stillbirths weren't unusual in Nigeria. But more than half of them occurred while the woman was in labor. Most happened in rural areas where skilled birth attendants or midwives weren't available.

That hadn't been the case for Hasana. But there were five major reasons for stillbirth. Childbirth complications, maternal infections, congenital abnormalities, fetal growth restriction and maternal disorders such as diabetes or pre-eclampsia.

Violet was running through all these in her head. The baby felt a reasonable size so there couldn't be a fetal growth problem. Urbi had told her there had been no complications during the pregnancy, so she was assuming pre-eclampsia, diabetes and maternal infections were not a possibility. There was no way to know if there were any congenital abnormalities—not until the baby was born.

Back home in the U.S. women were screened for congenital abnormalities and things were often picked by obstetricians doing detailed scans. But Hasana had had none of these tests available to her. They wouldn't be able to tell if something was wrong with the baby until he or she was born.

Hasana's muscles contracted tightly again—another contraction. And Violet held up her fists and scrunched up her face, miming pushing.

Hasana let out a cry, pushing with all her might. The time for being silent had obviously passed. The baby's head appeared between her thighs.

Violet's actions were second nature. It didn't matter that this baby was already dead. She'd gone back into junior doctor phase and was checking around the baby's neck for a cord. There was nothing there. Nothing restricting the baby's breathing. Nothing that could have led to its death.

Another push and the shoulders appeared, quickly followed by the rest of the slippery body. Violet caught the little baby in her hands, grabbing one of the blankets to wrap it in.

A baby boy. Hasana had a baby boy.

She wiped his little face. Praying against everything that he would breathe. But his pale lips against his dark skin showed that would never happen.

He was perfect. In every single way.

Her heart felt as if it could break all over again.

Hasana lay panting, exhausted after the delivery of her sleeping child.

There was no obvious congenital abnormality. No obvious reason for this baby to have been born asleep.

Just like hers. Just like her own daughter.

It didn't matter that nothing here reminded her of home and her own experience. It didn't matter that this forest floor was about as far removed from an Atlanta hospital as it was possible to be.

All that mattered was the perfect little boy in her hands. The little boy who should have been breathing.

She lifted him to her shoulder and held him for a few seconds. The umbilical cord was still attached, still making him part of his mother. She would deal with that in a few seconds.

She took a deep breath. Baby. New baby smell. It surrounded her in all its wonder. If only this moment could be different. If only she could be handing over a screaming baby to his mother.

She didn't care about the potential kidnappers in the forest. She didn't care about being silent anymore. She only wanted to will this little baby to life.

A single tear dripped down her face.

Life was so unfair. This little boy should be taking his first breaths. This little boy should be allowed to grow. He should have a life ahead of him.

He should be able to learn to crawl and to walk and talk. He should be part of a loving family. He should grow from childhood to teenage years, to adulthood. A life probably with intermittent hardships but a life worth living.

Instead, in her arms she had a silent, beautiful baby boy.

She helped Hasana sit up. She didn't have syntometrine to inject and help with the third stage of delivery. She was lucky to have something to clamp and cut the cord.

There was no one to translate for her now. Hasana spoke mainly Hausa, and she herself only English. But, here in the middle of the forest, they would have to muddle through.

She handed over the baby to Hasana. "You have a beautiful son, Hasana." She couldn't help the tears that fell down her cheeks. Hasana would think she was crying for her son—and in a way she was. She was crying for every sleeping baby that had ever been born. As only a mother could.

She wrapped her arm tightly around Hasana's shoulders, watching her embrace her little boy. She watched as Hasana dropped kisses on each of his eyelids and lifted his hands from the blanket and counted his tiny fingers.

It was almost as if she was embracing his perfection. The fact that in every way he looked like a healthy baby.

Her shoulders were racked with sobs and her tears soaked Violet's *buba* shirt. The light was beginning to dim among the trees. But Violet didn't want to pull her watch out and check the time.

Time here was more precious than anything. Hasana needed this time to spend with her son. To mourn his loss. To start the long grieving process that Violet knew inside out.

The hopelessness.

The despair.

The endless questions.

Everything would change once they returned to the village. Her family and friends would take over. Probably arranging a burial and blessing for the baby. Doing what they thought was best for Hasana.

But right now, right here, there was no need for any of that.

This was a time for mother and son to be together.

And although the rest of the world might not understand, this was the most precious time of all.

The one thing you could never get back.

And Violet had all the time in the world.

CHAPTER ELEVEN

LUKE PULLED THE truck over to the side of the road. "Now we go on foot."

Evan's eyes scoured the surrounding area. They hadn't reached the village yet but the last thing he wanted to do was announce their arrival.

They'd met Jaja on the road. He'd been hysterical and had wanted to come back with them. But it was obvious he wouldn't be of any use. He was jabbering incessantly and still shaking with fear. It had taken all Evan's self-control not to shake him by the shoulders to get some sense out of him.

Finally, they'd managed to find out a little more. The men had arrived in the village around 3:00 p.m. There had been four of them, all in one truck. They'd fired shots into the air and had demanded to know where the American doctor was.

Jaja had been on the other side of the compound, next to the truck in which Violet and the rest of the community workers had arrived. He hadn't had time to look for the others. He knew that Violet had been with the local midwife, Urbi, and the others working between houses in the villages. The armed men had been between Jaja and his colleagues. And as he'd jumped into the truck and sped away to raise the alarm, they'd fired at him. The evidence was all around the body of the truck.

Evan had quickly checked him over and sent him back to the camp. There was still no further information from headquarters.

"You know we should wait, don't you?" he said to Luke as they walked alone the edge of the dusty road.

Luke raised his eyebrow. "Are you going to wait?"

Evan couldn't meet his eyes.

"Then neither am I. But you do exactly as I say. I don't have a gun, we don't have any kind of weapon. We're going to skirt around the outside of the village and see if we can work out if the kidnappers are still there."

Evan glanced at his watch. It was nearing seven o'clock and the light was beginning to fade. The village was nearly ninety minutes away from camp, but the journey had seemed much longer.

His brain had computed a million possibilities in that time, most of which he didn't want to consider. He hated the way he kept falling on the worst-case scenario. He hated the way the rational part of his brain had ceased to function.

As their truck had sped along the dusty road he had kept praying someone from the village would make contact via the satellite phone but no one had heard a word. And they had no other form of communication.

In the shadows the outline of the village houses started to appear. Luke signaled him to get behind him as they crept slowly around the edge of the first house. Everything was silent. A quick glance told them no one was inside.

They worked their way systematically toward the center of the village. From the deathly silence on the outskirts they started to hear the gentle hum of voices. As they moved closer the noise level increased.

Evan tilted his head to one side as they strained to hear. "It sounds like panic," he whispered. "A lot of shouting, mainly in Hausa, with a little English."

Luke gave him a nod. "I'm going to get a little closer." He put his hand up as Evan tried to move behind him. "You're the doctor. Stay here. It will only take me a few seconds. Once I know for sure there's no one with guns, I'll signal you." His dark eyes flashed. "I mean it, Doc, don't move. There might be people in the village who need your help. I don't want you to get injured."

He moved away silently around the edge of one of the houses, virtually invisible in the fading light.

Evan strained to hear. The voices just sounded like a rabble to him. But there was no gunfire. No shooting. He hated having to stay here. His legs were itching to run—to run and find Violet. To make sure she was safe.

But if the kidnappers were still in the village, they would be only too happy to find another American doctor, and he knew that. Luke was right. He had to wait a few minutes and then see if any of the villagers needed attention. He knew all about his duty as a doctor. But what about his duty to Violet?

"Evan! Come out, you're needed!" Luke's deep voice cut through the dying light. Evan's blood started to pump and he ran toward the voice.

The noise around him increased rapidly. It seemed as if every resident of the village had made their way into the village center. That's why all the houses were empty and silent. There were several people on the ground. He recognized one of them immediately. Urbi. The village midwife.

He was at her side in seconds. Luke appeared at his

shoulder. "The men left the village little over an hour ago. They couldn't find Violet. They searched everywhere."

One of the community workers touched Evan's elbow. Her dark face was filled with anxiety. "We had to hide Dr. Hunter. When the men appeared, we had no choice but to hide among the villagers."

Evan was examining the deep wound on Urbi's head. "What happened?"

"Urbi was knocked unconscious. She delayed the men from reaching Violet. She told them Violet had already left the village. They hit her with a rifle butt."

His stomach was clenching. Violet. This woman had been injured trying to save Violet.

He couldn't stop himself. His head flicked frantically around. "Where is she? Where is Violet?"

He took a pack of swabs from his bag and held them to Urbi's forehead. Her small hand reached up over his. "We don't know, Dr. Hunter. She must have heard me shouting. When they got to the birthing room she was gone. She was helping me with a patient." She winced as he tried to stem the flow of blood. "They discovered some of her things in the birthing room. She must have dropped them. That's when they hit me."

Evan's stomach flipped over again. "But they didn't find her?"

One of the other villagers was shaking his head. "No."

Luke was kneeling next to another man. His shoulder had been grazed by a bullet. Another seemed to have been punched and one of the village elders had a similar wound to Urbi's.

Evan looked around at these people—most that he didn't know—who had hidden his staff and saved their lives. "Thank you," he said. "From the bottom of my heart, thank you for looking after the health workers."

A hand appeared on his shoulder and a variety of items were deposited on the ground next to him. Violet's bag. Her smashed satellite phone. Some of the polio supplies.

The sight of her battered belongings in front of him tore at his soul. It was obvious why no one had been able to contact them. The men had obviously destroyed the satellite phone once they'd found it.

He cast his eyes over the patients. Luke was a physician's assistant in the U.S. There was nothing here he couldn't deal with. He stood up. "Luke, can you deal with these people, please? I need to look for Violet."

Luke nodded briefly. The danger was past. There was no reason for him to stop Evan.

"Urbi, do you have any idea where Violet could be?"

"She was with a patient. A villager who was in labor. They must have gone somewhere to hide."

"But where could they have gone?" His eyes took in the surrounding area. The uneven rows of houses around them. The backdrop of the forest.

The forest. The ideal place to hide a conspicuous white face.

Urbi's hand reached out to his. "Dr. Hunter—the patient..."

He knelt back down. "What is it? Was something wrong with the patient? Was that why Violet didn't leave her?"

Urbi's expression was guarded. She gestured for him to move closer so she could whisper in his ear. "The baby. It was too late for the baby. There was no heartbeat. But the mother still had to deliver it."

Evan nodded. Violet must have been worried about

complications of delivery for the mother. That's why she'd stayed by her side. That's why she'd taken her with her.

But there was something else. Urbi pulled him a little closer. "Dr. Violet. She understood. Once she realized the baby was dead. She said she wanted to stay. She wanted to help."

Evan pulled back a little. Violet was a compassionate person. He didn't think she had much experience in obstetrics, and he knew there was a high stillbirth rate in Nigeria so she must have wanted to help.

"Please find them." She squeezed his hand.

Finding Violet was all he could think about right now—all he could focus on. Someone pressed a torch into his hand. "You might need this."

He stared down at the torch. The confusion in his brain didn't matter. The way that things were circling in his head didn't matter. There was movement beside him and he looked. A number of the villagers had formed a group around him.

His understanding was instant. In the poor light it would be difficult to find anyone in the forest. He had no idea how far Violet and the woman in labor might have traveled. It could be anything from a few hundred yards to as far as they had been physically able to.

Again, the people in this village were prepared to help. He was touched.

He drew his shoulders back. "Okay, Luke?"

Luke nodded. "No problem. I'll be waiting for you when you get back." The unspoken words were there. *When you get back with Violet.*

Evan nodded at the people around him. "Thank you. Thank you so much." They walked swiftly through the houses to the edge of the forest. There, the villagers started to talk among themselves and split into groups.

He pulled out the laptop he'd been given and reloaded the GPS software. The little red blip on the aerial view was still evident. He held up the laptop so the people around him could see, showing the view of the forest and where the red blip lay. "That should be Violet," he said out loud. He tried to picture where they were on the map. "We need to head in that direction." It seemed as though Violet had veered off to the left and headed into the forest for about half a mile. A hard trek in these conditions—let alone with a pregnant woman in labor.

There were no obvious paths into the forest, no tracks leading in different directions. Several of the stronger men had brought stiff canes with them, obviously to beat back some of the thicker leaves and jagged bushes.

Evan took one that was being held out toward him. He watched as several others starting beating at the bushes in front of them, clearing a path into the forest.

He started doing the same. Several of the men followed him, their torches helping to light up the dark forest. Shadows and outlines seemed to loom everywhere. The noise of the insects around them increased with every step they took further into the forest. He started slapping at his skin. Mosquitoes. He hadn't even thought about insect repellent. By the time they finished they would be eaten alive.

The deeper they went, the denser the forest became. The ground around his feet seemed alive. Every step crunched on something underfoot. The trees were closer together now, their trunks thicker and leaves slapping around him. The distance between the groups was increasing as they spread out to cover more ground between them.

Evan wasn't really sure which direction they were heading in any more. The forest could be disorientating. Especially at night. How would Violet be feeling? Would she be scared? Would the patient be in trouble?

He stopped for a second, looking around, sweeping his torch through the leaves and bushes.

There was no point in pulling out the GPS software now. It was only useful if you knew where you were in relation to the signal. He could hear shouts around him. The other searchers were obviously getting disorientated. Was it safe to continue?

There was no way Evan was going back to the village without Violet. No way at all. "Violet! Violet!" He started shouting like the others, stopping every few seconds to listen for any response.

Nothing. Were they heading in the right direction? He started to move a little more left, his torch trying to find an easier path for their feet.

His shoulders and arms were aching relentlessly as he tried to beat the bushes and leaves back. At least Violet would have been able to see these in the daylight and duck out of their way. He could hear some muttering behind him. How long had they been out here? Were the villagers starting to lose heart?

His torch caught a glimpse of something unusual. A color he didn't expect to see. He dropped to the forest floor and scrabbled about. A notebook. Violet's notebook with the distinctive purple flowers. His heart leaped. They were heading in the right direction.

"Look! It's Violet's!" He showed it to the men behind him, who instantly shouted to the other groups.

His adrenaline surged. The pain in his arms was forgotten. She must be close. She must be nearby. "Violet! Violet!"

Every step had renewed vigor. His calls were louder than before. His shouts echoed through the forest. All the men were repeating them over and over.

Then he heard something. Something different.

"Quiet!"

He stopped moving and held his breath.

Then he heard it. A hoarse reply. "Evan?"

He'd never heard anything sweeter.

He flung his stick aside, crashing through the forest toward the voice. He burst through into a little clearing. Dark moss, set among some trees. Violet huddled on a fallen tree trunk, her arm around another figure and a little wrapped bundle in her arms.

"Evan." The relief in her voice washed over him. Her pale face could be picked out easily in the dark night. He crossed the clearing in a couple of strides and pulled her into his arms.

"Are you all right? I've been so worried. No one knew where you'd gone." His eyes caught the woman to her right. "Did the delivery go okay? Is there something we can do for your patient?"

Violet shook her head silently. The men from the village had heard the shouts and crowded into the clearing. One of them rushed forward and took Hasana in his arms, shouting with relief.

Violet felt the tears on her face instantly. She laid a gentle kiss on the baby in her arms. She whispered to him, stroking the skin on his face as she talked to him a little longer.

And in that instant, Evan knew.

It felt as if a hand was squeezing his heart inside his chest. It was the tenderness, the look on her face. Pieces of the puzzle started dropping into place.

Violet was a good doctor—she'd always been a good

doctor. But she'd risked her life to stay with this woman. She'd trekked through a forest to keep her, and a baby that she already knew was lost, safe.

Evan's skin prickled.

No. Not Violet. That couldn't have happened to Violet.

Things started to jumble around in his brain. The look on Violet's face when he'd told her she would be working with the midwives.

He hadn't been able to place it at the time. Had it been fear?

Violet had seemed so at ease with the young children and the babies. Surely she wouldn't feel like that if she'd experienced a stillbirth? Surely she would want to run in the other direction?

He racked his brain. He tried to remember all the types of work Violet had covered in the past few years at the DPA.

None had been with children and families. None at all. Had she been avoiding that kind of work?

Other things started to come back. The few things that she'd said in the quiet moments they'd had together.

The fact she hadn't been ready to have a relationship six months ago. Why hadn't she been ready? He'd wanted to press her, had wanted to ask, but it hadn't seemed appropriate.

The fleeting look in her eyes when he'd told her about his friend who worked at Atlanta Memorial. It had the biggest maternity unit in Atlanta.

Was it because she'd had a stillbirth? Was it because she'd had a stillbirth there?

But why would no one know about it? The thought of Violet going through something so heartbreaking made him feel sick.

Was this why he'd never heard of Violet having a relationship in the past three years?

Had she been getting over a stillbirth?

His throat was instantly dry. He couldn't swallow. He'd been in bed with this woman. He'd spent hours in her company.

Why hadn't she told him about this?

He hadn't been able to be around her when he'd thought he was keeping secrets from her. That's what had made him blurt out something he'd kept deep inside for six years.

He'd had to share with her. He'd had to get it off his chest. Because his relationship with Violet hadn't stood a chance without him being honest with her.

So why hadn't she told him anything?

He felt a little fire build inside him. There was more than the personal side here. There was the professional side. He was her team leader.

If a personal event could have affected her ability to do her job out here, he should have known about it.

She should have told him. It should have on her personnel file. Someone should have told him.

Nothing made sense to him.

Hasana was talking to her husband. She was sobbing and obviously tired and distressed.

Her husband looked over toward Violet and didn't hesitate for a second, he held out his hands for his son.

Violet held him out with trembling hands and he took him, putting his arm around his wife and the two of them sat together, crying quietly. He cradled his son, stroking his face then looked at his wife. "Bem." She nodded and put her head on his shoulder as the two of them sat, looking at their child.

Not for Bem the traditional village naming ceremony in seven days' time. His mother and father wouldn't have the usual cause for celebration. But naming their baby was still precious to them, and Violet understood that.

Violet could hear the murmurs of the men around her. She heard one of them speak to Evan. "His name— it means peace."

Violet stood up moved to the edge of the clearing. She wanted to give them space to grieve together as a family, but she also felt as if she was suffocating.

The darkness and heavy air was closing in around her. She was struggling to breathe and she clawed at the loose *buba* shirt at her neck.

"Violet, what's wrong?" Evan stood in front of her, his wide chest blocking her line of vision. White. He was wearing white. And it cut through the blackness.

His hand touched her cheek, catching a tear with his finger. He pulled her back toward him and cradled her head against his chest, letting her feel the rise and fall of his chest. Her breathing slowed and her panic ebbed. His other reached up and stroked her hair. "You're safe now."

And she did feel safe. It was a relief to finally have some other people around her, to share the burden of being alone in the dark forest with a traumatized patient.

To feel the warmth and strength of someone's arms around her. But the tightness in her chest was spreading. Sobs rose up in her throat.

She'd just witnessed something very precious. Hasana's husband was grieving for his son as much as she was. He'd held his hands out for his son without hesitation and had looked at him with such tenderness it had broken her heart.

Her daughter had never had that. A father's love. A father to grieve over her. Blane had sent her a simple card when he'd heard the news. He hadn't been there to see how precious their daughter had been. How perfect. How beautiful.

He hadn't touched her little cheek or held her close to his chest.

Not the way Hasana's husband had for their son.

And it hurt. Just when she thought she was moving on, she realized there was something else to regret about her daughter's birth.

Evan lifted her chin so she faced him. His eyes were looking straight at her, illuminated by the torchlight around them. His blue eyes were dark, with the gold flecks standing out in the dim light. There was intensity about them she'd never seen before.

And even though she could see a hundred questions in his eyes he didn't hesitate—he pulled her into his arms and just held her. Held her as if he'd never let her go.

It was as if he knew, for those few seconds, exactly what she needed.

They stood in the darkness like that for a few minutes. She could feel his strong heartbeat beneath his chest. It slowed her and steadied her. Gave her room to breathe. The comfort from his arms felt like the warmest blanket she'd ever been wrapped in.

She wasn't alone in the forest anymore.

His lips brushed the side of her cheek. "Why didn't you tell me, Violet?" he whispered. "Why didn't you tell me about your baby?"

The words caught in her throat. How could he know? How could he know how raw she was feeling? How much she had pent up inside her?

Every muscle in her body was tensed, every hair standing on end.

He looked hurt. He looked upset.

"How, Evan? How can you know that? I haven't told anyone."

He shook his head. "I didn't need you to tell me, Violet." He ran his finger down her cheek. "It was right here for me to see. I just needed to notice the signs."

The words hung between them and Violet sucked in a breath. She couldn't stand the tension. "What about Urbi, the midwife? How is she? Did they hurt her?" She couldn't stand the thought of that. She couldn't stand the thought they might have hurt the woman who had tried to warn her. Tried to save her.

Evan shook his head. The obvious change of subject must have hurt him. "She'll need some stitches. But she'll be fine. Luke is taking care of her."

The men started to move, to organize themselves to help carry Hasana back to the village. Her husband still stood with his baby in his arms, his head held high.

Evan pulled Violet over to one side. He kept his arm around her. "I don't understand Violet. I don't understand why you didn't tell me. It's such a huge part of your life—so important. Why couldn't you share that with me?"

She shook her head. "I couldn't, Evan. I haven't even told my family."

He looked horrified. "What?"

"You don't understand. My mom and stepdad are just so frail. After what happened with Sawyer…" Her voice tailed off and she shook her head again. "Blane and I had decided to split up. I was doing it on my own. They would have been worried sick. And Sawyer, I didn't know how to contact him."

"I can't believe this. I can't believe you had to do this alone. You had *no one* with you?"

"I had a few close girl friends. They were fantastic. I couldn't have asked for more."

"Yes. Yes, you could. You could have asked for a whole lot more." There was an edge of irritation to his voice. Frustration about a situation he'd had no control over.

She sighed. "Nothing like that was meant to happen to me. I hadn't even considered it. I'd had a fairly easy pregnancy and expected to have my baby then let my mom and stepdad know. They would have been delighted. A grandchild would have been the joy to help heal their wound." She couldn't help the wistful tone in her voice.

She'd been hoping for salvation for her family—a new start for them all.

All she'd been left with had been a dark, heart-wrenching hole.

The villagers started to move past them. And they had to follow or be left behind in the forest.

Evan reached down and intertwined his fingers with hers. "There's so much I want to ask you, Violet, but this just doesn't seem like the time or the place." He stretched his other arm in front of them. "We've got a long walk ahead. I want you to tell me. I want you to tell me about your baby."

There was such a calm and determined manner about his words. He made it sound so simple. It was like an open invitation. An open invitation to share her daughter with someone else.

It seemed huge. It seemed enormous. No one had ever asked about her daughter before. How could they, when they hadn't known?

She'd thought she'd put this behind her.

But she'd left the most crucial part of her healing out.

The ability to share.

To share the joy and pain of her daughter.

And now she finally could.

They walked for a long time. She held up her head as they walked through the dark night. She had the strangest feeling around her.

Relief.

Relief to finally talk about her daughter. Yes, she'd spoken with the doctors and the coroner. Yes, she'd spoken with her friends. But her circle of friends had been so small that after a time she'd felt as if she'd had to stop.

This was entirely different. This was a chance to share with someone she cared about.

Loved.

The word shot out of the dark like a bullet to the brain.

Love? Was that how she really felt about Evan?

He was the first thing she thought about in the morning and the last thing in her dreams at night.

She spent the whole day waiting to see his smile or to feel his skin against hers.

Even when she was mad at him, she couldn't stop thinking about him.

The man had well and truly got under her skin.

What was the measure of love, anyway? Because, for her, right now, it felt as if there was only one.

Could she share with him about her daughter? The pain, the terror and the hidden parts of joy?

Yes. Yes, she could.

She squeezed the hand that was holding hers. "My daughter's name was Daisy," she began.

His step faltered then he gave her a smile. "What a beautiful name." He nodded knowingly. "A perfect name for a daughter." They walked for another few steps. "Violet and Daisy. Perfect combination."

She felt a little swell in her heart. A swell of pride that he appreciated the name that had come to her straight away. As soon as they'd told her that her baby was going to be a girl, she'd known exactly what she would call her.

And it felt good to say her name out loud rather than just look at it on a memorial wall. On a little plaque only she visited.

She took a deep breath. This wasn't as hard as she'd thought it would be but, then, she'd been so afraid to do this. Maybe it was all about timing. Or maybe it was all about sharing with the right person.

"She was perfect, Evan. There was nothing wrong with her. Full term. No complications. She had fine blond hair and blue eyes. And her skin...it was perfect." She could see her right then—as if she were right before her eyes. She inhaled deeply, trying to remember her gorgeous baby smell. The silky touch of her unblemished skin. The tiny eyelashes and soft fingernails.

He gave her hand a little squeeze. "She must have taken after her mom, then."

It felt good. He was helping her give Daisy some perspective. Giving Daisy her place in the world as a permanent part of her.

She heard him draw a deep breath. "The perfect part. Was that the hardest? Because I think that would have been the hardest for me." In the dark, his words sounded husky, as if he was struggling to get them out.

Wow. The words that cut right to her heart. The hardest thing of all. It almost took the breath from her lungs. How could he understand like that? Was it the doctor in him—or was it just Evan?

"Yes." Her voice was wavering but she couldn't help it. He understood. He actually *understood* what the hardest part to get over was. "I wanted a reason. I hated being a statistic, a number. I couldn't apportion blame anywhere. It made me think about every single thing I'd ever done during my pregnancy, every single thing I'd ever eaten. Every twinge. Every restless night. There was no one left to put the blame on but myself." She shook her head, her voice drifting off. "It was a normal day. We were planning on a delivery date. It was a routine scan."

She didn't need to say the rest. The horror of there being no heartbeat. The ominous silence in the room. The darting looks between the staff. And the crumpled chart in her hand that revealed her baby's movements. Right up until an hour before.

He released her hand and wrapped an arm back around her shoulders. Then he did something she didn't expect. He pulled her close and walked with his other hand on her belly.

She could feel it. She could feel it all around them. The way he was trying to comfort her. To be there for her. If she believed in auras Evan would have surrounded them in a green healing glow.

She'd thought the walk back through the forest would be long. She'd thought it would be tough. But it felt as if it was passing in the blink of an eye.

This almost felt cathartic to her.

His voice was quiet, just loud enough for them both to hear it. "I think I would have felt the same. It's the doctor in you, Violet. You look for a rational, reasonable explanation. When the world is full of 'don't knows' it makes it so much more difficult to move on."

He wasn't just talking about her. He was talking about him too.

It was strange. She hadn't seen any similarities in the things they'd had to deal with—probably because they'd never discussed them. Now they seemed crystal clear.

Two entirely different scenarios, one affecting Evan, both affecting her. The individual effects had been devastating.

And they'd both struggled. Someone else understood. For the first time it felt as if someone else understood.

But would he understand what she had to do next?

"I know what you mean, Evan." She looked around her. They were nearing the edge of the forest. The denseness of the trees was diminishing. The foliage was thinning out. Even the darkness was fading a little thanks to the moon, high in the sky.

Their journey was coming to an end.

The men were still carrying Hasana between them. They were a little ahead, starting to weave their way through the houses. Shrieks came from the villagers who spotted them and ran to embrace them in relief that they'd been found.

Almost automatically she could hear the level and tone of the voices changing. Discovering the outcome for Hasana's baby. Then she heard Urbi's voice above the rest—strong and authoritarian, ordering them to take Hasana and her baby to one of the houses. She heard her speaking to some of the men, telling them to prepare the village burial ground. Hasana, along with many of the villagers, was Hausa and would follow the Islamic burial principles. They would bathe and wrap Bem's little body and perform a blessing prior to his burial.

She turned to face him. The burial would take place in a few hours. She wanted to wait for that, but then she had to go. She had to leave.

She reached up and touched his cheek.

"Thank you for finding me, Evan. Thank you for finding *us*."

He knew. He could obviously sense it. The emphasis on that tiny word. He gave her lazy, sexy smile that she loved. "There was always going to be an *us,* Violet. It was written in the stars."

This was going to be so hard.

The hardest thing she'd done in the past three years.

It would be so easy to step into his arms and forget about the day she'd just had. It would be so easy to chalk up everything that just happened to the stress of the moment.

A reaction.

To allow herself to go back to their camp with him and into his bed.

But she had to be true to herself.

She didn't want to stumble on for another few months. Enjoying the days and nights with Evan, knowing that there was an inevitability to their relationship. She didn't want to wait around for the long silences and fights about family.

She had to do this now.

Before the strength left her completely. Her legs were already starting to tremble.

She stared into his eyes and took a deep breath. "You know now, Evan. You know about my daughter. You know about my life." She paused for a second. "And I know about yours." She willed back the tears that were pooling in her eyes. "And now I need to do the hardest thing of all."

His brow furrowed, almost as if a sweep of dread had just come over him. "What is it, Violet? What's wrong?"

She lowered her eyes and laid a hand on his chest. "I can't take the final steps with you around me, Evan. I can't heal. Because you won't let me." He looked as if he wanted to interrupt and she shook her head. "You have to let me finish. And somehow I realize you're not as far along the healing process as I am. You have to find your own way."

She looked around her. "I thought I was ready. I thought I'd waited long enough—kept myself out of harm's way. That's why I spent the past three years hiding in an office at the DPA instead of being out in the field. But being here has taught me that there are still a few steps I have to take."

She lifted her eyes to meet his. It took all her strength to continue. She could already see the panic start to flare in his eyes. "I have to talk to my family. No. I have to *share* with my family. I have to let them grieve for the niece and granddaughter that they never knew. I have to let them know where I am in this life. I've got to stop thinking about them for a little while. I've got to stop trying to protect them. And I've got to start thinking about me. I need to let them take care of me."

She could feel her voice start to become more determined. She knew this was the only way forward for her. "And I can't deal with your grief and mine. It's too much, Evan. It's too much for one person to take. I thought I needed to get away from you before. Before I came here. Kissing you that night unleashed a whole lot of demons I didn't know how to deal with. I was feeling attracted to someone again. I was feeling lustful."

Her voice dropped. "I wanted to do the kind of things that could get me back in a situation I couldn't control before. But you've helped me. You saw me through that part. I know I can have a relationship again. I know I can feel free to love someone again."

She drew a deep breath.

"But I can't do this with you, Evan. I need to be free. Free to finally move on."

She took a step back and pulled her hand away from his chest. She had to put some distance between them. "You have to take the next step for you. No matter what that might be. And what I really need to do is get away from you. I love you, Evan. But I can't love you like this."

He couldn't hold his tongue any longer. His arms automatically reached out for her and she had to back away. "No, Violet. You don't need to leave. We can work through this together. Whatever you need to do, that's fine with me." He tried to brush his fingers against her cheek. "I'll wait. I'll wait until you're ready."

"You're the one who's not ready, Evan. You're the one who's not ready for me."

She stepped back even further. She had to stay strong. She loved him, but he wasn't ready to be with her.

The sorrow in his eyes was killing her. This was hurting them both. She looked straight into his dark blue eyes. She needed him to understand how far this whole experience had taken her. "Never in a million years did I think I'd end up in this position. I would never have set foot on a plane to Africa if I could ever have imagined this. I knew I would be working with children and families. I knew I would be working with babies. But I thought I was ready. I felt ready. I felt as if I was moving in the right direction."

She threw up her hands. "But a stillborn baby? In the middle of a forest, fleeing from kidnappers? I could never have predicted that. I could never have realized how important to me that could be."

She wanted to leave him with something positive. She couldn't bear the haunted expression on his face.

"This wasn't a bad experience for me, Evan, but it was life-changing. Life-changing in a good way. I'll never see anything like that again. If I'd stayed in Atlanta I would never have been put in that situation. But I was. And I'm glad. Not glad for Hasana and her son but glad that I was able to be there, able to help. Able to understand. Once I've attended Bem's funeral it will be time for me to go back home. It's time for me to make my peace, once and for all."

And then she saw it, the tremble at his throat and the shine of tears in his eyes.

She could only whisper, "Don't make this any harder, Evan. If you love me as much as I love you, you'll let me do this."

And she turned and walked away before her heart could break all over again.

CHAPTER TWELVE

Two months later

HE WAS WAITING. Waiting in arrivals. His dark hair still shaggy, a baseball cap stuck on his head, wearing a pair of jeans and a pale blue shirt.

He didn't look happy.

Evan heaved his bag over his shoulder and carried his case in his hand, reaching him before he could change his mind and walk away.

"This had better be good. This is the second time in two months someone's asked me to meet them off a plane. Last time didn't go so well."

Sawyer hadn't changed. There was still that animosity between the two of them that had always been there.

"Did you know? Did you know about Violet?"

Evan shook his head. "I had no idea, Matt. Truly, I didn't. I only found out when we were over there."

Sawyer's eyes ran up and down his body then lingered on his face. Obviously trying to decide if he believed him or not. Finally his shoulders sagged a little. "Well, that's okay, then."

He turned toward the exit. "What is it you want to talk about, Evan? We've never exactly been friends."

Evan stomach churned. He wanted to get this over

and done with. He should have done this years ago—but Sawyer hadn't been around.

His throat was dry and his mouth parched. Nineteen hours of travel could do that to you.

A red neon sign caught his eye and he said the last words in the world he thought he ever would. "Sawyer, let's get a beer."

Sawyer raised his eyebrow. "Seriously?"

"Seriously."

They waited a few minutes while the bartender got their beers then sat down at a table in the corner of the bar.

"So what's the story with you and Violet?"

Evan felt the hairs stand up on the back of his neck. Sawyer was her brother. It was an obvious question. He took a quick swig from his bottle then put it back down on the table. Maybe he should have waited. Waited until he'd drunk a few more of these before talking to Sawyer. "Nothing. I'm not here to talk about Violet."

"You're not? What do you want to talk about, then?" Sawyer looked confused.

"Helen."

"What?"

He looked across the table at Sawyer. He had the same pale green eyes as his sister. It was kind of disturbing.

"I need to talk to you about Helen."

"You've left it kind of late. It's been six years, Evan."

"I know exactly how long it's been." His words were curter than he'd intended. But he could feel the pressure building in his veins. He had no idea what Matt's reaction would be.

Sawyer's finger was running round the top of his bottle. As if he was trying to decide what to say next.

It was now or never.

"Helen told me she wasn't feeling well."

Sawyer's head shot straight up. "What?"

There was no need for any preamble here.

"That day—of the mission—I was checking the inventory and Helen said she wasn't feeling one hundred percent."

Sawyer's eyes fixed on the table. "And what did you do?"

There was silence for a few seconds. He'd started now and he had to finish. No matter what the outcome.

"Nothing, Sawyer. I did nothing." His finger traced a circle on the table of the wet outline from his bottle. "I have no excuse. I didn't pick up on it until later. I wasn't paying attention. I didn't remember what she'd said until it was too late."

"And you've waited six years to tell me that?" The tone in his voice was clear.

"I didn't know what to say."

"Sorry would have been a start."

"You think I'm not sorry? You think I haven't gone over and over this in my head? That if I'd stopped and asked Helen more questions that day she might still be here, still be married to you?" His voice was rising and heads were turning in the bar.

He ran his fingers through his hair. "I wish I could turn back time. I wish I could go back to that day and that throw-away comment and *stop*. Stop and ask her what was wrong, why she didn't feel great. If there was anything else. If there was a possibility that she was pregnant."

Sawyer leaned back in his chair. His fingers hadn't moved from the top of his bottle. "You think you're the only one, Evan? The only one who hasn't gone over that day time and time again, wondering if there was anything different you could have done, different you could have said? Welcome to my life, Evan Hunter." He picked up his bottle and took a long slug.

Evan hesitated. "Violet said...Violet said you had no idea Helen was pregnant." He met Sawyer's eyes. "For a long time I thought you did know. I thought you and Helen might have been keeping the news under wraps. I'm sorry."

Sawyer stared at him for the longest time. "I know. Violet told me." He took off his baseball cap and flung it on the table.

"She told you?"

Sawyer nodded.

"What else did she tell you?"

He shook his head. "Only that. I knew there had to be more to the story. But she only told me that you thought we'd kept you out of the loop. She also told me she put you straight."

Evan felt a little flutter of relief. And he couldn't help the wry smile on his face at the mention of her name.

Sawyer straightened up. "Let me be frank. I agonized over Helen's death for six years. She was the light of my life. My reason to get up every day. When I married Helen I truly believed that we would grow old together. That we would end up with a pair of rockers out on our porch."

Evan smiled. He could almost picture the scene in his head.

He leaned across the table. "The only person I blamed for Helen's death was me, Evan, not you. *I* should have figured out my wife was pregnant. *I* should have stopped her going on that mission. I should have been able to save her. Not you. Not anyone else. Because I was the person she trusted most."

The color was building in his cheeks, the blood obviously pumping in his veins. But he stopped and took a deep breath. "But you know what? It's been six years. And I've got past it. I've had to get past it. Because there's a whole other life out there, Evan. And I know that Helen would have been the first person to tell me that."

Evan listened to the words. Even he could see the change in Sawyer. "Callie?"

Sawyer nodded and took another swig from his bottle. "Callie."

There was an inevitability about all this. A natural way for this conversation to go.

The tightness that had been in his stomach for the past six years was finally starting to unfurl.

"I didn't get it, Evan. I didn't get everyone else's loss. I was selfish. I was too focused on myself. Then I met Callie and my whole world changed." He snapped his fingers. "Just like that. I didn't think I'd ever get the chance of something like that again. I didn't think I'd ever deserve it. Being with Callie has changed everything for me. I've got a reason to get up in the morning again." He paused. There was regret written all over his face.

"When I think about what Violet has gone through on her own I feel so helpless. And so angry at myself. She's my sister. She needed me and I wasn't there."

Evan nodded slowly, raising his eyes. "Kind of angry with you about that myself."

Their eyes met. In quiet understanding.

And they sat for a few moments in silence.

"About Violet…" Evan started.

"Yeah, about Violet," countered Sawyer.

"What are we going to do about that?" The words hung in the air between them.

Sawyer took a final slug of his beer and stood up, stretching his back and sticking his baseball cap back on his head. "Guess you're going to have to stop hating me so much if you're going to be part of the family."

Evan raised his eyebrows. "I've never hated you, Sawyer." He stood up too and threw some bills on the table. "I just never liked you much."

Sawyer threw his head back and let out a laugh. They walked toward the door.

Evan put his hand on Sawyer's arm. "Violet? Where will I find her?"

Sawyer quirked his lip and touched the peak of his cap. "You'll figure it out."

CHAPTER THIRTEEN

VIOLET WALKED SLOWLY along the path. It was another beautiful day in Atlanta. It seemed as though the sun had been shining constantly since she'd got back.

Almost as if something was trying to remind her that she should still be in Africa.

The garden was quiet and she was grateful. The last few times she'd been here her mom and stepfather had been with her. They needed time and a place to grieve too, and the memorial garden was probably the most appropriate place.

But she was still trying to adjust. Trying to adjust to sharing her grief with other people. She was used to the calm of the garden, the tranquility. The first few times her mom had come with her it had almost felt like an invasion of her privacy.

Her family was still tiptoeing around her. Even Sawyer. Which was strangely uncomfortable.

She wasn't quite sure if it was what she'd told him or the presence of Callie in his life that was keeping him so even-tempered. But he'd changed. Changed in a good way.

It was good having her brother back in her life. And he was slowly but surely finding a path back into the

DPA. Which was just as well, as she'd taken a leave of absence for a while.

The director had been very understanding. He'd told her to take as much time as she needed, had offered her counseling and let her know that any career path within the DPA was open to her.

Violet approached the little granite plaque. It was attached on the wall next to hundreds of others. Sometimes she stood and read them all. But today she was only interested in her own.

She ran her fingers along the letters. Feeling the bumps and outlines beneath the pads of her fingers.

Daisy Connelly.
Born May 16th. Died May 16th.
A little flower lent not given, to bud on earth and bloom in heaven.

There was a lump in her throat—there would always be a lump in her throat when she came here—but today, for the first time, she wasn't crying.

She arranged her flowers in one of the little vases underneath the plaques. There were too many plaques for everyone to have an individual memorial flower vase, so the people who visited had to share.

She always brought the same flowers, a mixture daisies and violets for her daughter from her mommy.

A little array of pink flowers caught her eye with a little white card attached. She couldn't help but peek at the text. *Today I brought you petunias.* They were cute. Obviously hand-picked due to the haphazard way they'd been placed in the vase.

Her eyes looked along the line. There were more of them.

Today I brought you marigolds.

Today I brought you sky-blue pansies.

Today I brought you poppies.

Today I brought you Livingstone daisies.

They were beautiful. Flowers everyday. Were they from a newly bereaved parent?

She could feel the hairs stand up on the back of her neck. And she knew. Instantly.

Her head whipped around and her breath caught in her throat.

Evan.

Sitting on one of the benches. Watching her. Waiting for her.

Her legs were on autopilot. She was standing in front of him before she knew it.

His tan was deeper, his hair lighter, his eyes just as blue as she remembered.

He gave her the smile she loved so much. "Hi." After two months. One word.

"Hi." Her voice croaked. Her fingers itched to reach out and touch him. But she couldn't. Not yet.

"I came to meet Daisy. To talk to her."

She felt her heart squeeze in her chest. "The flowers are from you?"

He nodded.

"But they're so unusual. Where did you find them?"

He gave a little shrug. "My mom has a beautiful garden of flowers. When I told her why I needed them she made sure I had something different every day."

Wow. He'd told his mother about her. She didn't dare to think what that might mean. She counted along the wall. Ten lots of flowers that were obviously from him—some looking a little worse for wear.

She felt a little startled. "You've been coming here for ten days?"

His eyes met hers. "I knew that I'd meet you here eventually. I just had to learn a little patience."

She sat down on the bench next to him. Her eyes fixing on the wall covered in hundreds of individual plaques. So many little lost lives. So many families grieving.

His hand slipped into hers. It felt so natural, his fingers intertwining with hers.

But she held her body rigid. Keeping a wall up around herself.

"When did you get back?"

"Ten days ago."

Ten days. As soon as he'd got back he'd brought some flowers for Daisy.

One of his fingers started tracing a little circle inside the palm of her hand. It was comforting. It was soothing.

"I met your brother."

"What?" Her head shot up.

He nodded slowly. "I called him. Asked him to meet me at the airport." He lifted his eyebrows at her. "We had a beer."

She was imagining this. This couldn't really be happening. This was like one of those crazy dreams that woke you in the middle of the night.

She could feel her heart fluttering in her chest. She squeezed her eyes shut tightly. Maybe she would wake up now and everything would go back to normal.

But all she could feel was the cool summer breeze skittering across her skin.

"Violet?"

She opened her eyes again. The glare from the sun made her blink. She definitely wasn't imagining this.

She was scared to ask. It would have been a show-down between two of the most important men in her life. Surely that couldn't have gone well?

"How did it go?"

She held her breath. Sawyer hadn't said a word to her yesterday. Why not?

"Better than I could have expected. We talked about Helen. Sawyer told me he's tortured himself enough and it's time to move on."

"Oh?" If she held her breath much longer she would burst.

"He mentioned something about being part of the family."

That was it. This must be a dream. This couldn't be happening. She grabbed hold of a little bit of skin and pinched. "Ouch!"

"Violet? What are you doing?"

She jumped up and rubbed her leg. "What do you think I'm doing? I'm pinching myself, trying to work out if this is real."

He stood up next to her and put his hands at her waist. "Oh, it's real all right. Can I do something else to convince you?"

She didn't have time to answer. Because his lips were on hers. Kissing away any doubts. Kissing away any fears.

His warm body was pressing against hers. One hand at the back of her head and the other on her cheek.

"I want to spend the next fifty years convincing you, Violet," he murmured in her ear.

She could feel herself melting. The past two months had been the longest of her life. Working through the grief with her family had been tough. But it was the final act. The final piece of the puzzle.

She wanted to go forward. Go forward and embrace life.

And this was the man she wanted to do it with.

He started kissing around her neck and ears, sending tingles down her spine. "So, this thing with Sawyer, it's over? It's really over?"

His lips moved back to her face, dropping kisses on her nose and eyelids. "It's really over."

A warm wave washed over her. She believed him. She really believed him.

Maybe they could all finally start living their lives again.

She pulled back a little. "Then there's something I want to do."

Her voice was serious and she could see the instant wariness in his face.

She slipped her hand into his and walked back over the wall.

It was time. It was truly time.

She lifted their hands together and placed them on Daisy's plaque.

"Daisy, honey, there's somebody I want you to meet…"

EPILOGUE

"WHAT'S GOING ON? A C-section doesn't take this long." Sawyer paced up and down the corridor.

Callie gave her husband a smile and adjusted the toddler in her lap. "Sit down, honey." She glanced over to where an elderly couple was sitting. "You're making the expectant grandparents nervous."

The doors burst open behind them. *"It's a girl!"*

Evan's face was scarlet, as if he was about to burst with excitement.

Sawyer was up at him in seconds. "Is everything okay? Is she okay? Is Violet okay? What took so long?"

Evan put his hand on Sawyer's arm, his voice steadying as he spoke. "Everything's fine. My wife is beautiful. My daughter is beautiful. Six pounds three ounces, with a perfect Apgar. Her mom's just given her her first feed. I just didn't want to leave their sides. I didn't want to miss a second." He pulled his scrub hat from his head and opened the door behind them. "But now the newest member of the family would like to meet everyone else." He bent down and swooped up the toddler from Callie's lap. "Particularly her big cousin, Riley. Want to see the baby, Riley?"

Riley wrinkled his nose. "Baby," he repeated. "Baby."

Callie laughed and grabbed her husband's hand,

holding the door for Sawyer's mom and stepdad. "Let's go, folks. Let's meet the newest family member."

Violet stared down at her daughter. Perfect in every way.

She stroked her finger across her pale skin and downy hair. Leaning forward and taking a deep breath. She just didn't want to let her go.

Evan had been more than an anxious father throughout this pregnancy—even though he'd tried not to show it. In the past few months she'd been scanned every week and when they'd mentioned yesterday that they wanted to deliver her due to the position of her placenta they'd both had a minute of heart failure.

Even though a C-section hadn't been what she'd planned, the most important thing in the world was having a healthy baby.

She dropped more kisses on her daughter's eyelids, watching the rise and fall of her little chest. Moments like these were precious. And all she wanted to do right now was count her blessings.

The doors swung open and the family invasion began.

"She's beautiful!"

"Let me see her!"

"Can I hold her?"

Evan slid on the bed next to her and wrapped his arm around her shoulders. Riley looked at the baby and shuddered. "How are my girls doing?"

She loved it. She loved the way he said it and the tenderness in his eyes.

"We're doing fine." She snuggled against him. "But you were away too long."

She looked up at her family. She could see the tears

in her mother's eyes as she leaned over to see her new granddaughter. She could see the relief written across her brother's face.

She watched the smile that he and Callie exchanged as he reached over for his squirming toddler and balanced him on his hip. Becoming a dad suited Sawyer, more than she could ever have imagined.

"Do you have a name?" he asked.

Violet turned to Evan and smiled. "Are you sure it's okay?"

He nodded. "It's beautiful and it suits her perfectly."

Violet turned to her family. "We thought long and hard about a name. I was worried about family traditions." She wrinkled her nose. "Evan's family has a whole host of unusual names. But we've settled on one we both love." She tilted her daughter upward, pulling the blanket down from under her chin. "So, everyone, meet Rose. Rose Hunter. My beautiful daughter."

She smiled as Evan turned to her with a gleam in his eye. "And just think of all the other flowers we've got to choose from."

* * * * *

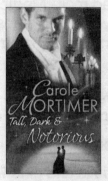

Join the Mills & Boon Book Club

Want to read more **Medical** books?
We're offering you **2 more** absolutely **FREE!**

We'll also treat you to these fabulous extras:

 Exclusive offers and much more!

 FREE home delivery

FREE books and gifts with our special rewards scheme

Get your free books now!

visit www.millsandboon.co.uk/bookclub
or call Customer Relations on 020 8288 2888